MEN IN

BURNING
for the
FIREMAN

MEN IN UNIFORM:
COLLECTION

January 2017

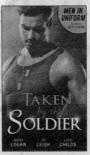

January 2017

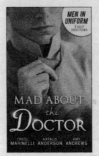

January 2017

February 2017

MEN IN UNIFORM:

BURNING
for the
FIREMAN

BARBARA   EMILY   LESLIE
McMAHON   McKAY   KELLY

MILLS & BOON

First Published in Great Britain 2017
By Mills & Boon, an imprint of HarperCollins*Publishers*
1 London Bridge Street, London, SE1 9GF

MEN IN UNIFORM: BURNING FOR THE FIREMAN © 2017
Harlequin Books S.A.

Firefighter's Doorstep Baby © 2010 Barbara McMahon
Surrogate and Wife © 2006 Emily McKaskle
Lying in Your Arms © 2013 Leslie Kelly

ISBN: 978-0-263-92795-5

09-0217

Printed and bound in Spain
by CPI , Barcelona

FIREFIGHTER'S DOORSTEP BABY

BARBARA MCMAHON

To First Responders everywhere—
thanks for all you do to serve and protect
every day. FDNY, we will never forget.

Barbara McMahon was born and raised in the south USA, but settled in California after spending a year flying around the world for an international airline. After settling down to raise a family and work for a computer firm, she began writing when her children started school. Now, feeling fortunate in being able to realize a long-held dream of quitting her 'day job' and writing full time, she and her husband have moved to the Sierra Nevada mountains of California, where she finds her desire to write is stronger than ever. With the beauty of the mountains visible from her windows, and the pace of life slower than the hectic San Francisco Bay Area where they previously resided, she finds more time than ever to think up stories and characters and share them with others through writing. Barbara loves to hear from readers. You can reach her at PO Box 977, Pioneer, CA 95666-0977, USA. Readers can also contact Barbara at her website: www.barbaramcmahon.com

CHAPTER ONE

MARIELLA HOLMES stood on the small stone patio and gazed at the lake. Some daredevil was racing the wind on a Jet Ski. A spume of water arced behind it. The soft rumble of its engine faded as it sped across the surface of the water. She glanced into the cottage. Dante was still sleeping. She looked back at the reckless idiot on the Jet Ski; if the noise had woken the baby she'd have been more than annoyed. It had taken her longer than usual to get him to sleep.

What was the maniac doing anyway? If he fell in the water he'd be frozen in no time. Late October was so not lake weather. Yet even as she watched, she felt a spark of envy. He looked carefree skimming along at warp speed. If he was on vacation, he was certainly making the most of his time.

She gazed around the tree-covered hills that rose behind the lake. This would be lovely in the summer. She could picture children swimming in the water, canoes or rowboats dotting the surface. Imagine even more daredevils testing their skills with the Jet Skis; chasing the excitement, exploring the limits of their skills. Her gaze drawn back to the man, she continued to watch as she hoped this one wouldn't crash. There was beauty in the arc of water spewing from behind him, in the soft wake that radiated from the path of the Jet Ski. Sunshine sparkled on the water, causing a misty rainbow when he turned.

She pulled her sweater closer and drank in the clean mountain air. Beautiful and peaceful. She had never visited this area before. She hadn't known what to expect. Forested hills, quiet lakes, small villages. It was enchanting. She wished she could explore everything, but they wouldn't be here that long. Whichever way things went, it would be a relatively short visit. She'd had a lull in work and so had acted on the spur of the moment when she'd decided to come see where Dante's father was from.

A loud smack of the Jet Ski on the water as it bounced over its own wake had her drawn again to the man. At this distance she could only see the dark hair and broad shoulders as he sat astride the machine. He seemed fearless as the engine roared louder and he went even faster. She could imagine herself flying along, the wind blowing all cares away.

Shivering, she stepped back inside the cottage. This would have been a perfect chance to call Ariana, tell her how much she was enjoying Lake Clarissa, and that she'd seen a man who fired her imagination. She still couldn't believe her best friend would never call her up again to talk a mile a minute about life. Would never get to hold her son or watch him learn to walk or start school. Mariella brushed the sudden tears from her cheeks. Ariana had been there for her when her own parents had died, but she was not here now. It was Mariella's turn to step up to the plate.

Time healed all hurts, Mariella knew that. She had gotten over the worst of her grief after her parents' untimely death when she'd been in New York during her first year at university. Her grief over Ariana's death would gradually ease too. She knew in her mind she'd remember her friend with love as the years went on. But sometimes she felt raw, burning pain. Ariana had only been twenty-two. Her life should have stretched out until they were both old ladies. Instead, it had ended far too soon.

Shaking her head to dislodge depressing thoughts, Mariella focused on the future. She had Dante. She had a job. She had a quest. One day at a time. It had worked so far. So what if she felt overwhelmed some days? Caring for an unexpected baby wasn't easy. At least they were both healthy, well fed and comfortable. And she was getting the hang of being a mother. She hoped Dante would never remember her inept first attempts.

Crossing the small living room, she checked on the infant sleeping in the baby carrier still locked in the stroller. Checking the time, she knew he'd awaken soon for a bottle. She had a few minutes to unpack the groceries she'd brought and prepare his next meal before the first stirring.

She'd booked the room for a week, thinking that would be enough time to wander around and get a feel for the place and see if anyone here recognized the picture she had of Ariana. If not, they'd move on to Monta Correnti. She had no firm clues, no certainty she was even in the right place. She only knew this was the place Ariana had spoken about. The only clue she had given about Dante's father.

Ariana had been so sick and afraid those last weeks. Mariella wished her friend had called upon her earlier, but she had waited until graduation and Mariella's return to Rome before sharing the prognosis for the disease that ravaged her body. And, despite all Mariella's pleading, she had not revealed Dante's father's name. Only the bare fact that he came from this area, and they'd spent a wonderful weekend at Lake Clarissa.

The only child of older parents, Mariella was now alone in the world—and the guardian of an infant to boot. She'd always wished for brothers and sisters, aunts, uncles and cousins galore. She wished that for Dante as well. Maybe she could find his father, tell him of his son and discover he came from a large loving family who would take the baby into their hearts.

She glanced over to him again, her heart twisting. She loved this child. But it was so hard to be suddenly a mom. If she found his father, would she be able to give the baby up? Would a big family be best for him? She was still uncertain. At least she didn't have to make any decisions today. First she had to see if she could even locate his father. She'd decide then what course of action to take.

Cristiano opened the throttle full blast as the Jet Ski skimmed across the waves. The air was chilled, causing his blood to pump harder to keep him warm. The thrill of speed, the challenge of control, the sun glittering on the water all made him feel more alive than he had in months. All other thoughts and worries and memories evaporated. If the Jet Ski could go even faster, he would have relished the exhilaration, however short-lived. He pushed the machine to the max.

The injured ankle had healed. He'd been unable to use the Jet Ski during the warm summer weeks, but now, in the waning days of fall, he had the lake to himself. Power roared beneath him as he bounced over the small waves. The shore blurred by as he pushed the throttle surging to that last bit of power. He felt invincible. He'd cheated death once this year. He would not be taken today.

Drawing near the shore, he slowly banked toward the right, not sharp enough to capsize, but enough to swerve away from the rocky land that was fast approaching. He could ease back on the throttle, but what challenge was in that?

The Jet Ski bumped over its own wake and he stood up

to cushion the smacks as it slammed down on the water. Now his ankle ached a bit, reminding him he was not yet totally fit. Another circle and he'd return to the dock. It was cold enough that his toes were going numb. But there were few enough sunny days at this time of year. He'd take all he could get to enjoy being on the lake.

A few moments later, he slowed the ski and made a figure eight, then angled near the shore to make a big sweep that would take him back to the dock. Lake Clarissa was empty, the beach deserted. He was the only person in sight. The summer tourists had long left and the few people who came in the winter had not yet shown up. He had the place to himself.

As he skied past the row of cottages the Bertatalis rented, he noticed the far one was occupied. Lake Clarissa didn't offer the nightlife that Monta Correnti did. Most people weren't foolish enough to venture into the cold lake at this time of year. They had more sense than he did. It was probably some older couple who wanted to watch birds or see the leaves change. It wasn't that far to Monta Correnti they couldn't still drive over for some nighttime entertainment.

He pulled the Jet Ski up to the dock and in only moments secured it in the small floating ramp in the berth he rented. He tied it down and headed back to land. His wet feet left footprints on the wooden dock as he walked to his motorcycle. Drying himself, he quickly donned the jeans and boots he'd left across the seat, and pulled on a heavy sweater. It felt good to get warm. Donning the helmet, he mounted the bike and kick-started it. The rumble was not unlike the Jet Ski. Did power equate noise? He laughed at that idea and pulled onto the street. The small amount of traffic still surprised him after his time in Rome. Vacations in Lake Clarissa had always been fleeting, too much work waiting at home when he'd been a child. Once grown, he'd preferred his exciting life travelling the world with his job, or the challenges of extreme sports, to spending much time in this little sleepy lakeside village.

Until the bombing had altered everything.

Shortly after one Cristiano got off his motorcycle on the side street by Pietro's Bistro. Lunch here would beat cooking for himself. His father would be horrified his own son didn't like cooking. It wasn't that he didn't like it precisely, it just didn't seem worth the effort for only one.

There was a wide patio for dining, empty this time of year. It wasn't that cool, yet the breezes blowing down from the higher elevation carried a chill. He entered the warm restaurant and paused a moment while his eyes got used to the dimmer light. Pietro's smelled like home. The restaurant he'd worked in most of his childhood, that his father still owned, was even of a similar rustic theme. Bella Rosa had more patrons and more bustle than Pietro's, but Pietro's was free of the ties to Cristiano's past he was trying to flee.

There were couples and groups eating at various tables—it was more crowded than he'd expected. Some people he recognized and nodded to when they looked up and waved. When Emeliano appeared from the kitchen, white apron tied neatly around his waist, heavy tray balanced on one hand, Cristiano watched. His arms almost ached at the remembered tiredness he'd felt after a long day at Rosa. He hadn't worked there in years, but some memories didn't fade. Even when he wished they would.

"Cristiano, sit anywhere. I'll be there soon," Emeliano called out as he deftly transferred the tray from his hand to the stand beside the table he was serving.

Cristiano walked toward his favorite table, near the big window overlooking the town square. It was occupied.

He walked past and sat at the next one, then looked at the woman who had taken the table he liked best.

She had blonde hair with copper highlights. She was cooing to a small baby and seemed oblivious to the rest of the restaurant. He didn't recognize her. Probably another tourist. Even keeping to himself, he still kept tapped into the local rumor mill—enough to know if someone local had a new baby visiting. Italian families loved new babies.

The woman looked up and caught his gaze. She smiled then looked away.

He stared at her feeling that smile like a punch to the gut. From that quick glimpse he noted her eyes were silver, her cheeks brushed with pink—from the sun or the warmth of the restaurant? Glancing around, he wondered idly where her husband was.

"Rigatoni?" Emeliano asked when he stopped by Cristiano's table, distracting Cristiano from his speculation about the woman.

"Sure." He ordered it almost every time he ate here.

"Not as good as what you get at Rosa," Emeliano said, jotting it on a pad.

"I'm not at Rosa," Cristiano said easily. He could have quickly covered the distance between Lake Clarissa and Monta Correnti for lunch, but he wasn't ready to see his family yet. Sometimes he wondered if he'd ever be ready to go back home.

"Saw you on the lake. You could get killed."

He and Emeliano had played together as kids, challenging each other to swim races, exploring the hills with his brother Valentino. Cristiano grinned up at him. "Could have but didn't." Didn't Emeliano know he felt invincible?

"You need to think of the future, Cristiano. You and Valentino, why not go into business with your father? If

Pietro didn't already have three boys, I'd see if he'd take me on as partner," Emeliano said.

"Go to Rome, find a place and work up," Cristiano suggested, conscious of the attention from the woman at the next table. He didn't care if she eavesdropped. He had no secrets.

Except one.

"And my mother, what of her? You have it great, Cristiano."

He smiled, all for show. If only Emeliano knew the truth—all the truth—he'd look away in disgust. "How is your mother?"

"Ailing. Arthritis is a terrible thing." Emeliano flexed his hands. "I hope I never get it."

"Me, too."

Cristiano met the woman's gaze again when Emeliano left and didn't look away. She flushed slightly and looked at the baby, smiling at his babbling and arm waving. Covering one small fist with her hand, she leaned over to kiss him. Just then she glanced up again.

"I saw you on the Jet Ski," she said.

He nodded.

"You fell in the water."

"But I didn't fall."

She shrugged, glancing at the infant. Then looked shyly at him again. "It looked like great fun."

"It is. How old is your baby?" He looked at the child, trying to gauge if it were smaller than the one from last May. He wasn't often around infants and couldn't guess his age.

She smiled again, her eyes going all silvery. Nice combination of coloring. He wondered again who she was and why she was at Lake Clarissa.

"He's almost five months."

A boy. His father had two boys and a girl. Wait, make that four boys and a girl. He still couldn't get used to the startling fact his sister shared a few months ago—about two older half-brothers who were Americans. Too surreal. Another reason to keep away from his family. He wasn't sure how he felt about his father keeping that secret all his life.

The infant had dark hair and dark eyes. His chubby cheeks held no clue as to what he'd look like as an adult, but his coloring didn't match hers at all.

"Does he look like his father?"

"I have no idea. But his mother had dark eyes and hair. Maybe when he's older, I'll see some resemblance to the man who fathered him. Right now to me he looks like his mom." She reached out and brushed the baby's head in a light caress.

"He's not yours?"

She shook her head.

"A nanny?" So maybe there was no man in the picture. Was she watching the baby for a family? She seemed devoted to the child.

She shook her head again. "I'm his guardian. His mother died." She blinked back tears and Cristiano again felt that discomforting shift in his mid section. He hoped she wasn't going to cry. He never knew how to handle a woman in tears. He wanted to slay dragons or race away. Unfortunately he all too often had to comfort women—and men sometimes—in tears at their loss. He always did his best. Always felt it fell short.

Emeliano arrived with a tray laden with rigatoni, big salad and hot garlic bread. He glanced at the woman, then Cristiano. "Want to sit together?"

"No," Cristiano said.

At the same time she replied, "That would be fine, if he doesn't mind."

"Oops," she said immediately. "I guess you do mind." She put on a bright smile. "I'll be going soon."

He felt like a jerk. He hadn't meant to embarrass her. "Come, sit with me. I could use the company while I eat." He tried to make up for the faux pas, but she just gave a polite smile and said, "No, thanks anyway, I have to be going. This guy likes to ride in the stroller to see the sights." She fumbled for her wallet and began pulling out the euros to pay her bill.

Emeliano served Cristiano, gave him a wry look and hurried away to look after another customer.

By the high color in her cheeks, he knew she was embarrassed. They'd been talking; it seemed churlish to refuse when his friend made the suggestion. Now he wished he had waited a second, thought before he spoke.

She rose and gathered her purse and a diaper bag and quickly carried the baby to the front of the restaurant without looking at him again. There he saw the stroller he'd missed when he first entered. In a heartbeat, they were gone.

His sister would have scolded him for his bad manners. His father would have looked at him with sadness. Of course his father seemed perpetually sad since their mother had died so long ago. He'd never found another woman to share his life with.

Cristiano began to eat. The food was good, not excellent, but good. What did it matter? Seeing the baby reminded him of his friend Stephano's young daughter. Too young to have lost her father. Cristiano still couldn't believe his best friend had perished in the instant the second bomb had exploded. Many days he could almost believe he was on leave and would go back to work to find Stephano and the others on his squad ready to fight whatever fires came their way.

But his friend was gone. Forever.

Cristiano ate slowly, regretting his hasty refusal of sitting with the woman with the baby. Learning more about her would have kept his mind off his friend and his other worries.

Mariella bundled Dante up and placed him in the stroller. She couldn't get out of the restaurant fast enough. She felt the wave of embarrassment wash over her as she remembered offering to have the man sit at her table. He had definitely been annoyed. He probably had women falling over themselves to gain his attention with those dark compelling eyes and the tanned skin. He looked as if he brought the outdoors inside with him. He towered over the waiter. When he'd sat at the table next to hers she'd been impressed with his trim physique, wide shoulders and masculine air. He had such vitality around him.

She'd also been too flustered to ask the waiter if he'd ever seen Ariana in the restaurant. She'd even brought the picture of her friend to show around.

A moment later the thought popped into her head that the man talking to the waiter could even have been Dante's father. He had the dark eyes and hair for it.

"So who's your daddy, sweetie? Did he live around here or only bring your mother for a visit?" she asked the baby as they moved along the worn sidewalk. Shops enticed, but it was difficult to maneuver the stroller through the narrow aisles of the small stores. She needed a better plan to try to find Dante's father than simply showing Ariana's photograph to every man she saw and asking if he'd known her. Why ever would anyone admit to it if there'd been a problem with their relationship?

Stopping near the church, she sat on one of the wooden benches facing the town square. It was peaceful here.

Dressed warmly, she was comfortable on this sunny afternoon despite the cooler temperatures. Checking on Dante, she was pleased he was warm and animated, looking around at the different buildings, up at the leaves on the tree partially shading the bench.

"Tree," she said. She knew Dante probably couldn't care less what that was called as long as she fed him on time and kept him dry and warm.

She still felt stressed dealing with the baby and hoped this trip would not only help her find out more about his father, but bring them closer together, too. She'd read every book she could get her hands on about newborns, had enlisted the help of a couple of friends who had children. But nothing had prepared her for the task of being an instant mom twenty-four-seven. At least most mothers had months to get used to the idea. Plans and dreams—usually with a partner—centered on the new life arriving. Psyching themselves up for the challenges.

Instead, Dante had been Mariella's instant baby. She had known about him for less than a month before she became his mother. No warning, no preparation, and definitely no partner to share the task.

Dante was dozing when Mariella thought about returning to the cottage she'd rented. He'd sleep better in the crib she'd had set up for him. And she could finish unpacking and settle in. They'd be here a week so she needed to get organized, then she could decide how to go on.

"I didn't mean to run you off." She looked to her left and saw the man from the restaurant. He paused beside her. The sun glinted on his dark hair. His dark eyes looked straight into hers and caused her heart to bump up in rhythm. For a moment she couldn't breathe. She felt a flare of attraction sweep through her. It made her almost giddy. Certainly not the way a mother should react. She hadn't expected to see him again—especially so soon after the restaurant.

"I was ready to leave," she said. She looked away. He was gorgeous—tall, tanned and fit. Was he on holiday? Why else would he be Jet Skiing and then taking a long lunch in the middle of the week? Or did he live around here and have the kind of job that allowed mid-week excursions to the lake? She wanted to know more about him.

He sat beside her on the bench, staring at the fountain at the center of the square. She flicked him a glance, but he seemed oblivious, still focused on the fountain. She noted no rings on his hands. She looked where he looked. The honey-colored stone blended well with the mountain setting. The cobbled street gave testimony to the age of the village. Surely he'd seen it all before. As if reading her thoughts, he turned and looked at her, offering his hand.

"My name is Cristiano Casali. Emeliano's suggestion caught me by surprise. You have a baby and I thought it best—never mind. I apologize for my rudeness."

She shook his hand and then pulled hers free. Tingling from the brief contact, she cleared her throat and tried to concentrate on what he said and not on the amazing feelings suddenly pulsing through her. He was just a man being courteous.

"Not to worry. I'm Mariella Holmes." She didn't dare look at him. Let her get her roiling emotions under some control first.

"So the mystery of the baby intrigues me. And if you knew about how things have been with me lately, that's surprising. How is he yours? You look too young to be a guardian of anyone." He glanced at the baby, then back at her.

"I'm twenty-two and old enough. I have friends who didn't go to university who married young and already have two children." She would never confide to a stranger how unprepared she felt being a new mother. If she'd just had more time to prepare, maybe she'd feel better suited to the role.

"Okay, you're old enough, but how?"

"His mother died. Before she did, I agreed to be his guardian. Ariana had no other family." She was proud she could say her friend's name without bursting into tears. Studying him as she spoke, she saw no start of recognition when she said her friend's name.

"The father didn't object?" he asked.

"I don't have a clue who the father is." She'd asked as many of Ariana's friends as she knew if they had known the man. No one had. It was a secret her friend had taken with her.

Cristiano frowned at her statement. Mariella elaborated in a rush, feeling the need to explain.

"Dante's mother was my best friend, Ariana. She met some guy and fell in love. Apparently when she told him she was pregnant, the man abandoned her. I didn't know any of this. I was in New York when I got her phone call shortly before Dante was born. She was sick and asked me to come back to Italy. I did, instantly. When she asked me to take Dante, how could I refuse? We were as close as sisters, yet she never told me his father's name though I asked many times." She looked at the child, feeling the weight of her commitment heavy on her shoulders.

"What happened to your friend?" Cristiano asked gently.

Mariella took a moment to gather her composure. It was still hard to talk about the death of her very dearest and longest friend. "She died of leukemia. She found out she had it while pregnant and refused any treatment until after the baby was born. He arrived healthy and strong, though a couple of weeks early. She died when he was two weeks old."

Mariella tried to blot out the picture of her friend those last weeks. Her thin cheeks, lackluster hair, sad, sad eyes. Ariana had known she wouldn't live to see her baby grow up. She'd implored Mariella over and over to promise to raise Dante for her. The day the guardianship paper had been signed, Ariana had smiled for the last time and soon thereafter slipped into a coma, which led to her death.

"You still seem awfully young to be tied down with a baby. Shouldn't you be out enjoying life at this stage?"

"Thanks for your concern, but I'm fine with being Dante's guardian." She didn't need some stranger questioning her ability to watch the baby. It was a huge responsibility, Mariella knew that already. And she often questioned her ability herself when lying awake at night, trying to anticipate all she needed to do to raise Dante. Mariella considered it an honor to be chosen to raise her friend's baby.

No one needed to know how overwhelmed she felt. And how while she loved Dante, it was not the deep maternal love she knew other mothers felt immediately for their child. Mariella loved this baby, but couldn't help feeling a bit cheated of her best friend. If Ariana had not been pregnant when she'd found out about the leukemia, she might be alive today. Mariella felt alone in a way she'd never experienced before; isolated even more by the demands of an infant.

Not that she'd tell anyone in a million years. What if it ever came back to Dante? She did love him. She did! But she had loved her friend for far longer.

"I need to go," she said, jumping up. She had to escape her thoughts. She could do this. She would do this. Or find his father and make sure Dante had a loving family to welcome him.

"Seems like I run you off at every turn," Cristiano said.

She started pushing the stroller. Cristiano rose and fell into step beside her. "Why are you here at this time of year? Most tourists come in the summer months, when they can use the lake," he said. Glancing at the baby, he added, "And they come when their kids are older and can play by the water. We'll be getting rain before long. It's already colder now than a couple of weeks ago. Not very conducive to sitting by the lake."

"I thought maybe I could find out about Dante's father. But now that I'm here, I'm not so sure." It had been a foolish thought. Clutching at straws, that was what. The man could have brought her friend here for a get-away weekend. She only knew Ariana had been happy at Lake Clarissa.

"What do you know about him?" Cristiano asked.

"Nothing. Ariana wouldn't talk about him at all."

They approached the small resort on the lake. Traffic was light on the street. The quiet of the afternoon was interrupted only by birdsong.

"You have the last cottage, right?"

"How did you know that?" Mariella asked, looking at him. He had obviously shortened his stride to stay even with her. She wondered if he'd come to the cottage and stay a while. She'd love to put the baby down and have some adult conversation—especially with a man so unlike others she knew.

"I saw it was occupied when I was skiing."

"Do you live here year round?" she asked.

"No." With that one word, he changed. She glanced at him, but his expression gave nothing away. He looked ahead as they walked, not elaborating on the single-word response. But she could feel the difference, the way he closed himself off. A bleakness in his eyes that hadn't been there before. What had she said?

"Visiting?" she probed. He'd asked enough questions, she could ask a few. Her curiosity grew. If Ariana had been around, she'd have called her up to tell her about the daredevil and how he was a poster child for sexy, virile Italian male. And speculate why he was at Lake Clarissa and discuss ways she might get to know him better.

"Staying a while," was all he said.

Her curiosity arose another notch. But she didn't know him well enough to pester with a lot of questions. Though a dozen burned on her tongue.

The path to the cottage was packed dirt lined with rocks. Bumpy and uneven. It was a bit of a struggle for Mariella to push the stroller, but Dante loved being bounced around. He gurgled and looked enchanted with the bouncy ride.

"Here, let me," Cristiano said at one point, reaching out to take the stroller. His hand brushed hers as he reached for the handle and she folded her arms across her chest, savoring the tingling. Walking beside him made her feel sheltered and feminine. This was how a family should be, father, mother and baby. She blinked. No going off in daydreams, she admonished.

"Thanks," she said when they reached the fifth cabin. The trees shaded in the afternoon. The small stone terrace had two chairs and a small table to use when sitting to watch the lake.

The wind had picked up a bit and it was definitely cooler than before.

"I can manage from here," she said with a smile. "I hope I see you in town again," she said, feeling daring. It would be too awful to have this be their sole encounter.

He stepped away from the stroller and looked at her.

Mariella had the feeling he wanted to say something. His eyes seemed full of turmoil. But he merely nodded and said, "Maybe you will. I come to town often. Goodbye."

She watched as he walked back along the path, his long legs covering the distance in a short time. One minute he was there, the next gone. And he took some of the brightness of the day with him.

She should have shown him the picture. Maybe he had seen Ariana. Where did he live? Why had her question caused the change? One minute he seemed open and friendly, the next closed and reserved. Not that it was any of her business. But she couldn't help the curiosity. Was he married? Separated or divorced?

She hoped she saw him again before she left.

Cristiano walked back to the square wondering if he was losing his mind. It had been months since anything had caught his attention as strongly as Mariella Holmes had. She was pretty—granted. But he'd seen other pretty women.

But not like her, something inside whispered. Her hair had that healthy glossy sheen that caught the light and reflected golden highlights. It looked thick and silky. He wished he could have touched it to verify the satiny feel. Her eyes were clear and honest. Her emotions shone through as they changed from steel grey to silvery.

He tried to ignore the image of her that kept flashing in his mind. Her gentle touch with the baby, her bright smile. The way she had of brushing back her hair when the breeze blew it in her face. Was he ready to risk a normal life now? Had things finally turned for the better? He had too much baggage to think of getting involved.

Yet she also came with baggage—a baby.

He'd never envisioned himself as a father. Or even a husband. He liked speed, challenges, adrenaline-producing activities that confirmed over and over he was alive and living life to the fullest. His job as a firefighter was exhilarating, but dangerous. Other men on his crew were married, but he'd never felt it fair to constantly risk his life if someone was depending on him.

He stopped along the sidewalk and gazed over the water. He knew he might never join his crew in battling a blaze again, or, then again, he might be fit to return to duty next week. No one knew what the future held. Maybe his held a silvery-eyed beauty. But he knew he had better be damned sure before going down that path.

Mariella Holmes had domesticity written all over her. She was not for a holiday romance. It'd be best for both their sakes to stay away from her.

Reaching the motorcycle, he sat on it a moment, watching neighbors and townspeople going about their business, shopping, greeting each other. Some waved to him and he acknowledged the greetings. Did they have secrets that would change lives? Did they have families who had kept secrets that were now coming out? Did they have sorrows and loss like those that had dimmed Mariella's smile?

Too philosophical for him. He put on the black helmet and started the bike. It was a short drive from the village of Lake Clarissa to the family cottage. He had liked being able to walk to the lake as a child. The happy times their family had once had seemed far away these days. Passing the driveway, he continued on, revving up his speed as if he could outrun the memories on the deserted mountain roads.

It was after dark when he pulled to a stop at the back of the family cottage. His excessive speed would give his father a heart attack. The harrowing hairpin turns provided a challenge he loved meeting. The fabulous scenery that raced by was a strong contrast to the smoke and dust and hell of his last weeks in Rome. He much preferred the vistas the hills offered to the memory of death and destruction and loss.

He entered the kitchen and ignored the dishes on the counter and in the sink. Going straight to the cabinet near the stove, he opened it and took down the bottle of brandy. It was far lighter than it had been last night. Not enough, now, to get rip-roaring drunk. He set it on the counter, reached for a glass, then stared at the bottle for a long moment. With a violent smash of his hand he knocked it on the stone floor where it broke into a thousand pieces, the smell of brandy filling the air.

He didn't need the stupor drink caused. Striding to his room, he stripped and went to take a shower, thinking of the bright smile on Mariella Holmes' face, and the love she showered on the baby. That was what he wanted. To feel connected. To feel passion and caring and hope for the future. To love. Dared he risk seeing her again?

CHAPTER TWO

MARIELLA rose at five to feed Dante. When he fell back asleep, she powered up her laptop and checked in on her clients, glad the rental cottage had Internet access. Working as a virtual assistant ensured she could work from home and at the hours that suited Dante's schedule. It was, however, a far cry from the work she'd thought she'd be doing after graduating from university.

She had often talked with friends in New York about setting up their own marketing firm. About setting New York on fire with their brilliant ideas and strong drive and determination. They'd fantasized about clients who would skyrocket them to the top of their field due to their impressive marketing.

Instead, she was quietly typing out another letter for a client miles away from the future she'd once envisioned. Yet she was grateful she'd found something that paid enough for their small flat and all their other needs. A baby was expensive. She could have been in worse shape.

By the time Dante woke from his nap in the late morning, Mariella had caught up on everything and had shut down her computer. Two of her major clients were away this week, which had freed enough time to allow her to start her search for Dante's father. It was a haphazard way to search for someone, but it was all she had to start with. Hiring someone would prove too expensive.

Bathing the baby when he awoke, then taking a quick shower after he'd been fed, she quickly prepared a light lunch. He was still awake and the day was lovely, so she took him in the stroller to the patio. Sitting on the wooden bench, she wished the cottage had come with a rocking chair. She had purchased one as soon as she'd known she would have Dante. It was soothing to rock the baby as he drank his bottle. Still, they'd only be here a week.

No daring Jet Ski riding today, she noticed. Or had Cristiano gone out earlier that morning and she'd missed him? She might have been busy with her work, but surely she would have heard the Jet Ski? She tried to ignore the pang of disappointment. She gazed at the deep blue of the water and the lighter blue of the sky. Contrasting with the dark green of the evergreen trees, it was an idyllic setting. She felt her heart lighten a bit. On impulse, she reached for the baby and held him sitting up in her arms as she absorbed the tranquility.

"Isn't this a pretty place?" she said, kissing the plump cheek. Dante gazed at her with wide brown eyes. Her heart expanded with love for her friend's child. He was such a precious little boy.

"Oh, Dante, what are we going to do?" she whispered. "I love you to bits, but I wish every time I see you that your mamma could see you. She loved you so much. One day I'll tell you just how much."

Then a noise caught her attention and she looked at the lake, almost grinning in surprised recognition. "It's him," she told the baby. "The man we met yesterday. Only you slept through most of it."

Cristiano sped across the water at a daring rate. She

watched, mesmerized. Did the man have no fear? She knew she'd be terrified to go at such speeds across the water.

He made it seem effortless. He and the machine seemed to be one as he banked and flew even faster toward the far shore. Soon she couldn't see him, only the arcing plume from the power ski. A moment later she saw the turn and then he was racing toward them. She stood, carried the baby to the edge of the patio and turned so Dante could also see the water. She had no idea if he was watching the Jet Ski, but she could scarcely take her eyes off the man riding. She remembered every inch of him—tall, tanned skin, dark hair shaggy and long. Remembering his dark eyes that had gazed into hers so intently had her heart racing.

She'd hoped to see him again. Wanted to learn more about him. Hear him tell about the village and the people who lived here. And tell her what he did in life, where he lived, what made him laugh. Was there a special woman in his life? She didn't think so, but would like to know for sure.

Was there any place in his life for her?

Foolish thoughts. She was only here for a short time.

As he approached the small dock in front of her cottage, he slowed, coming to a coasting stop as he cut the engine and glided to the wooden planks. Bumping slightly, he sat back and looked up at her.

She almost laughed in delight and, holding Dante firmly, she carefully followed the path to the dock, walking out the few steps to where he bobbed in the water.

"Hi," she said. "That looks amazing. How fast do you go?" She couldn't help her grin as she took in the broad shoulders, the muscular legs straddling the machine. For a moment she wished she'd checked her hair before coming out. But with the breeze, it would be windblown no matter what. Cristiano looked fantastic, tousled hair, ruddy cheeks, and those compelling brown eyes that about melted her heart.

"Not too fast. Want to go for a spin?" he asked with a cheeky grin, taking in the baby.

She laughed and shook her head, jiggling Dante a little. "Not with a baby, thank you very much. I'd never let him go on one of those."

"Maybe when he's older," Cristiano said, sitting casually on the floating machine, one foot on the dock anchoring him in place.

She eyed the machine with some wariness. "Too dangerous. Aren't you cold?" The breeze reminded her it was fall, no hot summer days to be refreshed by the water. With his dark eyes focused on her, she felt her temperature rise. The attraction that flared between them confused her. She'd never felt emotions like this with other men she'd known. Was Cristiano different in some way? Or was it just normal reaction after months of only dealing with Dante?

"My feet are freezing. I'm ready to head back. You going into the village today?"

Mariella hadn't been sure before, but this clinched it. "Yes. We'll be walking over in a little while. Are you planning to be there?" She gave him her best smile. Was she flirting with the man? Yes—and it felt great.

"I'll buy you an ice-cream cone." His eyes locked with hers, as if urging her to say yes.

She felt daring and excited at the same time. She nodded. "I'd like that." Trying to subdue the excitement from her voice, she said, "Don't fall in on your way back."

"No chance." He pushed off and in a moment the motor caught and he headed the short distance to the town's small marina.

She watched until she couldn't see him clearly.

"So, we've been invited to see him again," she said to Dante, hurrying back to the cottage to get the stroller. She could hardly wait.

Cristiano ran the Jet Ski up on the floating berth and turned off the motor. He'd left his clothes on the motorcycle again only this time didn't just pull them over his wet ones, but used the men's facilities at the public boathouse to change. He refused to examine closely why he'd stopped by the cottage to see her. He'd spotted her on the patio and impulse had driven him closer.

The only way to know if she was around, without being totally blatant about it, was to use the lake. When he'd seen her on the porch, the lure of the Jet Ski had vanished. He'd wanted to see her again.

Dressed, he bundled the wet clothes, strapping them on the back of the motorcycle. It would be a two-minute ride to the square. He had no idea if she'd already arrived. Maybe he should have gone home to get the car.

She was talking with the priest in front of the church when Cristiano entered the square. Stopping some distance away, he cut the engine and sat on the motorcycle as he watched, curious what she could be talking to Father Andreas about. The old man shook his head and then smiled down at the baby in the stroller.

In an instant the sunshine dimmed. Cristiano remembered the feel of the baby in the cradle of his arm, the small, terrified child clutched with the other. The baby cried and cried. The nightmare of smoke and darkness and wailing screams filled his senses. For a moment he was there, back in the tunnels of the metro, fighting for breath, for a foothold, for life itself with two children who were too young to die.

He could feel the heat of the fire behind him. Hear the shouts of other first responders, everyone trying to fight their way through hell. Screams of the dying, distorted shadows as the flames flared and waned. He could smell the smoke and dust as clearly as he had when his helmet shattered.

He couldn't breathe. He couldn't see. Which way was out? Which way lay sunshine and fresh air and life itself?

A shout sounded louder than the rest. Something bounced on his thigh and Cristiano blinked, looking down at the rubber ball that rolled away from where it had struck him. Two boys raced after it, their laughter and shouts echoing in the square.

He looked around. Mariella was pushing the stroller toward him. The priest was standing on the stairs leading into the old church smiling at the children who played around the fountain. The sun shone in a cloudless sky. A pastoral scene, one of peace and tranquility and the very fabric of life.

Taking a breath, he hoped he could keep his mind in the present. He'd thought he had these flashbacks under control. It had been days since—

"Hello,' she said as she approached, that wide smile holding his gaze.

No one seemed to notice anything out of the ordinary. Only Cristiano knew he'd had another flashback—thankfully brief this time. He never knew when they'd come, how debilitating they'd be. This one had passed quickly. Because of Mariella?

He didn't want her to know. They'd spend some time together today, enjoy each other's company and then he'd take off for the cottage, the bolt-hole he'd claimed when he had been released from the hospital. No one in his family had known he'd been injured far beyond the ankle that had broken.

"Are you all right?" Mariella asked when she reached the motorcycle, a questioning look in her eyes.

"Sure." He needed to change that subject quickly. "How do you know Father Andreas?"

"We just met. He was walking by and I showed him my friend's picture to see if he recognized her. He didn't."

She drew it from her pocket and held it out to Cristiano. He took it. The laughing expression on the unknown woman's face tugged at his heart. This was the young mother who had died. She didn't look as old as Mariella. Did Mariella feel the same tearing grief he felt whenever he thought about his friend Stephano? Did she regret time wasted when, if she had only known the future, she would have changed what she did in the weeks, days left before her friend's death?

Had he known Stephano would die in the bomb explosion last May, would he have done more in the days leading to that fateful time? Or would he have taken everything for granted as he had expecting them both to live forever?

It was a lesson well learned. No one could predict the future. Enjoy life while he could. As long as he could.

Handing it back, he said, "I don't recognize her. When was she here?"

"I don't know. Sometime within the last eighteen months is all I have. I thought at restaurants or shops someone would recognize her." She slipped the photograph back into her pocket and shrugged. "So far no one has."

"What are you going to do if you find him?"

"I'm still not sure. A baby should have his family around him. I'm hoping the father comes from a large family who would love Dante. I may never find him. But I want to tell Dante when he's older that I tried."

"Let your family be his."

She shrugged. "I have no family. Ariana was the closest thing to a sister I had. Both our parents are dead. Neither of us had any other living relatives. Maybe it's foolish to search for his father, but if it were me, I'd want to know. Easier maybe to find out about him now than when Dante is twenty-one."

Cristiano didn't know how he'd feel about finding out he had a child at some future date, after the child was grown. Had the man truly not wanted any connection, or had his initial reaction been panic that he now regretted?

In a way, his family's recent events paralleled Mariella's situation. He still didn't know how to deal with the newly acquired knowledge that his father had other sons, older than he was. They'd grown up a world apart. Would there be some connection should they ever meet? Would blood call to blood? Or would they forever be strangers?

Cristiano could never knowingly give up a child if he had one. How had his father done it?

He kicked down the stand and got off the motorcycle. "Have you questioned everyone in town?"

"So far only the priest and the proprietor at the resort."

"Come, I'll buy you an ice-cream cone and you can ask there. Seems to me your best bet would be restaurants and shops where visitors are likely to go."

"Maybe, but they could have simply come for a weekend at the height of the season when she'd have been just one of many," she said, pushing the stroller ahead as they walked around the square. The sun shone in a cloudless sky. The air was cool, but comfortable. And she was walking beside a handsome, attentive man. She didn't want to talk about Ariana and her lost love. She wanted to learn more about Cristiano.

The ice-cream shop was virtually empty.

"Not the time of year for ice cream. Want something else?" he asked.

"No. This will be good. I can give Dante a tiny taste. He's not eating real food yet."

They ordered, then went back into the square to sit on a bench in the sunshine.

"Did you once live here? The proprietress knew you," she asked.

"My grandparents were from Lake Clarissa. They had a small cottage nearby. We lived with them when we were children and papa was busy working. Summer days we would swim in the lake. Sometimes we'd camp out overnight in the forest."

He watched as Mariella licked her ice cream. The lonely existence he'd chosen these past few months melted away. He hadn't felt normal for a long time. What was it about this woman that changed that? He could forget the horror that haunted him when he was around her. Maybe he should take her home with him and keep her with him until the spell was broken.

Yet moments before he'd had another flashback. He looked away. He had no business coming to town. What if he had a major meltdown? He had to beat this thing before he could get his life back.

"Sounds like you had a lot of fun here," she said.

"Yes, we did, it was a happy time. My grandfather lived until I was almost an adult. He continued to live here even when we had all moved away from home, he was a part of the place. He gave our childhood an extra sense of fun and excitement, beyond playing in the forest or at the lake." Hard to think about the past when he listened to her voice, soft and lilting.

"Is that where you got your daredevil ways?" she asked with a teasing grin.

"Daredevil ways?" That grin felt like a kick to the mid section. For a moment he forgot where they were and wondered what she'd do if he leaned over and kissed her. Her eyes sparkled, there were freckles scattered across her nose, kisses from the sun. He looked away before he did something foolish, such as trail kisses over every one. They'd just met. It was too early to think about kisses.

Yet as the seconds ticked by, the thought would not fade. He'd like to take her hand and feel the soft warmth against his palm. Sit closer so he could feel every radiant bit of heat from her body. Lean in so she could only see him. Find out what fascinated him about her.

"Racing across the lake like you were trying to fly. I consider that amazingly like a daredevil," she explained, leaning closer.

Did she feel that same pull of attraction? He took a breath, taking in the scent of her, light and flowery. He held his breath for a moment to savor it. Then released it and shook his head. "I'm no daredevil. You should meet my brother Valentino. Now, he's the daredevil in the family. Today was just Jet Skiing."

She pointed to the motorcycle across the square. "That's a dangerous mode of transportation."

"Not if you know what you're doing. It's like flying along the road."

"So tell me about living here, especially during summer," she invited as they ate their cones.

Cristiano didn't want to talk about himself; he wanted to know more about Mariella. But if he offered something, he could have her reciprocate. He began recounting summer days playing at the edge of the lake, climbing around on the rocky shore and learning to swim. Then the nights he and Valentino had spent roaming the woods, feeling daring and grown up braving the darkness.

She laughed at his stories and from time to time admonished Dante to stop listening, she didn't want him to get ideas. The longer Cristiano talked, the lighter the world seemed to grow. He liked hearing her laugh. The more she did, the more outrageous he made the stories.

"Now, tell me about your summer holidays," he said when he'd wound down. They'd long since finished their ice cream. The baby had fallen asleep and Mariella seemed content to sit in the sunshine. It was as if she brought sunshine into his life where only darkness had once dwelt.

"We always went to places to learn more about history. My father was an accountant, but he loved history. So we visited Pompeii and Turin, Florence, of course, and Venice." She smiled in memory and Cristiano knew from her expression how much she'd enjoyed those vacations with her parents.

"Ariana went with us when we were teenagers. We flirted like crazy with the gondoliers in Venice. Of course they ignored us." She laughed, then her eyes unexpectedly filled with tears. "We should have had the chance to remember all those foolish activities when we were old with grandchildren running around. It's so unfair she died."

Cristiano wanted to comfort her, but only time would completely heal the pain.

"I had a friend who died last May. Life is unfair. I'm single with few responsibilities. He had a wife and two children. Why him? It should have been me."

She looked at him in shock. "Never say that. Who knows why some die young? But I have never thought it should have been me instead of Ariana. Life is too precious. We need to enjoy every moment. Maybe even more so because in a way we are now living also for our friends, experiencing life as they will no longer be able to."

The memories were threatening again. The fear he'd end up hiding beneath the bench they now sat on in the middle of the day, yelling for Stephano, was real. He had to get away before he cracked.

He stood. "I have to go.' The tightness in his chest grew. It was becoming more difficult to breathe. He held onto the present desperately.

"Thank you for the ice cream. And the conversation," she said.

He nodded and strode to the motorcycle. Staying any longer was flirting with danger. He knew his limits—and he'd passed them already. Time to get away.

He started the bike and looked over at Mariella. She was watching him, her head tilted slightly as if wondering what had gone wrong. If she only knew all that was wrong.

"Come tomorrow," he said.

She smiled and nodded.

Mariella watched Cristiano leave. He was the most perplexing man she'd ever met. She'd thought they'd been having a great conversation when he'd abruptly jumped up and left. She tried to remember what she could have said to cause such a reaction. They'd been exchanging memories and she had lamented the fact she and Ariana wouldn't grow old together.

So who was his friend who had died young? Such an odd thing for them to have in common, yet for a moment it brought her comfort. He was someone who could understand the sadness she felt for the loss of her friend.

The evening was quiet. Mariella played with Dante until the baby fell asleep. She liked this impromptu vacation. She was still working the odd hours to keep her clients happy. But she had more time to spend with the baby. And with several months' of experience behind her, she was growing more confident in her abilities than that first month as a stunned guardian with a tiny infant and no job.

She could not afford to stay in Lake Clarissa for long, however. She wanted to expand the search for Dante's father before she had to return to Rome. Stopping in a few shops, speaking with the priest didn't encompass all of the village. Tomorrow she'd make a concerted effort to visit more places. Then if she had no results, the next day she'd move on to Monta Correnti.

After the baby was asleep, she checked her laptop for any new assignments, then surfed the Net. She put in Cristiano's name on a whim and was startled when pages loaded. He was a firefighter. He'd been a first responder to the bombing in Rome last May. She read the compelling newspaper articles. The man was a hero. He'd gone down into the bombing scene time and again. He'd saved seven lives, become injured himself and still fought to bring a baby and small child through the smoke-filled metro tunnel to safety that last trip.

Wow. She read every article she could on the bombing. She'd been finishing up finals in New York when the terrorist attack had hit Rome. Once she'd been assured none of her friends had been injured, she'd relegated it and all other news to the back of her mind as she madly studied. Even if she'd seen Cristiano's name back then, she never would have remembered it.

She had suspected he had some physically demanding job. He was strong, muscular and fit. He moved with casual grace in that tall body. And being around him gave her a definite sense of security. She searched further hoping for a picture, but the only ones she saw were of firefighters and police in uniform, battling for people's lives.

It was late when she shut down the computer. Checking the doors and windows before retiring, she realized how much it had cooled down in the cottage. She switched on the wall heater and went to get ready for bed. Dante was fast asleep in one of the fleecy sleepers she used for him at night. She covered him with a light blanket and shivered; her fingers were freezing. Fall had truly arrived. At least the baby would be warm through the night, and once she was beneath the blankets she'd be toasty warm herself.

Cristiano sat upright with a bolt. He became instantly awake, breathing hard, the terror still clinging from the nightmare. He took deep gulps of breath, trying to still his racing heart. It was pitch dark—not unlike the tunnel after the bombing. Only the lights from their helmets had given any illumination in the dusty and smoky world.

He threw off the blanket and rose, walking to the window and opening it wide for the fresh air. The cold breeze swept over him, jarring him further. He breathed in the crisp air, relishing the icy clean feel. No smoke. No voices screaming in terror. Nothing here but the peaceful countryside in the middle of the night. The trees blotted out a lot of the stars. The moon rode low on the horizon, its light dancing on the shimmering surface of the lake, a sliver of which was visible from the window.

He gripped the sill and fought the remnants of the nightmare. It was hauntingly familiar. He'd had it often enough since that fateful day. Gradually the echoes of frantic screams faded. The horror receded. The soft normal sounds of night crept in.

Long moments later he turned to get dressed. There would be no more sleep tonight.

Once warmly clothed, he went to the motorcycle and climbed on board. A ride through the higher mountain roads would get him focused. He knew he was trying to outrun the demons. Nothing would ever erase that day from his mind. But he couldn't stay inside a moment longer. The wind rushed through his hair; the sting of cold air on his cheeks proved he was alive. And the lack of smoke was life-affirming. It was pure nectar after the hell he'd lived through.

Driving on the curving roads required skill and concentration. One careless moment and he could go spinning over the side and fall a hundred feet. The hills were deserted. No homes were back here, no one to see him as he made the tight turns, forcing the motorcycle to greater speed. He still felt that flare of exhilaration of conquering the challenge, his skills coming into play. At least he had this.

It was close to dawn when Cristiano approached the village. He'd made a wide circle and was heading back to home. A hot cup of espresso sounded good right about now.

He settled in on the road that curved around the lake. Soon he'd turn for the short climb to the family cottage. Then he smelt it.

Smoke.

His gut clenched. For a moment he thought he imagined it. He drew in a deep breath—it was in the air. Where there was smoke, there was fire. He slowed down and peered around. No one would have a campfire going at this hour; it was getting close to dawn. There, stronger now. To the left, near the lake.

For a moment indecision gripped him. Each breath identified the smoke as it wafted on the morning air. Forest fire? Building fire? He stopped the motorcycle, holding it upright with one foot on the ground. Every muscle tightened. He couldn't move. He felt paralyzed. Where were the village's firefighters? Why wasn't someone responding? Had the alarm even been sounded?

Seconds sped by.

Instinct kicked in. He slowly started moving, lifting his foot from the ground as the bike picked up speed.

He spotted a flicker of light where only darkness should be. He opened the throttle and raced toward the spot. In a moment, he recognized where he was—near the Bertatalis' row of cottages beside the lake. The flickering light came from the last one—the one Mariella and the baby were in!

He gunned the motor and leaned on the horn. In only a moment, lights went on in the Bertatalis' main house. He didn't stop, hoping they'd see the fire and respond. Seconds counted. Smoke inhalation could be fatal long before the actual flames touched anyone. Stopping near the cottage, he threw down the bike and raced to the door. He could see the fire through the living-room window almost consuming the entire area. The roof was already burning with flames escaping into the night. It would be fatal to enter that room.

Running to the back, he tried to figure out which window was the bedroom. Pounding on the glass, he heard no response. He hit his fist against the glass, but nothing happened. Quickly looked for anything to help; there—a large branch of a tree had fallen. Praying the baby was not sleeping beneath the window, he swung it like a bat, shattering the glass.

Smoke poured out. He could see the flames eagerly devouring the living room through the open bedroom door.

"Mariella," he shouted, levering himself up on the sill, brushing away glass shards, feeling the slight prick of a cut. He coughed in the smoky air.

"Huh?"

The sleepy voice responded. He jumped into the room and quickly assessed the situation. The door was open, the flames visible through the roiling smoke. Time was of the essence.

"Get up," he yelled, slamming shut the bedroom door, hoping it would hold the flames until he could get them out of the room. Where was Dante? He searched for the baby by touch in the smoke-filled room. There, near the wall, a cry sounded. He snatched up Dante and looked for Mariella. She was not responding. Had she already been overcome by smoke?

Stepping quickly as the crackling sounded louder, he found her still in bed and dragged her up.

"The cottage is on fire," he said as calmly as he could, trying to get through to her. He heard the sirens. Finally. Fear closed his throat as he looked overhead. An explosion paralyzed him. Was the tunnel caving in? Were there more bombs? Why wasn't his breathing mask working? He coughed in the smoke and moved toward the opening, pulling her with him. Echoes of men and women's screams sounded. The baby began screaming. Where was the little boy? Where was Stephano? Who could have done such a thing? How long did they have until everyone was safe?

"Cristiano?" Mariella's voice broke through. She coughed as she stumbled beside him. "What happened?"

"Don't know. Get out." They had reached the window and he scooped her up until she had her feet out the window, then pushed her gently until she jumped free. One leg over the sill, Dante in his arms, he didn't hesitate. A bright show of sparks and fire exploded as part of the front roof collapsed. Jumping free, he grabbed her arm and pulled her away from the cottage, the baby wailing in his arms. Past and present merged. Cristiano didn't stop running until he recognized the lake. Mariella kept up with him, coughing in the cold air.

The village volunteer firefighters were on their way. The sirens pierced the dawn air. Cristiano fought to keep his mind focused on the present, to be by the lake, to ignore the clamoring of his mind to relive the terror of a day in May.

In only moments the fire engine stopped, men scrambling to positions. Leaning against a tree, Cristiano stared at the fire, his throat tight. Tonight had not ended in tragedy.

"All my things," Mariella said, watching as the bedroom seemed to blossom with fire. "My laptop, my clothes. Dante's clothes. How could this happen?" She had tears running down her face. A moment later she was coughing again, shivering in the dawn light.

He pulled her closer, his arm around her shoulder, the baby screaming in his arms. "They are only things. You and the baby are safe, that's what's important." He offered up a quick prayer that he'd been able to save them. He'd faced his worst fear and come through.

Stephano and so many others hadn't been as lucky.

He watched the fire devour the cottage. In only moments it was completely engulfed in flames. He could feel the heat from where they stood.

She shivered again and he looked at her. The fire gave plenty of illumination. Shrugging out of his jacket, he wrapped it around her and handed her the crying baby. Her feet were still bare and must be freezing in the cold. Without a word, he picked them both up and headed toward the Bertatalis' main house. His ankle felt stiff, but it held. With grim satisfaction for the healing his body had done, he stepped carefully on the uneven ground, swinging wide around the burning cottage.

She coughed and tried to comfort the crying baby.

Signora Bertatali stood on the porch of her home, tears running down her cheek. When she saw Cristiano carrying Mariella and the baby, she hurried over.

"Thank God they are safe. Cristiano, thank you. Let me take the baby," she said, reaching out for Dante. "What happened?"

"I don't know," he said. "I saw the fire from the road and came to get them."

Mariella flung one arm around his neck. "I was asleep. Cristiano woke me up. How could the fire start?" She coughed again so hard, he almost dropped her.

"Try to take a deep slow breath. You're suffering from smoke inhalation."

"I don't know how this could happen. Oh, my dear, when I realized it was our cottage I feared the worst. Paolo has gone to help the firefighters. We'll know more after they tell us. Come, inside where it's warm. Did you leave the stove on or something?" Signora Bertatali asked, leading the way to her home. The warmth after the cold dawn felt wonderful. The baby stopped crying when in the light, blinking around, still looking as if he'd begin again in an instant.

"No. I turned it off after dinner," Mariella said.

"Oh, your poor feet. They're cut. Let me get some cloths and towels and take care of that," Signora Bertatali exclaimed, hurrying into the back bathroom, still jiggling the baby, trying to comfort him.

"I had to break a window to get into the bedroom. The living room was engulfed with flames when I arrived," Cristiano said, lowering Mariella down on a chair and kneeling in front of her to examine her feet as she began coughing again. She drew his jacket closer. A deep cut with a glass shard still in her left foot was bleeding; there were minor cuts on her right foot that had already stopped.

"This looks as if it needs stitches," he said, taking one of the towels Signora Bertatali brought and, after pulling the glass out, wrapped her foot.

The next while was chaotic. More volunteers arrived. Then the ambulance from Monta Correnti. Mariella and Dante were loaded up and taken to hospital while Cristiano stayed behind.

"I'll come to the hospital soon," he said as they drove away.

Now that the situation was under control, he watched from a distance until the fire was out. The adrenalin was wearing off. He could hear Stephano calling him. Feel the darkness closing in even as the sun broke on the horizon.

Retrieving his motorcycle, he roared off once more— trying to outrace the past.

CHAPTER THREE

MARIELLA braced herself against another bump as the ambulance sped toward the hospital. Dante cried until she picked him up to cuddle, trying to hold him around the oxygen nodules they both wore. He grew quiet at that and snuggled against Mariella. "Oh, sweet thing, we almost died." Tears pricked her eyes. She caught a sob. How could the cottage catch fire? And why had there been no alarms to alert them of the danger before it was too late? The first she'd known of the emergency was when she heard Cristiano calling her name. Smoke had filled their room and she'd almost passed out trying to get out of bed and to safety. Breathing had been almost impossible.

The next thing she remembered was stumbling into the yard with Cristiano while Dante cried. Thank God he was safe. They both were.

Her head pounded and her eyes watered again. Coughing, she felt she could not draw a full breath. A weight seemed pressed against her chest.

"We'll have you to hospital in just a short while. They'll bathe your eyes and continue the oxygen until morning," the EMT said, handing her a tissue to wipe the tears.

The baby had settled down, looked as if he was going back to sleep. She kissed his cheek, so grateful. Mariella wished she could drop off as he did and forget everything—if only for a few hours. Who would think such things happened while on holiday?

Once they reached the hospital, nurses swarmed around the ambulance. One gently took the baby, promising to take good care of him as she whisked him away to be seen by a doctor. Another helped Mariella into a wheelchair and pushed her quickly into the ER. It was quiet except for the two of them. In a short while a doctor had cleaned the cuts and stitched up the one on her left foot.

"Where's my baby?" she asked.

"He's in Pediatrics, on oxygen. A pediatrician has checked him out. Except for smoke inhalation, he seems fine. You can see him soon."

Mariella nodded. She already missed him. She needed to see again that he was all right. But patience was called for. For the first time she had a moment to think. Cristiano had saved them. She had no idea how he'd happened to be there, but she thanked God he had been. He was a hero. Without his intervention, she and Dante could have died.

After she'd been seen by the doctor, she was conveyed to a semi-private room by way of the pediatric ward. Once satisfied Dante was safely asleep, she allowed herself to be taken to her own room where she insisted she could bathe herself. After a quick shower, she gladly lay down, with oxygen, and tried to sleep—but the horrors of the night haunted her. What if Cristiano hadn't arrived? She and the baby could have been burned to death. What had caused the fire? What had brought Cristiano there at exactly the right time? It was much, much later before she fell into a fitful sleep.

Mariella stood by the window of the hospital room in the late morning gazing at the beauty before her. The gardens of the hospital gave way to the view of rolling hills that gave this area so much of its beauty. She knew the lake lay beyond her view. From her vantage point she saw only the edge of a bustling town and the distant serene countryside. The village was hidden behind a fold in the hills and no trace of smoke marred the crystal-blue sky.

Everyone went along with their daily lives. She had lost clothes and her laptop. And her photo of Ariana. Dante had only the sleeper he wore when they were rescued. Her livelihood depended on connections with her clients. She had to get another computer soon. She had backup files at home, so wouldn't totally start from the beginning. But this would certainly put a crimp in things.

The few hours' sleep she'd managed made her feel refreshed. She needed her wits about her to get back on track. Maybe she should consider returning to Rome immediately. But she wasn't sure when she'd have another break in her workload to look for Dante's father. If she didn't do some checking now, people would forget. Maybe they already had. But she owed it to the baby to find out anything she was able to.

Even with oxygen she still used she felt as though her lungs were on fire and it was difficult to breathe. Still, things were improving—she could go several minutes without the racking coughs.

She was declared healthy enough to be discharged, with a follow-up visit scheduled for a few days later.

She hurried to the pediatric ward, limping slightly because of the stitches in her left foot. She slowed in surprise to see Cristiano staring at the babies in the nursery.

"Cristiano?"

He turned and smiled when he saw her, giving her a critical look. "How are you today?"

She coughed, then smiled as she came up to him. "Much better. Doctor said I can go home and come back in a few days for another checkup." She looked into the nursery. "Is Dante in there?"

"No, these are newborns. Look how small they are."

She noticed the four babies and smiled. "Dante was tiny like that when he was born. Now look how big he's grown."

He turned and studied her again. "You really okay or are you pushing things?"

"I really will be fine. Let's find Dante."

Mariella was wearing clothes lent to her by a nurse on the night shift. Her feet didn't bother her much. The cut on the left gave her a bit of a limp, but the doctor had assured her it would heal quickly with no lasting damage. The scruffy slippers she wore needed to be replaced, too. Her mind spun with all she needed to do.

Cristiano led the way into the pediatric ward and in seconds they were in the room with the baby.

"The pediatrician made his round a short time ago," the nurse said. "Your baby's ready to go." She smiled at both of them. "He's a darling child. So attentive. But I know he misses his parents."

In a moment Mariella stood by the crib. Dante looked up at Mariella and gave her a wide grin. Lifting his arms, he came up easily when she reached out to pick him up. She held him closely, relishing the warmth of him in her arms. Her heart swelled with love. For a moment she almost broke into tears thinking about how close she had come to losing him. He was her precious son. The last link to her dearest friend. She gave silent thanks for his safety.

She turned to Cristiano. "You did a wondrous thing saving us. How could I ever thank you?" Mariella took a deep breath, taking in the sweet scent of baby powder and baby shampoo.

"Just get well fast. I'm glad I was there."

"And knew what to do. I don't even want to think about what could have happened."

"Don't. Let's get out of here," he said. "I'm not a big fan of hospitals."

As soon as they stepped outside he steered her to the black sports car parked nearby. Eying it dubiously, she asked, "Do you have a car seat for Dante?"

"The hospital is lending us one until you buy another. Then we'll bring it back. First thing, you need some clothes. Not that the outfit you're wearing doesn't have a certain cachet," he said, opening the door and pushing the passenger seat forward to access the baby's seat.

She laughed, then broke into coughing again. "Thanks. Nothing boosts a woman's ego more than compliments—" She stopped abruptly, before saying *from a man she cares about*. She had only just met the man. Taking the opportunity to end the statement while she put Dante into the carrier, she vowed to watch what she said in future.

Dante was oblivious to any tension. He babbled away in baby language and patted Mariella's face. Tangling his fingers in Mariella's long hair as she leaned over fastening the straps, he pulled.

"Ouch. You have to stop doing that," Mariella said with a laugh, grabbing his little hand and kissing the fingers. "That hurts!"

"He seems in fine form," Cristiano said.

Mariella smiled. "Seems as if no harm done. He's not even coughing."

Once she got Dante situated, she turned to Cristiano, so glad he'd come for her. "I have a million things to do. Are you sure you're up for it?"

"Who else?"

She bit her lip and nodded. Who else indeed? She had

no one except friends in Rome. If he was willing, she'd take all the help she could get.

"I have no identification—it burned in the fire. Along with all my money. I guess the first stop should be the bank, to see if I can get some cash."

"If not, I'll advance you some. Come on, it's breezy, let's get going."

Fifteen minutes later Mariella sat in a branch of her bank, talking with a manger to verify her identity and get money. Dante sat in Cristiano's lap, reaching for things on the manager's desk. He patiently pulled him back each time.

"That takes care of that,' the manager said as he hung up his telephone. "I'll get my secretary to bring you the money, and a temporary check book. You'll get imprinted checks sent to your home."

"Thank you. I appreciate all you've done for me."

The speedy transaction had been facilitated by Cristiano. The manager knew him and his family.

Once Mariella had money, Cristiano drove to a department store where she could get all she needed. He knew his way around Monta Correnti, for which she was grateful.

First purchase was a stroller for Dante, and a baby carrier. Once she no longer had to carry him, she felt better able to cope.

"Get a few things for him. I'll watch him, then, while you get your things," Cristiano suggested.

"You are a saint to do all this for me," she said. "I'm not sure I could have managed on my own."

He reached out and brushed back a lock of hair, tucking it behind her ear. The touch sent shockwaves running through her body. She smiled shyly and wanted to catch his hand and hold onto it, gaining what strength she could from him. But she kept still, treasuring the touch of his fingertips.

"You could have managed, I have no doubt. But why do it on your own?"

She nodded, knowing he'd made a special effort to help her. From comments Signora Bertatali had made, Cristiano had not left Lake Clarissa since he had arrived. She didn't know why he made an exception for her, but she was grateful.

"Next should be food for the baby. Once he's ready to eat, he lets everyone know in no uncertain terms—crying his head off."

"I bow to your assessment."

Mariella enjoyed shopping, the easy banter that grew between them. She held up baby clothes for his approval, which he gave after much mock deliberation.

"It really doesn't matter that much," she said, laughing at his posturing about the perfect outfit for Dante. "He's a baby. He doesn't know or care what he wears."

"Hey, he's special. He needs to make a statement—he's cool and he knows it."

She laughed again. Who could have suspected the devastation of the fire could lead to such a fun day-after? "I'll be sure to take pictures so he'll know when he's older."

Cristiano cocked his head at that. "Do you have a camera?"

"It burned."

"We'll get another."

"All the pictures I had on it are gone, too."

"All the more reason to make sure you start snapping new photos, so those won't be missed."

Her coughing was the only flaw in the day. She bought enough clothes to take care of a few days, shoes that didn't hurt her foot, and cosmetics—a definite necessity when she saw her face in the mirror. She probably should think about returning home to Rome. But she was enjoying every moment with Cristiano. She didn't want to think about being practical just yet.

Cristiano stood outside the dressing room, waiting for Mariella. Dante had been fed, changed, and was now asleep in the stroller. Idly he pushed it back and forth, but the baby didn't need soothing, he was out for his nap.

Glancing around the department store, he noted he was the only man, except for an elderly gentleman talking with his wife. If he'd ever suspected he'd be watching a baby this October day, that would have surprised him. Yet he couldn't imagine letting Mariella and Dante face this alone.

She came out of the dressing room wearing jeans that should have been banned—they made her figure look downright hot. The long-sleeve pink top highlighted her coloring and made her eyes seem even brighter silver. He could look at her all day. It wasn't just her looks that made it easy on the eyes. Her innate optimism shone from her eyes. He wished he could capture some of that for himself.

"Okay, I've gotten all I need, just have to pay for everything," she said, with a bright smile at him and a quick check for Dante.

"I'll be right here," he said, watching with appreciation as she walked away. Those freckles across her nose called to him. He wondered if she liked them. He'd heard from his sister when growing up that most women did not want freckles. He found them enticing. In fact, the more he saw of Mariella, the more he found enticing. She was pretty, sexy, and nurturing. He liked watching her with Dante. The baby seemed as fascinated with her as Cristiano was. "Probably a male thing," he murmured to the sleeping baby.

"All set," she said a moment later.

"Let's eat. You have to be hungry after all this and I know I am."

"Great. Where? Oh, dumb question, you probably always eat at your family restaurant."

Cristiano felt the comment like a slap. He had not been to Rosa for a long time. He'd been avoiding his cosseting family as much as he could, not wanting their sympathy over his injuries, and especially not wanting them to learn of his torment.

Excuses surged to mind. "I thought we'd eat closer to where we are. Rosa is across town. Then we need to get you two back to Lake Clarissa."

"Why? Where am I going to stay?"

"You could stay with me," he said. Then stared at her as the words echoed. Was he totally crazy? He'd been avoiding people to keep quiet about the flashbacks. He could not have anyone stay at the cottage. The first night he had a nightmare, the secret would be revealed.

"Thank you, really, but I can't stay with you. If the Bertatalis have another cabin available, maybe I'll stay a bit longer. I probably ought to return to Rome."

"Don't go."

He felt the intensity of her gaze. He could almost feel her mind working as she considered staying.

"Maybe for a few more days. I have no picture of Ariana to show around, few clothes, no computer."

"I have one you can use."

She slowly smiled. It was all Cristiano could do to refrain from leaning over and kissing her right in the middle of the department store. He caught his breath and forced himself to look away. Had he gone completely round the bend? He'd never felt such a strong desire to kiss a woman before. Obviously complete isolation was driving him more crazy than he already was.

"Then I'll stay for a few more days."

A man in his situation couldn't ask for more than that. At least not yet.

When Cristiano drove into the village by the lake, Mariella felt her stress level rise. The horror of the fire rose the closer they got to the resort. She wondered if she could ever fall asleep without fearing a fire would consume her lodgings.

He stopped the car near the Bertatalis' residence. The charred remains of the cottage could be seen clearly in the daylight. How had the fire started?

Signora Bertatali must have heard them as she threw open her door and rushed out to Mariella.

"Ah, Signorina Holmes. You are back." She hugged Mariella, baby and all. "I am so thankful. And the baby, he is well?" She greeted Cristiano and insisted on all coming into her home.

"We are devastated your cabin burned. Aye, when I think of what could have happened without the swift intervention of Cristiano. You will stay with us at no cost, we insist. That such a thing could happen is not acceptable. The fire chief thinks the heater's wiring overloaded. All are being inspected before we rent out another space. The electrician is here even now. I am so sorry. When I think of what could have happened—"

"We're fine, signora."

Cristiano nodded at her acknowledgment, staying near the door.

"Our insurance will cover everything. Please say you'll stay a little longer. We do not want you to remember Lake Clarissa with the horror from the fire. Do let us make it up to you. My husband has a contractor going over every inch of every cottage. They will be totally safe. I guarantee it. Please stay."

Mariella looked at Cristiano. "A day or two," she agreed.

"I am so grateful you are safe. And your baby. Come, let me prepare some tea and you sit. Please, come into the kitchen."

Signora Bertatali bustled around asking question after question. How did she feel? Did she get enough clothing?

"We are all so fortunate you saw the fire," she said to Cristiano. "How did you from your grandfather's cottage?"

He explained he'd been riding. Mariella wondered why he'd gone riding in the middle of the night. Not that it mattered. Thanks to him, they were safe.

Signora Bertatali poured the hot tea and sat at the table across from Mariella and Cristiano. Dante began fussing and Mariella reached into the baby bag to bring out a bottle. In short order it was ready.

"Let me. You drink your tea," Cristiano said, reaching for the little boy. Dante was light in his arms. For a moment Cristiano saw the baby he'd rescued. How was that child doing all these months later? He would have to see if he could find out.

"Thank you."

"And you, Cristiano, your family will be even more proud to learn of your rescue of last night. After that terrorist attack in Rome. I shiver every time I think about it."

He had no comeback. He didn't care if his family never knew of last night's fire. He was content to know he'd been able to function as his training had prepared him. No fear except for the woman and child.

Once Dante had been fed and changed, Signora took

to the cottage right next door to the Bertatalis' .e. It had been completely checked out and declared safe. Cristiano unpacked his car and brought in all her new clothes while Mariella put the baby down in the new crib.

Too tired to think straight, she thanked him and watched as he left, then fell on top of the bed and pulled over a blanket. Before she could mentally list any of the many steps she needed to take, she fell asleep.

The next morning Cristiano sat on the flagstone patio in front of the cottage and read from the latest manual his commander had sent him. Still technically on disability leave, he had plenty of time to keep up with the latest information and his commander agreed, sending him updates and reports to keep him current.

He heard a sound and looked up, surprised to see Mariella walking down the long graveled driveway. The sun turned her hair a shimmery molten gold shot through with strands of copper. She wore dark trousers and a sweater, though the afternoon was warm for October. He hadn't expected to see her here. How had she found the cottage? Not that it was hidden, lying right off the main road.

"Buongiorno," she called in greeting.

"Hello," he said, rising as he placed the manual face down on the small table. He hadn't expected her to make the long walk up a hill with a cut on her foot. Where was the baby?

"I came to say thank you for saving us," she said.

"You did that yesterday," he said, watching as she walked closer. He could see no lasting effects of the fire. Only the faintest hint of a limp showed.

"I know. I just wanted to see you again." She gave a shy smile and the effect on his senses was like the sun coming out after days of rain. For a moment, he felt elation. Then common sense intruded. He'd asked her to stay in Lake Clarissa, she had. Now she probably wondered why.

He glanced around. It was warm in the sun, but would cool down when the patio became shaded by the trees.

"Would you like something to drink?" he asked. He hadn't had anyone at the cottage since he had arrived. It felt strange to invite her inside.

"A glass of water sounds nice. It's warmer than I thought it would be today and that's a long walk."

"Especially with an injured foot."

She lifted her leg slightly and rotated the foot in question. "Actually, it didn't bother me that much."

He stared at the foot, then let his gaze wander up her body to those freckles. Her hair was curly and framed her pretty face. Her eyes were more silvery now than the other night. Then they'd been a stormy grey. The sun highlighted her hair, some of it the color of honey, some almost white gold. He wanted to touch those silky strands to see if they were as soft as they promised to be. Brush his fingertips across the freckles that dusted her face. Kiss her and feel the rise of desire being with a beautiful woman evoked. Prove to himself he was still alive, healthy and normal.

He resisted temptation. Dared he take the risk?

Every cell in his body clamored for closer contact with her. Temptation was never easily denied. He relished the feelings, the wanting, the anticipation, the desire. After staying alone for months, it was like an awakening, as if his body were coming alive after a long illness, painfully tingling. How ironic, he was attracted to a woman for the first time in ages and he dared not pursue the relationship. At least not beyond a casual friendship.

"Water's in the kitchen," he said.

She tilted her head slightly and smiled. "Usually is."

He led the way through the dark living area back to the kitchen. He opened the cupboard and stared for a moment. There were no glasses.

She followed him, looking around with curiosity. For a moment Cristiano scanned the room, noting the dirty dishes stacked in the sink.

He heard a giggle behind him and turned to find Mariella trying to hide her laughter. He scowled, knowing exactly what she was thinking.

"I've seen college kids with digs like this, but I never thought once people were grown up they'd continue to live this way. Or is it only guys?" she asked, the amusement bubbling in her voice.

"Dante would understand," he said, spotting a glass on the counter. He snagged it and quickly washed it. After it was rinsed, he filled it with tap water and handed it to her, still dripping. His sister would have his head if she ever saw the mess. His father would be speechless. Cristiano remembered how fastidious Luca had always been in the kitchen of Rosa.

She took the glass with a smile. "Thank you. I didn't mean to offend," she said. Drinking the entire glass in less than a minute, she held it out for more.

He filled it again. She coughed until she had tears in her eyes. Taking the glass, she sipped it more slowly this time, her gaze looking around the room as a smile tugged her lips.

"I've been recovering from an injury," he said gruffly, suddenly wanting her to know he didn't normally live this way.

Instant compassion shone in her face when she swung back. "I'm sorry. And on top of that you had the ordeal of carrying me away from the fire. I can't believe how fast the cottage burned."

"Entire houses can burn in less time given the right fuel and no safety precautions," he said. "How's the baby?"

"He's doing well. The Bertatalis are bending over backward to be accommodating. Did you know she has three children of her own, all grown now? She says she loves babies and almost begged to watch Dante for me while I walked here. Her husband has offered to take me on one of the fishing excursions on the lake."

"He leads fishing expeditions in the summer. Take him up on it if you get the chance—you'll like it."

"Hmm, maybe. It seems a little cool to be boating."

"I'll give you a ride back when you're ready to leave. Save walking on that foot."

"That would put you out. Which was not my intention. I truly wanted to thank you. You're a hero."

"No, I'm not." Why did people keep saying that? If they knew the truth— "I'll give you a ride," he said.

His motorcycle sat beneath the carport at the rear. Beyond that was a small building, door firmly closed.

Mariella followed, glancing around the kitchen again as she stepped outside.

"I could come back tomorrow and clean up the kitchen for you. As a token of appreciation."

Cristiano shook his head. "I don't need it."

He started the bike and helped her climb on. Instructing her to hold on tight, he didn't expect the jolt of awareness when she wrapped her arms around him. Her body was pressed against his back, her hands linked over his stomach. He closed his eyes, relishing the feel of her. Her hands were small, gripping over his belly. Her breasts pressed against his back and for a moment he wanted to turn around and pull her into a kiss.

"So how long will Signora Bertatali watch Dante?" he asked.

"No time limit."

"Want to take the long way home?"

"Sure."

"Will you be warm enough?"

"Oh, yes."

He started out slowly and then picked up speed when they reached the road. Turning away from the lake, he took the road he loved to ride when trying to outrun the demons and nightmares. It wound through the forest, dappled in shade in places, in full sunshine in others.

From time to time they could catch a glimpse of the lake sparkling in the distance. It was not as breezy today as other days and in places the lake looked like a mirror, reflecting sky and forest.

Mariella loved the ride. She felt free with the scenery whipping by. Seeing the lake when they turned from time to time was fabulous. Thankful for her rescue, she felt especially attentive to everything today. It was as if she were seeing things in a different light.

All due to Cristiano. And not only because he had saved them from the fire. But to take time yesterday to make sure she and Dante had all they needed was special.

But what she cherished the most was his request for her to stay.

He slowed and pulled off the road in a turn out that went to the edge of the open space in front of them.

"Oh wow," she said, gazing at the sight. The lake looked like a jewel nestled in a green setting. Beyond another hill and then another rose, until she felt she were on the rim of the world, looking out.

He stopped the motor. The silence was complete. Then the soft sighing of the breeze through the trees could be heard.

"This is beautiful," she said softly, so as not to disturb the moment.

"We can walk to the edge if you like," he said.

She hopped off the motorcycle and waited for him. Walking to the edge, she saw several rough-cut log benches.

"Others must come here for the view," she said, sitting on one sun-warmed log.

He sat beside her, gazing at the vista in front of them.

For several moments neither spoke, then Cristiano said softly, "I come here when I need to get away."

"A special place," she said, smiling, feeling as if she'd been given a gift. "I wish I had one. It gets overwhelming sometimes with Dante and working and trying to balance everything. I would love a place like this to just sit and be."

He nodded. "Maybe that's what is appealing, I can just be myself here."

She looked at him, tilting her head slightly. "Can't you be yourself everywhere?"

He met her gaze and slowly shook his head. "People expect certain things."

"And we always try to meet those expectations." She sighed. "Probably why I feel so inadequate with Dante. I expect to be wise like my mother and I'm not."

"She probably wasn't that wise when you were six months old," he said gently.

Mariella thought about that for a while. Was it true? Had her mother been learning as she went? "You might be right, but she always seemed to know what to say, how to explain things."

"You're a good mother to Dante. Don't doubt yourself."

Unexpectedly, Cristiano reached out and took her hand,

resting their linked fingers on his thigh. "It's beautiful here in winter when it looks as if powder sugar has been sprinkled on the trees. Now the trees are changing color, but spring will bring the new green of beginning leaves."

"Thanks for bringing me here," she said, returning her gaze to the magnificent view. The carefree feeling continued as if she had let all her worries vanish on the ride and the reward was this unexpected beauty.

They talked softly until the sun started slipping behind some of the trees and the temperature began to drop.

"Time to go," he said.

Mariella nodded, reluctant to end the enchantment of the afternoon. She would never forget this.

He continued the loop arriving in the village near the resort. He continued to the center of town to drop her by the small grocery store where she said she needed to pick up some things for Dante.

"Thanks for the ride home," she said, when she had dismounted. Giving into impulse, she kissed his cheek. "See you," she said and turned swiftly to enter the store.

Cristiano watched as she walked away, so alive and happy. He didn't want to think of the outcome had he not been riding that night.

But he felt like an impostor. He was no hero. He'd never tell her, or anyone, how fear engulfed him. How the nightmares of that incident in May haunted him unexpectedly day and night. Why couldn't he get the images out of his mind? Granted he could go several days without them. Just when he'd think he had it licked, they'd spring up and threaten to render him powerless.

Though he had been able to cope at the fire. Maybe, maybe, he was getting over it.

Mariella entered the grocery store and glanced back through the glass door. Cristiano sat on his motorcycle, staring at the door. Could he see her? She felt her heart beating heavily. She had never ridden a motorcycle before. She'd not known how intimate it felt, pressed against his hard body, feeling his muscles move against her as he drove the powerful bike. She still felt tingly and so aware of him. She hated to move, but people would begin to wonder if she stayed at the door staring like a moonstruck teenager at her latest heartthrob.

She almost giggled as she forced herself to move.

Would she ever get the chance to ride behind him again? Visit his special spot? Life seemed especially sweet today. It could almost as easily have been over for her. Instead, she had ridden with a sexy guy who intrigued her, fascinated her, set her hormones rocking.

She was curious about the injuries he was recovering from. Maybe he'd re-injured himself rescuing her, though he looked to be in perfect health to her. His broad shoulders and muscles beneath the shirt he'd worn attested to robust health. He looked as if he could jump mountains. And obviously was strong enough to carry her and the baby from a burning building.

With the loss of all her things—especially her computer—the sooner she returned home, the sooner she could pick up the pieces of her life. Maybe it was a sign she was not to look for Dante's father.

Fortunately her purchases fit into two bags and Mariella carried them back to the cottage. She also brought a bouquet of mixed mums for her hostess. She wanted to brighten the woman's day in gratitude for watching Dante for her. She wished the Bertatalis didn't feel so guilty. They had not known of the faulty wiring. All had ended well—except for the loss of her computer.

Was there a place in town she could use one? An Internet

café? Or, she could take Cristiano up on his offer and use his. Well, that was a no-brainer.

The next morning after tidying up, bathing and dressing the baby, Mariella set off for Cristiano's house. The road to the cottage was lightly traveled and easily navigated. However, it proved awkward pushing the baby stroller down the uneven graveled driveway.

The day was a copy of yesterday, sunny and balmy. Leaves had begun to change on some of the trees covering the hillside, bright spots of yellows and reds showed brilliant in the sunshine against the deep green of the conifers. She breathed the fresh air. What would it be like to live here year round? Nothing like New York where she'd been the past four years, with its concrete canyons and few open parks beyond Central Park.

Different from Rome, too. But that was home. Crowded, frenetic, yet comfortably providing all she really needed.

Rounding the bend, she saw the cottage. She studied it as she walked toward it. It was warm cream-colored stone, with a steep pitched roof of dark slate. The windows were wide with shutters on either side. It looked old, settled, perfect for its mountain backdrop. With an ageless look, it was hard to tell when it was built, but clearly a long time ago, she suspected from what she'd seen on the inside. He was lucky to have such a comfortable place to recuperate.

Cristiano was not on the patio this morning. She walked to the front door and knocked.

Cristiano opened the door a moment later and stared at her in surprise, then at the baby, his expression softening.

"What are you two doing here?" he asked, smiling at Dante.

"I came to take you up on your offer to use your computer. I need to check in with my clients."

"Come on in." He opened the door wide and she pushed the carriage in.

"It's dark in here," Mariella said, stepping into the living room. "Why is it all closed up?"

He looked around as if seeing the heavy drapes pulled over the windows for the first time.

"It suited me."

"How odd."

"They help insulate the windows."

"It's not that cold."

He stared at her a moment, then shrugged. "I'll get the laptop."

In less than five minutes, Dante was happily kicking his legs from the baby seat playing with a spoon and plastic cup while Mariella booted up the computer on the kitchen table. Cristiano had hooked it to a phone line. It wouldn't be the fastest connection, but at least she could check her email. Once Cristiano saw she was connected, he took off to give her privacy. She appreciated that, too aware of the man to concentrate on her work if he hovered nearby.

She gazed around the room while the computer booted up. It had a certain old-world charm that she loved. There was a huge fireplace, stone-cold now, at one end. She could envision a cheerful fire in the dead of winter when a sprinkle of snow might lie on the ground. How cozy this room would be. The large wooden table would seat a family of eight. The stone floor was cold, but, with a few rugs, could be comfortable in the winter months.

Which she would never see here in Lake Clarissa. For a moment the disappointment seemed too strong to bear.

CHAPTER FOUR

DANTE became fussy. Mariella prepared a mid-morning bottle and picked up the baby. She did not want to sit in one of the wooden chairs by the large table, balancing the baby and bottle, so she wandered into the living room. She'd like to tidy this room or at least open the curtains so she could see the magnificent views.

Sitting in a wing chair, she fed Dante, softly crooning to him as he ate. Maybe the dimness worked to her advantage as Dante began to fall asleep just as he finished the bottle.

Mariella continued to hold him after he fell asleep, relishing this quiet time with just the two of them. He was a beautiful child with dark brown eyes and dark hair. Ariana would have so loved this child of hers. Would Dante resemble her when he grew older? Or his unknown father? Tears threatened every time Mariella remembered her friend and her untimely death. How could she have borne having to leave this child behind? Love expanded within her heart and she wanted to hold the moment forever.

Cristiano came into the room from outside.

"Snack time?" he asked, studying her and Dante. He sat in the chair near her.

"Mid-morning feed." She gazed down at her sleeping baby. "I'll put him in the stroller and go when he wakes up. I still have to follow up on some work I was doing. I appreciate your letting me use your computer. We'll stay out of your way."

She rose and carefully placed the baby in the carrier, covering him lightly with a soft blanket.

"You're not in the way. Finish your work, then stay for lunch."

Cristiano knew he was grasping at straws, but he wanted her to stay. He wanted to talk to her, watch her laugh. Her skin was flushed slightly and looked soft and warm. Her hair curled around her cheeks, down her back. The sweater showed off the feminine body that awakened a need in his he'd thought long gone. When she was nearby, he had to fight the urge to find out more about her, see what she liked and didn't like.

And fight not to kiss her.

When he realized his thoughts had stayed on that point, he quickly looked away.

"You know that fire scared me. What if something happens to me? Who will take care of Dante?" she asked, covering the baby with a light blanket.

Cristiano's mother had died when he was a small boy. He remembered her smile, the fragrance she wore. The almost tangible love she'd given. No one got fully used to losing a parent. Had his father felt the same as Mariella? Worried about his children should something happen to him? Yet it wasn't the same. His father's sister lived in Monta Correnti, for most of his childhood Cristiano's grandfather had lived in this cottage with the rest of the family. There had always been family around. But one never got over the loss of his mother.

"My mother's dead, too," he said slowly.

"But not your father?"

"No, he's doing well." He guessed he was. Surely some-one would have told him if he weren't. Not that he'd been very receptive to overtures from his family since he'd taken up residency in the cottage. His bossy sister had made sure he knew her thoughts on that from the messages she left.

The flashbacks happened without warning. He couldn't be around people who knew him for long—they'd see how messed up he was and cosset him so much he'd never get his life back. He had to beat this thing.

Mariella gazed at him as if expecting him to say more. He stared at her for a moment, wondering if he was finally moving on. He had handled the cottage fire. He had not had a nightmare since that night. He drew a breath, smell-ing the sweet scent of Mariella. It brought a yearning that grew in strength every time he was with her. Yet he could not fall for this woman.

"Are you the oldest child?"

"Yes, Isabella is a close second, incredibly bossy. Our mother died when I was a child. She took on the house-hold work, and tried to keep us in line." For a moment he remembered some of the happy days they'd spent at the cottage, playing at the lake, just being with family. Life had thrown curves he'd never expected when he had been a child.

"Do your brother and sister still live close by?"

"Isabella still lives in Monta Correnti, along with Valentino," he said, smiling at the thought of his family.

"So you get to see them a lot. Must be nice. I was an only child."

He didn't reply. He had not seen them since they had visited him in the hospital after the bombing. His hospital stay had been lengthy and he'd missed his brother's wed-ding, and his cousin Lizzie's. Since his release from hospital Isabella called every so often trying to get him to go to family events. Mostly he let the answering machine take her call.

A lot had happened in his family over the recent months, including the startling revelation that his father had two older children by a first marriage. Cristiano still wasn't sure what to think about that. He had not met the two men—twins who had been raised in America. It was odd to think they shared the same father.

So far he'd found excuses that didn't raise undue suspicions. He was running out of time, however. How long could he keep his problem from his family? He wanted it to go away, wanted life back the way it had been.

He had loved this place as a child. It had been the first spot he'd thought of when wanting to retreat. His family was busy, fortunately. No one spent much time here anymore. Hiding hadn't changed a thing. Maybe he should open curtains. He was not in a tight subway tunnel, but had a view of endless miles.

"This is a terrific room. Do you use the fireplace when it gets cold?" she asked as she headed for the kitchen.

"Of course. It's the primary source of heat," he said, nodding toward the large wood-burning fireplace along an outside wall. He remembered rainy days in the fall when he and his brother Valentino would spend hours in front of the fire, trucks and cars zooming around. He hadn't seen his brother in months; he realized suddenly how much he missed him.

Cristiano followed her into the kitchen. She sat at the table and began checking her account. He crossed to the sink and leaned on the edge of the counter looking out the window over it. The view out back was opposite to the lake, to the rolling tree-covered hills that rose so high, offering peace and serenity. Dots of color presaged the coming of winter. Five months ago he had been working in Rome, settled with his life, his friends. Now he was practically a hermit, his closest friend dead, his job on hold.

But the hills didn't care. They remained the same year in and year out. Steadfast, secure, unchanging. It gave a longer perspective than short-time occurrence. Would he recover fully? Or was it time to begin to think of another way to earn a living? Would he return to Rome and the life he'd so enjoyed, or remain a virtual recluse cut off from friends and family?

"That was easy," she said a few moments later.

He looked over.

"Hardly any mail. I did send a note to two clients telling them I might be another day or two getting back in touch. Tomorrow I'll see about getting another laptop. Maybe in a shop in Monta Correnti."

"You are dedicated. I thought you were on vacation."

She looked at him. "I am, but I don't consider myself any more dedicated than you going into a burning building to save lives when you're recovering from injuries. You know I'll be forever grateful. Keep that in your heart. Now, do you have a printer?"

"Not here, why?"

"I wanted to print out a picture of Ariana. I found one I could use. The one I brought with me burned in the fire."

"Sorry. There's an Internet café in Monta Correnti, near the church on the plaza. They'd have a printer."

She shut down the computer and closed the top. "I'll go there, then. Thanks for the use of your computer today." She leaned back in the chair and looked at him. "So tell me, how did you get into firefighting? I think that's one of the most dangerous lines of work anywhere—pitting your life against a raging fire," she said.

"I like making a difference." A ready answer. It didn't explore the variety of reasons he chose fighting fires as compared to police work or mountain rescue. But all were similar kinds of jobs—first responders, never knowing what would await them. Challenges to be surmounted. Never boring.

She smiled, her eyes sparkling silver. Her hair shone in the sunshine pouring in through the side window.

Cristiano had a stronger urge to reach out and twirl some of those tresses around his fingers, feeling the silky softness, the heat from each warm strand. Those desires rose each time he saw her.

"Did your father want you to do something else?" she asked.

"Probably, though he never pressured any of us. My sister works with him at the family restaurant. My brother Valentino is home less than I am."

"Is your brother Valentino Casali? The racing daredevil?" She looked surprised.

Cristiano nodded. He knew Valentino had a reputation to match his daredevil ways. For the first time he wondered if their decisions had hurt their father. He took such pride in Rosa. It was a fine restaurant, but only Isabella had followed their father's path and worked in the family establishment.

"He got married recently, I saw that somewhere," she said. "Not my idea of a married man."

Cristiano shrugged. "What would be your idea of a married man?"

"Someone faithful."

"Valentino is fiercely loyal. He would always be faithful," Cristiano was quick to say.

"I'd also want my husband home more than he seems to be. And safe."

"Maybe now that he has a home and wife, he'll change. People do, you know."

She nodded.

"Other attributes?"

She frowned in thought for a moment. "Fun to be with, able to talk and share, and I'd want a husband to want the same things I do."

"Sounds like you've thought about it for a while."

"Ariana and I used to talk about our dream man. Hers turned out not to be the dream."

"And you?"

"Haven't met him yet. So what do you do here all day? Not working. No television I saw," she asked.

"This and that." He should tell her about the woodworking. Maybe later he'd take her to the shed to see.

"Did you always want to be a virtual assistant?" he asked, finding it an odd sort of job for such a bubbling personality like hers. He'd picture her surrounded by office workers, working as a team player, not in a solo job from home.

"When in university in New York, I planned to hit Madison Avenue big time. I majored in marketing—American style. But then my parents died, then Ariana. Things changed so much, I couldn't manage that on top of watching Dante. Maybe someday."

"I think I heard the baby," he said, hearing a noise in the living room.

Mariella jumped to her feet and went to check on Dante. Two minutes later she came back, carrying a bubbling baby.

"He was kicking his feet and saying something. I can't wait for him to talk."

"I'll start our lunch. I'll make you some of the world's best marinara sauce."

"The world's best?" she scoffed lightly.

"Hey, I challenge you to find better. It's from the family's restaurant. And you'll thank your lucky stars you get to have some."

"You made it?"

"No. My sister sends me care packages. I freeze the sauce until I'm ready to use it. It won't take long to prepare."

"Time enough for me to feed this little guy, then," she said.

"Again?"

"He eats a lot, that's why he's growing."

Cristiano took the sauce from the freezer, peeled off the wrapper and dropped it into a pan. Soon it began to simmer on the stove as he boiled water for pasta. He watched Mariella feed Dante while he worked. For the first time in months, he felt a touch of optimism. There was something about cooking long-familiar foods and sharing that touched that part of him that had once liked to spend time with friends. Stephano had loved the marinara sauce and every time he learned Isabella had sent some, he'd invite himself and his family over for dinner. He and the other guys at the station urged him to bring in enough for everyone.

For once the memory of his friend and the time they'd shared didn't hurt with the searing pain of loss. It was a bittersweet memory of times that would never come again. He missed his friend and probably always would.

But life went on. Stephano had loved life so much, he would have personally come to Lake Clarissa and knocked some sense into his head if he'd known Cristiano was secluding himself like this.

Except—the flashbacks were real.

Mariella's laugh pulled him from his thoughts and he looked up. The baby had something smeared all over his face, and his pudgy hands were spreading the mess to his hair.

"What is that?"

"Some kind of oatmeal cereal. The pediatrician is having me try it. Probably tastes like paste and feels better spread around outside than eating," she said, trying to catch Dante's hands to wipe them. She giggled. "He's a mess. I'm thinking this is not one of the better ideas the doctor had."

"You think? Hey, little man, would you like some of my papa's sauce?"

"He's not even six months yet. Too young for big people food."

"A taste won't hurt." Cristiano dipped his pinkie into the warming sauce and then carried it to the baby. Dante grabbed his hand and pulled it to his mouth. His frown of surprise had them both laughing.

"Maybe it's an acquired taste," Cristiano said.

The baby had eaten and Mariella settled him on a thick blanket on the floor when Cristiano served up their lunch.

"Wow, this was definitely worth waiting for," Mariella said after her first bite. "What makes it so great?"

"Family secret," he said.

"Ah. I bet Rosa has a line waiting for tables every night."

"The economy these days makes things unsettled. It does well enough, I think." Actually, from one or two comments Isabella had made, Cristiano wondered if that was true. Maybe he should check into it. If there was a problem, he might be able to help financially; he had some money saved.

"I know people are cutting back, but good food is always relished."

"My sister has been pestering me to talk about the situation for a while. It's her area, not mine. Whatever she decides is fine with me."

"Um. I just hope she decides to keep making this wonderful sauce. Does she sell it by the jar?"

He shook his head.

"She should. Maybe I can talk to her about that. She could consider an Internet mail-order business on the side. I bet folks would pay a premium. It obviously freezes well. I wonder how it could be shipped?"

"Ever the marketer?"

She nodded, but continued to look thoughtful.

"You said you went to university in New York? What was that like? Why there?"

"My dad was American, but he settled in Rome ages ago. Ever since I can remember the plan was for me to attend school there when I hit university level. After their death, it helped that New York is vastly different from Rome, so I didn't have lots of memories to deal with at every turn. Maybe it helped with the grief, too. To have the coursework to concentrate on."

"So now you're back settled in Rome?" he asked.

"I'm Italian, so is Dante. There is nothing waiting for us in New York. When he's older, I'll take him there and show him the sights. It's a fantastic city. But it's not home."

She looked up. "It was good to grow up in Rome, but I'm wondering if it might be even better to have a smaller town, where I could build a support group. A single mom will need help. I've lost touch with many of my friends from high school."

And lost her best friend, he remembered.

"I couldn't wait to move to Rome when I graduated. More vibrant, more things to do."

"Of course. But when you got hurt, you came home. There's a lot to be said for a country setting. Where in Rome can you get views like you have? Sitting on the patio, seeing the lake, the gorgeous hills. It's fantastic."

"Doesn't offer a lot of opportunity for young people, though."

"Ah, but that depends on what opportunities one's looking for. I have a job, a child. My opportunities now lie in different areas than when I was single and fancy free."

She smiled again and Cristiano was struck by her happy outlook. She seemed not to have a care in the world, though he knew differently. What was her secret to that optimistic outlook?

Not having to deal with post-traumatic stress disorder, for one thing.

"I think I'll take the baby to the lake later. Want to come with us?" she asked.

"Will it be warm enough for him?" he asked.

"In the sunshine. I guess you've done it a thousand times."

"It never gets old. The lake is beautiful all times of the year. My ankle was broken a while ago. I'm still getting it back in shape. The sooner I'm fit, the sooner I can return to work. Want to go Jet Skiing?"

She laughed and shook her head. "Sitting on the beach is enough."

CHAPTER FIVE

CRISTIANO drove them in the car back to the village. He and Mariella took the baby to the shore near the marina. The beach was a mixture of sand and pebbles sloping gently to the water's edge. There was a couple sitting in nearby chairs, reading. She waved to them while Cristiano settled on a spot some distance away so as not to disturb their tranquility with their presence.

He brought a blanket and soon Dante was taking tummy time facing away from the water, so he was facing up hill. When he grew frustrated, Mariella sat him up, holding him lightly so he wouldn't fall over. He could almost balance by himself. He settled in first gnawing on the plastic keys, then throwing them down. She retrieved them and handed them back.

Again

And again.

Cristiano stretched out beside them, laughing at the baby's antics. Mariella tossed him the keys.

"You try it," she said.

Dante turned to see the keys and grinned at Cristiano.

"Don't want to lose your keys," he said, dangling them in front of the baby. "Especially when you're older and that means wheels."

The tranquility of the setting soothed. Mariella coughed

again, wishing she'd get over the smoke problem soon. Her chest felt dry and tight. Taking a deep breath, she relished the clean air scented with evergreen. The sun sparkled on the water. In the distance she could see a boat bobbing near the center of the lake. Was that a fisherman?

Dante threw the keys again.

Cristiano retrieved them and handed them to Dante. He threw them again and looked at him, a wide smile on his face. Her heart contracted. She loved this precious baby.

"It's so lovely here, even if we can't swim today. Maybe we'll come back for a visit when Dante's older. Maybe continue the search for his father if we don't find him this time."

"How can you have spent so much time with your friend and not found out more information?"

"She was in the late stages of pregnancy and very ill. We spent more time talking about our shared memories, reliving good times. She changed the subject anytime I brought up who Dante's father might be. He could be named for the man, for all I know. She spoke of what she hoped for in Dante's future. The future she'd never see."

"Maybe she truly didn't want her son to know his father."

"Maybe." She wondered if she was doing wrong trying to find the man. He obviously wasn't as nice as Cristiano. She couldn't imagine any woman not want a child of his to know him.

"It's nice here," she said, turning slightly and fussing with the baby to cover the fact she was studying Cristiano's profile. He made her heart happy. He could have been in movies, she thought. The rugged hero rescuing the heroine from danger then kissing her silly. And her heart almost melted when he played with a baby. Why was a strong man giving his attention to a baby so sexy?

She sighed a bit, wishing he'd pay that much attention to her.

"Problem?" he asked, glancing at her, one eyebrow raised.

"No, just thinking how nice it is here and how horrible the other night was.' She shivered involuntarily. "We could have died."

"But you didn't." His voice came sharp.

She brushed her fingertips over Dante's head. He was perfectly content sitting on the blanket and throwing his plastic keys. She wished she could be so easily satisfied.

"I know that. As a firefighter, you've probably seen lots of death."

He frowned and sat up, resting an arm on his upraised knee. "It's not something anyone gets used to," he said.

"I imagine not." She could have bitten her tongue and not said anything. How many other lives had he saved, and how many had he not been able to save? There was more to firefighting than just pouring water on a fire.

"Do you think I can raise him?" she asked a few moments later.

"You can do anything if you want it enough. Remember that. From what I see, you are doing a fine job."

"Tell me more about growing up around here."

"Weekends are busy times for restaurants. My father worked hard. My mother with him, until she died. But even though we didn't see much of them our childhood was still magical. Especially when my grandfather was alive. His life was different from our everyday life. He knew the trees, the forest, fish in the lake."

She fell silent, thinking about the vacations she and her parents had enjoyed. It seemed so long ago and far away. Would visiting some of the spots bring the memories closer?

Or only emphasize she was alone? She wanted Dante to see all of Italy. They'd make new memories.

"I'm going into Monta Correnti tomorrow. The doctors at the hospital wanted to check me and Dante again, make sure there are no lasting effects. I need to get access to a printer so I can print up another picture of Ariana. Maybe check around in Monta Correnti to see if anyone recognizes her."

"Park near the town square. Easy to get to an Internet café, shops and the hospital."

"We'll find it," she said cheerfully, wishing he'd offered to drive them into town.

After visiting the hospital the next morning and getting a clean bill of health for both her and Dante, Mariella wandered the center part of Monta Correnti. First stop after the hospital was the Internet café where she was able to print a color photograph of Ariana. Staring at the picture of her friend, she remembered how vital she'd always been when younger. The illness had robbed her of so much.

Then she pushed the baby in the stroller, wandering down side streets, walking around the square. When she saw a likely tourist spot, she showed the photo. No one recognized Ariana.

It was after one when Mariella turned back onto the wide piazza and gazed at the buildings. Rosa seemed to leap out at her. That was Cristiano's family's restaurant—the one with the excellent marinara sauce. She pushed the stroller along, wondering if she dared try Dante in the restaurant. So far the baby had been in perfect harmony with all they'd done. But she'd hate to be in the middle of a meal and have him start screaming his head off.

As they approached, Mariella saw a nice open-air space

connected to the restaurant. Much better for the baby, she thought. The day was warm enough to sit outside.

Once seated, with a baby highchair for Dante, Mariella perused the menu. She'd try the tortellini with the famous sauce. She sat back to enjoy the ambiance while waiting for her order. The waiter had brought bread sticks and she gave one to Dante to drool on. He beat the table, put it in his mouth and looked surprised. She laughed. Hadn't he expected it to be food? He couldn't eat it, but she thought he could gum it a bit. Once it got soggy, she replaced it with another.

The courtyard was delightful. Tables were scattered around as if awaiting company, two others occupied. None too close to impede a private conversation. The bougainvillea spilled down a trellis, their flowers faded now as winter approached. She bet they were spectacular in the height of summer. A fountain's melody gave a pleasant sound to soothe and enhance enjoyment of the food. Mariella suspected the restaurant was a favorite of many.

When the meal was placed before her, Mariella smiled in anticipation. She looked at the waiter. "I can't wait to eat this. I had this sauce recently at Cristiano Casali's place. Do you know him?"

The waiter bowed slightly. "Of course. He is son of the owner, Luca." He frowned. "He has not been to visit recently. I shall tell his sister you are here."

Mariella took a bite of the tortellini. It almost melted in her mouth. The sauce was even better than she'd had at Cristiano's. She savored each mouthful.

"Signora?"

A pretty woman wearing an apron approached Mariella.

"Sì?"

"I am Isabella, Cristiano's sister. You are a friend of Cristiano?"

Mariella smiled. "He rescued me and my baby from a fire at Lake Clarissa. I consider him a hero."

"Ah. May I?" Isabella said, holding onto the back of a chair.

"Please."

"How is he?" she asked when she sat down.

"Fine. He said he is recovering from injuries?" How odd his sister asked a stranger for an update on her brother.

"He was a first responder to the bombing in Rome last May," Isabella said slowly.

"I knew that. That's where he was injured."

"A burn, a broken ankle. Yet it's taking a long time to heal. Does he walk okay?"

"Fine."

Isabella stared at Mariella for a long moment.

Growing uncomfortable, Mariella smiled again. "I had some of your marinara sauce at Cristiano's and so when I had to come to Monta Correnti and saw the restaurant, I thought I'd eat it again. It's delicious."

"Thank you. So you ate at Cristiano's home?"

"The cottage near the lake," Mariella clarified.

"I know where he's staying. Did he bring you here?" Isabella glanced around quickly.

"No, I drove," Mariella said.

Isabella looked at Dante. "What a blessing he is safe. Cristiano rescued him?"

"We're staying at the cottages rented by the Bertatalis. The unit we rented burned. Faulty wire in the heating device. I was asleep, so was the baby. We both would have been killed if Cristiano hadn't discovered the fire and come in to rescue us."

Isabella smiled. "So like my brother. You are going back to Lake Clarissa today?"

"Yes, for a few more days. I'm on a short holiday." She reached for her bag and pulled out Ariana's picture. "Have you ever seen her?" she asked.

Isabella looked at the photo and handed it back. "No. A friend?"

Mariella nodded. Another story too much to go into with everyone she saw.

"I have something for Cristiano. Would you take it to him for me? Things are hectic right now or I'd go myself. Not that he'd be happy to see me," Isabella said.

"Why ever not?"

"He's been avoiding me. Granted, I've had a few other things on my mind, but I wanted to make sure he was all right. He doesn't answer his phone most of the time. He was conveniently gone from the cottage the two times I went to visit. He's turning into a hermit."

Mariella laughed. "I don't think so. But he can be a bit moody."

"Cristiano? Doesn't sound like him. He has a very even disposition."

"Men hate to be sick. I know my father was grouchy when he was ill. My mother said not to worry, once he was better he'd be back to normal. Maybe Cristiano is frustrated with how long it's taking him to heal and is taking it out on family."

Isabella nodded. "Perhaps, but enough is enough. I shall get the letter and some more sauce. I'm glad to know he's eating what I left, anyway."

"It freezes well. I thought you might consider a mail-order side to the business. I'd love to be able to order this from my home and know I can have it whenever I wish."

"We are just a local restaurant."

"Think about it. I have a degree in marketing and could help set it up if you ever wanted to expand."

Isabella looked at her. "Would it cost a lot?"

"My contribution would be free. I owe Cristiano forever." She reached out and brushed back Dante's hair, smiling at the precious little boy. He rewarded her with a wide smile and drool on his chin mixed with breadcrumbs.

Isabella nodded. "If you would take the letter and sauce to my brother, it will be enough. Tell him his sister asks after him and to call me!"

By the time Mariella was ready to leave, a small bag containing a jar of sauce and an official letter was delivered to her table by the waiter. She placed in it the carry space of the stroller. After wiping Dante's face and hands, she placed him in the stroller and paid her bill. A few moments later they were walking around the square. She studied the restaurant that shared the small piazza with the family restaurant. It looked very upscale and trendy. Not the sort of place for a baby or a casually dressed tourist. Glad she'd had an excellent meal, and that Dante had not raised a fuss, she continued on her walk. There was more to see before returning to the lake.

The town was lovely, decidedly bigger than Lake Clarissa, yet nothing like New York or Rome.

But which appealed to her more these days—the big city excitement or the slower pace in these mountain towns? Would she like to raise Dante in a pastoral setting allowing him to experience nature in its raw beauty? Or would the experiences of museums, art galleries and opera be better to round his education?

Dante had fallen asleep by the time they returned to the car. Mariella couldn't wait to get him home and take a nap herself. The prognosis from the doctor had been good. But she still coughed from time to time.

* * *

The next morning, Mariella put Dante in the stroller, retrieved the sauce Isabella Casali had sent from the refrigerator and headed back up the road to deliver to Cristiano. Her nerves thrummed with anticipation.

On impulse, she stopped at the open-air market and bought a bouquet of mums. The fall flowers were vibrant bronze yellow and purple and she knew they would brighten the kitchen. She hoped he'd appreciate the gesture with the flowers. She wanted to brighten his day as he brightened hers.

Cristiano was sitting on the terrace when she arrived. She smiled when she saw him, already anticipating their time together. There was something about Cristiano that drew her like a lodestone. She watched his expression as it changed from surprise, to pleasure, to cautiousness. He rose and came to meet her.

"*Buongiorno.* We have brought you gifts," she said as she reached the terrace.

"I need no gifts." He watched her from wary eyes. He was several inches taller than she was and she had to crane her neck he was so close.

"Well, the flowers are from Dante, so speak to him about those. And this sack is from your sister, Isabella. She hopes you are well and you should call her."

"My sister?"

"Yes. She says you are becoming a hermit. I told her you weren't. Look how often we visit."

The amusement in his eyes lit a spark in her own.

Her spirits rose. She held out the flowers.

He stared at them and slowly took them. "Dante picked them out?" he asked.

"Well, that was the bunch he made a grab for. I figured they were the ones he wanted to give you."

"Or eat."

She laughed.

Cristiano stole another look at her. She was beautiful when she laughed. It was as if the sun shone from inside, lighting her eyes and making them look like polished silver. That pesky urge to wrap his hands in her hair and pull her closer sprang up again. He looked away before he did something stupid—like give into that impulse.

"And your sister sent you some more sauce." Mariella pulled a brown bag from the back of the stroller and held it out. Cristiano took it. Now both hands were full.

"I'll open the door so you can put the flowers in water and the sauce in the freezer or wherever you wanted to put it. I kept it cold. Delicious, even better made fresh. Still, I think your family could ship it frozen within the country at least. I think the sauce would do quite well—maybe they could send pasta, too. I printed a picture of Ariana, but no one I showed it to yesterday recognized her."

"Did you even take a breath in all that?" he commented, following her into the house and back to the kitchen. He put the sack on the counter, laid the flowers down and rummaged for something to put them in. Finally he settled on a tall glass. The flowers did look nice. But he wasn't used to getting gifts from women and wasn't sure how to handle this.

"I thought they'd look good on the table," she said.

"Sure." He set the flowers on the old table, struck by a memory of his mother doing the same thing. Now the forgotten memory flashed into his mind.

"My mother liked flowers," he said slowly.

"Most people do. I think they look happy. When we stopped at Rosa for lunch after our checkup yesterday, I told the waiter I'd had the sauce before and he apparently told your sister. She came out to meet me."

For a moment Cristiano wished he had given them a

ride, though he wasn't sure about visiting Rosa just yet. He realized he longed to see his father and sister. Find out how things were going at the restaurant. He had to make sure he was all right before risking it. "The outcome from the doctor?"

"We're both healthy. Though I still cough from time to time. The doctor said that would fade. So we had most of the day free after seeing him, so we set out to explore Monta Correnti. I recognized the restaurant as soon as I saw the sign. The food was superb. That's where I met Isabella. There's a letter in the sack for you as well."

Cristiano looked in the sack and took out the envelope. It was from the minister of the interior. Cristiano stared at it. It was addressed to his apartment in Rome and had been forwarded to the restaurant.

"Is it bad news?" Mariella asked, watching him.

"I have no idea." Although deep down Cristiano knew what this letter contained, but did not want to accept it.

"So open it and find out what it says."

He did. The letter confirmed what Cristiano had already known for a long time. He was being awarded a medal of valor for his rescue of the injured from the bombing. Immediately, he crushed the letter and threw it on the counter.

"Um, bad news," she guessed.

He shook his head. "It's a mistake, that's all."

Cristiano didn't want the medal, never had. Why him? Stephano had died. Others from his station had helped with the rescue. There had been so many who died. They had not been able to rescue everyone. Why would anyone want to award him a medal of valor? Especially if they knew of the flashbacks and attacks of sheer terror that gripped him. What kind of man deserved a medal when he couldn't handle all life threw his way?

"What's a mistake?" she asked.

"Never mind. Are you staying?"

"Gee, after such a kind invitation to visit and give you my impressions of Monta Correnti how can I refuse?"

She grinned that cheeky grin and Cristiano almost groaned at the sight. He wanted to pull her into his arms and kiss her until he forgot all the pain of the past. He wanted to feel that slim body against his, driving out the memories and offering an optimistic hope of the future. He wanted to lose himself in her and find that shining optimism she displayed.

He flat out wanted her.

Yet he had deliberately come to Lake Clarissa to avoid people until he could be sure the flashbacks had gone. Wasn't it risky to spend so much time with her? Yet she made him feel normal again, complete. And the baby was adorable. Cristiano wished he could remember when he was so young and innocent the future looked nothing but bright.

Dante began fussing and Mariella shrugged out of her sweater, tossing it on the counter, knocking off the letter. She picked it up and smoothed it out, her eyes drawn to the fancy letterhead. Skimming quickly, she widened them in shock.

"You're getting a medal! How cool is this!"

"I told you, it's a mistake. I don't deserve a medal. I certainly am not a hero!"

Mariella wasn't listening to him. Or attending to Dante, who looked as if he were working up to a fully-fledged screaming bout. She was reading every word in the letter.

"You saved seven people."

"Others saved lives as well."

"And at great personal risk you continued on with the last

two even though you were severely injured," she continued as if she hadn't heard him.

He didn't need the reminder. He saw it over and over every time he had a flashback. The shock, the anguish, the horror.

She looked at him, her eyes shining. "I knew you were a hero. Now it's been confirmed, and not just because of me and Dante. Wow, you must be so proud."

"I'm not going to accept it. It would be a farce."

"But—"

He snatched the paper from her hand, balled it up and tossed it into the trash before storming out of the kitchen.

CHAPTER SIX

MARIELLA was stunned at his reaction. But she had to see to the fussy baby before going after Cristiano. She lifted the baby from the stroller and tried to soothe him. Preparing a bottle one-handed, she soon shifted him to lie in her arm while offering the bottle. He fussed and pushed it away, wailing as if his world had ended. She jiggled him a little, singing softly as she tried the bottle again. Finally he took it, chewing on the nipple as much as sucking.

"Are you teething, sweetie?" She knew from the baby books that children began teething any time around five or six months, but this was the first time he'd pushed the bottle away. Maybe his gums hurt.

Finally Dante settled down to drink the bottle. Mariella walked into the living room, humming softly as he drank. The curtains were wide open today and sunshine flooded the room. It welcomed her and the baby. She sat in the chair that gave the best view of the lake and continued to hum as she fed Dante.

Her firefighter was an intriguing man. He was a hero, even the ministry confirmed that. Yet he seemed angry about it. Not at all satisfied with the heroic actions he'd performed.

So did that add to the fascination she felt around him? He was drop-dead gorgeous with his thick dark hair and haunted eyes. He looked fit enough to put out a blaze single-handed. She remembered those arms so strong when he lifted her and yet gentle enough for a small baby.

Her heart skipped a beat as she pictured the few times he'd smiled. She could watch him forever, she thought.

Except, he didn't seem to feel the same fascination with her.

Sighing softly, she tried to picture him as a child running around the piazza in Monta Correnti or the restaurant his father owned. She couldn't imagine it. She could see him here at Lake Clarissa, hiking in the woods, swimming in the lake in summer, racing Jet Skis. Chopping wood for a winter's fire. Chasing around a brother who looked like him.

Glancing around the room, she noted how family friendly it was. But she didn't see anything that looked as if it belonged to Cristiano alone. What were his interests? What did he do to combat the stress of rescuing people and battling blazes that threatened life at every turn?

Dante drifted to sleep. She rose and went to the door. As suspected, Cristiano was sitting on the patio, staring at the lake. She would always be able to picture him that way.

"Could you help me?" she asked softly.

He looked around.

"If you would release the back of the stroller, it lies down and I could put the baby there. He'll sleep fine in the stroller and be ready to go when I am."

The man nodded and rose. She watched him, no limp she could see, so why was he still on leave? Was he upset at taking so long to heal after being injured? Champing at the bit, so to speak, to get back to work?

She wondered why he was so adamant against the medal. Sure, others had died, but maybe they were also receiving a medal posthumously.

The stroller was still in the kitchen. He figured out how to recline the back and pulled the half canopy over it. He pushed the stroller, looking just a bit like a giant next to the tiny conveyance, over to Mariella.

She was swaying gently as she held the sleeping baby.

"Thanks, he's getting heavy."

He locked the wheels while she placed the sleeping baby down and covered him with a soft blanket.

"You take to being a mother," he commented, watching her. "Some women don't."

"It's still a struggle." She straightened and looked at the sleeping child with such an expression of love Cristiano caught his breath.

A strand of hair fell across her cheek. Before he could have second thoughts, Cristiano brushed it back, feeling the soft warmth of her skin. He tucked it behind her ear as she looked up and into his eyes. Her smile was warm. Her lips enticing. As if in a dream, he leaned across the slight distance and touched his mouth to hers. She was warm and sweet and so tempting. Kissing her lit a fire in his blood and he wanted the moment to go on forever.

Reality struck when she pulled back and blinked as she looked at him.

"I've wanted to do that for days," he said softly, his hands cupping her cheeks.

"I thought it was only me—I mean that the attraction was just one way."

"Oh, no," he said before he kissed her again, drawing her into his arms, holding her closely while the world seemed to spin around. Mariella was the only thing grounding him.

Rational thought vied with roiling emotions. The desire that rose whenever she was near had to be controlled. He refused to fall for Mariella. She was sweet and young and had bright expectations. He would never falsely lead her on when he had no clue if he could make it in the world again or not.

Holding her, touching her, kissing her, he could forget the horror of that day, the pain of losing his best friend, of the others in the squad that he'd been so close to. But it wasn't fair to her.

Slowly he eased up. They were both breathing hard. He wished for an instant the baby would sleep all afternoon so that he could whisk her into his bedroom and make love until they were both satiated.

"Wow," she said softly, the tip of her tongue skimming her lips. He almost groaned in reaction.

"Wow, yourself," he said, kissing her soft cheeks, seeing how long he could resist her mouth.

The baby awoke and started crying.

Mariella pulled away and hurried over to him.

"Oh, sweetie, what's the matter?" She picked him up and cuddled him.

"He was fussy eating, too," she said. "Maybe he doesn't want to sleep in the stroller. I'll take him home."

"I can drive you."

"No, we'll walk. It's still a pretty day. We'll be okay."

In only a couple of minutes they left.

He watched as she disappeared from view. Whether she knew it or not, the love she showed for the baby was strong. She would love that child forever. Her concerns on whether she was a good mother were for naught. When would she accept that?

He wished he could give her that knowledge.

Mariella pushed the carriage along the side of the road, not seeing the scenery, only halfway watching for vehicles. She was bemused with their kiss, concerned by the baby's fussy behavior. She was smiling, her heart still beating faster than normal, just thinking about Cristiano. She felt they were drawing closer. And he obviously felt that attraction she did, if his kiss was anything to go by. She wished they had not been interrupted.

"Not that you knew you were interrupting," she said to Dante. The baby was awake, fussy, his fist in his mouth.

She hoped Dante would nap in the crib. She wished to turn right around and go back to spend the afternoon with Cristiano. And share a few more blazing kisses.

Cristiano headed for the small shed in the back of the property. He entered, smelling the sawdust and polish. Slowly he relaxed. Whenever he came into the workroom he felt connected to his grandfather. His mother's father had been a craftsman in furniture making. He'd shown Cristiano the basics and had urged him to follow in his footsteps.

Cristiano had rebelled, as youth so often did, preferring the excitement of pitting his skills against that of a roaring conflagration and rescuing people from impossible odds— who would die if he hadn't been there. But always in the back of his mind were the quiet peaceful times he'd worked with his grandfather in this very workspace.

Since recuperating, Cristiano had built several small pieces of furniture. They were lined up against the side wall, polished to a high sheen, as if awaiting being taken home. He thought his grandfather would be pleased if he could see.

He went to the stack of wood against the opposite wall. He looked at each piece, selecting one of fine cherry wood. The overall dimensions were small, but would suffice for a project. Cristiano wanted to build a table and two chairs for Dante. The baby couldn't use a set for a couple of years, but Cristiano liked the idea of making something fine from Lake Clarissa. Once the boy was older, he'd learn of their visit to the lake. And Mariella could tell him of the fire-fighter who'd made him a table.

He put the piece of wood on the worktable, already envisioning the set. Small enough for a toddler, yet sturdy enough to last for years. Mariella would undoubtedly marry at some point—pretty women didn't stay single for long—and have more children. He hesitated a moment when thinking of her with another man. That idea didn't sit well. Unless he licked this hangover from the bombing, there would be nothing he could do about that.

He picked up a pencil and tape measure and began marking the wood for the first cuts.

When the phone rang half an hour later, Cristiano stared at it, debating whether to answer or not. It was most likely his sister or father. It might be Mariella. Though he had not given her the number, the Bertatalis had it. The ringing continued. Whoever was calling wouldn't give up. What had happened to the answering machine? He remembered—he'd unplugged it when hooking his computer to the Internet for Mariella.

Finally he reached for the phone to stop the sound.

"Ciao?"

"Finally. I was wondering if you'd ever answer," his sister's voice came cross the line. "How are you?"

"Fine." He leaned against the wall, wondering if he'd made a mistake staying away so long. Still, it was good to hear her voice.

"That's all? Fine. When are you coming here?"

"Why do I need to?"

"To see us. To see Papa. Surely you've recovered from your injuries by now."

"I have." At least the external ones. "But I've been busy."

"Come for dinner tonight."

"I told you I'm busy. I can't come for dinner."

"If not tonight, then later in the week?"

"Maybe." Not.

He heard her exaggerated sigh. "Tell me about your new friend, Mariella," she said unexpectedly. "I liked her."

He remembered their kisses. Swallowing, he hoped his voice came out normal. "She's visiting here, that's all."

"Where did you meet her?"

"I rescued her from a fire. She and the baby."

"She said she'd had the sauce at your house when you gave her lunch one day. That was unexpected. I sent another jar home to you with her."

"I know, thanks." The memory of their lunch surfaced. She had loved the sauce. If they shared a meal again, he'd get to see her delight in the flavor.

"Honestly, Cristiano, getting you to talk is like pulling teeth. Tell me something."

He laughed as a warmth of affection for his sister swept through him. He'd forgotten how much Isabella always wanted to know everything. Her curiosity knew no bounds. He missed her. "She came by to say thank you. I fed her lunch. End of story."

"So you're not going to see her again."

"Of course I am." A prick of panic flared at the thought of not seeing her again. One day soon, she'd return to Rome. But until then, he would see her again.

The surprised silence on the other end extended for several seconds. Then Isabella said, "I'm planning a family reunion at the end of the month. Actually, if you can keep it secret, it's a surprise for Papa."

"What kind of surprise? It's not his birthday." Cristiano was glad it was not a surprise party for him. Why did women want to have those?

"Just a surprise. But I don't want him to suspect, so, if

you're well again, I thought we could say it was a celebration of your recovery. That way he will know about it, but not that it's for him."

"I've been fine for a few weeks now."

"Not that any of us knew. I haven't seen you since you got home from hospital. If you're really okay, come by the restaurant one day. Come to dinner."

"I'll let you know."

"Keep the last Saturday free for the party."

Once he hung up, Cristiano almost groaned. Attending a party was the last thing he wanted. Yet how could he continue to deny his family? He missed them. He was fortunate to have a brother and sister, cousins. An aunt he didn't see much of. Still, maybe he could manage one evening.

He resumed his work on the child's table, thinking about the baby, trying to picture him growing up. The countryside was beautiful here. Maybe they could spend holidays in Lake Clarissa. There were endless acres of forest a young boy could safely explore. Water sports in summer on the lake. He worried Dante might dart into traffic in Rome or wander away and get lost and who would know him to help him home? No wonder Mariella worried—there was a lot to worry about when thinking of raising a child. His admiration rose at her willingness to take on that role.

He finished cutting the pieces by late afternoon, telling himself over and over their future had nothing to do with his. Cleaning up, he headed inside. The balmy fall weather couldn't continue forever. He'd eat his dinner on the patio if it wasn't too cold, watching the last of the sunshine as the shadows of night crossed the lake.

And he'd try to keep his mind off Mariella and the baby.

As he cooked dinner he realized it had been days since he'd had a nightmare or flashback. The night of the fire had been bad, but since then—nothing. Maybe he truly was getting better. Too early to know for sure. He'd gone several days between episodes before.

Still, if he continued this way, he'd make it back.

If not, he had a long, lonely life ahead of him.

Conscious of how fast her vacation time was speeding by, Mariella placed Dante in the stroller the next morning, making sure she had bottles and baby cereal, and headed out. The weather was ominous with dark clouds on the horizon and a breeze that was stronger than before. She hoped it wouldn't rain before she got to the cottage. Surely if it began after she arrived, Cristiano would give her a ride back to the village.

She wore her sweatshirt and jeans and wished when the wind blew that she'd bought a coat. But she had winter clothes back in Rome so had not needed to spend the money. She would have to return home sooner if the weather got worse.

Rounding the bend before the cottage, she shivered. It was growing colder by the minute and the dark clouds building on the horizon indicated it would surely storm before long. Maybe she should have stayed at the guest cottage. But her time with Cristiano was precious.

She reached the house and was disappointed not to find Cristiano sitting on the patio. Not that anyone in their right mind would be sitting out on a day like today, she thought. Knocking on the door, she blew on her hands. Unprotected while pushing the stroller, they were freezing. She checked Dante, and he smiled his grin at her. He was bundled up and felt warm against her fingers. Of course, they were so cold, how could she judge?

She knocked again.

There was no reply. Moving to the window, she peered

inside. The living room was empty; no lights were on even though it was growing darker by the moment. A gust of wind swirled a handful of leaves around, dancing near her, then moving off the patio.

Mariella heard a high whine from a power saw. She pushed the stroller around the cottage and heard the sound again, coming from a small shed at the far back of the cleared area. The stroller was hard to push on the uneven ground, but if Cristiano was there, she needed to find him. It looked as if it would pour down rain at any moment.

She found the door opened. Cristiano stood with his back to it, cutting a piece of wood. Pushing the baby inside, she was glad to be out of the wind. It felt much warmer in the shed, though she didn't see any sign of a heating unit.

She did see lovely pieces of furniture on one side. Cristiano cut another piece of wood and the baby shrieked at the sound.

He stopped suddenly and spun around.

"I didn't know you were here," he said with a frown. Reaching back, he turned off the saw. "Did you drive?"

"No, we walked. I think it's going to rain."

"It's supposed to storm." He took off safety glasses and tossed them on the wood. Walking over, he grinned at Dante.

"Hey, little guy. You warm enough?"

"Of course, I wrapped him well. I have a favor to ask." She had thought up the request on her walk up—to give herself a reason and not look so blatantly as if she couldn't stay away.

"What?" he asked warily, looking at her.

"Nothing dangerous, though I thought firefighters risked their lives daily for people. Are you telling me you wouldn't even do a little favor that does not involve risk of life or limb?"

"I'm waiting to hear what it is." He stood back up and crossed his arms across his chest, watching her.

Dante played happily with the plastic keys he was gnawing on. Mariella stepped around the stroller.

"Friday is Ariana's birthday. I wanted to go to the cemetery and put some flowers on her grave. A quick trip to Rome would enable me to get some winter clothes. Signora Bertatali said she'd watch Dante."

The thought of going with her to Rome made the bile rise in his throat. It was too soon. He wasn't ready. He stepped away, looking through the door, seeing the back of the cottage and the trees beyond. He couldn't see the lake from here. A moment went by. He wasn't flashing back to the subway tunnel. He took a deep breath, testing his reactions. Nothing. He could hear the baby with the keys, see Mariella from the corner of his eye. No flashback, no terror residual from the bombing.

He had to return to Rome sometime. What better than a fleeting visit knowing he could return to the cottage within hours? Maybe he worried for nothing. Maybe the worst was past and he could move on.

He could visit Stephano's grave.

Cristiano had not been able to attend Stephano's funeral. He'd been in hospital. Nor had he attended any of the many services for all the victims he had been unable to save. Rome had been in mourning for weeks. He'd escaped the worst of it drugged for pain and undergoing skin grafting for his burned hand.

He'd pictured it a thousand times, though. Stephano's coffin lowered into the ground. His wife weeping. His parents stunned with the loss of their only son. He drew in a breath, trying to capture the scent of sawdust to ground him in the present.

The faint hint of flowers caught his attention. Mariella's

special scent. He closed his eyes. The image of their kiss sprang to the forefront.

He opened his eyes, turned and looked at her, hungering for another kiss. He was lonely. Self-imposed or not, he didn't like staying away from his family or friends. Only the shame of not being able to handle things kept him isolated.

Until now.

She reached out and touched his arm, her touch light as a butterfly, yet as hot as a flame.

"Will you?" she asked.

He stared at her. He was thinking of kissing her, hugging her close to him, losing himself in her soft sweetness. And she was focused on a cemetery visit.

"All right, I'll go with you. For Dante. You can tell him you weren't the only one to mourn his mother's loss." He hoped he didn't have a flashback while standing by the graves.

A loud rumble of thunder startled them, causing Dante to begin to cry. Mariella rushed to him and lifted him from the stroller.

"There, there, little man, it's okay. Just noisy." She looked out the still opened door.

Rain poured down in torrents. The yard was already growing muddy as the rain splattered the dirt. The light was almost gone, making it as dark as twilight.

Cristiano breathed deeply the fresh, clean rain-laden air. The sky was a dark grey from horizon to horizon. The rain beat down ferociously. Mariella and the baby couldn't return to the village in this. In fact, they'd become soaked just running to his car. They were stuck for as long as the rain came so hard.

She came to his side, the baby settled on her hip and looking around. He gave his grin and lunged toward

Cristiano. He reached out instinctively to grab him and then was surprised when Mariella let go and he held the baby dangling in front of him. Bringing him close to his chest, he felt the light weight and looked at the baby. Dante gazed at him with dark brown eyes, as if studying a curious specimen. Then he grinned and bopped his head against Cristiano's cheek.

He was a goner. Who couldn't love a sweet baby like this?

"Rain," he said, pointing to the downpour.

The baby gurgled and patted Cristiano's cheek. He felt a tightening in his chest.

"His entire life is before him. What do you think he'll do when he grows up?" he asked softly as Dante settled against him to watch the rain.

"He can be anything he wants. I want him happy and healthy. And when he's older I'll tell him all I remember of his mother," she said, leaning against his left side. Cristiano put his arm around her shoulder. For long moments the three of them looked at the storm.

"And his father? What will you tell him about that man?" Cristiano asked.

"Ariana said he had vanished from their life. And the affair had been a mistake. But that, I would never tell their son. I'll just have to say he's gone."

"Do you think he's dead?"

"I have no idea. I had hoped I'd find something on this trip. People could have forgotten even if Ariana had been through here. Lots of tourists visit this area."

"Hmm."

"I hope it doesn't rain Friday," she said. "Cemeteries are sad enough without the heavens weeping as well."

"Well said. It rained on the day of Stephano's funeral. I think Heaven was weeping," Cristiano said slowly. He had never thought about it that way. He would have been weeping had he been at the church.

"Stephano was your friend?"

"My best friend."

"I'm sorry he died."

"He was killed in the bombing. We were on our third rescue foray when the second bomb went off. The roof of the tunnel completely collapsed, killing everyone still beneath it."

Cristiano wanted to step out into the rain, feel the cleansing of the water, feel the coolness, see the sky above him, know he was alive. But he held the baby, so remained sheltered in the doorway. The trust from Dante touched him. The baby knew the adults around him would care for him.

She reached around his waist, hugging him. "How horrible."

"The entire event was horrible."

"But you saved seven lives. If not for you, they would have perished in the second bombing."

"It wasn't enough. There were so many still trapped."

"It's amazing, that's what it is. How can you say it wasn't enough? It was more than anyone expected."

"I should have made sure Stephano was right behind me, not lagging behind—that he had not been in the tunnel when it collapsed. We lost seven men from our station." The anguish penetrated to his core. His duty was to save lives. His chosen way was to fight disasters and rescue people. He hadn't even been able to rescue his best friend.

She offered support the only way possible, her body warmth to chase the chill of torment. If only she could truly heal his sorrow. If only anyone could.

CHAPTER SEVEN

UNAWARE of the turmoil, the baby happily babbled, reaching out once or twice as if to touch the rain. The air grew chilled, but Cristiano didn't move. The child was well wrapped. He felt like the only warm spot in the world where he rested against Cristiano's chest. That and where Mariella touched him.

The silence extended. Yet it wasn't awkward. Instead, it was—almost healing. He took a breath, trying to let go the ache that plagued him with all the death and destruction.

"So how long were you and Stephano friends?" she asked.

Cristiano almost smiled. "I remember the first day I met him—it was at the training for firefighting. He came from Genoa, a man loving the sea. I came from here—hills and lakes. He was an only child, had a pretty wife and parents who doted on him. We both passionately loved soccer. We were paired up in training and the rest—"

He hadn't thought about those days in all the months since Stephano had died. Now, telling Mariella, he let the memories wash through him. They'd had fun times. They'd fought fires in Rome. Been sent to man the lines in raging forest fires worldwide. Practiced paramedical routines to save lives. And spent a lot of time together in their off hours.

"He was always up for adventure." Slowly Cristiano began to speak of his friend, remembering aloud the trips to the sea, the ski trip that had ended with both falling face first in the snow, and how quickly they'd progressed from that. The quiet times by a fire, sharing philosophies, plans for the future.

"His wife would probably like to hear from you," Mariella said as Cristiano wound down after telling her many of the shared experiences. "You haven't seen her since?"

He shook his head. "How can I face her when I lived and Stephano didn't?"

"You didn't kill him. The terrorists did. You and she have a shared love of the man—different, of course, but bonding nonetheless. I bet she misses you being around."

"I would remind her of Stephano."

"Maybe she wants to be reminded. Maybe she wants someone around who knew him, faults and all. Who can remember the happy times together. Celebrate his life, not ignore it."

"You don't understand."

She shrugged. The baby was growing more and more squirmy.

"He's probably hungry. I'll take him," she said, reaching for Dante.

He relinquished the child, feeling the cold air hit where the baby had been.

"What are you working on?" she asked, moving back to the workbench and looking at the wooden pieces.

Cristiano turned as well. The emotional toll started to overwhelm him. Needing a diversion, he crossed the small room and picked up one of the pieces that would be a chair leg. "A table and chair set for Dante."

"Wow, you can do that? Did you do all those?" She looked at the pieces lined up against the wall.

"It's been a long summer. I don't just ignore housework," he said, trying to lighten the mood.

"These are beautiful." She stroked a finger across the smooth polished top of a small half pie table. The cabriolet legs were elegant. The rich cherry wood gleamed even in the defused lighting.

"Those legs were hard to do. I ruined more pieces than I wanted." Temper had played a part, but he didn't need to tell her that. Impatient with his recovery, feeling helpless, he'd taken it out on the wood.

"And this, what a beauty this is. Did you make it for someone?" The small console table had classic lines and a band of inlay lighter wood in the perimeter.

"Just made them to kill time while recuperating."

"I'd buy this one if it's for sale," she said hesitantly.

"You can have it. No charge." He wondered where she would put it. Could he visit her one day and see how she was using it? It made him think of a connection between them. For as long as she held onto the table, she'd be holding onto a part of him.

He turned back to the workbench.

"Go on and work if you wish. Looks like we're going to be here a while with the rain. We won't get in your way," she said with a smile. "I can't wait to see what Dante's going to get. He's one lucky boy, isn't he?"

That damned optimism. Cristiano shook his head. How could she think that? The kid had no mother or father. No known relatives. He placed a terrible burden on the young woman now his mother. Yet Mariella seemed sincere in her comment.

Cristiano began working on the leg. At first he was conscious of Mariella watching him. But soon the pleasure he took in working with wood took over.

He was aware when she fed the baby, of the soft lullaby after he ate. Then when she put him down in the stroller for nap. She came back to stand beside him.

"Circle of life sort of thing, isn't it?" she said.

"What is?"

"You fight fire and destruction, and now create things of beauty. A balance. Is that why you do it? To balance out?"

"No. I do it because I like it. My grandfather taught me."

"And your father taught you to cook?"

"A bit. I do like good food prepared well."

"I can boil eggs," she said impishly.

He laughed. He couldn't help it. She'd been to America and back. Was capable of taking on an infant. And couldn't cook worth beans?

"So you and Dante will live happily ever after on boiled eggs."

"I might have to expand my repertoire," she said, wrinkling her nose. "Maybe you can give me some hints." She frowned. "You don't think that will be a problem in the future, do you? I mean, I can learn. And for now he's just beginning to eat baby food, so no worries."

"I'm sure that's not a condition of growing up healthy. Though to enjoy eating, you do need to know more than how to boil eggs." He shook his head. All the members of his family knew how to cook. Well, he wasn't sure about the newly found half-brothers from America. But if they lived alone at any time, they would cook for themselves.

"So tell me what you're doing now," she said, pressing closer. She was a toucher. He hadn't been touched since he left hospital. Until now. Every time Mariella came close, she reached out or bumped against him. He liked the human contact. The thought of pulling her into his arms grew stronger by the second.

He cleared his throat and began to explain, hoping talking would get his mind off what his body was craving—contact up close and personal with Mariella Holmes.

The worst of the storm seemed to be easing. The baby slept in the stroller. And Cristiano showed his work to an interested party. Mariella exclaimed over the craftsmanship and he felt the tightness ease. He might not be a hundred per cent yet, but he still had the ability to build something beautiful.

He glanced at his watch, surprised to see the morning had fled.

"I can give you a ride back. The worst of the rain seems over."

"Beats pushing the stroller. Plus it's decidedly colder after the rain."

Once in the car, Cristiano looked at her. "Since we're going out, what about lunch?" He surprised himself, then knew it was the right thing to do when she gave a happy nod.

"I would love that. I'm hungry. Do we have time to go to Monta Correnti? We could eat at your family's restaurant."

Cristiano hesitated. There was Pietro's in the village. He'd much rather eat there. He hadn't been to Rosa since long before the bomb. He felt a moment of panic. What if he had a flashback in the restaurant? What if he completely lost sight of reality and ended up beneath a table? His family would be horrified.

He knew he had to face his family at some time. The longer he delayed, the more suspicious his absence would become. His sister and father already complained they never saw him.

Yet, he wasn't ready.

Would he ever be?

"Never mind. Forget it. Pietro's is fine. Of course their sauce is not as good," she said.

"Fine, we'll go to Rosa." With any luck, his sister would be too busy to stop to talk to him. Though lunch during the week wasn't normally as crowded as dinners—or weekend crowds. With real luck, he'd act normal for the time it took to order and eat. Then get out of Monta Correnti and back to the safety of the cottage.

He drove through the intermittent rain testing his will power. He tried to gauge his feelings as they approached the town his family lived in. So far so good.

As they reached the outskirts of Monta Correnti she spoke for the first time since leaving the village.

"It's really pretty, even in the rain. I can see why Ariana spoke so fondly of it. And the memories I think were happy even though the end of their affair brought pain."

The closer he drove to the restaurant, the more the tension rose. It would be the first time he'd seen Isabella in months. The sporadic phone conversations didn't count. She would have a hundred questions. He'd be trapped until lunch was over. Had he made a mistake coming here?

They parked the car and walked quickly through the rain. Cristiano held a large umbrella he kept stashed in his car. She carried the baby and they moved in step, close together, to avoid the drizzle. It wasn't too late to turn back, he thought as they approached the door. He didn't know how he'd explain the situation to Mariella if he broke down, but he'd come up with something.

Entering the restaurant, Mariella took a deep breath.

"If we could bottle this aroma and pipe it into other

streets, people would flock here," she said. "It makes my mouth water."

Cristiano took a breath. To him it was home, as familiar as ever. The awkward stress grew until he felt it was almost tangible. He could taste the uncertainty and fear. One of the waiters came over. The two men greeted each other.

"We haven't seen you in a long time," the waiter said.

"It has been a while. Is my sister or father in today?"

"No. They are both at some meeting they had to attend."

"We'll sit in the back, if there's room," Cristiano said, letting the relief wash through him. One worry avoided. Now he just had to remain normal until the meal ended.

"Quiet today. Rain keeping people away, I think," the waiter said, leading them back to one of the small tables near the rear wall.

The wooden paneling gave the restaurant a cozy feel, contributing to quiet enjoyment, mixed with anticipation of the meal to come. When the waiter brought the high chair, Mariella strapped Dante in and handed him his plastic keys.

She opened the menu and scanned the offerings. Everything looked delicious. Choosing only one item wasn't easy.

Once they had ordered she leaned back and looked at Cristiano. "Do you know everyone here?"

Cristiano glanced around and shrugged. "I know most of the wait staff and I bet most of the people in the kitchen. My father has owned this place since before I was born."

"Sorry you're missing him today."

Cristiano pushed a glass toward the right a fraction of an inch. "It's just as well."

"Why?" she prodded.

He glanced up. "No reason."

She narrowed her gaze but didn't push the issue.

Breaking a bread stick, she handed half to Dante and began nibbling on the other half. She studied the decor. "When we ate here before we sat on the terrace. It's lovely. I really liked that. Too bad for the rain."

Just then there was a commotion by the door. Cristiano looked over and frowned.

Mariella turned around to see.

A woman in her early sixties was arguing with one of the waiters. She turned as if in a huff and then spotted Cristiano.

"Oh-oh," he said softly even as he began to rise as she stormed over.

"Cristiano." She reached him and kissed both cheeks. "I thought you were injured and recuperating." She ran her gaze from head to toe. "You seem fine to me. You were always such a good-looking boy."

"Aunt Lisa. I am fine."

"Hmm. So I see. Where is your father? What meeting is he attending?"

"I don't know. I expected him to be here."

She looked at Mariella. "How do you do? I'm Lisa Firenzi, Cristiano's aunt."

"Mariella Holmes."

"Holmes? Are you from around here?"

Mariella shook her head. "Rome originally. Most recently, New York."

"Ah, there they have fine restaurants that are appreciated by everyone." She looked around a bit and shook her head. "Cozy. Who wants cozy? Tell your father I want to talk to him. Or your sister. Perhaps Isabella would be easier."

Cristiano smiled slightly. "I'll make sure they know."

She gave a wave and headed back outside.

"Wow, a whirlwind," Mariella said.

"She actually owns the restaurant next door. Even though she's my father's sister, they have barely spoken to each other in years. I wonder what she wants."

"Maybe she appreciates the family she has. I wish I had family somewhere, besides Dante, of course."

"He's lucky to have you. Many people would not consider the child your responsibility. It's such an awesome one."

"Don't you want children?" she asked. "I mean after you marry and all."

He did not want to go there. On the surface, he looked normal. Only he knew what turmoil lurked inside his mind. He could not subject anyone to that. Fearful of what the flashbacks could lead to, he had to make sure no one came in harm's way. How could he enter any kind of intimate relationship with a woman if he could go off the rails without warning?

In fact, it was a risk to be away from the isolation of the cottage for this long.

Not that he'd had a problem since the night of the fire. Twice he'd thought he was coming close, but one look at Mariella and he'd staved off the threatening flashbacks.

For a moment he hoped he was recovering. Maybe he would be able to go back to work before long. It was still too early to say with complete confidence, but he might touch base with his commander in the next week or so.

"Maybe, if I marry," he replied.

"I'm so surprised you didn't go into this business. A ready-made family affair that you could take over when your father retires," Mariella said a short time later when savoring the first bite of her rigatoni. The sauce had a piquant flavor that she relished.

"It's my sister's thing. My brother and I couldn't wait to leave. It always felt too settled here, I guess you'd say."

"So you two chose the opposite extreme. You with your job, he with his races. Why do you both put your lives on the line like that? At least your actions are for some greater good, but just to challenge the laws of physics and risk death in car races seems a bit reckless."

"Ah, but there is that awesome feeling when he succeeds. Can't be measured."

"Is that how you feel about fighting fires?"

"It is always a challenge. No two fires are exactly the same."

"Scary."

He shrugged. He wouldn't admit it, but he had felt fear a few times. Overcoming it to come out on top was another kind of high. One that he could not achieve with the aftermath of the bombing.

"Enough about me and my family. Tell me about New York."

"It's so vibrant. I worked as an usher at theaters to get in to see the shows for free. Spent many rainy or snowy afternoons roaming the museums. I majored in marketing at university. I was not the only non-American in my classes. There were also students from the UK and Japan."

"You would have more chance of a high-paying job if you didn't have the baby."

"My entire life would be different if I didn't have Dante. I was set to partner with a fellow student in New York in a marketing firm."

"Must have been tough to give that up," Cristiano said.

"The reality turns out to be different from my dreams. I love Dante. I am gaining a bit of confidence. It's not forever. When he's in school, I can try something else, use the education I have. There are a lot of single moms out there. They all manage."

"And single fathers, but it still works better if there are two."

She fell silent. A moment later she looked up.

"I'll see if Signora Bertatali can watch Dante when we take a run up to Rome."

He'd take her to the cemetery, then swing by the station and talk to the commander. Check on his own apartment, which had stood empty these last months. He had held onto it with the intent of returning if he could lick the PTSD. And he'd go to see Stephano's widow.

He'd like to see where Mariella and Dante lived, too. He'd take her there to get her clothes. Then they could have dinner on the way back. For the first time in a long while, he felt the stirring of anticipation.

"We'll leave early."

She grinned at him. "How early is early?"

"Seven?"

"Fine. Are you going by the ministry to talk about the award?" she asked.

He'd forgotten about that. He shook his head. "No."

She narrowed her eyes. "Why not?"

"People died in that bombing. Good people. Men who tried to rescue others. I was luckier than most, I got out alive. But there were many more who didn't."

"You saved seven people. Including two children." She reached out to touch his arm. "It must have been terrifying as well as horrific. So many people lost their lives."

Including Stephano. Cristiano began to feel the stirrings of a panic attack. His vision was growing dark around the edges. His heart began pounding in remembered fear.

Her hand slipped into his and he gripped it, focused on her silvery eyes. And that dusting of freckles across her nose. What would it be like to kiss each and every one? She looked like happiness personified. He knew she'd had some hard knocks herself, but they didn't get her down. For a moment he envied her. He'd give anything to turn the clock back. To be the man he once was.

The moment passed. Another. The restaurant came back into focus—people enjoying the good food, the laughter and conversation conveying their pleasure. He drew a deep breath.

"Did you want dessert?" he asked, withdrawing his hand. Mariella was like a lifeline. Was that the clue? Not lock himself away but be with her all the time?

He'd give almost anything to do just that.

They decided against dessert. Soon they headed back to the car, glad the rain had stopped—if only temporarily. The dark clouds showed the storm had not completely passed.

She remained sitting in the car when Cristiano stopped in front of the Bertatalis' home. Dante was asleep in his car seat, the stroller folded in the trunk.

"It's been a nice day despite the rain. Thank you for lunch," she said.

"My pleasure."

"Your family's restaurant is so nice. I really like it. You're lucky to be a part of that, even if you don't work there."

That might change. If he couldn't return to firefighting, what would he do? Join his sister in the restaurant?

No public job. If he got that bad, he would never be able to be certain he wouldn't have another flashback. He gripped his hands on the steering wheel. Better he'd been killed in the bombing instead of injured. No one would ever have known about the reactions he couldn't control.

He would do his best to make sure no one ever found out.

"Thanks again," she said, opening the door.

"I'll get the stroller." Cristiano got out and retrieved the stroller from the trunk while Mariella took Dante, car seat and all, from the car.

The nightmare woke him again. Cristiano came awake amidst terror. He clenched his hands into fists and fought the tattered memory that wouldn't let go. Flinging off the blanket, he rose and went to the window. Breathing hard, he pushed open the window and drank in the cold night air. Gradually he calmed. He hadn't had a nightmare in days. He'd thought, maybe—was he forever doomed to relive the bombing?

He flung on some clothes and went to the kitchen for some coffee. No going back to sleep after that. He glanced around as he waited for the water to boil, feeling frustrated and angry. Noticing the laptop still on the table, he forced himself to remember Mariella using it. He could picture her blonde hair falling forward when she leaned closer to the screen. Her fingers had flown across the keys. Just thinking about her lowered his anxiety level. He almost smiled, wishing he could see her right now.

Of course starting any relationship with a woman he could scare to death if they slept together and he awoke in the throes of a nightmare would be foolish beyond belief. The kettle whistled and he turned to make the coffee. Still, the thought tantalized. She brought sanity into his life, made him hope for more than he had in a long time. He liked being with her. Wanted to know every speck of information about her life, her hopes, her dreams, now that she had a child to raise.

He wanted her in his life. Dared he risk such a chance?

Once he filled his cup, he prowled around the cottage. He considered going to the workshop and continuing with his project, but felt too edgy. Draining the cup, he grabbed the keys to the motorcycle. He'd ride through the remainder of the night and hope to find peace come dawn.

The roads were lonely, scarcely used even in the summer. No traffic. Few residences scattered miles apart. The world seemed different at night. No people. No animals he could see. Just the strip of asphalt illuminated by the headlight, the rest shadows whipping by, undefined vague splotches of black melding together as he increased the speed of the bike.

He made the circuit he'd completed many times before. Slowing as he approached the village, he looked toward the Bertatalis' cottages. The last time he'd done that one had been on fire. No sign of flames tonight. But the cottage Mariella was staying in was lit up; light spilled from every window.

He turned into the lane that led to the cottages. Stopping by hers, he considered his next step. Knock on the door to see if all was well? Would that scare her? A knock in the middle of the night? What if she'd merely fallen asleep with the lights on?

He glanced toward the east. A slight lightening of the darkness. Dawn was not that far away.

He heard the baby cry.

Quickly he went to the door and knocked.

A tearful Mariella and wailing baby opened the door.

"Cristiano, what are you doing here?"

"What's wrong?" he asked, stepping inside.

"He's been crying most of the night. I can't get him to stop. I've checked everything, given him warm milk, but he doesn't even want the bottle. I don't know what to do." With that she burst into tears.

"Here, give me the baby," he said, preferring dealing with a crying child than a woman's tears.

She complied and then wiped her cheeks. "I'll be right back." She fled.

The baby continued to cry and Cristiano juggled him, remembering another baby who had cried. The smoke and cement particles floating in the thick air had only exacerbated his distress. He would never take fresh air for granted again.

He bounced the baby gently. Watching Dante, he took a breath, testing the limits. Nothing but a warm cottage and a crying baby.

"Hey, little man, none of that. You've kept your mamma up all night by the looks of it," he said easily.

The baby scrunched up his face and looked ready to let fly again.

"Now, now, what's wrong?"

Cristiano rested him against his chest, upright so his head was by his own. Slowly he rubbed the baby's head with his cheek.

Dante hiccuped and then stopped crying, swaying back enough to look at Cristiano. His face was wet with tears, his eyes red. But he looked at Cristiano as if examining a wondrous thing.

"That's better. Give your mother a break. People normally sleep at night."

Mariella entered, having washed her face and pulled on a sweatshirt over her nightgown.

"What are you doing up so late at night? People normally sleep. And how did you get him to stop? He's been crying since before midnight!" Mariella peered at the baby. He still looked as if he'd start crying any second, but so far he was distracted by Cristiano.

"I woke early, took a ride."

"It's freezing outside."

He shrugged. Nothing colder than the way he felt after the nightmares.

"Well, I'm glad you did. Do you think he'll feel like going to sleep?" she asked hopefully, worried eyes studying the baby.

"I don't know, but you look like you could keel over without a problem."

She nodded and brushed her hand lightly over Dante's head. "I am *so* tired. But if he can't sleep, neither can I. I think he's teething. It's what the baby books say for this age. He won't eat, won't sleep, I don't know what else to do."

"Take a nap. I'll watch this little guy."

She looked at him.

The hope brimming in her eyes made Cristiano laugh.

"Really?" she said.

He nodded.

She reached up and pulled his head down for a fleeting kiss. "Thanks. I'm so tired I can hardly stand on my feet. Call me if you need anything." With that she turned and went to the bedroom.

Cristiano watched, feeling the soft press of her lips against his. The lurch in his heart had surprised him. Without wanting it, without knowing it, Mariella had captured his heart. He'd give anything to have her kiss him every day. To share the tasks of caring for the baby, of seeing her sleepy and ready for bed. Desire shot through him and he shook his head. He had a cranky baby in his arms, she was dead tired, and all he could think about was her in that bed, alone. How her blonde hair would be spread across the pillow, soft and silky. Her skin would be warm and smooth.

He turned away from the door and his thoughts and he looked at Dante.

"Your mother weaves a spell on men, watch out," he said.

The baby looked as if he was dazed, his head weaving back and forth.

"Okay, let's get comfortable."

He put Dante down on the sofa to shrug out of his jacket. He hadn't even dropped it on the chair before the baby started crying again.

"Hey, none of that. Your mom needs sleep." Cristiano scooped him up and walked him around the small living room. The child was light and warm. Cuddling him gave Cristiano a sense of peace he hadn't had in a long time. He remembered the infant he'd saved. How was he doing these days? Would he ever have even the faintest remembrance of that awful day? He hoped Dante never had anything more difficult to face than teething.

A few minutes later Dante's head fell against his shoulder. Looking at him, Cristiano realized the baby had finally fallen asleep.

He sat on the sofa, careful not to disturb the sleeping child. Rubbing his back slowly, he let the peace of the cottage take hold. If he could bottle this and take it with him, any time a flashback threatened he'd be instantly cured.

Slowly dawn arrived. The baby slept; Cristiano relished the feel of him in his arms. But his thoughts winged to Mariella. He knew she was sleeping, but he wished she'd wake up and come talk with him. They could discuss options to make Dante's teething easier on all concerned. He wish he knew what the future held.

Even more than that, he wished he'd kissed her back when she'd kissed him.

The sun was well up when Mariella came back into the living room. She'd had several hours of much-needed sleep. Stopping in the doorway, she smiled at the sight. Cristiano was sprawled on the sofa, holding Dante. Both were fast asleep. Even in sleep, his arms cradled her son, keeping him safe.

She stared a long time, longings and wishes surging forward. He was a marvelous man. Strong, sincere and capable. Plus sexy to boot. The beginning beard gave him a rakish look. The muscular chest made the baby seem all the smaller—yet well protected and loved.

She went into the adjacent kitchen and quietly prepared coffee. While it brewed, she looked into the refrigerator for breakfast. She'd feed her savior of last night and send him on his way. She didn't want to impose on his time. He'd already helped more than she should have any reason to expect.

Hopefully Dante would sleep most of the day and she could get another nap.

She heard the baby fussing before she finished boiling the eggs she planned for breakfast. She knew she was no cook, but they could have eggs and toast. And coffee. She excelled in coffee.

"Something smells good," Cristiano said when he walked into the kitchen carrying Dante.

"Coffee. And I boiled us each an egg."

He laughed and, as naturally as if they did it all the time, he stepped closer, leaned in and kissed her sweetly on the mouth. Mariella savored the touch, too quickly ended.

"I like boiled eggs," he said a moment later.

Flustered Mariella could only stammer, "And toast. I can do toast."

"A feast indeed."

"Thank you for letting me sleep," she said, stepping away, feeling overwhelmed with the sensations spinning out of control. She wanted to put Dante in his crib and grab Cristiano with both hands. But she had responsibilities.

"Let me take him and feed him," she said.

"I can hold him while you get things ready. But I would take a cup of coffee."

"Done."

They worked together as if they'd done so before. Soon Dante was nursing on his bottle, but still fussy. Mariella encouraged him to eat, conscious of Cristiano only a few feet away. She wished she'd taken more care in dressing, had put on some makeup.

"I wish he could tell me for sure if he's teething. Babies start getting teeth at six months and he's almost that old already," she said as she teased his lips with the nipple. Dante chewed on it for a moment, then sucked some more, then looked as if he would cry.

"Ask Signora Bertatali what she did for her children— she had three," Cristiano suggested.

"Good idea."

When Dante fell asleep, Mariella smiled and kissed him gently. "Let's hope he stays asleep at least long enough for us to eat," she whispered, rising. "I'll put him in the crib."

Cristiano had started the toast when she returned. She quickly put the eggs into cups and set the table she used for dining.

"Best boiled eggs I ever had," Cristiano said.

She laughed. "Sorry, I'm just not a cook. I ate out mostly in New York—everyone seems to, or order in. My mother cooked at home, but I never wanted much to learn. I bet you're a great cook."

"Could be said by some. Not my father, but those not in the restaurant business think I can make some fine dishes," he agreed. Gazing into her eyes, he smiled.

Mariella felt her heart turn over, then begin to race.

"I could cook dinner for us tonight if you like," he said softly.

"I'd love that," she replied, still caught in the gaze of his dark eyes.

They finished breakfast and, by the time Dante woke again, white fluffy clouds dotted the sky. The chance of rain remained high, but for the short term it looked pleasant outside. Mariella fed and bathed Dante while Cristiano sat nearby to watch. They spoke of myriad things, from her favorite restaurants in New York, to his vacations skiing in the Swiss Alps.

"Come back to my place," he said when the baby was dressed for the day and had smeared oatmeal cereal everywhere.

Mariella merely laughed as she cleaned him up again, looking over at Cristiano. "To do what?"

"You can help me make the table and chairs."

"I know nothing about making furniture."

"Sanding doesn't take a lot of previous experience. Come on, it'll get you out of the house. But I can't bring you two on my motorcycle. You'd have to drive yourself."

"Or we can walk there. Dante loves the stroller."

"So I'll see you soon."

She smiled and nodded, glancing out the window again. "We'll be there soon. But if it looks like rain, we'll have to scoot for home. Maybe I can use your computer again. I want to check the status of the one I ordered. If it's already shipped it might be in Rome when we go up."

Cristiano waited until she had Dante bundled up and in the stroller. He took off on the motorcycle while she began to push the stroller up to the cottage. It was noticeably cooler than it had been. Tomorrow they'd zip into Rome. She'd do what she needed and he'd do what he needed and then she'd return to the lake to finish her vacation. She looked forward to spending the day with him without the baby. With just the two of them, and a carefree day, who knew what might happen?

When she reached the cottage, Dante was asleep. Poor thing, he was probably exhausted from being up all night. She went straight to the workshop in back. As she walked closer she could hear the raspy sound of sandpaper against wood. He had already started.

Parking the carriage just inside the doorway, she stepped further into the workshop. Better for Dante to be near the fresh air than one laden with sawdust. If it began to rain, he would be sheltered and she could get to him quickly.

Cristiano glanced up.

Taking a breath, she relished the scent of furniture oil and fresh-cut wood. "I love the way it smells in here."

"Me, too. Are we set for tomorrow?"

"I checked with Signora Bertatali and she said she'd be delighted to watch Dante. I'm looking forward to our drive. She also said it did sound like Dante is teething. She said to give him something cold to chew on, like a cold damp rag or a rubber toy that's been in the freezer."

He nodded, beckoning her over to watch as he continued with the sanding. She stepped closer and peered at the smooth piece that would become a leg.

Reaching out a finger, she rubbed it in the direction of the grain. "It feels like velvet," she murmured. She looked up. Her face was mere inches from Cristiano's. She could breathe the scent of his aftershave lotion. See the crinkles near his eyes from squinting in the sunshine. Feel the heat radiating from his body. Mesmerized, she gazed into his dark eyes, seeing tiny specks of gold near the irises. For an endless moment time seemed suspended.

A moment later Cristiano leaned forward the scant inches that separated them and kissed her. Mariella closed her eyes, relishing the warmth of his mouth on hers, the excitement that rocketed around within her. The way time felt suspended and only the two of them existed. This kiss was perfect: no pulling away, no fretful baby making noise in the background. Just a man and a woman sharing a special moment.

He pulled back, gazing into her eyes for a long moment, then took a breath and looked around—almost as if he weren't sure where he was.

She smiled and reached out to touch the wood again. Maybe she wasn't the only one knocked off her equilibrium by that kiss. She felt almost giddy with delight. The day seemed brighter than before. The colors more vibrant everywhere she looked. Cristiano seemed happier than she'd ever seen him. She loved watching him.

"Then we're set, we leave early in the morning," he said with a smile, his dark eyes gazing directly into hers.

CHAPTER EIGHT

CRISTIANO picked up some sandpaper and handed it to Mariella. "Rub it along the length of the leg. We want it totally smooth. No splinters for the little fella." His fingers deliberately brushed against hers in handing her the sandpaper. She smiled and nodded, feeling that tingling awareness that sparked whenever Cristiano was around.

Mariella had never done home projects so she was thrilled to be able to assist. She perched on the stool he had vacated and began rubbing the way he showed her. There was something soothing about the long, slow strokes. She couldn't wait to see the finished table and chairs. She'd never helped to build anything before. Glancing around, taking in everything, she would always remember the quiet time spent in this workshop.

Cristiano was focused on the piece he worked. The quiet was complete except for the sound of sandpaper and the rustling of the wind outside the door. She looked outside. It was growing overcast. She rose and checked the baby. He was fast asleep. Touching him, she knew he was warm beneath the fleecy blanket. She looked around. The beauty of autumn in the hills was evident everywhere she looked. Golden leaves, red leaves, and the occasional brown leaf looked a bit dull in the flat light beneath the clouds. She had seen them with the sun shining on them and they'd made her breathless.

Could she be happy in such a quiet setting?

"What do you do all day?" she asked, returning to the worktable.

"What do you mean?"

"It's quiet. Not many shops in the village, no nightlife to speak of. Do you listen to music or watch television?"

He shrugged. "No television broadcast service up here. Sometimes I listen to the news on the radio. I like the silence."

"Your family lives close enough though. How frequently do you visit them?"

"Not often. They have their lives, I have mine—"

"If I had a family who owned a restaurant, I'd eat there at least once a week. The pasta is so delicious and that sauce. Maybe you get tired of it if that's what you've known your whole life."

"I don't get tired of eating there. It's complicated."

"When do you go back to work?"

"Soon."

Dante began to fuss. Mariella dropped the chair leg she was sanding and went to pick up the baby. He rubbed his face and began to cry. She cuddled him close and walked around, rocking him gently.

"Does he need a bottle?" Cristiano asked, coming over.

"I don't know. He should be sleeping longer than this. If you could prepare a bottle, I'll try that. Maybe he's hungry because of being up so late last night."

Cristiano pushed the empty stroller to the kitchen. In only a moment, following Mariella's instructions, he had the bottle warmed for the baby.

Dante did not want the bottle. Taking the nipple, he

sucked for a moment then let out a wail. He pushed the bottle away and cried.

"Oh, honey, don't fret." Mariella held him up against her shoulder, walking around the stone floor. "Do you think it's more than teething?"

"I think your guess about teething is still likely. I remember Stephano's baby when he was teething. You could check with Signora Bertatali again, if you want. After that, if you aren't convinced, we can try the doctor."

She used his phone and checked with the woman again. When she hung up the phone Mariella looked at him. "She said it still sounds like teething. Give him something to chew on—soft so he won't hurt himself, but firm so he can feel it when he bites down. She said the process could go on for weeks or months."

"Oh, great. Do you have a rubber toy we could put in the refrigerator until it gets cold and let him chew on?"

She shook her head, jiggling him as Dante rubbed his face and cried.

"Maybe a cold washcloth?" she asked.

"That I have. I'll be right back."

In less then five minutes, Cristiano had a cold damp washcloth—soaked in ice water for a moment, then wrung out.

When he offered it to Dante the little boy stopped crying long enough to look at Cristiano. He lunged for him.

"Whoa." Surprised, he took the baby. Holding him in one arm, he offered the cloth again, wrapped around his finger. When Dante clamped down on it he smiled.

"He's got some bite. He keeps biting and releasing."

"At least he's stopped crying. Poor baby." Mariella brushed his downy hair. "This goes on for months? I'll never sleep."

"This might calm him down."

But as the afternoon wore on it was obvious to both adults the child had staying power. He chewed on the washcloth, then cried. They'd swap it out for another cold one, and he'd be content for a little while. Cristiano insisted on taking turns with Mariella as they walked the baby, trying to get him comfortable.

Dante drank a bottle, alternating between chewing on the nipple, crying and sucking. Finally, late in the afternoon he fell asleep.

Mariella held him close. "I think we should go home now," she whispered.

"I don't think the sound of our voices will wake him, he's out," Cristiano said. Hearing a noise, he looked at the windows. "It's raining again. Pouring more like. You don't want to take him out in this. Stay."

She looked at the rain. "So you're stuck with us."

He brushed his fingertips down her cheek. "No problem. The worst is behind us. I'll dash out and make sure the workshop is closed up. We can start dinner, eat a bit early and, when the rain stops, I'll drive you back to the cottage."

She nodded. "If this keeps up, I can't go to Rome tomorrow. I can't leave him when he's not one hundred per cent all right. I wanted to visit Ariana's grave on her birthday, but she'd understand I couldn't leave her son."

"Rome will be there whenever we go, no problem. Truth be told, I'm not sure I'm ready."

"Ready for what? Driving to Rome? Does your ankle hurt?"

"No, not that. I'm not sure I'm ready to face Stephano's wife. He had so much to live for. Why was he killed and not me?"

"We don't know why things happen. I'm sure every

family who was affected by that bombing questions why it happened."

"He saved several people before he was caught in the second blast."

"So he's a hero, too."

"Small help to his family now."

"There is comfort in knowing that, Cristiano," she said gently, reaching out to touch his arm. "I can only imagine how devastated his wife must feel, but she and her children can be proud of what he was doing when he was killed. And I know she would love to see you. I love visiting with friends of Ariana's who were close to her those last months when I was still in New York. Talking about her, remembering her hurts—but it also heals. She didn't have such a great life but she loved life. She was optimistic almost to the end."

"At least you had time to prepare."

"One is never prepared. Go to your friend's wife, talk to her of Stephano. You two probably knew him best in the world. She would want that contact."

He looked away, searched the ceiling, wondered how to truly convey the fear that flooded. "It's not that easy."

"No one said it was easy. It's just important."

"He was a good friend."

"So was Ariana. I think special friends are rare. I wonder if I'll ever have another that I feel as close to as I did with her."

He thought about it for a moment. "Probably not. Another friend that's close, I expect, but not as close. Stephano and I shared a strong bond from the training and the fires we fought together. We took holidays together. He and AnnaMaria always included me in family events."

"She must be hurt you haven't contacted her," Mariella said.

"I thought she wouldn't want to be reminded—"

"She'll need you for the memories you share. You can tell Stephano's children about their father. That'll be special for them."

Cristiano hadn't considered that. He missed his friend, but the best way to honor his memory was to make sure he was never forgotten. He hadn't given his friend's wife the attention she deserved. She would have been even more devastated to lose her husband than he had been to lose a friend. How could he have ignored her pain while dealing with his own?

"Cristiano?"

He looked at Mariella. "What?"

"You looked like you were in a trance."

"Just thinking about Stephano's family. I do need to see them."

"Yes. And your own."

"Why do you say that?"

"You're so lucky to have a big family to rally around when things are tough. They are there for you. I think the bombing must have been very hard on them. You need your family. You need people who know you, who love you, to support you no matter what. They are your support group that will never fail."

"Did you know I found out a few months ago that my father had a wife and two sons before he even met my mother? Yet he never told any of his second family about them. So maybe our family isn't as close as I once thought."

Mariella looked astonished. "You're kidding. What happened?"

"I don't know all the details, it all came out when my father and aunt were arguing. Isabella said the first sons live in America, but they have visited the family here, however I've never met them."

"How odd,' Mariella murmured. "How do you feel about that? I can't imagine learning I had siblings at this age. Is that why you aren't spending time with your family while you recover?"

He hesitated, the urge to explain growing stronger by the second. Yet he couldn't bear to see the disappointment in her expression when she realized he couldn't control his own mind. "It's complicated," he repeated.

"How?"

"For one thing, I can't believe my father never told us we had older siblings. Strangers who share our blood. Apparently he lost touch with them. Isabella didn't give a lot of details."

"So you have even more family than you thought. That's so cool."

He looked at her. "You have a most annoying habit of seeing everything through rose-colored glasses. What about my father's lack of trust in this family, his keeping them secret? His ignoring them for many, many years?"

"Maybe you should ask him why," she suggested. "I'd give anything to belong to a large family, to have people who loved me around to help when I need it. Or just to share good times with. What's wrong with being happy about things? Are you a pessimist?"

"No. A realist. Bad things happen to people. Things that can't ever change. Life is not all sunshine."

"True. But for the most part, it's an exciting adventure. There will be tough times, but happy times, as well. We need to search for the happy. Hold onto it as long as we can to balance the other times."

"Are you happy? You lost your friend, your parents, you're saddled with an infant, working at a job that's not what you planned for. No prospects for change in the near future that I can see."

She nodded and smiled at him. "Today I am happy. The baby is sleeping, you are cooking dinner for me, and I'm healthy. Just because I'm not doing what I thought I would be doing career wise right now doesn't mean I won't at some point in life. I've come to realize these last few days that I could never give Dante up. I will still look for his father so he'll know about him, but I don't know if I'll approach him. I need to make sure Dante stays with me. He's so precious."

"Don't you want to get married, have your own family?"

"Dante is my family. And, yes, I'd like to get married some day. But if that's not in the cards, I'm not going to pine away. Do you want to get married?"

He shrugged. "I'll let my brother and sister take care of future generations."

She laughed. "There's more to marriage than having children. I see it as a partnership of two people sharing their lives together. My parents had a great marriage. In a way, much as I wish things had been different, I'm glad they died together. I think either would have been lost without the other. That's the kind of marriage I want if I ever find the right man."

"Wonder if that's what my father thought he was getting—each time. The first wife left him. My mother died young. He's been a single dad most of his life."

"And, what, five kids? That's got to be sort of nice."

Dante fussed again and she went to quiet him down before he could fully wake up. Cristiano continued preparing the meal while the rain ran down the windows. Had his dad regretted the past? Wished he were closer to the grown sons he had in America. Cristiano had never doubted his father's love. But it seemed as if his entire world had gone topsy-turvy and he didn't like it.

"This is a nice place," she said when she had wheeled the stroller into the darkened living room. "Tell me some more about being a kid at the lake."

The rest of the afternoon passed with both sharing memories of happier times when they'd been younger.

Dinner was delicious.

"If you ever decide to give up firefighting, you could get a job cooking anywhere," Mariella commented as she complimented him on the pasta dish.

He looked at her sharply. "Why would I give up firefighting?"

"I don't know. It's not exactly the kind of job you do in your eighties, is it?" She licked her lips.

"No, it's not a job for an old man. But I've years ahead of me before I'm eighty."

She nodded, laughing softly. "I'll say."

Almost as if he knew dinner was finished, Dante began to cry again. He was not easily placated. They tried the cold washcloth for him to chew on. Tried rubbing his gums with their fingers, wincing when he bit hard. But nothing seemed to work.

Mariella fed him again, a hit or miss with him spitting out the nipple more than he drank from it. "I should be going," she said at one point.

"Stay a bit longer. No need for you to have to handle this alone. I can help."

"If this is like last night, you wouldn't get any sleep."

"We'll trade off. If he screams all night long, I'll take him for a while so you can sleep. I don't need much sleep."

"Thanks, but he's my problem."

"Actually, he's your son, not a problem. This situation can be shared. Let me help, Mariella."

She swayed from side to side trying to soothe the baby. "You don't know what you're in for."

"I do. I saw him last night. And today. We'll be fine. Let's try another cold washcloth."

As they took turns holding the baby and walking the floor with him, the hours slowly passed. A little after midnight Mariella gave into Cristiano's suggestion she go lie down in one of the bedrooms and sleep for a little while.

"What about you?"

"I'll be fine. I'll wake you when I need to go to sleep, unless this little guy finally gives in."

She nodded and closed her eyes for a moment. "I'm dead on my feet," she said. "Thanks, Cristiano. Which room?"

"None of the beds are made but mine. But there are fresh sheets and blankets in the closet along the hall."

"I'll make do."

It was almost three when Dante finally nodded off, tears still on his sweet face. Cristiano continued holding him in the large chair they'd been in for the last couple of hours. The child was in such discomfort nothing seemed to work. Now he would escape that by sleep. Cristiano envied him. He'd love to sleep and escape everything. But he never knew if the nightmares would rage or if the night would be restful.

The rain continued. The sound on the roof reminded him of days in the past when he and his brother and sister had to stay inside because of rain and how they'd railed against the weather.

He missed seeing them. Missed being a part of their lives. Valentino had married! He was trying to adapt to knowing his younger brother was married. And his sister, too! Mariella was right, he had a close family who would rally to his aid, if there were anything they could do.

Time and again he returned to wondering about the newly learned-of brothers. Dante lay across his chest. Cristiano brought up the baby blanket to cover him. He'd leave him right where he was for a while. He knew his father must have held those early babies—twins. Had his father planned a future for his sons? How devastated he must have felt when the boys had to go to America.

Had their mother had family to help out? Or had she been a single mother like Mariella? He'd want to share in all his child's growing—seeing him learn to walk, hear the cute sayings he'd come up with, watch as the amazement of learning blossomed on his face. If he ever married, ever had a child.

"What of you, little man? What will you become? Anything you want. A doctor? Maybe an artist.' He felt a pang when he thought of not seeing the baby again after Mariella left.

What of when Mariella left? He hadn't known her for long, but the feelings that had exploded had nothing to do with length of time knowing her. If things had been different, he'd make sure she didn't disappear back in Rome. He'd court her the old-fashioned way—flowers, dancing, long walks where they could talk about their hopes and dreams and fall in love.

Unfortunately, his future was on hold. Maybe gone.

He reached out and turned the lamp to the lowest setting, dimming the light. He'd see if he could doze a bit while Dante slept. Who knew how long he had?

Mariella woke in daylight. For a moment she wasn't sure where she was, then she remembered. Jumping out from beneath the duvet she'd drawn over herself last night, she hurried out to the living room. The house was silent. Where were Cristiano and Dante?

She stopped at the doorway. One lamp was on, giving little illumination. Cristiano was stretched out on the comfortable chair, his long legs straight out, his head resting on the back. Cradled against his chest, the baby was sound asleep, covered by one of his little blankets. Just like yesterday. She could get used to this.

For a long moment Mariella stared, imprinting the image on her mind for all time. She let herself dream for an instant that this was a usual occurrence. She'd be asleep and then awake to find Cristiano with the baby. She'd waken them and they'd spend their days together. And their nights. Dante would not always need extra care. He was good about sleeping through the nights normally.

She went into the kitchen to clean up from dinner and get something started for breakfast. If only coffee.

Then she needed to make plans to return home. Not for a brief trip, but back to their normal lives. She was falling in love with her firefighter and he was not falling for her. She blinked back tears, feeling the pain of disappointment deep inside. She wished he would, but there was an intangible barrier. Every time she thought they were drawing closer, he'd pull back.

What she felt for him went far deeper than any emotions she'd had before. From time to time growing up, she'd thought she was in love. A boy in high school. A young man in New York. But soon the feelings had faded. Knowing Cristiano showed her how pale the emotions before were compared to her feelings for him now. He was strong, generous, helpful. He saved people's lives. He was a hero several times over. And he made her feel so very special.

Which reminded her of the medal ceremony. He should attend. If not for himself, then for the others he spoke about who were heroes but couldn't be there. She wanted the world to know what a true hero he was.

She wondered how she could convince him to attend. Could his family help? She wasn't even sure they knew. To come right out and tell them seemed a breach of confidence, though Cristiano had never told her not to tell anyone.

She still had the letter. From what she'd read, the award was being made—whether Cristiano accepted it in person or not.

The cottage was quiet. Cristiano's computer sat on the table from before. Mariella turned on the computer, surrounded by the warmth of the cottage kitchen, redolent with the fragrance of coffee brewing. She checked messages, contacted her clients to let them know she was on top of things. Then she looked up the award ceremony. There was quite a bit of press about the event, honoring those who had responded to the bombing, both living and dead.

It would be held at the Parlamento addressing both the Senato della Repubblica and the Camera dei Deputati. The Prime Minister himself was presenting the awards.

The ceremony was given by a still-grieving nation doing what it could to honor those who had first responded at great personal risk and sacrifice.

The rain finally ended. She closed the laptop and rose to go to the doorway, opening it a crack and breathing in the fresh air, cool and damp. It raised her spirits. She had been on a fool's errand, trying to locate a man who had never wanted to know he had a son. If he'd left Ariana, she should have taken that as a sign. Longing for family of her own should not have had her going against her friend's wishes, however much Mariella wanted Dante to have an extended family. Her limited attempts to locate anyone who had known Ariana in this area had proved totally futile. Another sign?

She did not regret coming, however. If she hadn't, she never would have met Cristiano.

"Be happy, my love, whatever the future brings you," she whispered to the wind, wishing she dared whisper it to him face to face.

Time to go home.

to five directions, found himself bending over Mariella, who was instead scanning the Remington Arms factory to the left for someone, hoping it—

"How are—" There—

CHAPTER NINE

THE phone rang.

"Get that, would you?" Cristiano called from the living room. Mariella hurried to the counter and picked it up.

The woman on the other end was obviously surprised when Mariella answered.

"Who is this?"

"Mariella Holmes." She recognized Cristiano's sister instantly.

"Where is Cristiano?" Isabella asked as soon as Mariella identified herself.

She explained how he was watching the fussy baby. "Hang on, I'll get him for you."

"A moment, please, Mariella. Do you know about the awards ceremony for those who rescued people in the bombing last May?" Isabella asked.

"Yes, I was just reading about it on the Internet, actually."

"You know Cristiano is getting a medal, don't you? Is he still refusing to attend?"

"I believe so." She was hesitant to confirm or deny anything. "You need to talk to him." Mariella hurried into the living room and held out the phone.

"It is your sister." She gently picked up the sleeping

baby and rocked him a bit, walking out of the room. But she could still hear Cristiano's side of the conversation.

He was arguing with his sister.

She knew he felt he'd done nothing extraordinary—it was his job to respond to any emergency. He should have done more at the bombing site. He focused on those who hadn't made it, not the ones he'd saved. Somehow he had to see he'd done more than most and merely because he lived didn't mean he hadn't been willing to give all. He hadn't needed to this time.

She heard an expletive, then silence. She stood by the back door, swaying with the baby. Was Cristiano angry with his sister? More likely just angry—at fate, at the way things had turned out.

She didn't know how long she stood there, but when she heard the car in the driveway a short time later she knew it had been long enough for Isabella to drive from Monta Correnti. Mariella watched as Isabella got out and walked quickly to the house. Her long wavy black hair blew in the wind. Her blue eyes looked stormy.

"Hello," Isabella said when she stepped inside.

"Cristiano is in the living room," Mariella said, wondering if she should leave or stay. "Do you want coffee?" She could put the baby in the stroller and prepare coffee—it would give her something to do.

"Yes, please." Isabella took off her jacket and draped it over the back of a chair, then headed to the living room.

Mariella was soon scooping coffee grounds and listening to the raised voices arguing in the living room. It wasn't anything she had not already heard. Cristiano did not want to accept a medal. He didn't feel he'd done anything special. He kept going on about those who had died.

Finally there was silence. Mariella checked the brewing

coffee and then stepped to the doorway. Brother and sister glared at each other.

"I think, Cristiano," Mariella said softly, "that this is something you have to do."

He began to protest, but she raised her hand. "I'm not finished. I've been thinking about it, and reading about it. It's a way for our country to honor those who went to help. What else can we do? We were not there with you. We did not die like your friends and comrades. We did not see the horror. What we did see was the bravery of the first responders who plunged into the inferno without knowing what they would find, or if they'd make it back out. You did—time and again and you saved seven lives to prove it."

"Stephano—" he began, but she raised her hand again and frowned at him.

"Listen to me! You must accept because of Stephano. He is not there to be awarded. Go and represent him and all those men and women you knew who died. Let our country honor your bravery, your courage and the unselfishness you demonstrated by risking your life to save strangers. Our country needs this, Cristiano. No matter what you think, the rest of us know you are a hero and we want to express our appreciation in a way the entire world will understand."

The anguish in his eyes was beyond her understanding. But she was steadfast in facing him. He needed to do this for himself and for those who had died. The tension stretched. Finally he gave an abrupt nod and turned to stride out the front door. "I'll think about it," was all he said.

"Whew," Isabella said, watching him leave. "Thank you, Mariella. You put it eloquently."

"It's only true. He carries this feeling he failed because his friends died, but he didn't. And I know every single one of the seven he saved will bless him all their days."

They returned to the kitchen to pour the coffee. Sitting at the table, Isabella looked at her for a moment, then said,

"His accepting the medal is an even better excuse to have the party. Dad will never suspect anything else."

"Like what?" Mariella asked, confused.

"What I'm telling you is in confidence. You can't tell anyone," Isabella said, leaning closer, dropping her voice slightly.

Mariella blinked. "Okay."

"My father and my aunt each own a restaurant in Monta Correnti. Many years ago, before I was born even, they were joint owners of Sorella. Then they had a major falling out. Dad left the restaurant to Lisa and started Rosa."

Mariella nodded. Where was this going?

"Economic times have been tough lately, people aren't eating out as much. Both restaurants have taken a hit, especially Rosa. For a while there we thought we'd have to close. One way to carry on is to merge the two and find economy of scale to have them both operated as one. They'd still keep their different menus, but economies can be achieved which would go a long way to turning things around. The restaurants would complement each other and continue to thrive."

"So is merging a problem? Are your aunt and father still feuding?"

"Actually, Dad turned the day-to-day operation of the restaurant over to us—Scarlett and me. I've been talking with my aunt and we've decided this is the best way to handle things. We wanted to surprise my father with this merger. I want a fait accompli. He loves the restaurant. I expect he'll go along with anything that keeps it open—even joining forces with his sister. Plus, there's another situation."

Mariella asked, "What is that?"

"Did Cristiano tell you about our American brothers?"

Mariella nodded slowly.

"I want a way to bring the entire family together—a reunion, if you would. So this is perfect. Everyone loves Cristiano. We've been worried about him these months. To celebrate this honor for him would raise no suspicions. I'll have Alex and Angelo visit from America and I'll make sure Aunt Lisa and her family are present. Then we can mingle, celebrate and announce the plans for the merger. It's perfect!"

"What's perfect?" Cristiano stood in the doorway.

"The excuse for the party I told you about. We'll change it to celebrating the medal."

Cristiano frowned. Isabella ignored him.

"Dad will be so proud of you. We'll have the celebration at the restaurant, of course. Everyone will come." She glanced at her watch. "I've got to go. I'll call you with details." Isabella glanced at Mariella, giving her a wink. "Bring Mariella as well."

When Isabella left, Cristiano sat at the table, looking drained.

"Are you all right?" Mariella asked. "Want some coffee? It's fresh."

He nodded. When he took the cup, he spoke, "There's things you don't know anything about. Other reasons I don't want to accept the medal."

She reached out and took his hand, feeling warmed when he turned to clasp hers. He studied their linked hands for a long moment, then raised his gaze to hers.

"Will you come with me?" he said.

"I can't go." She was stunned. "Someone close to you should go—Isabella or your father."

"You or I don't go at all."

She blinked. "Why me?"

"Because if you're ganging up with Isabella in pressuring me to go, I want you there. I'm sure families are allowed. I'll find out. Otherwise, the deal is off. I don't go."

"Okay, then. I'll go." She would be thrilled to be in the audience when he accepted the medal.

Dante woke and grew fussy. Mariella prepared him a bottle and then had the difficult task of getting him to eat when he was so miserable.

"Can I help?" Cristiano asked, watching them with concern.

"I'm getting the hang of it. You had him earlier."

"There's no time limit. I like that little guy," he said.

She smiled down at the cranky baby and kissed his forehead. "He does grow on you, doesn't he? Go do some woodworking. We'll come out when he's finished eating."

"What makes you think I want to go work?"

"It'll soothe you, you said so—maybe not in so many words, but it shows."

Cristiano went to the shop in back and switched on all the lights. He was in turmoil; the thought of accepting the award not sitting well. And the worry he'd have another flashback in the midst of it all was enough to make him want to flee.

He was sincere in wanting Mariella there. He would look at her, not see in his mind's eye the devastation and horror of that day. He'd focus on her silvery eyes, her optimistic smile, and know he'd risk a hundred forays into hell to see her smile.

"It's an excuse, you know," Mariella said a short time later when she arrived pushing the stroller.

"What is?" He looked up, already feeling better for seeing her and the baby.

"Your medal celebration. Isabella wants a party to announce the merger of Rosa and Sorella."

"What?" He stared at her in stunned surprise. That was the last thing he'd expected to hear.

Quickly she told him what his sister had said.

"And Dad's okay with this?" he asked.

"Apparently it's to be a surprise, but Isabella said he turned things over to her and Scarlett and this is their decision."

"He'll flip."

"Or be proud of yet another offspring—for her business acumen. I still want to talk to her about a mail-order outlet for that sauce. Actually, the place could use a website just to let people know about it. I do have a degree in marketing— maybe I can help."

"Who will be at the party?"

"Just family, and me and Dante. Unless you don't want us to go."

"If I go, you go," he said, pulling her close with his arm around her waist. He leaned in and kissed her.

Wishes do come true, Mariella thought as she savored his kiss, giving back as much as she was able. Maybe she should start wishing for the moon. It could happen he'd fall in love with her, couldn't it? His month moved against hers, leaving to trail kisses across her nose.

"I've wanted to kiss those freckles since I first saw you," he murmured, trailing kisses across her cheek, down to her jaw, lower to the pulse point at the base of her throat, wildly beating as the blood rushed through her. She was floating in delight. Seeking his mouth, she sighed in contentment when he covered hers with his and deepened the kiss.

Long moments later they were both breathing hard. He pulled back a scant inch. "Is the baby okay?"

"I haven't heard him. I'll check."

Cristiano did not loosen his hold.

"Or maybe I'll just listen from here."

He kissed her gently.

"If he makes it through okay today, let's try Rome in the morning," he said. "We missed your friend's birthday, but it'll still be close."

She nodded, still in the circle of his arms, where she'd like to stay forever.

"You'll be okay about the medal?" she asked softly.

He groaned softly and rested his forehead against hers. "We'll just see, won't we?"

"What does that mean? Sometimes you're a bit cryptic."

"We'll just see."

Cristiano didn't want to talk. He wanted to hold her, kiss her, make love to her. His feelings were already entangled with Mariella Holmes. He couldn't take things any farther until he knew if he'd come through this a whole man.

He would never tie anyone to a man who couldn't function in today's world.

The thought seared his brain. He wanted her. He wanted what others had—a life's companion that would share the journey through the years. Share good times and bad, laugh with friends, children. He needed to affirm life, to relish the ordinariness of the day. Take what the day offered and not worry about the future. One day at a time. How far could that take them? Would it be enough?

Cristiano breathed deeply of the fresh, clean country air, the scent of wood and oil. The sun shone from a cloudy sky. The air was crisp and cool after the rain. It was a perfect day. And he vowed he'd spend it with Mariella and the baby. Time was fleeing, he had to make the most of every moment.

They took Dante for a walk in the stroller after lunch to

keep him occupied. Even though he was fussy, the change seemed to work. Cristiano had never imagined he'd be content to walk alongside a woman and baby on a quiet country road. Where was the adventure of Rome, the exciting life he'd demanded before? Stephano had told him how much richer life was married to AnnaMaria. He'd been over the moon when his son had been born, then his daughter.

"You're quiet," Mariella said.

"Thinking about Stephano's son. He's three now. His daughter is almost two."

"Go visit."

"When I drive you to Rome." It would be perfect, time constraints keeping it short. He could handle that. At least he hoped so. Would seeing AnnaMaria bring up all the anguish? Was she missing him as Mariella suggested? Or would she rather he not barge in? It had been six months; maybe she was getting on with her life and didn't need a part of the past.

"I was thinking of returning home. Not just for a quick trip," she said slowly.

That surprised him. "I thought you had some more vacation time."

"I do, or at least less demands on my time until my major clients return. But I'm going to stop trying to find Dante's father. The more I think about what you said, the more I question if I truly want him found. What if he tries to take Dante from me? I couldn't bear that. I used to think it would be okay, his father could tell him about Ariana. But they weren't together for long. And a man who could walk away like that isn't the one I want for a father for Dante. Better he stays with me. Some of my rationale in searching was the fear of being the sole person responsible for this child. But it looks as if that's the way it'll be. I think I can do it. I'll have to, won't I?"

"You'll probably marry some day. Then Dante will have a father. Pick a good one."

She avoided his eyes as they strolled along. Had he touched a nerve?

"Problem?"

"No."

He waited. Mariella usually wasn't so quiet. Something was wrong; even he could figure that out. "What?"

She glanced at him. "Nothing. Just—not many men will want to take on a ready-made family."

"Hmm, wonder if that's what kept my father silent all these years."

"What do you mean?"

"What would you do if you found out your father had been married before your mother, that all your life until you were thirty—well, all your life up to now—you thought you were the oldest of your father's children and suddenly you find out you have two older brothers?"

"I imagine I'd be thrilled. But then I think I have a different take on family than you seem to."

"It's not what it's cracked up to be."

"Why not?

"My grandmother made a mistake a long time ago, resulting in my father. His half-siblings never forgave her or him. It wasn't his fault he was born. But it still split the family. What I remember about my aunt and father was the constant fights and altercations. I know that when Dad hit a bad patch he asked his sister for financial help. She refused. So I should rejoice in finding more family?"

"If your sister asked for help would you refuse?"

"Of course not. I'd do anything for Isabella."

"And your brother?"

"Yes."

"How about your aunt?"

"Never."

She laughed. "Careful, she's going to be even closer tied if the merger goes through."

"That's another thing—what is Isabella thinking of?"

"Maybe of a way to get this split family back together acting like a solid family, with no secrets and no division. Who knows, you might like having older brothers."

"Twins."

She laughed again. "Oh, Cristiano, I wish you'd known them when you were younger. Think of the mischief four of you Casali boys could have gotten into. That would have given your father such joy."

"You have the most annoying habit of being right." He stopped her in the middle of the street and kissed her. "Okay, I'll go to the blasted awards and then Isabella's party and do my best to make nice with strangers, but if the twins start bossing me around—"

She hugged him. "Then you give back as good as you get. My money's on you every time."

The next morning when Mariella walked into the living room after a fitful few hours of sleep, Cristiano was balancing a happy baby.

"Come," he said, beckoning her over.

Taking her hand, he folded three fingers and held her index finger. Gently he rubbed it against Dante's lower jaw.

"A tooth!" she exclaimed. "Oh, baby, you have your first tooth."

"Don't let him bite down, it hurts," Cristiano said, smiling at the baby. "I know."

She opened the baby's mouth. "I can hardly see it."

"It just broke through during the night, I guess. Anyway,

until the next one, I think this kid is going to be back to his normally pleasant baby self."

"I hope I can sleep through the night."

"Me, too."

They grinned at each other.

Then Mariella said, "So I can head for Rome tomorrow. I can never thank you enough for everything. Saving my life—"

"Stop. I told you no debts."

"I know, but still. And helping these last few days with such a cranky baby."

"You sound as if you are saying goodbye."

"I am, sort of. I need to go home."

"Not yet. You have vacation time to finish. Stay, Mariella. Please?"

She hesitated, then wondered if she was thinking clearly when she agreed. "For a little longer." She didn't want to leave—not leave Cristiano behind. But he never mentioned returning to his life in Rome. How long would it take for him to fully recover? Then what? Was staying good or bad? Would she fall even more for the man only to face heartache a few weeks later?

"Today I'll finish the table. Tomorrow we'll go to Rome and take it to your place."

"No rush, it'll be a while before he can use it," she said.

"The table will be done. The chairs a little longer. I like knowing something I've made will be in your home. Maybe you'll think about me from time to time."

She couldn't speak. If he only knew! She loved him. She was going to hate returning home.

"I'll fix coffee," she said with a strangled voice. "And boiled eggs."

"I'll cook breakfast," he said quickly.

Mariella laughed, blinking to keep tears at bay.

The entire time Mariella fed the baby and then ate the delicious eggs Benedict that Cristiano prepared, she felt on the verge of tears. There was nothing to hold her in Lake Clarissa. She had her own life to get back to. But she didn't want to go. She wanted to stay with Cristiano. Was it a good thing he asked her to stay longer? Could they find a future together? Was he even thinking along those lines?

Yet she wanted to hold onto every moment, imprint every second on her mind in case there was not a shared future. The way Cristiano looked by the stove. The smiles he gave the baby, who was in a much better mood today. The way the sun shone on his dark hair when he passed by the window. Taking a deep breath, she smelled his scent, uniquely his. Her heart pounded and she had to take another breath to avoid breaking into tears. She longed for the right to ask him to hold her, kiss her. Make love with her. To be part of his breakfast every morning and sleep with him every night.

Soon after she ate, she insisted on returning to the rental cottage. She needed some breathing room and a serious talk with herself to make sure she didn't give away her feelings. She'd take a few more days' vacation and then return to Rome for good without ever letting him know how much she loved him.

The next morning Mariella kissed the baby goodbye and gave Signora Bertatali a dozen last-minute instructions.

"Go, have a good day. I know how to take care of *bambinos*." The older woman practically shooed her from the house.

Cristiano waited by his dark sleek speed machine. The instant Mariella sat inside she felt carefree and adventurous. She loved Dante to bits, but she was elated to be free of responsibility for a few hours.

It was an awesome car, much more suited to couples than families. And its driver drove as if he were in a grand prix or something. Smoothly taking the curves, accelerating on the straight ways. The ride was exhilarating.

"We'll be there in ten minutes, at this rate," she said.

"Too fast?"

"Not if you can handle it," she replied. For the first time in months she was totally on her own—no baby demanding her every moment. She missed Dante, but knew she'd be back with him in a few hours. She needed the break.

And who better to take it with than the man of her dreams? The car suited her image of him, fast and yet in control. Risking life and limb fighting fires, yet considerate and always looking out for others. He was a caring man and there were few of those around.

"Are you going to see Stephano's wife?" she asked.

"I'll see her once I drop you off at your place after we visit the cemetery."

She looked in the back and the small table wedged in. Reaching back, she ran her fingertips over the satiny wood. "It looks amazing. I can't wait to have it in the apartment. Who else will you see?" she asked. "Are you stopping by the ministry?"

"No. I called them yesterday and got all the information I need for the ceremony," he said. "We have to be there by seven. The actual ceremony begins at eight." He reached out and took her hand. "Wear something very pretty."

"And your family party is the next night. Tell me more about your family. If I'm to meet everyone, I need to know who's who, the relationships and how much you like them— or not," she said.

"What does it matter if I like them or not?"

"No sense wasting my time on people you don't like. I wouldn't like them either."

He laughed and squeezed her hand, then rested it on his thigh. "I don't know the older brothers, but I don't think I'll like them."

"Not fair, you have to meet them first. Who else?"

The rest of the drive was accomplished with Cristiano telling her about his aunt, his cousins, his brother and sister and what little he knew of the unknown men from America.

Reaching the outskirts of Rome, Mariella gave directions to the old cemetery. The visit was brief. Cristiano held back while Mariella went right to the small headstone marking the final resting place of her dearest friend.

He looked around. Stephano was buried in the cemetery closer to his home. He had yet to visit the grave. Maybe soon. But not just yet.

"Thank you. It was important to me," Mariella said when she rejoined him.

He nodded, wishing he could do more to ease her grief. Wishing his own would vanish.

She directed him to the apartment building housing her flat. It was on an older road, stone façade looking weathered and ancient.

He carried up the finished table. Entering, he looked around. "Nice." It was simply furnished, but every item was in good shape. The upholstered pieces looked comfortable. There was enough baby paraphernalia to tell the world a baby lived there, but not too much clutter in the small apartment.

"There, I think?" she said, pointing to a spot beneath the window. "When he's older, he'll have a place to play blocks or color with crayons. I can't wait."

Cristiano wished he could be there to see Dante toddling

around. Running in to tell his mother some exciting news, or bringing some friends over when he was older.

"I'll be ready to go after three," she said.

"I'll pick you up then." He brushed her lips lightly with a kiss and headed out. Time to stop in and see his chief and then go see AnnaMaria.

It was shortly before three when he stopped in front of Mariella's apartment building. The meeting with his captain had gone well. As soon as he received the release from the doctor, he was free to return to work.

AnnaMaria had welcomed him with open arms. Once the initial awkwardness had passed, he'd felt right at home. The only difference was he had expected Stephano to walk in at any moment. AnnaMaria had even commented on that. It helped her through the days, she said, imaging he was just away.

Their son had grown and talked a mile a minute. Cristiano couldn't help thinking of Dante in a few years. He'd be much like Stephano's son. Would the two boys like each other? In another time and place, they might have been friends like him and Stephano. The little girl was napping, but he could see Stephano's features in a feminine version on her face when he peeked in at her.

The afternoon sped by. Cristiano vowed to stay in closer touch with AnnaMaria and told her to call on him for any help she needed. They talked of the future, near and distant, and the fact Stephano was getting a posthumous award and she'd be there to receive it.

Arriving at Mariella's apartment a few minutes earlier than planned, Cristiano thought about waiting before going up—not wanting to appear anxious. "Forget this," he said, climbing out of the car. So he was early. If she wasn't ready to go, he'd wait in her flat. At least he'd be with her. Then they'd drive back, maybe eat dinner at Rosa, show his sister his face so she would be reassured. Talk about their day, make further plans for the award ceremony that he was now resigned to attend.

Mariella greeted him with a smile. "Come in. Want something to drink before we leave?"

"No. I'm not in a hurry."

"How did it go with AnnaMaria?"

He told her a little of the afternoon. "It was odd with Stephano not there. I always think of her with him."

"It must be hard for her."

He nodded.

"I'm almost ready. The new computer is set up. I had a lot of things stored on my backup drive, so could just reload." As she chatted about how she'd spent her afternoon, Cristiano settled in on the sofa, enjoying the normalcy of the moment. Feeling cautiously optimistic he wondered if he dared risk returning to work soon.

And if he dared take this relationship with Mariella another step.

"We could stop for dinner on the way home," he suggested.

"Terrific. In Monta Correnti?"

He nodded.

"Rosa?" she asked.

"Would you like to try Sorella? See the competition my sister wants to merge with?"

"Is it as good?"

"Not the sauce, but my aunt doesn't do anything by halves. No deadline to be home for Dante?"

"I checked with Signora Bertatali about a half-hour ago. He's doing fine."

She finished loading the computer. Shut it down and packed it in its carrying case. "I have this to take and another suitcase of clothes. I'm tired of wearing the few things I bought after the fire. And I have more for Dante. I think he's already outgrowing the clothes I bought last week."

"All set, then."

They headed out to the car. Cristiano placed the suitcase in the trunk, reached to take the computer from Mariella when the wail of sirens filled the air, growing louder by the second. The klaxons sounded at the intersection as two large fire engines roared down the street, the noise amplified between the buildings.

Suddenly the neighborhood vanished. He crouched low as the debris fell. The air was acrid with smoke, so thick he couldn't see two feet in front of him. The baby screamed in his arms, the child he carried whimpered softly, clinging fiercely. "Stephano," he yelled, fighting to keep going. The roof was collapsing. A second bomb had blown. Where were the stairs leading up from the subway station? Searing pain hit his leg, his ankle. He couldn't breathe, couldn't see. His helmet faceplate was broken, smoke and dust surrounded him, blinded him.

The wailing sirens filled his senses, the smoke impossible to see through. Heat scorched from behind from the fire. Concrete rained down. Chaos and confusion reigned. "Stephano?" He yelled again, heard nothing but the roar of the world collapsing around him. He couldn't move. Couldn't go forward, couldn't go back. He had two children to save. Where were his fellow first responders? Was he alone in a world gone mad?

"Cristiano!"

A voice called. It wasn't yelling. He could scarcely hear it over the klaxons echoing from the apartment façades.

"Cristiano, what's happening?"

He recognized that voice. What was Mariella doing in the subway? Had she been trying to catch a train?

"Cristiano, stop, you're scaring me." She shook him, patted his cheeks.

He closed his eyes and the world went black.

CHAPTER TEN

"CRISTIANO!" Mariella clutched his arm, shaking him again. She was stooped down beside him. When he fell against the car, she looked around. One of the men on the sidewalk hurried over. Panic filled her. What was wrong with him?

"Do you need help?" the man asked, leaning over.

Cristiano opened his eyes and gazed up at them, dazed.

"Yes. He's had a seizure. If I can get him standing, I think I can get him to my apartment," she said. "I can call an ambulance from there."

"No—no ambulance. I need to sit for a minute," Cristiano said, shaking his head as if to clear it.

The man helped Cristiano get to his feet.

"You sure? An ambulance could be here in a few minutes," he asked.

Cristiano nodded, his arm over Mariella's shoulder. "I've had this before. I know how to deal with it. I just need to sit."

"*Grazie*," Mariella said, leading Cristiano into the apartment building. In only moments they were back in her apartment.

"I'll be okay," he said, still leaning slightly on her.

"Good. Sit on the sofa. I'll make some tea. Do you need to see a doctor? You scared me half to death."

"I don't need any doctor." He sank onto the sofa, elbows on his knees as he dropped his head into his hands.

"You scared me. Are you sure you'll be all right?"

"I'm sure," he said, his voice muffled.

Mariella watched him for a moment, biting her lip in indecision. Finally she headed for her kitchen. "Wait here, I'll make some tea."

She hurried into the kitchen, the initial fear fading. What had happened down there? It was as if he'd spaced out, ducking and yelling. She peeked back to the living room. He hadn't moved.

It seemed to take forever for the water to boil. As soon as she had the tea ready, she hurried back.

He still hadn't moved.

She placed both cups of tea on the coffee table and reached out to touch his shoulder.

He shrugged off her touch, rose and paced to the window. Gazing out, he still seemed dazed.

"Sorry about that," he said with some effort.

"Post-traumatic stress disorder," she said, picking up her cup to take a sip. Wanting her hands to have something to hold since he wasn't letting her hold him.

He swung around. "What do you know about it?"

"You forget, I spent the last four years in New York. America is home to PTSD. The terrorist attacks, hurricanes, major forest fires, earthquakes. Between first responders and the military, there are a lot of people suffering from PTSD. I have a friend whose brother was in Iraq and suffers from it daily. It can be quite debilitating. Is that what you have?"

He nodded. "Now you see why I am not a hero," he said,

turning to gaze back out the window at the scene on the street.

"What does that have to do with anything? You are a hero. Even more so, rescuing me and Dante after what you went through in May." She rose and crossed the room to stand beside him. Reached out to touch him, wanting contact; she wasn't going anywhere.

"Cristiano, you are a hero."

He hit his forehead with the palm of his hand. "Except I'm not right in the head."

She shook him slightly. "My friend calls her brother whacko, but loves him to bits. He does the same thing, goes off into the horror none of us can share."

"I can't get the images out of my head. I wake in the night. Sometimes during the day, out of the blue, I'm suddenly back in that hell. What kind of man does that make me?"

"Human."

He glanced at her, looked back out the window.

"Truly, I don't think we were designed to witness the horrors of modern life. The human mind can only absorb so much. Then it kicks in its defense mechanisms," she said.

"What are mine? Reliving the day forever? It's like I'm stuck in some repeat loop—the smoke, fire, crashing concrete, cries of the dying."

She hugged him, leaning slightly against him until he lifted his arm and put it around her shoulders. "I don't know that much about it. I've heard it can get better with counseling. Sometimes not. There are Vietnam War survivors still suffering from it forty years later. It's an awful payback for being heroic, for doing your best for others. I don't know how you can get over it. Maybe you never will, but it does not diminish who you are or what you've done."

"If I can't function in the world, they might as well lock me up and throw away the key," he said, letting his frustration show.

"Wait a minute—is this the reason you've become a recluse in Lake Clarissa? Does your family know?"

He turned and gripped her shoulders hard. "Do not tell them—do you understand?"

"Why not? It's nothing to be ashamed of. It's not something you can predict, or cure. It's not even something you caused."

"They think of me as some fearless, reckless adrenalin junkie. Daring danger in the line of work. I don't want them to know what a pitiful creature I've become."

"You are not the least pitiful. You are strong, brave, courageous and dependable." She gripped his wrists and shook him as much as she was able. "Pay attention, Cristiano, this isn't your fault. You are a fine man."

"Sure, like just now. Sirens go off and I'm a puddle on the pavement."

"A trigger, right? You heard them and flashed back to that day. From what I read on the Internet, it was horrible. You saw things you'll never forget, terrible things. People dying you couldn't save. Your own friends dying. You were almost killed yourself. Why wouldn't that bother you? You would be a very cold person if it didn't affect you."

"I can't get past it. It's been months. I need to get back to work. But I'm afraid that'll never happen. I ride the trucks that have the sirens. What good would I be if I have a flashback and put others in danger because I can't control what I see?"

Mariella didn't know what to say. Her heart ached for the burden he bore. She could tell by the anguish in his expression that this was something he'd been dealing with since May—alone. She encircled his waist with her arms.

For a moment he held himself rigid, then brought his arms around her. Clinging almost desperately.

"Your ankle was broken when the second bomb went off, wasn't it?" she asked, hoping she was going along the right track. She wished she knew more about PTSD, what triggered it, what might avoid an attack. How people moved beyond it.

"Yes."

"And it healed, but it took time. So, look at it as if your mind got bruised or something. It will take time but it will heal." She prayed she was right. She knew some men never got over the horrors they'd experienced. She hoped Cristiano wasn't one of them. But a man needed hope. She needed him to know that anything was possible.

"Have you seen a counselor?" she asked.

He shook his head. "The doctor at the hospital recommended one, but I left for Lake Clarissa as soon as I was out. There aren't any there."

"Monta Correnti?"

He shrugged.

"There's no shame in being injured," she said gently.

"There's shame when a man wants to be productive and dare not risk going among other people in case something like today happens. What good would I be anywhere? What if I'd been driving? I can't be a risk to others. I was a fool to leave Lake Clarissa today, to hope because I haven't had an episode recently that I was cured. To wish for a normal life like others. It isn't going to happen."

"You don't know that."

"I know I want what I had before—life that was carefree and suited me perfectly. Stephano and his family. My own family. The hope of falling in love and getting married. What of all that?"

"You can still fall in love and get married," she said.

"You still have your family and Stephano's wife and children."

"What woman would want to take on someone like me?" he bit out.

She stared at him. "I would," she said softly. Her heart ached for him. All the more painful for feeling his pain, his frustration when she had so much love to offer.

"Now you sound as crazy as I am," he said. Despite the words, he tightened his embrace and rested his head against hers, holding her firmly against him.

"Neither of us is crazy," she said, her voice muffled against his shoulder.

"If I weren't I'd court you like I were crazy," he said softly.

Her heart skipped a beat and then raced. "Don't play with me, mister," she warned.

He laughed. "I can't offer you anything. I will always cherish the days we spent together at the lake. But you need someone who's whole and free of flashbacks that could wind up injuring you or your son. I wish things were different, but they're not."

"So that's it? You are withdrawing from the world because everything is not perfect in your world?" She pulled back and glared at him.

"It has to be that way."

"No, it doesn't," she said, pushing free from his embrace. "You aren't the type of man to give up easily. Do you love me, Cristiano?"

"I have no right—"

"That's not what I asked." She glared at him. This certainly was not the way she'd expected to find out a man loved her. She had thought of roses and fine dining and dancing.

He took a deep breath, studying her face as if memorizing

it for all time. "I love you, Mariella Holmes. Your sunny disposition brightens my life. Your laughter makes my heart sing. Your devotion to your friend's son is heartwarming. I want you in the worst way—to spend nights in loving you, days in keeping you happy. But I have nothing to offer. I don't have a job I can go back to yet. I don't have the coping skills to make it with PTSD. I'm a mess."

She smiled at him and stepped closer. "I love you, too, Cristiano. I thought the way you were always pushing me away meant that you didn't care for me. But you do. Together we can face anything!"

"Didn't you hear me? There's no future together!"

"I'm ignoring what I don't want to hear. We can manage this. We can. I love you for who you are. I never knew you before, so this suits me perfectly."

"And if I have another meltdown like a little while ago?"

"Then we'll deal with it. Maybe you can start counseling to see if that helps. You can't be the only man from that day suffering from this. Who have you talked to about it? Who have you told?"

"No one."

She shook her head in exasperation. "I pictured you a fighter."

"I am. When there is something I can fight. This—I have no resources."

"So go find out all you can, find the resources to deal with it. Call your captain and tell him. Ask who else is having this problem and what they're doing about it. Oh, Cristiano, don't throw away what we could have together for some misguided notion you are in this alone. Your family would rally around in an instant. Your friends. Everyone. Me especially."

"I can't deal with it."

"Yes, you can. We can."

The silence stretched out for endless moments, then, with a soft sigh, he pulled her into his arms and kissed her. "What did I ever do to deserve this?" he said softly.

Sometime later he rested his forehead against hers and said, "It's not what I want for you. You should have a healthy, perfect man. You'd be getting damaged goods."

"How would I be getting that?" she asked saucily.

"I love you, sweetheart. Would you think—in the future, after we know more about this PTSD and what the prognosis is—would you consider marrying me?"

"Yes! And I don't need to wait for anything. I love you, Cristiano. I want to be with you always. No matter what, we can face it together. Besides, I come with baggage. Dante will need a father."

"Another thing that couldn't be better. I love that little boy. I want to see him grow up, see what kind of man he becomes. And have a part in that, showing him right from wrong, watching him discover the world."

"What better for him than a hero? Remember, you saved his life, it belongs to you."

"His biological father is a fool. I'd be honored to be Dante's father. So you'll marry me? As soon as we know—"

She put her fingertips over his lips. "As soon as we want. We're not waiting for some nebulous time in the future when you decide the stars align right or something. I want to be with you now, starting our memories and traditions. And helping if I can until you lick this thing."

"I have no job."

"I do. If we can live at the cottage for a while, we can manage. Don't say you don't want me unless everything is perfect. Love isn't like that. It takes good and bad, ups and downs. Now that I know you love me, I don't want to be apart. I'm alone in the world except for Dante. With you, I feel whole, complete, part of a family."

"What if I don't get better?"

"Cristiano, what would you do if I got sick?"

"I'd take care of you."

"Yet you want to deprive me of the same opportunity? I want to love you, be with you. Cristiano, that was a proposal and my answer is yes. Not yes someday, plain old yes!"

Her heart sang when he lifted her up to spin her around. "I love you!" he shouted.

She shrieked with mock fear as he spun them both around. "I love you!" she shouted back, then laughed with joy.

They spent the rest of the afternoon kissing, making plans, kissing, calling Cristiano's chief, kissing, and finally departed to return to Lake Clarissa.

"I can't wait to tell Dante," she said as she drove through the streets of Rome. Cristiano had insisted she drive, fearful of another episode if a siren sounded.

"He's six months old, what will he understand?"

"That you're going to be his daddy. That's so special."

"I think it's even more special that you're going to be my wife."

"Will your family approve? When will you tell them?"

He groaned. "Do you know every one of my cousins and siblings got married or engaged in the last six months. Must be something in the water."

"You're kidding!"

"Hey, we're all about the same age, natural, I guess. Only I didn't think I'd find anyone—especially after last May."

"So we can tell them at the party."

"After today I don't know if I should go. What if—?"

"Hey, they'll understand if something happens. You can't cut yourself off from the world. They'll be so proud of you receiving that medal."

"Oh, God," he groaned. "I can't go there."

"Of course you can go. I've known you for weeks and this is the first time I've seen you have a flashback. As long as there are no sirens, you'll probably be fine, don't you think?"

"What I think is if I can just look at you the entire time, I'll be able to do anything," he said, lifting her hand from the wheel and kissing the palm, then replacing it.

"Do you think your family will like me?"

"Yes."

She glanced at him. "That was positive."

"How could they not? You are adorable."

She laughed. "Keep that thought in mind forever."

"That's how long I'll love you. Forever."

CHAPTER ELEVEN

MARIELLA was dressed in a long gown, a rich dark burgundy velvet, suitable for the most formal of events. Her hair had been done up. Her nails polished to match the gown. She felt the butterflies in her stomach and knew Cristiano had to feel even more stress.

He was picking her up in another ten minutes. She had prayed all week that no sirens would mar the night. She so needed her man to receive his medal, to stand with those who had served beside him in rescuing all they could possibly save. And to stand in place of those comrades who had fallen and were only present in the memories of the minds of those present.

Promptly at the appointed time he knocked on her door. Her downstairs neighbor was watching Dante tonight. Nothing would interfere with the ceremony he so richly deserved.

She opened the door and exclaimed at how handsome he looked in his dress uniform.

"Wow, I'd want you to save me from all burning buildings," she said, leaning forward for his welcomed kiss. She'd only been alone for a day, but she had missed him as much as if they'd been parted a week or longer.

"Don't know if I ever will be able to do that," he murmured, pulling back to look at her. "You are beautiful."

The warm glow seeped through her. She hoped he always thought so.

"I'm ready," she said, reaching for her coat.

"That makes one of us," he said wryly.

"You'll do fine."

"If I end up a puddle on the floor, you'll be to blame."

She squeezed his arm, wishing she could take away every bit of turmoil and uncertainty. Wishing she could make him whole again. Perhaps time would do so, but not tonight.

Tonight was about Cristiano and Stephano and all the others, alive and dead, who had experienced the horror of the bombing together.

He'd hired a limo for the occasion and it was waiting outside her apartment. In only moments they arrived at the Parlamento building, brightly lighted for tonight's event. Reporters and cameramen flanked the cordoned-off entry, calling for sound bites and taking photos and videos of all entering.

"AnnaMaria will be there?" she asked as the limo stopped and Cristiano began to open the door.

"Yes. Her parents and Stephano's will be with her." He stepped out amidst the flashing lights and demands for tell-us-how-you-feel, coming from all directions.

"I probably should not confess to live cameras that I feel like I might throw up, hmm?" he said softly for her ear only.

She laughed and then smiled at the reporters. "I'm so proud to be here with you."

"Then let's walk tall and remember the fallen," he said, offering his arm and escorting her inside.

The buzz from outside was muted once inside the impressive building. Escorts took them to the Senato chamber where Cristiano moved to stand with other recipients while

Mariella was escorted to a seat in the second row. She saw him clearly when he walked in with the others, tall and proud. He looked amazing.

The actual event was full of pomp and ceremony. Television cameras captured everything. The national anthem was played. The Prime Minister spoke about the horror of the day, the attack on a country who had never anticipated such a cowardly assault, the great debt of gratitude the country had for those who had first gone in.

Mariella looked at Cristiano; his gaze was fixed on hers. She tried to relax, to be there for him as a means to hold on and not give way to the fear that plagued him. His eyes did not waver. She hoped he felt at ease.

The names of the men, women and children in the subway trains who perished were read. Relatives and friends sat in the audience. Mariella could hear quiet sobs as names were spoken.

The names of the first responders were then read, each one present stepping forward to receive their country's highest medal for bravery and service above and beyond the call of duty. She clapped wildly when Cristiano's name was called, when he stepped proudly forward to receive the medallion on a banner of Italian colors, green, white and red. He bowed slightly toward Mariella when he received them, his eyes glittering.

She was so proud he loved her. She wanted to stand up and tell the world that brave man had chosen her for his wife. But she merely clapped until her hands were red and stinging, and smiled as broadly as she could.

Then the names of the fallen responders were read. Mariella blotted tears at the moving ceremony, her heart aching for those men and women who had plunged into hell to save and ended up giving their lives. How fortunate their country was to have such brave people.

When the ceremony was over, everyone was invited to a reception. Cristiano found her as soon as the broadcast portion ended.

"Let's get out of here," he said, running his finger around his collar.

"No, first we go to the reception. Those you saved will be there. You must see them. For them to thank you and for you to know you did a miraculous thing that day."

"I don't want thanks."

"Sometimes you have to accept so others can give it. They need closure, too, Cristiano. Don't deny them that."

He drew in a deep breath.

"Very well, but we're not staying long."

The large reception hall was not crowded, though there seemed to be several hundred people present. Mariella met AnnaMaria and conveyed her sorrow on the loss of her husband. People came to congratulate Cristiano, to slap him on the back and some to give hugs. When a man came forward carrying a baby, Mariella watched closely. The child wasn't too much older than Dante.

"You gave me my son," the man said, reaching out to grasp Cristiano's hand. "How you managed I'll never know. I lost my wife, but I have my son, the best part of her. Thank you."

Cristiano smiled at the baby. "He doesn't look any worse for his ordeal. I'm glad."

A young boy came over, looking wary and overwhelmed. His grandparents were with him. "This is Emelio, the last one brought out—with the baby. He is our pride and joy, thank you," they said. "Our daughter and her husband perished, but we have our grandson."

"Thank you for saving me," the little boy said, grinning when Cristiano raised his hand in a high five, slapping it hard.

The young woman he'd first carried came over to thank him, and introduce him to her husband and daughter, both delighted to meet Cristiano and add their thanks.

So went the evening until everyone had greeted the man who had saved their lives.

"Tell me now you don't think you're a hero," Mariella said softly when the last man limped away.

"I was just doing my job. I wish I could have brought more out."

"I know. I think we could leave now," she said. She was exhausted with the emotions of the evening. How much more so must Cristiano be?

They found AnnaMaria and the rest of Stephano's family and said goodbye, with promises to get in touch when they returned to Rome.

Finally they were in the quiet of the limo, speeding through darkened streets.

Mariella squeezed his hand. "You did it, no episode at all!"

"Luck."

"Good luck, then," she said, snuggling close to him.

"I couldn't have done it without you, you know that."

"So we make a good team. I love you," she said.

"Not as much as I love you," he said, leaning over to kiss her.

Just one night later Cristiano parked his car near the piazza in Monta Correnti.

"I'm nervous," Mariella said, looking at the lights over the restaurants.

"We don't have to attend," Cristiano said as he switched off the engine and turned to look at her.

"Yes, we do," she said promptly. "Though if you felt

like this when we went to the medal ceremony, you're even more a hero than I thought."

He reached for her hand and kissed her fingers. "I'd just as soon forget the entire situation and go back to the cottage. You, me and Dante. It's cold enough for a fire, we could sit and talk until he's asleep and then make plans."

It was tempting. But she had to meet the rest of his family some time and maybe it would be better all at once. She had memorized all the names and tried to keep the relationships straight. Plus she didn't want to disappoint his sister. She had worked hard to make sure everyone was there.

"The timing is perfect. We need to let your family celebrate. Besides, remember, this entire gathering is really for your father, the medal award is the excuse."

"I know, but we'll still get more attention than I want now." He took a deep breath. "I hope you're right about their understanding."

"Oh, Cristiano, of course they'll understand. They all love you. If one of them was hurt, you'd be the first there to help. Let them have that same privilege."

"It's not quite as visible as a broken ankle."

"But just as real."

Mariella still marveled that this dynamic man loved her. They had made plans for a quiet wedding before Christmas. For the foreseeable future things would continue much as they had been: she'd work her virtual-assistant job, Cristiano would make furniture—and see a counselor to help him cope with the PTSD. They were very hopeful in time he'd be able to return to Rome and his job. It might take a few months or maybe even a year or so. And if not, he had his woodworking, which he enjoyed. Mariella was convinced he could name his price for the fine pieces he made.

Mostly she was just glad he had not held firm on waiting

to get married until he thought he was cured. She couldn't wait to be his wife, spend her days and nights with him.

"Let's do it, then," he said, opening the car door. They took the baby carrier, though Mariella carried Dante. They'd use the carrier when Dante needed to rest.

In only a moment they were walking into the wide piazza that led to the restaurant. The large stone patio between the two restaurants was illuminated by soft lighting. The chairs were all empty as it was far too cold to sit out at night in November. The front doors of both establishments had prominent signs declaring they were closed for a private party. Mariella heard the voices from Rosa and felt a touch of panic. What if the family didn't want him to marry her? What if he changed his mind? Shaking her head impatiently, she knew she was acting stupid. As if anyone in the family could tell Cristiano what to do. She looked at him for support. She loved him so much she could scarcely believe it. And he loved her! That was the most amazing thing. She'd been deliriously happy these last weeks. And knew once married she'd be even happier. She would have her family—Cristiano and Dante. And maybe a few more babies. But if not, she would feel her world complete.

"Ready?" she asked with a smile.

"As I'll ever be."

With that he opened the door to his father's restaurant and the three of them entered.

"Feels like home," he murmured as they walked into the main room. The tile floor, warm wooden trim and fall colors in the decor were so familiar.

They were immediately spotted by his brother, standing with a small group on one side.

"The hero of the hour!" Valentino called, raising a glass in his honor.

Cristiano looked around. "I don't recognize half these

people. I thought Isabella said it was family," he murmured as he spotted his sister.

"About time. I was worried you wouldn't come," Isabella said, rushing over to give him a hug. "You haven't exactly been a frequent visitor since you started staying in Lake Clarissa." Then she hugged Mariella and Dante. "Welcome. We saw the presentation of the medals on the television. I cried through almost all of it. You looked so tall, so distinguished. I'm proud of you, Cristiano. It's not every day we have a hero in our midst."

Mariella saw him wince and stepped closer. "You've had him all along, maybe you just didn't recognize he was such a hero."

"Well said," Valentino said, giving Cristiano a bear hug as others crowded around, calling greetings. "You remember Clara," he said, reaching for the pretty woman at his side. The love shining from Valentino's face was obvious to the world.

"I remember you," Cristiano said. "Congratulations on marrying this guy. I hope he treats you right. If not, you let me know."

"Oh, he treats me really fine," she said. Rubbing her stomach, she smiled. "The truth will be seeing how he does when the baby comes."

"Congratulations, I didn't know," Cristiano said, shaking his brother's hand and slapping him on the back. "Beat you in the family department, though," he said with a smile at Dante.

"*Ciao*, Cristiano," another voice said.

"Scarlett, I haven't seen you in a while." He smiled at his cousin, and put his arm around Mariella's shoulders. "I'd like everyone to meet Mariella Holmes. My fiancée," he said proudly.

The exclamations and congratulations flew back and forth.

"We have news ourselves," his cousin Lizzie said, coming up to him. He hadn't seen her in years. She was glowing.

"You have new cousins you haven't met yet," she said, giving him a warm welcome. "They're sleeping right over there." She pointed to a double stroller sheltered in the one of the corners of the room, away from the main activity, but close by.

"Twins?" he asked.

"Yes. Must run in the family."

She gave him a hug and laughed. "You haven't seen anyone in a while from what I hear. Glad to see you made it out from that attack with only a broken ankle. That was horrible, for all of us."

The others greeted him, met Mariella and exclaimed in delight over Dante. The baby smiled his one-toothed grin and was soon being passed around as everyone seemed to want to hold the happy baby.

Then Cristiano looked across the room, seeing his half-brothers for the first time. The twins stood near each other, each with a beautiful woman beside him. They looked like their mutual father—only with lighter hair and lighter eyes. Almost as if it had been choreographed, the others parted as Cristiano and Mariella walked across the tiled floor to the two men.

"I'm Cristiano," he said, hesitating only a moment before putting out his hand.

"Angelo," the one with the blue eyes said, reaching out to shake his hand.

"Alex," the more muscular one said.

"Here's Aunt Lisa," his sister said, tugging on his sleeve. "We'll have lots of time tonight to catch up on everything.

Dad should be here soon. We're having drinks and appetizers here, then dinner will be at Sorella. Fingers crossed Dad accepts the merger."

"You can wrap him around your little finger. He'll be pleased things are going to continue, no matter how that happens."

He stepped back a bit and pulled Mariella closer.

"This is more than I expected. Everyone is either engaged or newly married, so we've just doubled the family. But I didn't realize they'd all be here tonight."

"A tribute to you and to your father," Mariella said.

Luca Casali entered the restaurant and greetings were called again. He made the rounds, clasping hands, hugging, getting kissed by most of the women. He looked pleased to see his American sons. Cristiano felt a twinge of uncertainty. He'd always been the older brother. Now he had two older than he. Still, he rejoiced for his father to finally connect with those children he'd had to give up so long ago. He glanced at Dante, being held by his cousin Jackie, and knew it would devastate him if he had to give up the child and never know if he'd see him again. He loved that little baby. He would be the best father he could be for him.

"Son," Luca said, reaching Cristiano. He gave him a big hug. "You have done us all proud," he exclaimed, smiling broadly. "Who knew those fearless escapades when you and Valentino were little would push you to become a man who does such daring rescues? I'm glad you came home to heal and hope you'll visit often after your return to Rome."

"There's something to talk about, Dad, but not here or now. I'm not going back right away."

"Good, I hope we see more of you than we have recently."

"From the looks of things, everyone has had plenty to keep them occupied."

"Luca." His sister Lisa came over. "So, we are united tonight as we have not been in many years. I think Mamma would be happy."

He nodded, glancing around. "I'm sure of it. All her grandchildren here, each with the one special person who will share life's journey with them. It is a happy day. And for me, especially to see my first sons again after so long."

"Attention." Isabella raised her voice above the conversations. Everyone stopped talking and looked at her. Smiles broke out. Glances to Luca were made, then back to Isabella.

"First, I'm so glad everyone could attend tonight. It means a lot to me and, I know, to my father." She smiled at him.

"We are gathered to celebrate my brother receiving a medal from the ministry for his heroic actions after the bombing last May. He was injured in the last moments, yet still managed to keep the children he carried safe and rescued a total of seven people. He also rescued Mariella and Dante from a fire at Lake Clarissa. And that sure had a happy ending."

Everyone laughed, Cristiano with them, leaning down to kiss Mariella quickly. He still had moments of doubt he was doing right by her, but her love was steadfast and he couldn't bear to turn his back on all she offered. He would always do his best to keep her safe and happy.

"But there is another reason we are gathered. Many years ago, my aunt Lisa and my father were left a restaurant by their mother, our grandmother Rosa. They ran it together for a while, then they parted. Different restaurants, different cuisine. Same family, however, though going in different directions. Now we come full circle."

All eyes turned to Luca. Cristiano hoped his father would be pleased.

"We are merging the two back. We will keep the differences in decor and menus, to attract a wide variety of patrons. But Rosa and Sorella will be operated as one unit. Dad, we do this for you. No one could have been a better father given all the setbacks and hardships you faced. This is our thanks to you."

Luca looked stunned. He looked at his sister, surprised to see her smiling.

"I don't know what to say," he said a moment later when no one else spoke. "I can't believe it. It's what Mamma wanted. After all these years—"

Lisa nodded. "You can blame me. I was at fault over a lot. But here's to good fortune for the family from today forward," she said, raising a glass of champagne high.

"Hear, hear."

Each raised a glass to join the toast and drank. Then laughter and conversations started again.

Cristiano walked to his sister. "You did it. He looks amazingly happy."

"I'm so glad. It's the best thing for both restaurants, but it was a risk. The breach was long."

"Healing comes through love," the man beside her said.

"Cristiano, meet Max—my husband," Isabella said.

Cristiano looked at Isabella. "You never introduced us before."

"You weren't exactly Mr. Approachable. And then I was more concerned with getting this off the ground."

Mariella took Dante from Jackie. "I hope he didn't drool on your beautiful suit," she said.

"Not at all and it wouldn't matter if he did. Have you seen my new nephews?"

"No, but I'd like to."

They went to the stroller. The babies slept peacefully, both adorable in their little blue sweaters and hats.

"The only bad part is they'll be growing up in Australia and I won't get to see them all the time. Lizzie has promised photos every day over the Internet. When they are all older, they and Dante can play together when they visit Italy."

"A ready-made family," Mariella agreed.

"Congratulations on your own forthcoming wedding," Valentino said, coming over to Cristiano as Max and Isabella moved to talk with Scarlett and her fiancé, Lorenzo Nesta. Cristiano knew Lorenzo from his years of working at the restaurant. The change in the man since the last time he saw him was amazing. He looked younger and far happier than Cristiano had ever seen him.

"Thanks. So you're going to be a father, Val. Hard to believe," Cristiano said.

"That's something, isn't it? Never thought it would happen," he said, his gaze focused on his wife halfway across the restaurant. "You know, I almost lost her before we got things straight. Life's fleeting. Look at our mother, dying so young." His face twisted in remembered pain.

"Let it go," Cristiano said gently. "She would be happy for all of us tonight." He knew Valentino always blamed himself for not being able to save their mother, but he'd been a small child. Even adults could not have saved her. "Mariella and I are adopting Dante."

"He's not her son?" Valentino asked in surprise.

Cristiano quickly explained things, then reached out to grip his brother's shoulder. "I want to make sure my son always knows he's mine, no matter who donated the sperm. You have always been Dad's son, no matter what. And always my brother."

Valentino nodded, looking for Clara again. "I've

changed. Love and family is the most important thing to me now. And whether it's by blood or love, families evolve and are there for us."

"Even brothers we have never met before?" Cristiano asked.

"I wasn't too excited about getting to know them when I first learned they existed. But the full story is sad. Dad did his best, couldn't keep them, so sent them to live with their mother. He couldn't afford anything until after he and mamma married. They have their own problems with the situation. I hope in time all of us feel the tie I know Dad does."

"Takes some getting used to."

"No more than realizing Lisa is actually welcoming the reunification of the restaurants and that Lizzie married an Australian and had twins," Valentino said.

Cristiano laughed, feeling things were getting back to normal. "Or Isabella married."

"To a prince, no less."

"What? Neither mentioned that."

"Prince Maximilliano Di Rossi," Valentino said.

"Does Isabella plan to leave the restaurant?"

"Not a chance. She's the best thing to happen to it. Who would take over completely if not Isabella?"

"Isn't that guy with Jackie the man she dated years ago?"

"Yes. Guess love's even better the second time around. He's okay. It's the Aussie I have trouble talking with. His Italian, as far as I can tell, is limited to I love you, my darling, which he says every so often to Lizzie."

Cristiano laughed. It warmed his heart to be with his family again. The PTSD hadn't abated. He could have an episode without warning, but Mariella had been right. If he did, the family would rally round. He'd forgotten that in his first months of hiding. He wasn't perfect, but neither was anyone in the family. They all did the best they could with what they had.

Mariella was walking his way, her smile lightening his heart. He would never tire of looking at her, or being with her. Whatever the future held, they were in it together.

"So, I've met the baby twins and the older twins. Now, do you think we run the risk of twins? I have to tell you, one baby is a lot to handle."

He brushed his lips across hers. "Whatever comes, we can face it together."

"Good answer. I love you, Cristiano."

"I love you, sweetheart. What a welcome to the family, huh?"

"Well, I've met an actress, a baseball player, two ranchers, a fashion designer. How is that for a diverse family?"

"Don't forget the prince."

"What?" she exclaimed, looking around.

He explained and laughed. "I hide away from the world for a few months and everything changes."

"All for the better. A few months ago I had no one, my best friend was dead, my parents gone. Now I have you and the baby and all these amazing relatives-to-be."

"And they'll have amazing you as part of their families. I will never be able to let you know how much I love you and how much your love means to me. You've given me back my life."

"You would have reclaimed it sooner or later. I'm just glad to be a part of it now and forever. Let's just promise we won't make any of the mistakes others have made. We will be happy forever."

"Forever."

Cristiano pulled her over to one side for a kiss. Behind the pillar, his aunt was talking with a man he hadn't yet met.

"It's a new age," he heard his aunt say.

"Same old Lisa," the man retorted.

"Single, but maybe thinking of marriage. I mean, look at everyone here tonight. I never saw so much love and devotion in one room," she said.

"You always wanted to be free," he said.

"I always wanted you," she replied. "Will you marry me?"

Cristiano peered around the column. The older man with his aunt had eyes only for her. Catching his movement, they both looked at him.

"Oh, don't you breathe a word," Lisa said. She glanced at the other man. "Rafe, are you going to answer?"

"Yes, but when we are alone," he said, his eyes dancing in amusement.

"It's time for dinner," Isabella announced.

"Ah, but first one more toast," Luca said, going to stand beside his daughter.

"To the legacy of our mother, Rosa," he said, raising his glass.

"To Mamma's legacy," Lisa echoed.

"To Rosa!" the entire family said as one.

SURROGATE
AND WIFE

EMILY MCKAY

Emily McKay has been reading romance novels
since she was eleven years old. Her first Mills &
Boon book came free in a box of Hefty garbage
bags. She has been reading and loving romance
novels ever since. She lives in Texas with her
geeky husband, her two kids and too many pets.
Her debut novel, Baby, Be Mine, was a RITA®
Award finalist for Best First Book and Best Short
Contemporary. She was also a 2009 RT Book
Reviews Career Achievement Award nominee for
Series Romance. To learn more, visit her website,
www.emilymckay.com.

One

"We're pregnant."

Kate Bennet did her best not to roll her eyes at the absurdity of her sister's remark. "Yeah. I know."

As a surrogate mother for her sister, Beth, and her brother-in-law, Stewart, Kate knew all too well that "they" were pregnant. Her hand drifted to her belly where the baby was just beginning to show. Her stomach seemed to flip over, making her curse the first trimester nausea that had yet to fade. She picked up the mug of hot peppermint tea Beth had made for her.

Beth reached across the kitchen table and put her hand on Kate's wrist. Kate paused, mug halfway to her mouth. "What?"

"We're pregnant. Stew and I."

Kate lowered the mug, struggling to make sense of the words. "You and Stew?"

"Yes."

"Pregnant?"

Beth nodded, her smile so beatifically maternal her face all but glowed. Her eyes sparkled with happiness.

Kate's stomach did another flip, the nausea building now. She pressed her palm to her belly. "With another baby? In addition to the baby I'm carrying for you?"

"Yes."

Kate bolted from the chair and dashed to the hallway bathroom. She barely made it to the toilet bowl before emptying the remnants of her breakfast.

She knelt there for a long time on the bathroom floor, leaning against the cabinet, eyes pressed closed, until her stomach stilled and tile bruised her knees. Only the sound of Beth knocking on the door roused her from her stupor.

"Kate? Are you okay?"

Was she okay? Well, she felt as if her world had just been turned inside out—along with her stomach. Other than that, she was just ducky.

She hoisted herself to her feet to wash her hands and rinse out her mouth before opening the bathroom door. Resting her shoulder against the doorjamb, she stared at her sister. "How is this possible?"

Beth grasped her elbow and guided her away from the door and down the hallway. "Come back to the kitchen. I'll make you a fresh cup of tea."

Kate let herself be pushed gently into the Windsor chair and watched as Beth bustled around the simple, homey kitchen.

"We were as surprised as you," Beth said.

"But you and Stewart can't have children. It's impossible. Isn't it?"

"Highly improbable. But not impossible."

In fact, their chances were viewed as so slim, the doctor had recommended not using Stew's sperm to inseminate Kate. Instead, Stew had asked his best friend, Jake, to be a sperm donor.

Still reeling, Kate said, "I thought you said there was only a 0.2% chance of you getting pregnant on your own."

"We were just very lucky." Beth set a mug of steaming water in front of Kate and held out a bowl of teabags. "Peppermint or chamomile?"

"How can you be so calm?" Kate felt hysteria rising up inside her as the full implication of Beth's pregnancy began to sink in. Kate snatched one of the offered packages, ripped it open and dunked the teabag rapidly in and out of the water.

"I guess, because I've had more time to get used to the idea."

Kate's hand instantly stilled and her eyes sought Beth's face. "How long have you known?"

"A week. I suspected for longer, but I didn't dare hope. My periods have always been so irregular—and after so many years of trying—well, I'd trained myself not to hope, even when I missed a period. Or four."

"Four? How far along are you?"

"Eighteen weeks."

"Eighteen weeks? That's a full month further along than I am. A full month." The very thought made her mind whirl and she sank back against the chair. "So all those sympathetic pregnancy symptoms you've been going through that I thought were so charming weren't sympathetic ones at all. They were real."

Beth smiled wryly. "I hadn't thought of that." She reached for Kate's hand. "Look, I know this makes everything very complicated, but ultimately Stew and I just really want to be parents."

Kate sat forward. "You still want this baby, right?"

Beth gave her another beatific smile. "Well, Stew

and I talked about it and agreed that decision should be up to you and Jake."

"Up to me and Jake? What's that supposed to mean?"

"Technically, it's your baby and—"

"No. There's no technically about it." Okay, *technically* she was both egg donor and genetic carrier, so the baby was biologically hers, but still… "This baby is yours. Yours and Stew's. That was the agreement."

The tension inside Kate threatened to boil over. She leaped to her feet and began pacing, glancing incredulously at her sister. Under the circumstances, Beth didn't seem nearly as distressed as she should be.

Beth stood following Kate's movement with her gaze. "Yes, of course that was the agreement. But things have changed."

"You can't refuse to take this baby. I won't allow it." Kate spun around and pinned Beth with her most judicial stare. At least, she tried to pin Beth with a stare, but a wave of dizziness left her groping for a handhold on the nearby countertop, which ruined the effect.

Beth rushed immediately to her side. "Come and sit down. You shouldn't be pacing like that. It can't be good for the baby."

"You know what's not good for the baby?" she quipped irritably. "This whole conversation." Still, she sank gratefully into the chair.

"Naturally, Stew and I will still take the baby. If you decide you don't want it. But we want you to at least think about keeping it. The baby is biologically yours. And whether you're willing to admit it or not, you feel a connection to it already."

For a second, Kate didn't know what to say. Didn't Beth get it? Didn't she understand that the only way

Kate had been able to do this was by doing everything she could not to feel a connection to the baby?

"I don't—"

"I know you do," Beth said, cutting her off, "So there's no use arguing with me about it. The point is, we have two healthy babies here. Stew and I would love to have them both, but we knew all along we were asking a lot of you and Jake. So if either of you—"

"Jake? What's he have to do with this?"

Beth shot her an exasperated look. "That baby you're carrying is his, too. If either of you decides you want to keep the baby, Stew and I are willing to step aside."

Suddenly struck by the absurdity of the situation, Kate dropped her face into her hands and choked back laughter. "If either of us wants to keep the baby? You realize how completely absurd that is, don't you?"

But Beth, who merely looked at her with a slight frown, apparently did not.

"Let's face it," Kate explained. "I have all the maternal instincts of a paper clip. The only idea sillier than me wanting to keep the baby is Jake Morgan wanting to keep it. He's hardly 'daddy' material."

"Jake's not so bad," Beth protested.

"Hey, he may be a great guy, for all I know. But we're talking about a man who runs into burning buildings when everyone else runs out."

"Actually—" Beth lifted her chin stubbornly "—now that he's moved up to arson investigation, he doesn't run into burning buildings anymore. Just smoldering ones."

"Right. Smoldering ones. Big difference."

Beth flashed an impish grin. "Well, at least his kid won't play with matches."

Kate pointed a finger at her sister. "You can laugh now, but these are the genes your child is going to have."

Beth just chuckled. "I'm not worried about Jake's genes. He's smart, handsome, charming, and—"

"Exactly. He's one of those annoying people who thinks he should get whatever he wants just because he *is* handsome and charming." Hoping she hadn't revealed just how appealing she found Jake—or how much that annoyed her, she said quickly, "What does my opinion of Jake have to do with anything?

"It's not like you to be so judgmental."

Beth was right, of course. So Kate smiled wryly and said, "I'm a judge. We're supposed to be judgmental. Besides, I know I'm right about this. With all the broken homes and bad parents I see in my courtroom, it's my job to cull the good from the bad. I promise you, neither Jake nor I will want this baby."

"Just think about it. You might change your mind."

"Yes. And I might turn into a pig, sprout wings and fly. It's not impossible, just highly improbable."

Despite her determination to put it out of her mind, Kate was still thinking about her conversation with Beth the next evening as she tried to finish up paperwork at the office. It was after six on a Monday; nearly everyone else in the courthouse annex had gone home. But she'd long since given up any hope that the relative quiet would help her concentrate.

How could she not think about Beth's offer to let her keep the baby? Kate rested her hand upon her belly where her baby was growing inside.

Her baby.

Her breath caught in her throat as she felt emotion tighten her chest. For once she didn't try to squash it or shove it aside. What would happen if she did allow herself to keep the baby?

Her heart filled with anticipation. As if keeping the baby was what she'd been subconsciously hoping to do, even though every logical bone in her body had told her doing so would be selfish and irresponsible.

She already loved this baby. Even though it was too early to tell the baby's sex, Kate's gut told her the baby was a girl. Kate's gut had been pretty vocal lately. Every instinct she had demanded her baby girl would want for nothing. So Kate had spent the past three months following to the letter the advice not only of her doctor but also every pregnancy book she could get her hands on. By golly, this was going to be the happiest, healthiest baby ever born. And if she had anything to say about it, this baby would have the best of everything.

That included the best parents. Kate knew, beyond a shadow of a doubt, that Beth would be a much better mother than she would be.

She saw the evidence all the time in her family-law courtroom. Some women—like Beth—were born to be mothers. Others just weren't. In her professional opinion, Kate knew she fell into the latter group.

Suddenly angry with herself for dwelling on the issue for so long, she shoved the files she'd been reviewing into her briefcase and headed for the door. The brisk walk to her car made her feel no less grumpy. When she reached the parking lot to find *him* leaning against her Volvo, her mood plummeted even further.

She'd never quite been able to pin down what it was, but something about Jake Morgan just rubbed her the wrong way. It wasn't only his confident charm—a trait she'd learned long ago to neither like nor trust in men. Maybe it was that slow, sensual gaze of his that seemed to undress a woman and make love to her all at once. Or maybe it was just the pure testosterone that emanated from him in waves. He was just too much. Too masculine. Too charming. And entirely too smug.

Not to mention too in her way.

"What are you doing here?" she asked as she approached her car.

His long legs were crossed at the ankles. The faded denim of his jeans stretched taut across his thighs. His only defense against the unusually cold May evening was a long-sleeve flannel shirt worn unbuttoned over his T-shirt. With the sleeves rolled up, no less.

Typical. Probably thought he was too manly to need a coat. Or maybe he knew how good he looked and didn't want to ruin the effect.

She pulled her keys from her coat pocket and used the remote to pop the locks. With a shrug of his muscular shoulders, he pushed himself away from her car.

"I came to see you."

"I assumed as much." She opened the rear door and slid her briefcase onto the seat. She made no move to climb into the car herself. He was standing too close to the driver's door for her to comfortably edge past him. "You always lurk in parking lots by women's cars? That could be construed as stalking."

A slow smile spread across his face. "And here you always pretend not to have a sense of humor."

Even though she had been joking, his insinuation annoyed her. So she said, "I don't joke about that kind of thing."

"No, of course not." He faked a serious frown, but his twitching lips gave him away. "By the time I got here, the building was closed for the night."

"The guards usually leave at 5:30."

He nodded. "I figured as much. But this was my only free evening this week and I think we need to talk."

"Why?"

This time he chuckled. "Don't look so suspicious. I just want to talk about the situation with Beth and Stew."

"So talk."

"You really want to discuss this in the parking lot? We're just a block away from the restaurants on the square. Besides, it's too cold."

The thought of sharing a meal with Jake sent a shiver of apprehension through her. Georgetown, once a sleepy college town, had grown as the sprawl from Austin crept up IH 35. Like many small Texas towns overtaken by suburbia, Georgetown struggled to maintain its own identity. The historic town square, situated around the Williamson County Courthouse, with its collection of locally owned stores and restaurants was one of the ways Georgetown distinguished itself from larger, more liberal Austin.

While food sounded good to Kate, the romantic atmosphere of one of the local restaurants did not. Dinner was entirely too intimate. Too datelike. She sniffed dismissively. "Then you should have worn a coat."

"I meant for you. You're shivering already."

He was right, of course. Ever since the pregnancy, she'd been unusually cold. Which, for some reason, she didn't want to explain to him. Talking about pregnancy symptoms seemed even more intimate than dinner.

Suddenly she was aware how intimate their relationship already was. The bond they shared was so much deeper than just the sexual bond that usually accompanied intimacy. They'd created a life together.

A part of Jake was in her.

The thought unnerved her, so she fisted her hands on her lapels and pulled her jacket more closely around her body. She didn't want to eat dinner with him. Didn't want to do anything with him. Yet there probably were things they should talk about.

"Okay, then. Dinner it is."

Fifteen minutes later she found herself opposite him in a booth at one of the restaurants on the square, a mug of hot tea in front of her, a bowl of tortilla soup and a plate of cheese enchiladas on the way.

As she sipped her tea, she studied him over the rim of her mug. He sat in the middle of the bench with one arm stretched across the back, making his shoulders appear even wider so that he seemed to take up the entire booth.

Jake was so different from all the other men she knew. Men with manicured hands and suit jackets custom-made to make their shoulders appear wider than they were. Her gaze drifted down to Jake's hand where it rested, palm down on the Formica beside his beer. His hands were big, muscular even, with long tapered fingers that ended in clean but unmanicured nails. They were unquestionably masculine. Tough, almost.

Had she ever noticed a man's nails before? She didn't think so. There was something oddly personal about looking at Jake's hands. Warmth swirled through her body, pooling somewhere deep inside of her. Where she carried his baby.

She jerked her gaze back to his, cursing the blush she could feel on her cheeks. His eyes were practically gleaming with amusement. As if he could read her thoughts and knew just how unsettled he made her feel.

A scowl settled on her face and she sat up straighter. "Don't—"

"Let me stop you right there," he interrupted. "We both know you don't like me."

"I don't know you well enough to like you or not," she protested.

"Okay, don't *approve* of me."

Well, she couldn't really argue with that. They'd only met on a handful of occasions and she'd never been able to relax around him. She saw right through his laidback charm to the testosterone-fueled masculinity beneath. It was less that she didn't approve of him and more that she simply didn't know what to do with him. Which made her very nervous. She also couldn't deny how drawn to him she felt. Why now? Why Jake of all people?

Maybe this sudden attraction she felt was just some weird pregnancy thing. Maybe her body somehow knew he was the father of the child she carried. If that was the case, all the more reason to maintain her distance.

So she stiffened her spine as well as her resolve, and said, "No, I don't."

"Regardless of that, we're in this together now."

"I disagree. If anyone is in this together, it's Beth, Stewart and me. Your part in this is, thankfully, over."

"That might have been true before, but now—"

"Nothing is different now."

"You can't really be that naive."

She bristled at his words, even though there was nothing objectionable in his tone. She leaned forward over the table. "Trust me. I am anything but naive. I understand exactly—"

"Okay, not naive then." He held up his hands in a gesture of innocence. "But you've got to admit, things are going to be a lot different than any of you planned."

"Yes, they'll be different, but I'll manage."

He continued as if he hadn't heard her concession. "You were planning on Beth and Stew helping you out. Taking care of you. Things are going to be different now. They've got their own pregnancy to contend with."

"You think I can't take care of myself? Trust me, I've

been doing it for years. Far longer than most women my age, actually."

"That's not what I meant."

"Then what did you mean?"

"From what Beth has said, you haven't had an easy first trimester, but it's only going to get worse. The second trimester won't be too bad, but by the time you hit the third trimester, you'll—"

"What makes you such an expert? Have you taken some sort of course in prenatal care?"

He grimaced. "No, but five of my buddies have had babies in the past eighteen months. I've heard my share of complaints about late-night cravings and women who can't tie their own shoelaces."

"Well, unless you're planning on moving in with me, I don't see how you could help with either one of those situations." She chuckled, but the sound died in her throat when she realized he wasn't laughing with her. "Oh my God. You can't be serious." She gaped at him in disbelief, waiting for him to crack a smile and laugh at her expense. He didn't even blink. "You *are* serious. You think we should move in together."

Two

Kate jerked away from him and shrank back into the booth. "Are you insane?"

Okay, that could have gone a little more smoothly.

"Just hear me out—"

"I mean, I knew you were crazy in that, anyone-willing-to-run-into-a-burning-building kind of way, but *this?*"

Okay, a lot more smoothly.

"Or are you joking? Because this just isn't funny."

"I'm not joking. And if you'll just give me a chance to explain—"

But before he could, the waitress approached with their food.

Kate fumed in silence while their plates were distributed, glaring at him from across the table as if wishing she could charge him with contempt of court.

"Okay, talk," she ordered as soon as the waitress was out of earshot. "But make it good, because I'm having a hard time believing that you've been nursing a secret desire to cater to the whims of a second-trimester pregnant woman."

She continued her diatribe for a solid four more minutes. He didn't bother interrupting—she wouldn't have let him, anyway. Instead, he took the opportunity to study her.

With her ivory complexion and thick black hair pulled back from her face, he'd have to be dead not to notice how beautiful she was. She wasn't anything like the women he normally dated, but she piqued his interest. Smart, sexy and fiercely independent. Challenging enough to keep things interesting without ever being clingy or emotionally demanding.

Not that he'd dream of pursuing her now. That would only screw up an already complicated situation. To make matters worse, he couldn't help admiring how she resisted his help. Even though it made things more difficult for him.

"I wouldn't have to actually move in," he pointed out once she seemed to lose steam. "But I could still help out." Changing tactics, he said, "Beth and Stew are worried about you."

She rolled her eyes. "Beth and Stew always worry about me. Trust me, if it wasn't this, it'd be something else. The part of town I live in or the hours I work. Beth is a worrier."

"Well, this time she feels responsible." He leaned forward, bracing his elbows on either side of his plate. "Whether you like it or not, your life is changing. I can help you."

"What exactly is it you think I need help with?"

"Whatever." He shrugged. "Laundry, grocery shopping, cooking. The point is, you don't have to be so stubborn. You don't have to do everything on your own."

Her eyes flashed as she leaned forward and spoke with barely concealed annoyance. "I'm not being stubborn. I *can* take care of myself. I am not your problem. I—"

He recognized the slipup as soon as the words were out of her mouth. The way she broke off, then pulled away from the table to toy with her napkin as if flustered, only confirmed that she hadn't meant to give so much away.

Maybe he should have just let it go, but he couldn't resist digging a little. I never said *you* were."

She wiped her fingers on her napkin and tossed it to the side of her plate. "Fine. The *baby* is not your problem. None of this has anything to do with you."

"Ah, come on. Even *you* have to admit it has at least a little to do with me."

She waved her hand dismissively. "Yes, yes, your part was very important. I certainly didn't mean to belittle your contribution of spending thirty minutes in a locked room with a plastic cup, but I daresay you've done enough. This end of the deal—" she gestured to her belly "—is all my responsibility."

Suddenly he didn't feel like teasing her anymore. "You don't have to do it all on your own."

She cleared her throat. He could practically see her struggling for a flip response, but in the end, her answer came out sounding as serious as his had. "Yes, I do."

"But—"

"Look, even if your intentions are good, we're talking about the next six months of your life. You're bound to get bored of playing house."

"I'm not—"

"I didn't mean that as an insult," she reassured him. "We're talking about half a year of giving up your spare time to coddle a pregnant woman. You'd have to be a saint to do that. And, let's face it, you're no saint."

"You have no idea," he said, unable to shake from his consciousness all the sinful things he'd like to do to her.

He knew this discussion was affecting her as much as it did him, because her voice sounded brusque when she replied, "Which only proves my point. Do you really think you're going to want to spend your time off doing *my* laundry when you could be out on a date? Right now, all this pregnancy stuff may seem fascinating, but, trust me, the novelty will wear off."

"And you think I won't stick around after the novelty wears off."

"I'm not about to start depending on you now, only to find out you won't."

He leaned back in his seat and stretched his arm across the back of the booth. "You don't have a very high opinion of me, do you?"

"Don't take it personally. There aren't a lot of people I do have a high opinion of."

"That's a pretty cynical attitude."

"Not cynical. Realistic. Every day at work, I see people at their absolute worst. I know what men—and women—are capable of. How they can hurt and betray the people they claim to love the most. If there's one thing I've learned after four years on the bench, it's that the only person you can really trust is yourself."

"What about Beth and Stew?"

"Of course I trust them. But I certainly don't expect them to take care of me. Especially not now that they've got their own baby on the way. I'll be fine on my own. Just like I've always been."

And with that she grabbed her purse, dropped a twenty on the table and scooted out of the booth. She left the restaurant without even a backward glance.

He stared at the money for a minute before the irony

sank in. This was the biggest commitment he'd ever tried to make to a woman and she hadn't even let him buy her dinner.

After he dropped his own twenty on the table, he pulled his cell phone from his pocket and dialed Stew.

"You were right," he said as soon as Stew answered.

"I told you she wouldn't go for it."

"She sounded insulted."

Stew chuckled. "Of course she was insulted. Basically, you told a grown woman you thought she couldn't take care of herself. Not just any grown woman, either. This is Kate we're talking about here. She's been on her own a long time and she's always prided herself on her competence. Which you just questioned."

"Not exactly." At least, he didn't think he had. "I think she doesn't like me."

"No, she probably doesn't. You haven't made a very good impression on her."

Great. Of all the women he'd known in his life, and gotten along with just fine, the one who didn't like him at all was the one carrying his baby.

He'd been eight years younger and stupider when they first met. Too young to know that some women found charm suspicious. It hadn't helped that she'd been so much fun to tease. She'd never gotten past that first impression of him and he'd never made the effort to convince her he wasn't a total jerk.

"What're you going to do now?" Stew asked.

"Not much I can do. The ball's in her court. If she can't see the logic of my offer, there's nothing I can do about it." Then he muttered, "Why couldn't she be more like Beth? Beth would have said yes."

Stew chuckled. "Because Beth is a one-of-a-kind woman."

So was Kate, Jake couldn't help thinking a few minutes later as he tucked the phone back into his pocket and made his way to his car.

Kate was unlike any woman he'd ever met. Tough, cynical and stubborn. Boy, she was stubborn.

He knew he was right—she would need help in the coming months—but he had no idea how to convince her of that. Still, he couldn't help admiring her for clinging so passionately to her independence. She was a complex and intriguing woman. Way too intriguing.

Under the circumstances, he should probably be thanking his lucky stars she'd refused his offer. He was off the hook. Not even Stewart could say he hadn't tried.

So why couldn't he shake the feeling that something really important had just slipped through his fingers?

He couldn't explain—not even to himself—why he wanted so desperately to be a part of this pregnancy. Surely his offer to help Kate was nothing more than that. Help. It certainly didn't have anything to do with this inexplicable pull she suddenly had over him.

Shaking his head, he shoved the thought aside. As he steered his car toward home, he knew he should be rejoicing in his freedom. And he didn't let himself wonder why he wasn't.

Her week—which had started out so badly—only got worse.

From the news about Beth's pregnancy, to the bizarre dinner with Jake, to this—being called on the carpet by Judge Hatcher first thing Thursday morning.

Two years ago Hatcher had been elected a district judge on a platform of conservative family values. Since associate district judges like Kate were merely appointed, Hatcher was essentially her boss. She wasn't happy about it, since they shared years of barely concealed animosity, dating all the way back to when they'd both worked in the Georgetown D.A.'s office. However, since he had the power to make her life very difficult, and since she knew this position was only a stepping-stone to further his political ambitions, she'd stayed out of his way. Until now.

As she made her way back to her chambers in the courthouse annex, she struggled to calm herself. She found Kevin Thompson, the other associate district judge, waiting for her, noisily poking through the papers on her desk.

"How'd it go?"

Still feeling bristly, she glared at him. "How did you know about my meeting with Hatcher?"

"Are you kidding? In this office, gossip spreads like wildfire."

She grimaced. As if she needed that reminder.

Kevin propped himself on the edge of her desk. "So, how did the meeting go? Did he just want to rake you over the coals a little?"

"It went about the same as all my meetings with him go. He was patronizing and rude. I kept my mouth shut."

"Good girl. I know he drives you crazy, but it's best to keep your head down and your nose clean. And look at it this way, in six months he'll be out of here."

She sank into her chair. "That's not reassuring. In six months the elections will be over. If he's out of here, that means he's been elected to the Texas Supreme Court."

Kevin shrugged. "True, but at least he'll be out of our hair. And let's face it, ever since he announced he was running, he's been a pain in the patootie."

Kate sighed. That was sure the truth.

Meeting Kevin's gaze, she said, "He wants me to step aside and let him handle the McCain case."

Kevin let out a low whistle. "Guess we should have seen that coming. Are you going to do it?"

"Step aside? No. Not if I can help it. That case has been on my docket for months now."

"A high profile divorce like that? To be honest, I'm surprised this is the first time it's come up."

Roger and Shelia McCain had worked for a local personal computer company during the boom. The millions they'd made thrust them into the local limelight. Everyone in town wanted to know the details of their divorce settlement. "Until recently, it's only made the local weekly," she reasoned. "But now that the story is being picked up by the *Austin American-Statesman* and the *Houston Chronicle*, he can't resist getting the press. Guess he figures it's good for the campaign."

"Good for the campaign? That kind of daily press would be worth a fortune. Maybe you should just let him handle it."

She shot Kevin an incredulous look. "And let that viper turn those poor people's divorce into a media circus about waning family values? Think about what that would do to them. Worse still to their kids. I'm not going to give him the case unless I don't have any other options."

"Oh, honey." Kevin shook his head slowly. "Just be careful."

"I won't be bullied by him," she insisted. "Sure, he can make my life difficult, but that won't further his political ambitions."

Kevin raised his eyebrows pointedly, as if she'd missed something obvious.

"What else can he do?" she asked with false cheer. "It's not like he can fire me." Her chuckle died in her throat when Kevin didn't join in. "You think he's going to fire me? That's ridiculous. Even *he* wouldn't try to have someone removed from the bench. Would he?"

"I think if you gave him a reason to he would. Especially if he could pin you with something morally questionable. Think about it, you'd be the first associate district judge fired in over forty years. It'd be all over the press, so it'd be a chance to remind everyone of the hyperconservative values he stands for."

She studied her friend. "Are you worried about *your* job?"

"Me?" He shrugged. "Not really. I'm very careful, and you're the only one around here who knows." Kevin didn't dare utter the word *gay* in these conservative halls. "Besides, it's not me he hates. And if he gets rid of you, he could swoop in, take over the McCain case and maximize his media exposure."

As she listened to Kevin, she felt a sinking sensation deep in her stomach. What if he was right? What if Hatcher was just looking for a reason to fire her?

She'd been perfectly behaved, perfectly respectable her entire life. Except…

Except now she was pregnant. With no plans of marrying.

Back when she'd first agreed to be Beth and Stew's surrogate, it had seemed a simple enough matter. Of course, that was a full five months ago, before Hatcher had announced his plans to run for the Supreme Court. Yes, it had occurred to her that some of her more conservative colleagues might raise their eyebrows, but surely no one could fault her for being a surrogate mother for her sister. But now that Beth was pregnant herself, would people question Kate's pregnancy?

Kevin must have read the distress on her face, but he

hastened to reassure her. "Don't worry, hon. You're way too smart to give him a reason."

Kevin's reassurances did little to pacify her fears. "What if I had done something wrong?"

"You?" Kevin raised his eyebrows. "Little Miss Perfect you? You haven't made a misstep in decades."

"Hypothetically, let's say I did do something…questionable in Hatcher's view. He's just one judge. Wouldn't he have to convince the other seven district judges in order to get me removed?"

"I'd say it all depends on whether they think your 'questionable' behavior impairs your abilities or position of authority. In this conservative political environment, it might not take much. Especially with Hatcher focusing his campaign on moral values. The last thing the other judges want is to appear morally lax. Good thing for you you're squeaky clean, right?"

She smiled lamely and hoped it didn't look too much like a grimace. "Right. Lucky me."

By the time Kevin left for court, Kate's head was reeling. All she could do was stare numbly at her desk, asking herself over and over again, Could he be right?

Unfortunately, the only answer she could come up with was *Yes*. Very soon she was going to appear to be an unmarried mother-to-be. That seemed like exactly the kind of morally questionable behavior Hatcher would use against her.

Three

Standing outside Jake's apartment, waiting for him to answer the door, Kate was practically shaking in her boots. Or she would have been if she'd been wearing boots. As it was, she was merely shaking in her sensible, size-nine black pumps.

"Can we talk?" she blurted out when the door finally opened.

Jake stared at her blankly for a long moment.

Long enough for her to be reminded how handsome he was. How purely masculine. Of course, it didn't help matters that he was bare-chested.

But the thing that really got to her, that actually made her heart stop beating for a second, was how the sheer size of him made her feel feminine. Delicate. Almost frail, even.

She was a solid five-nine, barefoot. No one made her feel delicate.

No one except Jake.

She didn't like the feeling one bit. And she couldn't help wishing that Beth and Stewart had picked some other man to be the donor. Someone who didn't make her feel so distinctly at a disadvantage. Preferably someone who didn't make her feel anything.

Someone who didn't look as if he'd just tumbled out of bed.

"Oh, God," she muttered, finally breaking the silence. "You're not alone." The naked chest, the disheveled hair, the sleepy stupor. She'd have put it all together sooner if she hadn't been so distracted by the…well, the naked chest and disheveled hair. Mortification spread through her and she spun on her heel to leave. "I'll come back another time. Or better yet, just forget I ever came here."

But before she could make it even a few steps, he grabbed her by the arm.

"Oh, no, you don't. You got me out of bed. You might as well say whatever it is you came here to say."

"I…"

He pulled her into the apartment, not roughly, but with enough force to remind her—again—how much stronger he was. Toeing the door shut, he wheeled her around to face him.

"I, um…" she began again, only to have all thoughts evaporate the instant she realized how close she was to his bare chest.

"What's wrong? You look…sick, or something."

Or something, indeed. "I'm a little faint," she lied, pulling her arm from his grasp. "I've been having dizzy spells lately." Which wasn't entirely untrue. He did make her head spin.

He reached for her arm again, carefully steering her to the nearby leather sofa. "You should sit. Can I get you something to drink? Water? No, wait, milk. Can I get you a glass of milk?"

Great. Here she was wrestling with this unexpected attraction to him, and he wanted to make sure she was properly hydrated. Just great.

"No, nothing. Look, I'm sorry I interrupted your…evening. I should have called first."

"You didn't interrupt anything. I was asleep." He smiled wryly as he grabbed a flannel shirt that had been left dangling over the back of a chair. He slipped into the shirt, buttoning enough for modesty, but not enough to block the occasional glimpse of his muscles. "Alone."

"Oh. I see." Except she wasn't sure she did. It was Friday night. And it was only nine-thirty.

He must have noticed her looking at her watch because he explained, "I have to be at the firehouse pretty early in the morning."

"Oh. Then I'm sorry I—"

"Why don't you stop apologizing and go back to the part where you said we need to talk."

He lowered himself into the club chair beside the sofa. Again he seemed entirely too close.

"I…um…" The words caught in her throat, trapped there by a giggle rising to the surface. This was absurd, but so was the question she couldn't see a way out of asking. So finally she just said, "Will you marry me?"

Jake froze, his expression blank for the second time this evening. Then shock registered, and his voice rose sharply as he asked, "What?"

"I need to get married." Then she added in a rush, "And you did offer to help out with the pregnancy. You said you'd do anything you could."

"I meant I'd help with your laundry. I didn't think you'd want to get married."

"You said you would help."

"Sure, but married? You want to get married?"

"It'd be a marriage in name only," she reassured him. "Just until after the baby is born. Maybe not even that long."

"Let me see if I've got this right. Four days ago you didn't even want me to do your grocery shopping, and now you want to get married?"

"Yes. Well, not exactly." She frowned, trying to sort through the logic of her proposal. "See, here's the thing. There's a slight chance that if I have this baby out of wedlock, I'll be fired."

She watched his expression carefully, looking for any hint of his emotions, but he remained stoic. After several seconds he asked, "How slight?"

"Slight-ish."

"Can you give it to me in a percentage?"

"Maybe forty…" She paused, then added honestly. "Ninety percent."

For another several seconds, he stared at her, then he sprang to his feet and marched to the kitchen. She heard him open and close the refrigerator door. A minute later he reappeared with a bottle of beer, half of which was already gone, as if he'd had to take several fortifying gulps before facing her again.

He rested his shoulder against the doorway to the kitchen and leveled his gaze at her. "So there's a 'slight' ninety percent chance you'll get fired when you have this baby and you didn't think to mention it until now?"

"I didn't think it wasn't an issue before Beth and Stew got pregnant." As briefly as she could, she explained about Hatcher's bid for a seat on the Texas Supreme Court and his moral-values campaign. "So you see, being a surrogate mother for your sister who can't get pregnant could be considered noble. Claiming to be a surrogate for your sister who's already noticeably more pregnant than you is definitely suspicious."

He eyed her doubtfully. "You really think anyone will even notice that you and Beth are pregnant at the same time?"

"Yes, I do. Beth and Stew know a lot of people. Half the town shops in their health food store. Trust me, people are going to notice she's pregnant."

"So, you just have to explain the situation. Most people will believe you."

She sighed. "You're right, of course. Most people will. But Hatcher doesn't have to convince 'most people' in order to get me fired."

"Do you have some kind of morality clause or something in your contract?"

"I'm an associate district judge," she explained. "We're appointed by the district judges. We don't have contracts."

"This Judge Hatcher can just fire you on a whim? His decision doesn't have to be based on your performance? That's bull."

"I couldn't agree more." Even under the circumstances, she couldn't help being a little amused by his vehement reaction. "Of course, it's not his decision alone. There are eight district judges total. They'd have to vote on it. All Hatcher really has to do is call a press conference questioning my morality. A public outcry from a few concerned citizens would be enough. He only needs a simple majority to vote me out of office. That's just four other people."

"And you think he can convince them?"

"I think it's possible. He doesn't even have to convince them that what I've done is wrong. He just has to convince them that supporting me could risk their reputations. With reelections right around the corner, how many judges do you think will stand against him?"

Jake didn't answer, but the clenching of his jaw muscle said it all. The situation pissed him off almost as much as it did her.

"He'll have to convince the other district judges that I'm morally unfit to preside over a court of law, but—" she shrugged "—Williamson County is one of the most conservative counties in the state, maybe even the country. If there's anywhere being labeled an unwed mother could cost me my job, it's here."

He didn't argue with her, which only confirmed that she was right. The simple truth was that people held judges to a higher standard of behavior. And Kate, for one, expected no less.

"I still don't see how our getting married will help things. You think people will notice that you and Beth are pregnant at the same time, but not notice six months from now when we get divorced and they adopt your child? You don't think anyone will question your morality then?"

"That's just it," she countered. "By the time I have the baby in November, the elections will be over. Regardless of the outcome, Hatcher could no longer use me as a pawn in his or anyone else's campaign." She sensed she'd almost swayed him, so she added, "It'd only be until November."

After a long moment of studying her, he shook his head ruefully. "Look, the situation sucks, but—"

She stood. "You said you would help."

"I know I did, but—"

She crossed the room until she was standing right in front of him. "You said you would do anything you could to help out."

"I know. And you said you didn't trust me to stick around."

"So prove me wrong." She met his gaze head-on. As disturbing as it was to stare into his eyes at this range, she didn't let herself blink.

"What makes you think I'll make an even halfway decent husband?"

"I don't need you to be a decent husband. I just need a ceremony and a ring."

He chuckled. "Lowered your standards a bit, have you?"

"Don't make this harder than it is."

If possible, his smile broadened. Apparently whatever panic he'd initially felt had dissipated. "Why shouldn't I? You certainly made my initial offer to help difficult."

Only Jake could find humor in *this* situation. "I was surprised," she said through gritted teeth. "That's all."

"'Are you insane?' I believe those were your words."

Hearing him parrot her words back to her, she felt ashamed by how badly she'd treated him. Yet he didn't seem hurt. Didn't even seem angry. If anything, he seemed amused.

"Don't you take anything seriously?" she asked, suddenly feeling peevish.

"Very little."

"Not even insults to your mental stability?"

He just shrugged. "I've heard a lot worse than anything you can come up with, Katie."

She spun on her heel, needing to put distance between them. "This is never going to work. You're not the crazy one. I am."

But before she could make a move, he was beside her, his hand on her shoulder, easing her back to her spot on the sofa. "Hey, calm down. I was just teasing."

"Well, stop. This isn't the time or the place. What we're talking about is very serious."

"If you say so."

"I do say so." She desperately wanted to jump to her feet and pace. But doing so would probably mean being touched by him again. Since she wasn't willing to risk that, she scooted to the far corner of the sofa, then crossed her legs to keep herself from tapping her foot. "If we're going to do this, we need to be as businesslike about this as possible. We need rules. Boundaries."

Shirts that buttoned all the way up, she thought, wisely keeping it to herself.

"Gee, you're just suckin' all the fun right out of this."

If his amused expression was an indication, she hadn't sucked any of the fun out of it for him.

"I'm serious."

"I know you are. That's what makes it so damn cute."

"Cute?" She wasn't cute. No one called her cute. She was a judge, for goodness' sake. Judges weren't cute. She was pretty sure that edict had been written into the Texas Constitution.

"Now, don't get all huffy on me," he said in his most placating tone.

"I am not getting huffy."

"Sure you are."

"No, I'm—" She sucked in a deep breath. "This is exactly why we need boundaries."

"This?" he asked archly.

"This." She waved her hand back and forth between them. "If any kind of arrangement between us is going to work, we can't have this kind of flirtatious banter."

He raised an eyebrow, studying her with obvious humor. "Flirtatious banter? So you think I'm flirting with you?"

Despite his teasing manner, there was a spark of intensity deep in his gaze that unsettled her even more than his flirting.

Boundaries, she reminded herself. Get back to setting boundaries.

"I think you'll flirt with any woman within earshot." He didn't seem insulted by the observation. Or perhaps he just didn't see it as an insult. "But I don't want you to flirt with me. It would lend too much intimacy to the marriage."

"'Too much intimacy to the marriage.' Now there's a phrase you don't hear very often."

"And while we're on the subject…" She felt her throat beginning to tighten, and paused just long enough to clear it. Discreetly, she hoped. "I'm sure you'll agree there should be absolutely no…intimacy between us."

His lips twitched as if he was barely containing his laughter. "No intimacy? You mean like no flirting? You already covered that."

"No, I mean no intimacy." She felt her cheeks begin to burn. Damn it, why should this discussion embarrass her? She was a grown woman, for goodness sake. "No physical intimacy."

She'd forced herself to say the words without hesitating or stuttering. But she couldn't force her mind not to stumble over the images automatically produced. The two of them together, lying naked in a tangle of sheets.

Her reaction surprised her. She didn't want Jake Morgan. She *couldn't* want him. Not in their present situation. Not ever.

The only thing that surprised her more than her reaction was the flash of corresponding heat she saw in his gaze.

In an instant it was gone. Replaced by a teasing twinkle in his eye and a cocksure grin on his lips.

"So you think I won't be able to resist you? You

think once we're living together, we'll both cave to temptation unless we set up all these rules beforehand?"

"Certainly not. It just seemed wise to— Wait a minute, what do you mean once we're living together?"

"Well, there's no point in us getting married if people aren't going to see us living together, right? I was thinking your place, 'cause I assume it's bigger, but if you want to bunk down here, be my guest. But I've got to warn you, in your condition, I don't really think you should be sleeping on the sofa, and there's only one bed. I may be willing to give up my social life for this, but I'm not willing to give up my bed."

Her mind reeled as he babbled on about the comforts of his bed. He wanted them to *live* together? How could she possibly maintain her equilibrium—her emotional distance—with him living under her roof?

"No. Absolutely not." She shook her head, hoping she sounded very judicial, hoping her tone brooked no argument. "Cohabitation has disaster written all over it."

Either he didn't pick up on her no-one-argues-with-the-judge attitude, or he just didn't care. Because he said, just as firmly, "No, if we're going to do this, we're going to do it right. If we're legally married, but don't live together, that's way too suspicious. Hatcher—or someone else—will figure out something's wrong."

"You're right, of course." She sighed with resignation. "So what now?"

"We'll need to have a real ceremony," he said. It doesn't have to be in a church if you don't want it to, but we'll both have to invite some friends. Preferably friends from work, so that plenty of people will know. We'll need a story for how we met and why we're getting married so quickly. We can mention the baby if you want, but we don't want it to look like that's the only reason we're getting married."

"Not the only reason? You can't expect people to believe we're actually in love."

"That's exactly what I expect them to believe. For this to work, we need to *make* people believe it."

Four

In less than a week she'd be married.

They'd tentatively scheduled the wedding for Friday at the courthouse. She'd make the appointment Monday when she went in to work. Sure, being married by a J.P. lacked romance, but in this case that wasn't a bad thing. Besides, it had the added benefit of guaranteeing that everyone she worked with would know about the wedding within hours, Hatcher and the other district judges included.

But no matter how many times she told herself this was the only solution, it did nothing to diminish the sinking feeling in her belly. Or her racing thoughts. She was getting married. To Jake Morgan of all people!

Sunday night, as she lay in bed, trying to sleep, she couldn't keep that one terrifying thought from pounding through her head.

She'd gone to bed early, exhausted from spending the

day emptying out her spare room for Jake. Despite her protests, he'd insisted on giving up his apartment entirely, since it would look suspicious to keep it. So all of his furniture would be incorporated into her house or kept in the storage shed out back. After all her work she'd been sure her fatigue would take over and allow her to sleep. Yet here she lay, eyes wide open, heart beating too fast, thoughts racing too quickly for sleep to settle over her.

She felt so jittery, she actually jumped when the phone rang. Alarm shot through her as she snatched the phone from its cradle.

"Stew?"

"No, it's Jake." His voice sounded low and lazy through the phone lines. "Were you expecting Stew to call?"

Soothed by the tone of his voice, she sank back against her pillow. "No. But usually no one calls this late, so…never mind. It's silly."

"So you assumed something was wrong with Beth?"

"Yes." You only needed one alarming late-night phone call to fear them for life, and she'd had several. Mostly when she was young and she and Beth still lived with their mother. She didn't like that he found her so transparent, so she quickly changed the subject. "Did you need something, Jake?"

"I'm sorry I called. I wouldn't have done it if I'd known it would upset you."

"I'm not upset," she lied.

"In my defense, it's not that late."

She glanced at her bedside clock. Only 9:23. Dang it, he was right. Most people were still up watching the Sunday night movie.

"But I guess," he continued without waiting for her response, "that pregnant women tire easily and go to bed early. These are the kinds of things I'll have to get used to."

Now that was a disconcerting thought. "Why did you call, Jake?"

"I was thinking about our story."

In the background she could hear the faint murmur of a TV. "Our story?" she asked.

The sounds faded, as if he'd just turned down the volume with the remote. "The story of how we met, remember? We need to get our story straight, because when people find out we're getting married, they're bound to ask."

She could picture him so clearly in her mind. Lounging on that leather sofa, his legs stretched out onto the battered wood coffee table, phone in one hand, remote in the other, football game on ESPN.

Shaking her head to rid herself of the image, she said, "That's easy. We met at Beth and Stew's wedding."

"We met at their wedding eight years ago and now—outta nowhere—we're getting married? Naw, that doesn't make sense." He chuckled. "I bet you're a terrible liar."

Lying in the dark, she felt distinctly disadvantaged. So she flipped on the light beside her bed, stacked a couple of spare pillows behind her and sat up. "I'm a judge. We're not supposed to be good liars."

"Is that part of the job description?" he teased.

"No, but it should be," she said wryly. And then felt annoyed with herself for letting him lure her off the subject. "About this story, we should keep it as simple as possible. And close to the truth, if we can. If you think we really need one."

"Come on, everybody's got a story. And when a couple gets married, everyone wants to hear it."

"I disagree. Not everyone has an interesting story, and surely few people care enough to ask about it."

"How did Beth and Stew meet?" he asked.

"I don't know." She rubbed her temple as she thought about it. "I guess it was their freshman year at UT. She was working at that little sandwich shop across from campus." She couldn't keep from smiling as a few of the details came back to her. "Even though he was vegetarian, he'd always order a Philly cheesesteak, because they took so long to make and that gave him more time to talk to— Wait a second. Surely you've heard this all before."

Jake chuckled. "Of course I have, but you just proved my point. Everybody has a story."

"Maybe," she reluctantly admitted.

"Definitely. Tell me something. How did your parents meet?"

Kate chewed lightly on her lip, unsure what to say. Her parents had met in a bar during one of her mother's frequent bouts of drunkenness. Nine months later, when Kate was born, her mom couldn't remember her lover's name. Couldn't narrow the field of possible fathers down to just one guy, for that matter. The most Kate had ever been able to get out of her mom was, "He was probably either the cop from Austin or the salesman from Dallas. Or the trucker from Ohio."

Whichever guy it was, it didn't make for the kind of story she wanted to share. So she lied.

"They were high school sweethearts. Their first date was the homecoming dance. They married young." It wasn't entirely a lie. More an amalgamation of stories from her adopted parents and her various foster parents.

Since it would never hold up under questioning, she asked, "What about your parents? How did they meet?"

He didn't answer right away, and she thought she heard a refrigerator door open and then close on his end of the line. A second later she heard him take a drink.

Probably of beer. Instantly she pictured him standing with his shoulder propped against the kitchen doorway, the way he'd stood the other night.

Why did he feel the need to get a beer before answering such a simple question? Was it possible she wasn't the only one prevaricating about her past?

"Jake?" she prodded. Then felt guilty for being so nosy. And for jumping to conclusions. "Never mind. You don't have to tell me."

"Actually, he rescued her from a burning building. Saved her life."

"Really?" Now that she hadn't seen coming.

"Yeah, really. It was…"

When he didn't speak for several seconds, she offered, "Very romantic, I imagine."

She could picture it. The terror of being trapped in a burning building. The certainty that death was near. And then, out of the smoke, appears a handsome, broad-shouldered firefighter come to carry the damsel in distress to safety. It was the stuff of fantasies.

"Romantic? Sure. But it's a really bad way to start a relationship. When my dad was injured in the line of duty and had to take early retirement, I think my mom was more upset than he was. I don't think she ever forgave him for being just a man."

Something in his voice tugged at a part of her deep inside. He sounded so serious. So pensive.

This vulnerability disconcerted her. She didn't know how to talk to him when he was like this. Didn't know how to keep up her barriers against him. So she said nothing.

There was another long pause from his end of the phone. More sounds of him swallowing.

The image of him drinking from a beer bottle crept into her head again. She could practically see him. The way he tipped his head back. The way his Adam's apple slid up and down the column of his neck as he swallowed. The beads of condensation that formed on the bottle, moistening his fingers.

She wasn't a fanciful person. In fact, she'd been accused on more than one occasion of having no imagination at all. So why couldn't she turn off the images of Jake in her mind?

Was it merely the unnatural intimacy that came from talking to him on the phone while lying in bed?

That must be it.

"Look, I should go." She glanced at the clock. "Now it really is late. At least for a pregnant woman."

"Yeah, I suppose so—wait, we don't have a story yet."

"Can't it wait till tomorrow? We could talk after work."

"By then it'll be too late. You're making our appointment with the justice of the peace tomorrow, right?"

"Yes. I was going to do it over lunch."

"When you do, the women you work with will want details."

"The women I work with? What's that supposed to mean?"

"Oh, come on, don't pretend to be offended." That teasing warmth was back in his voice. "Women are the worst about this kind of thing."

She opened her mouth to disagree, then snapped it closed. He was right, of course. There would be at least a dozen women at the courthouse pumping her for information the second she scheduled an appointment with the J.P. Her court clerk, Meg. All the female court reporters. Not to mention the other judges. And Kevin would be just as bad as any of the women.

Did she dare share the truth with even him? If she did, there would be the inevitable questions about why she hadn't told him about the pregnancy in the first place. What a mess.

"You've gotten pretty quiet over there. You fall asleep?"

I wish.

"Okay, so we need a story by tomorrow. Surely you have some idea already or you wouldn't have brought it up."

"What about Beth and Stew's New Year's Eve party?"

"What about it?"

"We could say we 'fell in love' that night. We were both there, right?"

"Yes." She went every year, even though she normally didn't enjoy large parties. But on New Year's Eve it just seemed wrong to stay home watching repeats of *Law & Order.* "But so were about fifty other people. All of whom would know we barely spoke to each other that evening."

"Come on, no one will remember that. It was a New Year's Eve party. A lot of people were drinking."

"I wasn't," she pointed out.

"Well, of course you weren't."

"Hey—"

"I'm sure you never drink in public. Wouldn't suit the image of the judge, would it?"

Actually, she didn't drink out of fear of turning into her mother. But that certainly wasn't the kind of thing she wanted him to know.

"But even you," he continued, "as sober as you were, do you remember what every other person at the party was doing?"

Mostly she remembered the unending boredom of listening to Paul—Beth and Stew's accountant—describe his two-week glacier cruise to Alaska. But other than Paul, she couldn't remember how anyone else spent their evening. And despite how long it had felt, her conversation with Paul had lasted only twenty or so minutes.

"Okay, then," she conceded. "We 'fell in love' at the party. So we're set with a story."

"We need a few more details than that, don't you think?"

She let out a frustrated sigh. "What kind of details?"

"Well, if I remember right, it was a pretty warm night for December. We could say we went into the backyard to sit by the chiminea."

"That would explain why no one saw us together," she pointed out. Beth and Stew's house sat on more than half an acre of land. The long, narrow backyard was scattered with live oaks. For parties, Beth draped the limbs of the trees with lanterns. On a winter night, gathered around the warmth of the fire in the chiminea, it would be an undeniably romantic setting. The perfect place to fall in love.

"It does sound nice," she murmured. As soon as she heard how dreamy her tone sounded, she sat up straighter. "For the purposes of the story, I mean."

"Oh, of course. For the story."

He sounded amused. As if he sensed that she'd momentarily gotten caught up in the fake memory they were creating to pass off their fake marriage as real.

Part of her wished she could adopt a similarly cavalier attitude about the situation. But then, it was her job that was at stake, not his.

Which probably meant she should be more grateful that he'd come up with a story about how they'd fallen in love.

His attitude might seem cavalier, but he was taking their arrangement as seriously as she was. Maybe even more so.

"What about dating?" she asked, determined to do her part.

"What about it?"

"We certainly didn't go on any dates around town. Someone would have remembered that."

"Good point. I guess—" she heard a rustling of fabric in the background and for a second his voice was muffled "—we dated in Austin."

"We kept our relationship secret, though. Why would we do that?" she asked.

"I wanted to protect your reputation."

For some reason, that struck her as funny. So she was laughing as she replied, "That's awfully noble of you."

"What?" Mock offense laced his tone. "You don't think I'm noble?"

"Hey, you're marrying me to protect my reputation. I don't think it gets more noble than that."

"Right. Don't forget it, either."

"Don't worry. If you go through with this wedding, I'll really owe you one."

"Speaking of the wedding. I was, um—" he cleared his throat "—wondering what you wanted to do about the honeymoon."

"The honeymoon?" she finally choked out.

"Yeah. People will expect us to go away somewhere."

Dang. A honeymoon? Why hadn't she thought of that? And why, now that he'd mentioned it, did her mind suddenly fill with images of the two of them alone together in some romantic location. An exotic beach or quaint bed and breakfast.

"No," she said abruptly. "Absolutely not."

Letting her imagination run away with her was one

thing. Actually fulfilling one of those daydreams by letting Jake take her on a romantic getaway? That was out of the question.

He must have heard the pure horror in her voice, because he said, "Hey, it's not like I'd take you to the Bates Motel or anything. I was thinking something more along the lines of a B&B in Fredericksburg. Just for a night or two."

Right. A couple of nights in one of the most charming historic towns in Texas? She'd prefer the Bates Motel.

"No," she said firmly. "We're not going anywhere."

"But—"

"We're going to spend the weekend moving your stuff into my place like we discussed. We can tell people we're planning a big trip in the fall, if you want."

Before he could protest further, she said good-night and ended the call.

Five

"I can't believe you're doing this."

Beth sat in the spare chair in Kate's office. Her normally serene features were twisted into a frown, just as her hands were twisted into fretful knots where they lay on her lap.

Kate squelched her nerves and forced her attention back to her computer screen and the open document she'd been reading when Beth arrived at the courthouse a full hour early for the wedding.

"I know," Kate said, hoping to placate her sister's nerves. "I can hardly believe it myself."

"The thing is, Stew and I…" The tension in her voice drew Kate's gaze back to her. "Well, we never meant for this to happen. I mean, we knew we were asking a lot, but…"

With a sigh, Kate finally gave up on getting any more work done and closed the document on the screen. She rounded her desk to stand by Beth's chair. "I know you didn't. No one could have predicted things would turn out like this."

Beth looked up at her and Kate was surprised to see her sister's eyes brimming with tears. At the sight, the tension that had been building inside Kate over the past two weeks began to seep away.

"Hey." She leaned down and rubbed Beth's arm. "There's no need for tears. Everything's going to be fine."

Beth stood and clutched Kate's hands. "So you don't hate us?"

Kate hadn't realized it, but until that instant, she had been harboring some resentment.

Not for having to marry Jake. No, she blamed only herself for not realizing sooner the threat Hatcher posed to her career. But she did resent Beth because being pregnant had made Kate realize all that was missing from her life. Made her yearn for things she couldn't have, but that Beth could. But faced with Beth's obvious remorse, that, too, disappeared. "No," she reassured. "I don't hate you. How could I?"

"Because you…" Beth's voice broke. "You have to marry Jake. You hate Jake," she finished with a wail.

Even though there was nothing at all funny about the situation, Kate couldn't help chuckling. "I don't hate Jake." She glanced at the door to her office, verifying—again—that it was firmly closed.

"You were right about him, you know?" Kate admitted. "Jake is a really good guy."

More and more, Kate was realizing just how distorted her initial impression of Jake had been. When they first met at Beth and Stew's rehearsal dinner, she'd been put off by Jake's charm and good looks. She'd assumed they were all he had going for him. Funny, how wrong she'd been, when she was usually such a good judge of character. She couldn't think of any other man—not even Stew—who would marry a virtual stranger under such circumstances.

Beth smiled weakly. "He is a good guy, isn't he?"

"Absolutely. So you don't need to worry at all. Everything is going to turn out just fine." Kate smiled gamely and hoped it hid her own nerves. Despite her reassurances to Beth, she wasn't at all sure that everything would be anywhere near fine.

Beth must not have sensed any of the doubts plaguing Kate, because she offered a wobbly smile of her own.

"I brought you something. For the ceremony." She held up a brown paper shopping bag from her store the Health Nut. "I was hoping you'd wear it."

Kate felt a wave of sinking dread. "Oh, Beth…"

"I know you don't think of this as a real ceremony, but you should still have something nice to wear," Beth said in a rush. "It's not fancy. Not a real wedding dress or anything." She laughed nervously. "Not even I would bring you a real wedding dress in a grocery sack."

"I appreciate the offer, but I'm okay wearing what I have on."

"Please, Kate," Beth all but pleaded. "Let me do this. You never let me do anything nice for you."

"It's really not necessary."

"But I still hope you'll wear it. It would mean a lot to me."

Reluctantly Kate took the bag from her sister and pulled out the dress inside. It was a simple, cream-colored dress that would fall nearly to her ankles, with short cap sleeves and lace around the deep, heart-shaped neckline. Very feminine. Definitely the kind of thing she'd wear only to mollify her sister.

"I know it's not what you would usually wear," Beth began before Kate could protest. "But it matched the shawl."

With a sense of resignation, Kate reached back into the bag. She knew what she would find before her hand even touched it.

The delicate lace shawl that Beth had worn with her own wedding dress. The shawl that Stella—their adoptive mother—had worn with hers.

Shaking her head, she tried to hand the heirloom back to Beth. "I can't accept this."

But Beth refused to take the shawl, pressing it back into Kate's hands. "Stella would have wanted you to wear it."

No, Stella had wanted Beth to have it.

Kate and Stella had rarely gotten along during the nine years Kate lived with Stella and Dave—the adoptive parents that Beth adored and Kate could barely stand.

Before Kate could log any more protests, Beth squeezed her hand and said, "Please, do it for me. This way I'll know you've forgiven us."

How in the world was she supposed to say no to that?

"Besides," Beth added with a grin, "you can't wear what you have on. You look like a waiter."

Kate looked down at her outfit of wide-legged black crepe pants and tailored white shirt. "A waiter?"

So she caved. As she usually did when Beth looked at her with those big sad eyes. Funny, Beth was the older sister, yet Kate had always felt like the tough one. The one in control. The one who got things done and held things together.

Because she'd always been the tough one, she'd never been able to stand seeing Beth upset. Which—she admitted to herself as she was changing into the cream dress in the bathroom of the courthouse annex—was what had gotten her in this situation in the first place.

Just before sending Kate off to the bathroom to change, Beth had whipped out a brush and sparkly hair clip. She'd twisted and smoothed until Kate's scalp ached, forcing the black waves into some semblance of a style. Now, Kate smoothed the dress over her hips and eyed herself critically in the mirror. She was now fifteen weeks pregnant. The fabric clung a little snugly across her belly, but not noticeably so.

Never in a million years would she have picked this dress for herself. It was too frilly. Too girly. Exactly the kind of thing she thought she looked ridiculous in.

Kate looked longingly at her folded pants and shirt. Maybe she had resembled a waiter, but at least she'd looked like herself.

Now she looked like freakin' Snow White.

As she and Beth walked across the park to the main courthouse, she half expected birds and little woodland creatures to scurry to her side, chirping music.

Just outside the J.P.'s office, Kevin caught up with them.

"I'm sorry I'm la—" He cut himself off as he looked at Kate. "Whoa."

She glared back. "You're not late. And don't you dare say anything about how I'm dressed."

He held up his hands. "I was going to say you look great." He caught Beth's eye as he leaned in to brush a kiss hello on Kate's cheek. "This your idea?"

Beth smiled. "Absolutely."

He smiled. "I heartily approve."

Kate narrowed her gaze. "You are worthless as a best friend. First you're late and now this?",

She reached for the handle of the door to the J.P.'s office, but Beth plastered herself against the solid wood.

"Hold on, you can't go in there."

"What? Why not?"

Beth clucked disapprovingly. "Because they might not be ready for you. You can't go in until they are, otherwise the groom will see you before the wedding and that will be bad luck." Beth cracked open the door and peeked inside. "Jake and Stew are already inside. I'll just check on things."

Kate opened her mouth to protest, but snapped it closed when Kevin caught her eye.

In front of him, she couldn't point out that it hardly mattered if Jake saw her before he wedding, because this wasn't a real wedding. So she kept her mouth shut, fumed silently and tried to ignore the satisfied smile Kevin was bestowing on her.

After several moments, she gave in to her curiosity and demanded, "What?"

"What?" he parroted.

"You're looking entirely too smug. Why?"

"I don't know what you mean." He smiled innocently.

"I hope you don't have anything silly planned be-cause—"

Before she could finish with her threat to make his life miserable, Beth opened the door to the J.P.'s office, revealing exactly why Kevin looked so smug.

Kate had expected to see five people at most inside Judge Walthen's chambers. Instead, dozens of people were crammed into the already small room. Judge Walthen stood behind his desk, which had been cleared to make room for several large vases of day lilies. Her favorite. To Walthen's left, stood Jake—looking so breathtakingly handsome that he...well, he took her breath away.

She hadn't seen Jake in a suit since Beth and Stew's wedding. The crisp white shirt showed off the tanned

column of his throat. And his broad shoulders did things
for a suit jacket that should be illegal.

But it was his expression that stopped her in her tracks.
As he turned to face her, the cocky grin he usually wore
faded, replaced by delight as he studied her.

She couldn't help feeling a bubble of feminine pleasure at the appreciative gleam in his eyes. For a second
he looked almost like a man in love.

Then he ruined the effect by flashing her a grin accompanied by a quick wink.

And just like that, the bubble of pleasure she'd felt
popped.

To him this was all a joke. To her, it was little more than
an obligation. A trial to be endured. Not a celebration.

As for the friends who had shown up for the wedding…she was deceiving them. And she'd continue to
deceive them for as long as it took to keep her job.

Suddenly it felt right that Beth had forced her into
this frilly dress and heirloom shawl. It was the perfect
costume for this farce. She was little more than an actress who'd wandered onto stage during a play. Except
she didn't know which play she was in and she certainly
didn't know any of her lines.

Nevertheless, she forced herself to put one foot in
front of the other, and by the time she reached Jake's
side, her uncertainty had crystallized into anger. This
was all his fault.

The flowers, the guests—none of this could have
been done without his knowledge. Surely he could have
guessed she wouldn't have wanted any of this.

He leaned over to brush a kiss against her cheek and
whispered, "Smile. No one will buy this if you keep
looking like you want to kill me."

He pulled back and took her hand in his. Knowing he

was right, she plastered a smile onto her lips that she hoped passed for either "nervous bride" or "dopey romantic."

She could kill him later.

"I now pronounce you husband and wife."

Kate's hand felt clammy in his. At least, she no longer looked ready to faint. Or strangle him.

Her expression remained strained, but most people would probably write that off as nerves. Which would be normal, under the circumstances. He didn't know how men did this for real. Hell, he'd been a nervous wreck all day.

Except for the moment when he'd turned to see Kate standing in the doorway. In that instant everything felt right. Alarmingly so.

But he'd shoved the sensation aside. Just as he'd done with the well of emotion he felt while sliding the simple platinum wedding band onto her finger.

Whatever he'd felt, surely it wasn't pleasure. Pride, maybe, in living up to his responsibilities. Doing the right thing.

Satisfied that he'd pigeonholed his feelings, he returned his attention to the judge just in time to hear the words, "You may now kiss the bride."

A glance in the direction of the audience revealed a sea of expectant faces. Kate, on the other hand, looked as if she was wavering between feeling faint and wanting to stomp on his foot with the heel of her shoe.

But whether she liked it or not, he had to kiss her.

For a second he merely stared down into her wide brown eyes. Her lips were parted slightly and moist, because she'd licked them nervously during the ceremony.

Kissing Kate would be no hardship.

Part of him had been thinking about this moment ever

since he'd first agreed to marry her—maybe longer. His first kiss with Kate.

Maybe his only kiss with her.

He felt a surge of anticipation mixed with determination. If this was going to be their only kiss, then he was going to make it count. Why the hell not? She already wanted to kill him anyway.

So he wrapped one arm around her shoulders to pull her toward him and with the other hand he tilted up her chin in the instant before his lips came to rest on hers, he caught a 'Don't you dare' expression in her eyes. But he did dare.

Her mouth was soft and pliant beneath his. From surprise, most likely. Because as soon as she realized he wasn't pulling away immediately, her lips stiffened and her hands pressed into his chest. She could easily have pushed him away if she'd really wanted to, but she never quite mustered the resistance.

At the feel of her lips beneath his, the taste of her on his mouth, desire sprung to life, pumping through his blood. He found himself aching to press her against his body, to deepen the kiss. He barely restrained himself from sweeping his tongue into her mouth.

But he did manage to finally pull back. He didn't want her like this—kissing him because she had to. He wanted her eager. Warm and pliant. Hell, he just wanted her.

He nearly cursed as he let her go. Because his new wife was the one woman he couldn't have.

Six

"This isn't what we talked about," Kate muttered through clenched teeth forty minutes later as they stood in the private dining room of the 7th Street Bistro. The bistro was one of the trendy new restaurants that had opened on the square across from the courthouse.

Tonight the private room was filled with the guests who had come to help them celebrate. Champagne toasts were being made to their happiness. Large platters of appetizers were being passed around.

Jake held a glass of champagne in one hand but kept his other arm draped over Kate's shoulder, partly for appearance's sake and partly to keep her by his side. The minute he let go, he knew she'd pull away from him.

"I hope this wasn't your idea," she said under her breath.

He'd guided her to the back of the room by a table laden with a two-tier cake and a dozen or so packages wrapped in shades of white paper. They stood slightly apart from the crowd, so there was no chance of being overheard. But they were being closely watched.

"Not a chance." He leaned in to brush a kiss on her temple and caught the scent of her shampoo. Something sweet and fruity. Damn, she smelled good.

She nudged her shoulder against his chest. "Stop doing that," she hissed.

"What?"

"Being all lovey-dovey. It's ridiculous."

"This is our wedding reception," he pointed out. "It'd be ridiculous if we *weren't* affectionate."

She made a disgruntled noise. "So, if this wasn't your idea, then whose was it?"

"Your friend Kevin. He's the one responsible." Just then Kevin caught his eye from across the room and smiled broadly. Not wanting to spoil the guy's fun, Jake raised his glass in salute before downing a healthy gulp.

"I'm going to kill him," she muttered. "When this is over, I'm definitely going to kill him."

"He just wanted to do something nice for you. Why is that so hard for you to accept?"

He studied her, genuinely curious about her reaction

"Nice?" Kate scoffed. "Nice would have been arranging for me to have the afternoon off. This is torture."

"Ah, it's not so bad."

"Not so bad? Half the town is here."

"Thirty people is hardly half the town." She merely glared at him, so he added, "Try to look on the bright side—"

"The bright side?" she asked sarcastically before he could finish.

He ignored her. "At least now everyone knows about the wedding. That was the idea, wasn't it?"

Turning to face him, she said, "Speaking of things

people know about. All of this might not have been your idea, but you knew about it, didn't you?"

He could lie, but what would be the point? "As soon as Kevin found out we were getting married, he started planning this. I found out on…oh, about Tuesday, I guess."

"And you didn't put a stop to it?"

"Don't you think that would have seemed strange? Besides, what's the harm?"

"What's the harm?" she asked incredulously. "If we're not careful—if we slip up at all, any one of these people could put two and two together and figure out that we barely know each other. And that we're certainly not in love."

"That's not going to happen."

"How can you be so sure?"

He nodded toward the room. "Look at them. Do any of them look suspicious? Even a little bit?"

She twisted to study the crowd, carefully examining each face. He allowed her a few seconds of paranoia before nudging her chin with his knuckle so she looked back at him. "The only thing that might make people suspicious is if we don't act like happy newlyweds."

Her mouth opened and closed several times as if she were considering a protest. Finally she snapped her mouth shut and just glared at him. She looked so damn cute when she was mad, he simply couldn't resist kissing her petulant lips.

Unlike the kiss after the ceremony, this time, she didn't put up much resistance. Too surprised, he supposed. Her lips parted beneath his almost instantly, and with one quick swipe of his tongue he felt her defiance give way completely.

She tasted just faintly of champagne.

When they first arrived at the reception, someone

had thrust a flute into her hand, and ever since then she'd been dutifully raising it to her mouth with every toast. Thankfully, no one else noticed the glass was full. Still, a few drops of the champagne clung to her lips.

The taste, so unexpected and sweet, surprised him. Just like she did.

He pulled back from her and studied her face. For a second she looked slightly shell-shocked. He suspected he did, too.

Then she shook it off and said, "Why did you do that?"

"Kiss you?"

She nodded.

"Because, we just got married. There are thirty people in this room who think we're so in love we couldn't wait long enough to plan a church wedding. Therefore, I should look like I can't keep my hands off you."

Doubt flickered in her eyes and for a second, he thought she wasn't going to buy it. Finally she nodded. And with an expression of resigned determination, she slipped her arm around his waist and turned to face the crowded room, where the wait staff was just beginning to serve an early dinner.

He felt a surge of relief that she hadn't pressed him for another explanation. Sure, the one he'd given her worked, but it wasn't the whole truth.

Just now he'd kissed her because he wanted to. The ruse they were perpetrating hadn't even entered his mind.

He was in for a hell of a long six months.

Kate awakened to the unfamiliar sounds of someone moving around in her kitchen. After a split second of alarm, she remembered that someone was Jake.

With a groan she rolled over and buried her head in

her pillow, wishing she could go back to sleep. Or wake up to find she'd just had a nightmare.

She'd lain awake half the night, trying to find fault with Jake's logic. But no matter how she approached the problem, his solution was the only one. Whenever they were in public, they'd have to appear to be in love. Which meant more touches, more kisses and more restless nights knowing he was sleeping just a few feet away in her tiny bungalow-style house's only other bedroom.

After a few more seconds of squeezing her eyes closed, she sat up to face another morning without coffee. Boy, could she have used the caffeine this morning. At least her morning sickness had finally passed.

She had her arms halfway into the sleeves of her robe before it occurred to her that she really didn't want Jake seeing her in her pj's and robe. There was way too much intimacy between them as it was.

So she took the time to dress in a casual pair of pants and long sleeved shirt that she knotted low on her waist to distract from the slight bulge. Then she made a quick trip to the bathroom to twist her unruly hair into a semblance of an elegant knot and to run a toothbrush over her teeth.

She found Jake in the kitchen, barefoot, dressed in jeans and a faded black T-shirt, scrambling eggs. Lots of eggs.

When she cleared her throat, he glanced over his shoulder. "Mornin', Katie."

Letting the annoying nickname slide, she said, "I don't know what pregnancy books you've been reading, but although pregnant women do eat a lot, they generally don't eat two dozen eggs for breakfast."

He chuckled. "God, I hope not. I couldn't afford to feed you. These are for the guys. Besides, it's not just eggs, it's breakfast tacos." He lifted the spatula from the frying pan and pointed toward the oven. "The first batch is in the oven. Help yourself."

"Breakfast tacos?" she repeated dreamily. In her mind, nothing beat the sheer joy from consuming eggs, bacon, melted Colby-jack and spicy salsa all wrapped up in a warm tortilla.

"Yep. Those are bacon, egg and cheese. These'll be sausage, egg, and potato, if you want to wait. And there's decaf coffee in the pot."

She was already fishing a couple of tacos out of the oven when he got to the part about the coffee. "Decaf? Is that what you normally drink?"

"Naw. Normally, I'm a double-shot espresso kinda guy. But Beth mentioned you'd given up caffeine. I figured, if you could do it, so could I."

"My gosh, you're a saint for giving up coffee if you don't have to." She dropped the tacos onto a plate and began gingerly peeling away the hot tinfoil he'd wrapped them in. "Where'd you get all this food? I could have sworn I didn't have five dozen eggs in the fridge."

"I went out to the store this morning."

She glanced at the clock. "It's only 8:30. How long have you been up?"

"Let's just say that inflatable mattress you blew up for me last night wasn't quite made for someone my size."

"Ah. Sorry. Not having a proper guest bed means unwanted guests don't stay for long. Sorry you had to pay the price though. On the bright side, it does give us an excuse to move your bed and furniture into my guest bedroom."

There hadn't been time before their wedding night to move in his bed. Which had left either the sofa or the inflatable mattress. "By the way, when you said these were for 'the guys' which 'guys' did you mean exactly?"

"The guys from the station." He dumped the scrambled eggs into the bowl of already cooked sausage and potatoes.

"Just so I know what to expect—" she spooned salsa onto her tacos "—will 'the guys' be coming over every Saturday morning for breakfast?"

"No."

"Oh, that's good."

She'd been teasing, but as she took a bike of taco, it occurred to her: What did she really know about Jake, other than the fact that he was an arson investigator and had been Stew's best friend since the tenth grade? And he made kick-butt breakfast tacos.

Everything else was supposition and extrapolation. And yet she'd invited him into her home—into her life—for the next six months. What in the world had she gotten herself into?

And did it really matter as long as he kept feeding her like this? she mused as she took another bite of taco.

With her foot she nudged a kitchen chair away from the table so it faced the counter where Jake worked. She lowered herself into the chair, held a napkin under her chin so she didn't drip on her shirt and took another bite.

Man, oh, man, she could get used to this.

Freshly made breakfast tacos. Hot coffee waiting for her. Jake sure knew the way to a woman's heart.

"The guys are helping to move my stuff in. I offered to feed them as payment." As he stirred the ingredients together, he studied her over his shoulder. "I told them—"

She looked at him over her taco. "What?"

"That's what you're wearing?" His eyebrows were raised, his expression dubious.

She glanced down, just to verify that her pants and shirt hadn't somehow morphed into a Big Bird costume. "What's wrong with what I have on?"

He looked her up and down with a thoroughness she found more than a little disconcerting. "Nothing. I guess."

She looked down at her clothes again, then back up at him. "Seriously, what's wrong with this?"

He shrugged, turning his attention back to filling the tortillas. "It's just a little formal for a Saturday morning, don't you think?"

"No, obviously I didn't think so or I wouldn't have put it on." She frowned at his back and added wryly, "But compared to your jeans and ratty T-shirt, I guess I am dressed somewhat formally."

He gave her a cocky grin over his shoulder. "Hey, it's moving day. Jeans and a ratty T-shirt are perfect."

"Yes, well, I don't have any jeans," she mumbled around a mouthful of taco.

He stilled instantly, then slowly turned to face her, an expression of mock horror on his face. "You don't own any jeans?"

She lifted her chin defiantly and met his gaze. "No, I don't."

"You don't own jeans," he repeated. "That's the damnedest thing I've ever heard. Why don't you own jeans? I'm only asking 'cause you must be the only person in the U.S. under the age of ninety who doesn't."

For a moment she gritted her teeth, then finally admitted, "If you must know, jeans don't flatter my particular body shape."

He let out a bark of laughter. "That's the stupidest thing I've ever heard."

"It's not stu—"

But he was laughing too hard for her to finish.

"What? You think they make your butt look too big or something?" When she didn't answer, he stopped laughing and studied her. "That's it, isn't it? You think jeans make your butt look big."

"I'm not even going to dignify that with a response."

He looked her up and down appreciatively. "You don't have to, 'cause I know I'm right. But let me put your mind at ease, Katie. Your butt is most definitely not too big."

She clenched and unclenched her jaw, unsure what annoyed her more: his use of the nickname Katie or the way his lingering gaze made her breath catch in her chest.

Finally she choked out the only response she could muster without embarrassing herself further. "My butt is not too big. I'll have you know that according to the current standards of the Surgeon General's Office, my pre-pregnancy weight was perfectly in line for someone my height and age."

He nodded, smiling. "Well, it's good to know the surgeon general and I agree. Now that we've got that settled, we need to do something about your clothes."

She looked down at herself again. "Isn't that what we've been talking about? Since I don't have any jeans, I don't see that there's much we can do about it."

He propped his hip against the counter and studied her with his arms crossed over his chest. "No, you're right. But it's not so much your clothes as it is your general appearance."

"Now you're insulting my 'general appearance'? What's next—my personal hygiene? My politics?"

He stroked his chin, seemingly unaware of how insulting this all was. "It's not that there's anything wrong with your appearance per se. It's that you don't look particularly...satisfied."

Humph. What was that supposed to mean?

She crossed her arms over her chest and glared at him. "Well, I'll certainly look a lot less dissatisfied if you stop insulting me."

He pushed away from the countertop and crossed the kitchen to stand before her, all the while sporting one of his arrogant grins. "Oh, I think we can do a lot better than 'less dissatisfied.'"

With him standing over her as she sat, he had her at a distinct disadvantage. So she bumped her chair back and stood. Unfortunately, that only brought her closer to him.

But she refused to be intimidated by his height. Or his nearness. Or the delectable way he smelled—like coffee and bacon and freshly showered man.

"I'll have you know, I think there's nothing wrong with my appearance."

His lips twitched in a way she was sure he knew irritated her. "Sure, if we were just going to hang out here all morning by ourselves, but…"

"But?" She arched an eyebrow.

"But the guys from the station are coming over."

"I've appeared in court like this." She propped her hands on her hips. "I certainly think this will do for your friends from the station."

He continued to study her, he scratched the back of his head as if he was trying to solve a very complex puzzle. "Well, there you go. That's the problem. You look like you're going to court."

"And that's a problem because…"

"Because you should look like you just tumbled out of bed."

Her heart seemed to skip a beat at his words. She sucked in a deep breath, but the extra oxygen didn't counteract what had to be some kind of weird prenatal heart arrhythmia.

She opened her mouth to speak, but all that came out was a weak, "I... I..."

"The way I see it, the morning after her wedding night, a woman ought to look thoroughly..."

Before she could stop herself, the words just popped out. "Thoroughly made love to?"

A wicked gleam sparked in his eyes. "I was going to say satisfied."

"Oh." She could feel a blush creeping into her cheeks and she floundered for a moment. "I, um..."

There were moments in life when she wished she was a completely different person. Someone witty and quick, instead of smart and serious. This was definitely one of those moments.

Another woman might have thought of something clever to say that would have put Jake in his place. Or shocked him into silence. She merely stood there, gaping like a trout.

In this game of witty repartee, it was Jake one, Kate big fate zero.

"Obviously, we need to start with this," he said, reaching up and pulling the clip from her elegant knot.

Her hair fell down about her neck as she heard the clip land on the table beside her with a clatter.

"Now it probably looks like I just tumbled out of bed." She grumbled in protest.

He grinned. "That's the general idea."

Instantly she brought one hand up to smooth her hair into place and reached for the clip with the other. Before she could repair the damage, he grabbed her arm by the wrist and tugged it away from her hair.

"Let me."

Let him what?

But before she could demand an answer, he finger combed her hair, gently parting it on the left.

Stop this! she ordered herself. But she didn't listen. His touch simply felt too good. Her eyes drifted closed.

"Your hair is beautiful. You should wear it loose more often."

"It gets frizzy," she said weakly. "In the humidity. And it doesn't do what I want it to. Looks uncontrollable."

"Wild?"

His voice was like a caress. Sensuous and a little rough. It sapped her strength and when she spoke her voice sounded weak.

"Yes."

"And you don't like that," he surmised.

"No."

"Being wild isn't such a bad thing. It's sexy."

Like Jake. He always seemed so wild. So reckless.

Well, her hair might be wild, but *she* definitely wasn't.

She forced her eyes open. Forced herself to meet his gaze and to suppress the wave of longing she felt rising up inside of her.

There was heat in his gaze, as well. Proof that this crazy awareness she felt wasn't one-sided. But wanting Jake would do no good. And giving in to the want would only cause more problems than she could imagine.

Yet before she could force herself to move away from him, he pulled his hands from her hair, only to lower them to the top button of her shirt.

"This shirt here. That's another problem." His voice was low and rough and grated against her already-sensitive nerves.

"It is?"

"Definitely." His fingers slipped first one and then

another button loose from its hole. His knuckles brushed against the sensitive skin of her throat and chest, sending flashes of heat spiraling down through her body.

She felt herself swaying toward him, suddenly unable to control her own body. Even though she knew what a mistake it would be, she found herself mentally urging him to keep unbuttoning. To pull her shirt right off her.

He must have had way more restraint than she did in that instant, because instead of ripping her shirt open, his hands dropped to where she'd knotted the hem of her shirt low on her hips. Patiently he loosened the knot.

She sucked in her breath as the tail of her shirt fell from his hands and his fingers continued unbuttoning.

With every movement of his fingers, she willed him to meet her eyes, desperate to see his expression. But he kept his attention focused on the task he performed with such painstaking gentleness.

By the time he retied the tail of her shirt into a loose knot just under her breasts, she felt light-headed and weak. In undoing the buttons on her shirt, he'd stripped away all of her defenses, as well.

Still, when he stepped back to eye his handiwork, her hands darted to the skin he'd exposed. He grabbed her wrists before she could cover herself.

"Don't."

"But my stomach is so much rounder than—"

"Leave it." Finally his gaze met hers and he seemed completely serious for the first time since they'd met. "You look…fantastic."

The doorbell rang. Jake dropped his hands to his sides. They both stared toward the front door.

She could hardly bear the intrusion. The reminder of how little this encounter must have meant to Jake.

After all, the past few minutes had been little more than skillful manipulation. When he'd said she looked "fantastic," what he'd really meant was that she looked "satisfied." Like a woman who'd just been made love to. Like the woman his friends expected to see.

As Jake moved to get the door, she snatched the clip from the table and quickly twisted her hair back into a knot. But of course, it was too late. Before she could repair the damage and redo the buttons on her shirt, Jake's friends were pouring through the front door.

They'd seen her hastily putting herself back together. The way their voices, one by one, dropped, from loud, rambunctious chatter into silence proved at least that much.

A scorching heat crept up her neck into her cheeks, fueled by embarrassment and kindled with more than a little anger. Anger at Jake for manipulating her, but mostly anger at herself for falling so completely under his spell.

She knew better, damn it.

At least, she thought she did.

What was the point of carefully constructing defenses against men, if she cheerfully threw open the gates and allowed in the first man with a charming smile and plateful of breakfast tacos.

Man, she was easy—when she looked at it in that light.

Jake had been in her home less than a day, and she'd melted like an ice cube. And to think, while he'd been plying her with tacos, she'd been telling herself how she could get used to this.

As Jake's friends flooded the kitchen and began fixing plates, pouring coffee and introducing themselves, she felt her determination hardening.

She might not be able to control her physical reaction to Jake, but, by golly, she was going to control her emotions. Make herself less susceptible to him. Which meant no more decaf coffee. No more hot breakfasts. No more morning intimacies. She was not going to "get used to this." Not if she could help it.

At least Jake's friends were polite enough not to say anything about what they'd seen, but their sideways glances and knowing grins said plenty. They'd inferred exactly what Jake meant for them to.

They assumed she and Jake had spent their wedding night the traditional way. Making passionate love.

Funny, she'd never felt less satisfied.

Seven

In the month since their marriage, Kate had certainly kept her distance.

She worked long hours, which Jake, of course, had expected. She went to the gym almost every day for pre-natal workout and yoga classes. And when she was home, she spent most of her time in her room, "resting," she claimed, which made sense, because he knew pregnant women needed lots of sleep.

All of that he could put up with. If only she'd let him help her. With anything. But she wasn't letting him.

He'd offered to help with her laundry. She'd refused and started sending it out to be done. He'd tried to cook dinner for her in the evenings. She insisted on eating microwaved frozen meals. Every morning he had a pot of hot decaf brewing by the time she emerged from her bedroom fully dressed. And every morning she walked right past it on her way out the door to Starbucks.

Yes, he'd pushed too hard the morning the guys from that station came over. He knew that now. For the life of him, he couldn't explain why he'd pushed at all. All he knew was that when Kate entered the kitchen dressed so primly, he hadn't been able to resist trying to ruffle her a bit. Maybe because he remembered how good she'd felt in his arms when they'd kissed. Or because he didn't like the thought of her coming to breakfast dressed so formally every morning for the next six months. Or maybe he'd just wanted to kiss her again and couldn't resist finding out whether she wanted that, too.

Frankly, he didn't know what to do anymore.

Which was why, one Thursday night after work, instead of heading home, he stopped by Beth's and Stew's to get their advice.

"We haven't seen you in a while," Stew said as he flipped a vegetarian hamburger on the grill in the backyard.

"If I'd known you were making burgers, I would have gotten here early enough to claim one."

Stew laughed. "You're welcome to one. But only one." With his spatula he gestured to the three burgers sizzling on the grill. "There's no way I'm taking food out of the mouth of a pregnant woman. You know what I mean?"

Jake chuckled and nodded. But the truth was, he didn't know what Stew meant. That was the problem. That was why he'd come here this evening for Stew's advice.

Carrying buttered hamburger buns for Stew to grill, Beth greeted Jake warmly, as she always did. He couldn't help noticing her clothes. Sure, she was a full month farther along than Kate, but Beth was already wearing in long, flowing maternity dresses, designed to show off her belly. Kate, on the other hand, was still dressing to hide her pregnancy. Something she wouldn't be able to get away with for much longer.

Beth set the buns down by the grill, then shot a pointed look at Stew. Not too subtle.

Especially when Stew cleared his throat a few seconds later and asked, "So how's Kate doing?"

Funny, he'd been about to ask them the same question. But apparently Stew and Beth didn't know any more than he did. "Okay. I think." He ran his hand down the back of his neck. "Has she always been so…"

He wasn't sure exactly how to finish the thought tactfully.

"Difficult?" Beth piped up.

"Closed off?" Stew supplied.

"I was going to say 'unwilling to accept help.'"

Beth nodded. "Yep, that's Kate for you. She's always needed to do things her own way. Frankly, it'd be annoying, if she wasn't usually right."

"She won't let me do anything for her. It's driving me crazy," he admitted.

Stew chuckled.

"What?" Jake shot an annoyed look at his friend.

"Man, this must be killing you."

"What's that supposed to mean?"

"Well…you know how you are."

"No." He gritted his teeth. "Apparently, I don't know."

"You need to save people. Be the hero."

"I need to save people?" Jake repeated. Then he scoffed at the idea. "I don't need to save people. That's ridiculous."

Stew and Beth gave each other an amused look.

"I don't need to save people."

Stew used his spatula to transfer the burgers from the grill to the waiting plate. "Sure you do. It's why you became a firefighter. It's why you agreed to marry Kate. It's—"

"I agreed to marry Kate because it was the right thing to do. She needed a husband and she needed someone to take care of her while she's pregnant."

"Right," Stew said. "And you want to be the one who takes care of her, because you need to save people. It's not a bad thing."

"It does explain why you're having so many problems with Kate," Beth said. "She doesn't need anyone to save her. She hasn't since she was a little girl. She doesn't need anyone, period."

And that—Jake realized as he drove home later that night—was the crux of the problem. Kate didn't need anyone's help. Not even his.

Maybe Stew was right and he did need to be a hero, because it drove him crazy that Kate didn't need him.

In some ways, the realization relieved the tension that had been eating away at him the past month. Kate had been getting to him. After all, she was a beautiful woman and they were living together. The physical attraction he felt for her was only natural.

But this was more than purely sexual. He thought about her all the time and had to resist the urge to call her at work. Just to check in.

He thought about ways to tease her. Things he could say just to get a rise out of her.

His growing attachment to her had become quite a problem.

But now…now he had a clue what was really going on. Stew was right. He needed to be a hero.

He'd married Kate so he could help her, and she wasn't letting him. All he had to do was get her to accept his help and—presto—his Kate obsession would disappear.

* * *

He crept into the house a little after eleven, expecting Kate to be in bed already. So he was pretty damn surprised to find her stretched out on the sofa, remote control in hand, a late-night rerun of a crime drama on TV.

She slept through him turning off the TV and pulling the remote from her hand, but woke when he tried to cover her with the throw from the back of the sofa.

"You're home." She wiped at her eyes with her fingertips as she sat up. She looked delightfully sleepy, mussed by her nap. She was dressed in baggy pajamas. Pink with fat ladybugs scattered across them. He'd never seen her in her pajamas before, since she always dressed before leaving her bedroom.

For that matter he hadn't seen her barefoot since that first morning. He glanced down at her feet. Sure enough, they were bare. Slim with high arches and red-painted toenails. Ladybug-red.

He never would have guessed her for red toenails.

She must have caught him looking at her feet, because she quickly hid them as she sat cross-legged on the sofa.

He forced his gaze back to her face. "You didn't have to wait up."

"I wasn't. I just—" She frowned and glanced toward the TV. "What time is it, anyway?"

"About eleven-thirty."

"That late?"

He wasn't sure if the hint of accusation he heard in her voice was real or a figment of his guilt. Either way, his knee-jerk reaction was defensive. "I called."

"I know. But you shouldn't feel like you have to report in. You can stay out as late as you want."

Having apparently said what she'd needed to say, she

unfolded herself from the sofa and stood. Only as she was headed toward the hall did he notice how tired she looked.

"If you weren't waiting up for me, why were you sleeping on the sofa?"

She hesitated in the doorway to the hall, and for a second he thought she'd just ignore his question altogether. Then she turned to face him, propping her shoulder against the door frame. "Insomnia."

Her arms were crossed over her chest in a defensive posture. Waiting for him to tease her, he supposed. She looked cute, standing there in her ladybug pj's and bare feet. Vulnerable in a way she almost never was. And that appealed to him.

Not that he wanted her to be weak. He just wanted her to let him in occasionally.

"Insomnia, huh?" he prodded, willing her to say more.

"I've had it on and off for years. Mostly on. I can usually cope with it pretty well."

"And sleeping on the sofa helps?" he asked doubtfully.

"A little. The doctor said I shouldn't sleep on my back. Apparently it restricts the flow of blood to the placenta. So, when I do fall asleep, every time I roll over, I wake up, afraid I've rolled onto my back. At least on the sofa there's nowhere to roll. But it's less comfortable, so I still have trouble falling asleep. Unfortunately, a lot of the things I usually do to relax, you can't do when you're pregnant."

"Like drinking a glass of wine?"

She smiled. "I was thinking more along the lines of taking a hot bath. That usually helped. But I'm not supposed to raise my body temperature above 102 degrees. So the hot bath is out."

Into his mind popped an image of her soaking in the bathtub, surrounded by bubbles, hair piled high on her head, skin silky and moist, gleaming in the flickering light from a nearby candle.

He shoved the image aside and cleared his throat. This was not the time to be fantasizing about Kate. That tended to lead to wanting Kate. And wanting Kate was what had scared her off the last time.

Now that she'd finally started to relax around him again, he didn't want to screw this up. He wanted to do the right thing. To be helpful, damn it.

"There's gotta be something you can do to help you relax enough to sleep. Back when I was fighting fires, I'd come home from the job all keyed up from the adrenaline. I wouldn't be able to sleep."

Her lips curved into one of her rare smiles. "Well, I did blow out a candle earlier. But that's hardly the same thing."

He smiled. "You're into the second trimester, right?"

"This is my nineteenth week, so yeah."

"Isn't that when women are supposed to feel all energetic? Clean a lot or something?"

"Right. Nesting. It's when women are supposed to go through the nesting stage."

"Exactly. Tonight when I saw Stew, he said Beth was driving him crazy. She'd reorganized every closet in the house and was having him paint everything that stood still."

She laughed. "I guess that explains why I got a message from her last week wanting to go through some old stuff of our adopted Mom's."

"So you're probably nesting, too. That's why you have so much extra energy."

"Right." Her smile faded. "Except, I have no nest. I mean, sure, I've got a house I could clean and paint and organize, but what's the point, really? I don't have a baby to get ready for."

Her tone sounded almost wistful, and before he could stop himself, he asked, "Having second thoughts?"

Her gaze darted to his. "About?"

"Do you want to keep the baby?"

"No." She shook her head. "Absolutely not," she said a bit too firmly. After a second she looked at him curiously. "You're not…"

"Not what?"

"Thinking *you* want to keep the baby, are you?"

"No. God, no." But even as he said the words he knew they weren't entirely true. Of course he'd thought about it. But what could a guy like him offer a kid that Beth and Stew couldn't? He took a moment to study Kate and he asked, "You're sure you're not—"

"Definitely sure."

"Good."

"Right." She nodded. But then she tilted her head to the side and studied him. "I know Beth and Stew have said they want us to at least consider it, but as far as I'm concerned, it's not even an option."

It wasn't any of his business, but he couldn't help saying, "Okay, I know why I'm not even considering it. I know how my own dad struggled to raise me alone. But what about you? Why are you so dead set against it?"

She shrugged. "Some women are mommy material. Some aren't."

"And you think you aren't?" he asked, because she sounded a little too sure of her answer. Who was she trying to convince? Him or herself?

"Isn't that rather obvious?" She didn't wait for him to answer, but shifted the conversation back to their previous topic. "I see your point about the nesting, though." Words poured out of her. It was her avoidance technique, he was beginning to recognize. Anything she didn't want to think about, she just talked through. "Let's face it, sitting on the bench all day isn't exactly a high-energy job. I guess I could use some of that nesting energy to do some reorganizing around here—"

She broke off when he chuckled.

Narrowing her gaze, she demanded, "What?"

He looked pointedly around the living room, gesturing to the perfectly fluffed pillows, the neat fan of this month's magazines and the woven basket that held the TV remotes. "I'm just wondering what exactly you'd organize. Maybe rearrange the DVDs by genre before alphabetizing them? Group the candles on the mantel by height instead of color?"

Her gaze got even squintier and he couldn't tell if she was annoyed with his teasing or trying not to laugh.

"Ah, come on, Katie, even you have to admit there's not a lot around here that needs organization."

She shrugged, pushed herself away from the doorjamb and moved toward him. "So, back when you were fighting fires, what did you do to relax? Besides get drunk and take bubble baths, I mean."

"Firefighters don't take bubble baths."

"That's a shame. You tough guys are really missing out on one of life's great pleasures."

Kate naked in a bathtub? Oh, man. One of life's great pleasures indeed.

He felt heat beginning to creep up the back of his neck just thinking about it. Man, he needed to change the subject. "I…um…"

Kate let out a bark of laughter. "I've embarrassed you."

"No, I—"

"I have, haven't I? Look at that—" she gestured toward his face "—you're blushing."

He was blushing?

He was really in trouble now. He certainly couldn't tell her that he wasn't blushing, just hot under the collar from thinking about her.

"I…um…" He fumbled for a suitable lie, but came up with nothing.

"Don't worry," she said, chuckling. "I won't tell anyone that the big tough arson investigator embarrasses so easily. And just at the thought of taking a bath. That's pretty funny." She cocked her head to the side as if something just occurred to her. "Unless it's because you really do take bubble baths."

"I don't take bubble baths."

"That must be it. You take bubble baths."

"I don't. Trust me."

"Okay." But her smug grin told him she didn't believe him at all.

"I don't," he insisted through gritted teeth.

"I believe you." She slanted him a mischievous look. "But just in case you're lying, don't worry. Your secret is safe with me."

He opened his mouth to respond, only to snap it shut again, his rebuttal left unsaid. Unless he really did want to tell her what he'd been thinking about, there was no point in protesting.

Still grinning like she knew his deepest secret, she said, "So, besides taking bubble baths, what do big tough firefighters do to relax after a fire?"

For him, the best way to come down off an adrenaline rush had always been sex. The release that came with a couple of hot sweaty hours in bed had always done the trick.

Of course, he hadn't always been in a position to use that form of relaxation. He was too smart to risk casual sex in this day and age. A trip to the local dive with the other guys was always his second choice. He'd never needed a third. Until now.

Now, he racked his brain trying to think of a suggestion.

"What about exercise?" he tossed out.

"Why do you think I've been going to the gym five times a week?"

"Not working, huh?"

"It helps me fall asleep, but inevitably I wake up after a couple of hours and I just can't get comfortable again. I usually end up out here on the sofa."

"With the TV on?"

"Usually."

"I can't believe that doesn't wake me up."

"I hate to break it to you, but you sleep like the dead."

"Must be my mattress. Anyone would sleep like the dead on it. It's one of those adjustable air-filled ones. It's really—" He grinned, suddenly remembering a childhood remedy for sleeplessness. "I've got it."

"Got what?"

"The trick to help you fall back asleep." He grabbed her hand and pulled her into the kitchen.

"What? You're going to feed me?"

"Better. I'm going to make you warm milk."

"Warm milk?" She stuck her tongue out. "Bleck."

He pulled out one of the chairs from the table and nudged her toward it. "Have you ever tried it?"

"No," she admitted.

"Trust me. You'll love it."

She crossed her arms over her chest. "It sounds gross."

He pulled a saucepan out of a cabinet and the milk from the fridge. "My mother used to swear by this stuff. She made it for me all the time when I was little." He poured about a cup of milk into the pan and cranked up the heat on the burner.

A few minutes later as the milk came to a simmer, he pulled the pot from the stove and poured the liquid into a mug. He brought the mug to where Kate was sitting at the table, but instead of drinking it there, she took the mug and returned to the living room where she curled up in the corner of the sofa. After a tentative sip, she nodded. "This is good."

As she drank, she appraised him in that serious way she had. "How old were you when she left?"

For a moment, he could only stare at her in surprise. "What do you mean?"

She shrugged. "I just assumed your mom left, because you said your dad raised you alone. Also, when you talked about how your parents met, you said she never forgave your father for being just a man, which implies their marriage ended badly. Just now you said she made this for you when you were little. So I assume she left when you were pretty young. It sounds like it was a pretty nasty breakup."

"What makes you say that?" He avoided her gaze, even though there wasn't a hint of condemnation in her voice.

"I've sat on the bench for more than four years now. You get used to reading the signs."

"The signs?"

"The signs of a marriage gone wrong. Of husbands and wives fed up with each other. Of children disappointed by their parents' behavior. Disappointed by life. After a while you can hear it in the tone of their voice. See it in their expression. They seem haunted."

She sounded so sad as she spoke. And beneath that sorrow was the faintest hint of pity.

He leaned forward, bracing his elbows on his knees

and templing his fingers as he met her gaze. "I'm not a child. Don't make the mistake of treating me like one."

She blinked as if surprised by the ferocity of his tone. But she didn't back down, and her gaze didn't waver from his. "I didn't say you were. But we never get over the disappointments we suffer as a child, do we? Not the big ones, at least. Those disappointments can feel like abandonment—say, if mother doesn't stick around when things get tough."

Just like that, she'd summed up his entire childhood in one easy convenient package. And frankly, it ticked him off.

He stood and paced to the fireplace. "Don't try to psychoanalyze me."

"I wasn't trying to. I was just—"

"I don't feel abandoned by my mother. She did what she had to do."

"Deserting her husband and child? That was what she *had* to do?"

Kate sounded so damn logical. So reasonable. So irritating.

"Dad made her miserable. I can't say I blame her. She married a man she thought was a hero. Turned out he wasn't."

"You mentioned he was injured on the job. Was that when she left?"

"Neither of them really got over his injury. Dad started drinking. He had bouts of depression."

"So she didn't just leave you. She left you with an incompetent parent. That's borderline criminal."

"She did what she had to do."

"I'm sure she did," she muttered in a voice heavy with sarcasm.

He spun around to face her. His tone came out harsher than he'd intended. "Let it go, Kate. My family's not on trial here."

Kate flinched at his words, instantly stirring his guilt. She tried to hide her emotions, downing the last of the milk, but he saw the flash of pain in her eyes.

"Well, I'm sure you're right. I don't know what I'm talking about." She stood, taking her mug with her. "Thank you for the milk. I'm feeling sleepy already."

"Kate, I didn't mean…"

In the doorway to the hall, she looked over her shoulder. "Good night, Jake."

And then she disappeared, leaving him standing in the living room, alone. Again.

Eight

She had lied to him. She was not sleepy. The milk did not help. And she lay awake for what felt like several more hours, staring out the window, trying to figure out where things had gone wrong.

As far as she could tell, their conversation had been going along quite nicely...until she stuck her big fat nose where it didn't belong.

"Sounds like you had a troubled childhood, Jake," she murmured to herself in a whiny voice. "Why don't you tell me all about it while I poke you with a sharp stick."

With a huff, she rolled onto her other side. Who did she think she was? His therapist?

She sighed, running her hand over the curve of her belly. She hadn't meant to be nosy. Hadn't meant to venture where she wasn't wanted.

She'd just thought to...to what? Offer absolution of some kind?

Guilt came along with resenting a parent. That parent could be the worst person in the world—irresponsible, immoral or abusive—and yet nothing could overcome a child's basic need to love his parents. And if that love eventually soured and faded, the child inevitably felt a certain amount of guilt.

She'd wrestled with those emotions herself for years before finally admitting that it was okay to be angry with her birth mother for abandoning them to the imperfect mercies of the Texas foster care system and with her adopted mom for loving Beth so much. Doing so had helped her finally make peace with her adopted mom. Though she'd never be as close to her as Beth was, at least they now talked occasionally. So often she saw those conflicting emotions on the faces of the children whose warring parents paraded them through her court.

Of course, making peace with her own emotions and pushing Jake to acknowledge his were two very different things. Perhaps it was for the best that he'd pushed back. After all, she was supposed to be maintaining her distance from him, not forging an emotional connection.

She thought of the baby growing within her. She was already so much more attached to this baby than she should be. Even though she had no intention of keeping the baby, part of her still yearned…for what? Some fairy tale ending in which she and Jake fell in love, decided to keep the baby and lived happily ever after?

The very thought was absurd. She'd learned long ago that happily ever afters weren't for her. The lesson she was taught by an uncaring mother and an impersonal social services system had only been reinforced by the men she'd dated. Men who'd found her independence annoying and her strong will troublesome. Jake would most likely be no different.

No, she'd learned long ago it was best to stand on her own two feet. To depend only on herself rather than on others. That was the only way to keep from getting hurt.

Yes, keeping her distance from Jake was crucial. Because the unseen bonds between them were already far too strong.

By the time morning rolled around, Kate was exhausted. Days of too little sleep, combined with nerves and the pregnancy, had worn her down. Still, she found herself unable to doze any longer. So she got out of bed around six, dressed, and headed for breakfast.

She stopped cold in the doorway. Jake sat at the kitchen table, the morning paper open in front of him, a mug of coffee cradled in one hand, a last bite of a croissant sitting on a plate.

Unsure if she was up for another confrontation, she eased back a step, hoping to sneak away unnoticed. But he raised his head and pinned her with his stare.

"You're up early."

Overcome by the sudden need to fidget, she had to make herself stand perfectly still. "So are you." She'd been sure that after his late night he'd still be in bed. Yet once again he surprised her.

"I figured you'd be up early. Since you've been having trouble sleeping." He motioned to the white paper bag in the center of the table. "I got you a whole wheat banana nut muffin. Giselle at the bakery said that's what you normally get."

The unexpected gesture warmed her. Last night she'd trampled all over his personal space—emotionally speaking—and yet this morning he'd still been thoughtful enough to get her breakfast.

Despite her promises to herself not to rely on him,

she couldn't bring herself to reject his peace offering. So she pulled out the chair across from his and tugged the bag toward her.

She tore the bag down the side and spread the paper out before her as a makeshift plate. To her surprise, she found not just the whole wheat banana nut muffin, but a chocolate raspberry croissant, as well.

Before she could protest, he jumped up to get her a glass of milk. "I didn't know what you were in the mood for," he said as he also handed her a plate.

As she stared at the choices before her, her self-control wavered. The whole wheat banana nut muffin was indisputably the right choice. The healthy choice. Better for her, better for the baby.

But she yearned for the chocolate raspberry croissant…as completely devoid of nutritional value and as laden with calories and fat as it was. Just looking at it made her taste buds prickle and her stomach growl.

She felt as if every emotional battle she'd waged in her life came down to this. What she knew was best versus what she desperately wanted.

In the end she knew she'd do what she always did. The right thing. Because if she didn't make the right choice, she certainly couldn't trust anyone else to do so, either. And this time, more than her own wants and needs were at stake. She was making this choice for the baby, as well.

With one last look at the croissant, she put the muffin on her plate and carefully wrapped the paper bag around the croissant.

She peeled back the paper on the muffin and tore off a bite. As she popped it in her mouth, she noticed Jake smiling.

"What?"

He shook his head wryly. "Somehow I knew you'd pick the muffin."

"There's caffeine in chocolate."

"Not much more than there is in your decaf coffee," he pointed out.

"The muffin is still the better choice. Whole wheat, protein from the nuts and even a little fruit. Lots of nutrients the baby needs."

"Sure." He nodded.

"You disagree?"

"Not at all. That's very logical. You're taking this surrogate mother thing very seriously."

"Of course I am," she admitted. "This is a huge responsibility."

"And you feel like you have to do everything just perfect."

"You say that like it's a bad thing." And then, because she didn't want to sound defensive, she added lightly, "Besides, I'm the only one who can."

"Well, sure, but…"

"But…" she prodded.

He held up the last bite of his own croissant. "But sometimes you have to spoil yourself. Just a little."

As she watched, he placed that last bite in his mouth. She could just imagine how it tasted. The sweet chocolate, the lingering tartness of the raspberries. The way the flakes of croissant would practically melt on her tongue.

By comparison, her muffin tasted dry and bland. No contrast. No depth. No decadence.

An unexpected wave of sadness hit her. Usually she liked banana nut muffins. She'd eaten them for breakfast without complaint for years.

Now she wondered if she'd ever enjoy one again.

Resolutely, she took another bite of the muffin and

forced herself to chew and swallow. After washing down the bite with a gulp of milk, she said, "I wanted to—"

"About last night—"

Laughing, Jake ducked his head, looking up at her from beneath his lashes. "You go first."

Kate felt the power of that glance deep in her belly. There was a rueful, almost bashful, gleam in his eyes that was way more appealing than his usually wicked charm. Which was saying a lot, since she often found his usually wicked charm pretty dang hard to resist.

Determined not to make a fool of herself if she could avoid it, she sucked in a deep breath and dove head-first into her groveling. "I wanted to apologize for last night. I didn't mean to pry into matters none of my business."

There was more she wanted to say, so she stuffed a chunk of muffin in her mouth to quiet herself.

"It's funny." He took a sip of his coffee. "I was going to apologize for being so defensive. I guess I'm just not used to talking about her."

"Well, most people have decent relationships with their moms. And if you do, it's hard to imagine a mom who's a little more difficult to get along with."

"Actually, we have a pretty good relationship now."

Her eyebrows shot up and she eyed him with doubt. "You have to have some lingering anger toward your mother."

"I don't." He shrugged with a nonchalance she didn't buy. "I did when I was young, but we get along fine now."

"So your mother abandoned you and you've just… what? Just forgiven her?"

"Yes. Why is that so hard for you to believe?"

She pushed back her chair, snatched up the remains of her breakfast and took them to them trash can. "It just is, okay?" She stomped on the foot lever that popped the top to the can and dumped her trash inside.

As the lid clanged closed, she realized how snappish she sounded. What a way to apologize.

She turned back to face him and leaned against the counter behind her. "I only meant that if you do have any lingering resentment, it'd be best to admit it. Parents are imperfect, too. It's okay to be angry with them."

He leveled his gaze at her. "Kate, it's also okay to forgive them."

Ah, so they weren't talking about just his mother anymore.

"What's that supposed to mean?" she asked, even though she suspected she knew exactly what he meant. His appraisal was too intense for her to miss his implication.

"You've never even tried to make peace with your mother, have you?"

"Make peace with her? No. Sorry. I can't make peace with what she did."

"Still—"

"The state took us away when Beth was ten and I was eight. Mom didn't even protest. Never tried to get us back." A sarcastic laugh struggled past her lips. "Maybe you think I should be grateful. Maybe letting us go was the best thing she ever did for us."

Jake just eyed her with what she was sure was pity. "All these years later and you're still letting the way she treated you affect your life."

"And I suppose now you're going to point out that Beth has handled this whole thing so much better than I have. That she—miraculously—has overcome all the hardships of our childhood, made peace with our mother's actions and learned to trust again."

"No," he said quietly. "I wasn't going to say any of that. This isn't about Beth. It's about you."

Suddenly her exhaustion caught up with her and she slumped against the counter. God, she hated it when she felt like this. Angry and bitter. Not just at her mother, but at everyone involved in her upbringing. All the overworked caseworkers who didn't have the time to do their jobs properly. All the foster parents who'd judged and found her lacking.

Sometimes—she was most ashamed to admit—she was even angry with Beth, who'd seemed to have such an easier time being shuttled from foster house to foster house. Who'd instantly been everyone's favorite and who seemed never to feel unwanted.

She forced herself to hold his gaze. "I guess you're right. It's not about Beth. But…"

"But…" he prodded.

"But sometimes I wish I was more like her. She coped with things differently than I did. Plus, our experiences have been different. She and Stew met and fell in love so young. For most of her life, she's had him to depend on. To trust. I've never had that." Uncomfortable with the personal turn of the conversation, she looked away.

God, she didn't want him to think she was fishing for something from him, so she forced an upbeat tone into her voice. "I've always been very self-reliant. That's the way I like it. I'm the one person I know I can always trust."

The smile she gave him felt tight. His gaze seemed to pierce right through her forced cheer, and she had to turn away from him to hide.

Rinsing her breakfast dishes proved the perfect diversion. But when she was done, she turned to find Jake standing right behind her.

Before she could protest, he pulled her gently to his

chest. Stroking her hair, he murmured. "There's nothing wrong with the way you've coped with things. You're strong and brave. And that's admirable. But you're not alone anymore. I'm here to help. You can trust me."

His arms felt so good around her. So strong and capable. His chest was solid beneath her cheek. His shoulders broad. Her eyes drifted closed, and she allowed herself to lean against him. He seemed so solid. So dependable. So much what she'd always wanted and never allowed herself.

Oh, how she wanted to believe him. To pretend, just for a few minutes, that he could share her burdens. That his presence in her life wasn't temporary.

He meant well, but in the end he was like that chocolate raspberry croissant. A temptation she didn't dare allow herself to enjoy.

Nine

By the time Kate arrived home Friday evening, Jake had already left for work and wouldn't return until after midnight. Normally he worked the day shift four days a week, but tonight he was covering for a buddy on vacation.

She wandered restlessly through the house, amazed that she'd become accustomed to his presence. Even though they rarely spent time together, she'd gotten used to having him around.

What would it be like once this was all over with and he left for good? She'd have neither him nor the baby to keep her company. The thought made her inexplicably sad.

No matter how many times she reminded herself that neither Jake nor the baby were hers to keep, she couldn't help wishing... *Wishing what*? the more logical part of her mind scoffed.

Keeping the baby was out of the question, no matter what she secretly yearned for. As for keeping Jake, what would be the point? She'd been independent her entire adult life. She relied on no one but herself for her happiness, and that was the way she wanted it. It was the only way to ensure she'd never be let down, never be hurt. She'd had more than enough of that during her childhood.

Still, she couldn't help wondering what it would be like if they were a different sort of newlywed couple.

Undoubtedly, she'd wait up for him. Plan some romantic encounter for when he got home after work. Pull out the lingerie she'd bought before the wedding and spend the evening relaxing in a tub scented with exotic oils. Or maybe she'd retire early after planning a romantic breakfast in bed for him the next morning.

Kate felt a slight throbbing deep in her gut in response to the images her mind had conjured. She would do none of those things, and the evening stretched endlessly before her.

Around eight, she opened the fridge, planning to make herself a grilled cheese sandwich, only to find a casserole dish with a note from Jake taped to the lid.

Don't worry, it's good for you. Lasagna with lots of veggies and whole wheat pasta. Maybe you'll eat the chocolate croissant for dessert.

She smiled. Like this morning, she couldn't bring herself to reject his peace offering. Besides, what he'd prepared was much better for the baby than the grilled cheese she would have made. So she nuked the lasagna in the microwave and ate it at the kitchen table with a glass of milk while reviewing papers. By the time her plate was clean and the last of her work seen to, fatigue settled over her like a heavy blanket.

She tried to nap on the sofa, but couldn't get comfortable. Her own bed was worse, inexplicably both lumpy and hard. Then she remembered what Jake had said about his mattress.

It helped him sleep like the dead.

She grabbed the pillows from her bed and marched down the hall to his room.

She stood in the doorway for a long moment just staring at his bed. She hadn't been in this room since he moved in, and somehow the changes surprised her.

His king-size bed was huge. He hadn't made the bed that morning, so the thick navy comforter remained pulled back, revealing cream-colored sheets beneath. A heavy dresser lined one wall and a chair sat in a corner, both draped in discarded clothes. The room looked...comfortably messy. Lived in. This was most definitely *his* space. And *she* was invading it.

She'd never dream of doing something like this, if she didn't need some decent sleep so desperately.

Just a few hours of decent sleep and she'd sneak back to her own bed.

Jake wouldn't be home for hours. He'd never know. After all, with her recent sleep patterns, she'd be awake long before he got home, to sneak back to her own bed.

She slid between his sheets. They were soft, worn from years of use, and they felt good against the skin of her arms and legs, left bare by the tap pants and camisole she wore—the last of her prepregnancy pajamas that still fit.

After propping her own pillows against her back, she curled into a ball on her left side and burrowed her face into his pillow. With every breath, she inhaled the scent of him, crisp and clean, with a slight hint of masculine muskiness.

And for the first time in weeks—maybe months— she relaxed into sleep.

* * *

When Jake pulled into the driveway a little past midnight, not a single light shone through the windows.

Inside, the house was quiet and Kate's bedroom door was closed. He could only hope she was finally getting some sleep.

Not wanting to wake her, he crept into the kitchen to make himself a sandwich. To his delight, he saw that Kate had eaten the lasagna he made for her dinner. But not the croissant. Well, at least he was making some progress.

He took a quick shower to rinse off the grime from sifting through the remains of the fire, and planned to read a little of his Dean Koontz book in bed before calling it a night.

Only, when he walked into his bedroom, a bath towel wrapped around his waist, he found a Kate-size lump in the center of his bed and realized reading wasn't going to be an option.

"Looks like someone's been sleeping in my bed," he murmured.

He crept closer, to get a better look. She was curled into a ball on her side, her fist tucked under her chin, like an infant. Her inky hair spilled across his pillow. Her bare shoulder and the thin strap of something silky and decadent, were visible above the sheets.

His resolve to keep his distance seemed suddenly doomed.

She was his wife.

She was carrying his baby.

And she was asleep in his bed.

The same bed he'd lain awake in countless nights thinking about her. Trying to piece together the puzzle of Kate. And—if he was honest with himself—wanting her.

And all she wanted was a good night's sleep.

He couldn't give her even half the things he wanted to, but he could give her that, at least.

As quietly as he could, he pulled a pair of boxers and sweat shorts from the dresser drawer. With his back to her, he yanked them on. He was creeping to the door when she made a cute little sniffling noise in her sleep, followed by a soft moan. He spun to look at her, waiting to see if she'd woken.

She wasn't fully awake, but as soon as she started to roll onto her back, her eyes flew open. When she spotted him standing at the foot of the bed, she sat bolt upright, clutching the sheet to her chest.

"I…I…"

He held his hands palms out to calm her. "It's okay."

"No, it's not." She swung her legs over the side of the bed, but she must have still been groggy and lightheaded, because she never made it to standing. "I didn't… I'm so embarrassed." She propped her elbows on her knees and buried her face in her hands. "I thought you wouldn't be home for hours."

She looked so adorably flustered, he couldn't resist comforting her. So against his better judgment, he rounded the bed to sit by her side.

"Hey, it's okay."

She peered at him through the cracks in her fingers. "What time is it?"

He glanced at the clock beside his bed, which apparently she hadn't seen. "A little after one."

She curled her fingers in so her chin was propped in her palms. "I slept for four hours. How is it possible I'm still tired?"

Her hair hung mussed about her face, with one heavy lock draped in front of her eyes. Almost of their own volition, his fingers rose to brush aside that lock of hair. "It's been how many days since you had a decent night's sleep?"

She scrubbed a hand across her face and sat up straighter. "Quite a few. Weeks, maybe." She stood, swaying slightly on her feet. "I guess I'll head back to my own bed."

For some reason he just couldn't pin down, he didn't want to let her do that. He grabbed her wrist. "Wait."

Her skin was warm and he could have sworn he felt her pulse leap under his fingers. You should stay here," he said.

Her eyes widened and she pulled her wrist from his hand. Her gaze darted to his bare chest, and he would have sworn he saw a flash of awareness in her eyes.

Tempting as hell, but not exactly what he'd had in mind.

He leaped to his feet before he said or did something really stupid. "Look, obviously you slept better in here than you have in your own bed. It only makes sense for you to sleep the rest of the night in here. It's just for tonight. You'll feel better in the morning."

He took her hand again and tugged her gently toward the bed. To his surprise she let him. The second she sat down on the bed, she seemed to relax.

"Where will you sleep?"

"I'll figure something out," he reassured her as he nudged her shoulder back.

She lay down, curling onto her side so that her back faced him.

"I won't be able to sleep," she muttered, her eyes already closed, the lines of fatigue on her face easing.

"Just give it a few minutes." He had the strongest urge to brush her hair back from her face, but leaned over her and murmured. "If you don't fall back asleep, you can get up and I'll take you dancing."

She chuckled, then sighed as she began to nod off. For a long moment he stood there, watching her. There was something so peaceful about watching someone sleep. So intimate. In that moment, he was seeing a side of her few people ever saw.

With a sigh of his own, he crept to the chair in the corner to retrieve one of the shirts draped across its back. He was reaching for the novel on his bedside table, when she started to roll over onto her back and once again jerked awake.

She blinked sleepily. "See, I told you I wouldn't fall asleep."

He sat down on the side of the bed and gave in to the urge to run his hand down her hair. "You were asleep. You just woke up when you nearly rolled over."

She groaned and buried her face against the pillow. "It's silly that I'm so worried about sleeping wrong, isn't it?"

"No."

She looked over her shoulder at him. "How long was I asleep this time?"

"Not long enough."

Then inspiration hit. He climbed into bed beside her and pulled her back against his chest so his body cradled hers.

"Jake!" she protested, trying to pull away from him.

"Shhh…it's okay," he murmured. "I'm just trying to help. You can't sleep because you're afraid of rolling over, right? Well, if I'm here, you won't roll over."

"But—"

"If you know you can't roll over, you'll be able to sleep."

She let out a puff of air. "Theoretically. But—"

"You can trust me." He chuckled to ease her fears,

even though there was nothing funny about having her body pressed against his. "I promise I won't take advantage of you."

"That's not what I'm worried about. No one would want to take advantage of a woman who's almost five months pregnant." She twisted to look at him over her shoulder. "But this is exactly the kind of intimacy we agreed it best we didn't share."

"I won't tell if you don't."

Again he smoothed her hair down with his palm and then, because he didn't know what to do with his hand, he rested it on her shoulder. She began to relax against him incrementally.

Just when he thought she'd fallen asleep, she said, "I'm just worried about doing everything right."

"I know you are." She tried so hard to make all the right choices for the baby. How could he help but admire that?

"I want…the baby…to be healthy and strong." She sounded as if she were struggling to stay awake. "I don't want…to disappoint Beth and Stew…. Or you."

He sucked in a breath, waiting to see if she'd say anything to explain that cryptic comment. But apparently she'd fallen asleep because she said nothing else.

Staring down at her, he couldn't help but be a little amazed. Until this moment he'd had no idea she was afraid of doing everything right. But wasn't that just like her? To keep her fears and concerns to herself?

He urged his body to relax, but found it impossible to do so. With her lavender-scented hair tickling his nose, her lush fertile body resting against his, and her warm round bottom nestled against his groin, it was all he could do to continue breathing regularly.

It was going to be a long night.

* * *

Kate woke feeling rested for the first time in weeks. Not just rested…secure. Safe. Completely at peace.

Slowly she became aware of her surroundings.

And of Jake nestled against her back.

The events of the previous night came rushing back. The embarrassment of being found sleeping in his bed, which just barely exceeded her embarrassment at being talked into staying there.

Oh, boy. This had not gone as planned.

The worst part was, she didn't immediately leap from the bed and preserve whatever dignity she had left. Lying next to Jake just felt too dang good.

With his chest cradling her back, his hand resting on her belly and the warm masculine scent of him surrounding her, whatever willpower she had possessed deserted her completely.

His breath, slow and even across her ear, sent tremors of pleasure radiating through her body and she just couldn't resist nestling deeper under the covers, closer to him.

Only then did she realize that the lean muscles of his chest and arms weren't the only parts of his body that were hard and unyielding. She felt a jolt of pure anticipation.

How long had it been since she'd woken up in a man's bed? Suddenly, it seemed like years. Geesh, maybe it was years. Long enough that she'd forgotten the intimacy that came from sleeping with another person.

Saturday-morning sex had always been her favorite. Slow and lazy. Relaxed almost. With no rush, no constraints on time. Just the steady building of passion and the ecstasy of release.

Before she could give in to temptation, she started

to pull away, but stilled when Jake's arm tightened over her belly.

"Don't go," he murmured against her ear.

She sucked in a breath. "You're awake?"

"Barely."

He sounded sleepy, but not just-woke-up sleepy. She twisted her head just enough to shoot him a suspicious look. "How long have you been awake?"

Propping himself up on an elbow, he looked down at her without removing his hand from her belly. "Long enough to feel you wake up."

He'd lain there beside her. His erection pressing against her buttocks, but saying nothing. Not even moving. Her pulse kicked up a notch. Was he as aroused as she was? Or was this just a standard physical response for him?

"And you didn't move?"

"I didn't want to wake you."

His answer was so simple. So logical.

Still, having him so close made her feel as if she could crawl out of her skin. "You should have—"

Just then the baby gave her a sharp jab, right under Jake's hand.

"Oh my God. Was that…?"

She again started to pull away from him. "I should really—"

He didn't let her get very far, but lassoed her with an arm and pulled her back to his side. Before she knew what was happening, he had her flat on her back and was pressing the side of his face as well as his hand to her stomach.

"You know—" she tried to protest.

"Shh," he said.

"It's not like you'll be able to hear her."

"Shh."

"I'm not supposed to be on my back like this."

"It's only for a minute," he said without moving his head.

Well, at least he wasn't shushing her anymore.

As much as she hated to admit it, he was probably right. A few minutes on her back couldn't do much harm. Which was kind of a shame, because she really could have used the excuse to get out from under him.

With his face pressed to her belly, she could feel the warmth of his breath through her camisole. And when she inhaled, she could feel the prickle of his unshaved cheek poking through the silky thin fabric.

His hand pressed low across her abdomen, his palm hot against her. Especially where the camisole didn't quite meet the top of her tap pants and he touched bare skin. If he lowered his hand just a few inches—five, maybe six, at most—he'd be touching her intimately. And her traitorous body wished desperately that he would.

It would be so easy to rock her hips up to his touch.

She sucked in a deep breath and squeezed her eyes closed. Boy, she hoped he couldn't hear the thundering of her heart. But how could he not? He wasn't deaf. Hoping to cover the sound, she said, "Jake, I really don't think this is—"

The baby gave another sharp kick, right to the spot where his cheek rested.

This time, they both sucked in deep breaths.

"I felt that." Awe laced his words. "I definitely felt that." Without moving his left hand from her belly, he raised up on his other elbow and looked at her. His goofy expression nearly took her breath away again. "Damn, that's something."

She could only nod in response.

"Was this the first time you felt her move?"

"No."

His smile faded. "And you didn't say anything?"

"I—" She bit down on her lip.

"How long have you felt her moving?"

"Three weeks. Maybe four. It's hard to say." His expression urged her to try, so she fumbled to explain. "At first it was so vague. I wasn't sure that's what I was even feeling. The doctor said it would feel like a fluttering. Like butterfly wings. But that's not what it felt like at all."

"What was it like? I mean, what is it like?"

He was staring at her so intently her throat nearly closed up on her. No one had ever looked at her so closely. Watched her with such an expression of curiosity. As if her next words would be the most important he'd ever hear.

"It's more like—" she struggled to put the sensation into words "—a twitch. Like a muscle spasm. Or maybe…" Then she hit on the perfect description. "Do you know the feeling when you're really nervous or you've been exercising really hard and you can feel your heart thundering in your chest?"

He nodded without taking his eyes from her face. His voice, when he spoke, was husky with emotion. "Yeah. I know what you mean."

For an instant her mind went completely blank and she lost herself in his gaze. Her entire existence seemed to shrink down to just him. Just this moment. Just his hand on her stomach, the look in his eyes, and the thundering of her heart.

Right…her thundering heart. The movement of the baby. That was what they'd been talking about.

She forced herself to finish her description, but her voice sounded breathless and weak. "That's what it's like. Like your heart beating against your ribs. But not rhythmic."

He looked back at her belly when the baby once again moved against his hand. "It's amazing."

"Yes." She nearly choked on the words. "It is amazing."

It truly was amazing. Not just the sensation of her baby moving inside her, but the way he'd looked at her.

No one had ever looked at her like that before. As if *she* was amazing. And she'd never in her whole life felt closer to another person.

She felt part of something far bigger and more important than any of the other things in her life—duty, justice, honor. Things she'd always thought of as so hugely important, but that seemed dwarfed by this baby and the connection it created between her and Jake.

It nearly broke her heart to think that this was all just an illusion. The connection she felt was not just frail; it was false.

Because the baby wasn't hers. And neither was Jake.

Ten

Kate had been distant from the moment she climbed out of his bed Saturday morning. She went out for breakfast and spent the day in her office. His only consolation was that she'd agreed to go to a barbecue with him on Sunday at a buddy's house. That would give him the whole day with her. A whole day full of excuses to hold and touch her.

When she finally did make it back to the house that night, she refused to sleep in his bed again. Even when he offered to take the sofa…which he thought was more than generous.

After several hours of staring at the ceiling, missing having Kate in his bed after only one night, Jake was finally almost asleep when he heard a low moan coming from Kate's room.

In an instant all his senses went to high alert and he was out of his bed and running down the hall.

Her door was shut. Without thinking, he twisted the knob at the same time he slammed his shoulder against the door. It flew open and ricocheted against the wall. He didn't bother searching for the bedroom light. There was no need. Light shone in through the window, revealing a tableau of Kate sitting up in bed bent over her leg. When he'd crashed through the door, she turned toward the noise, and now her face was clearly illuminated in the moonlight.

"What's wrong?" he asked frantically.

"Just a leg cramp," she said, turning her attention back to her leg.

Relief flashed through him. She wasn't sick. The baby was fine. Nothing was wrong.

Except that she was in pain. The thought pulled him to her side.

"Let me help." He lowered himself to the edge of her bed.

"I've got it," she muttered, trying to wiggle away from him. But her movements must have made the cramp worse, because she winced noticeably and reached again for her leg.

He blocked her hands with his palm. "Let me help."

She eyed him warily in the near dark but finally relented, leaning back onto her elbows, granting him free access to her leg.

He'd had leg cramps before and knew they could be painful, so he moved slowly. Taking the heel of her foot in one hand, he ran his other down the length of her calf. He gently massaged the tense muscles, willing himself to focus on the task, rather than the length of bare leg exposed to him.

He could go on forever touching her skin…sitting in her bed. If he thought for even a minute that she'd let him.

As much as he wanted to lose himself in the pleasure

of touching her, he tried to restrain his reaction. He was a certified EMT. He should have been able to detach himself from the situation. But he couldn't. Not with her. Not when he'd spent all day wanting her. Resisting her. Not when he'd spent all day wanting her. He just wasn't that strong. No man was.

His thumb found a particularly hard knot. As he tried to loosen it, she groaned. The sound was low and guttural and threatened his willpower.

But it also brought him back to his senses. She was in pain, not turned on.

He looked up at her face, trying to read her expression, but her eyes were closed, her head tilted back, exposing the length of her arched neck. "Too hard?"

Her head came up and her eyes blinked open. "No. It feels good."

"I'm going to try to stretch the muscle, okay?"

She nodded, her eyes wide.

Watching her carefully for signs of pain, he grasped the ball of her foot and slowly flexed. Her expression didn't even flicker. If she was in pain, she wasn't showing it.

He couldn't help but admire how tough she was. So independent, so sure of herself, so determined. Qualities he never thought about wanting in a wife. But he was glad she had them.

He flexed her foot several more times until he felt the knot beneath his thumb loosen and dissolve.

"Better?"

She nodded. "I'm sorry I woke you."

"Don't apologize. And don't pretend this isn't much harder on you than it is on me."

Even though the cramping had stopped, he couldn't seem to make himself release her leg. The soft spot just behind her knee was too tempting. He kept expecting her to pull her leg away from his touch, but she didn't.

Her lips curved into a half smile. "Well, maybe a little harder."

He shifted his weight, moving closer to her on the bed. As he did, his hand slipped from her calf to just above her knee. With his free hand, he brushed aside the lock of hair that had fallen into her eyes.

There were a thousand things he wanted to tell her. How beautiful she looked in the moonlight. How tempting her skin felt. How enticing she smelled. How much he wanted to kiss her.

How he'd wanted to kiss her all day.

Before he let any of those things slip, he forced himself to remember his past mistakes. Even the slightest nudge, and she'd scamper in the other direction.

So he shoved aside all the things he wanted to say and instead said the one thing he didn't think would spook her. "Has the baby been moving?"

"She's been a little active today. But I feel her more at night."

"You keep referring to the baby as a 'her.' Has the doctor—"

"No. It's just a gut feeling."

They were so close. In the half light from the moon, he saw her eyes widen. He heard her soft intake of breath. He wanted desperately to kiss her but knew he couldn't. She'd set out strict ground rules for their marriage.

For the first time in his life, alone with a beautiful woman in her bedroom he found himself wishing they were in a crowded place.

He forced himself to withdraw his hands and lean back. Now, if only he could force himself to return to his room. But, hey, he wasn't a saint.

Before he could chastise himself any more, she surprised him by asking, "What were you thinking just now?"

He surprised himself even more by answering. "I was wishing we were in public. If we were, I'd have an excuse to kiss you."

She leaned forward, her gaze dropping to his mouth. "You've never seemed like the kind of man who needs an excuse to do what he wants."

Hell, he had a hundred reasons to break the rules. And only one reason not to. If he did, he'd lose her. That was the one thing he wasn't willing to risk.

Still, there was a hint of invitation in her eyes. But how could he take advantage of her? How could he destroy the trust they'd only just started to build?

He stood, putting some distance between them. "Don't tempt me, Kate."

She stiffened. "I don't know what you mean."

"Sure, you do. You made me promise this would be only a business arrangement. No intimacy. Those were your rules."

Defiance flashed in her eyes as she met his gaze. "So?"

"If you want to change the rules, then *you* have to change them. I won't break them for you."

But, damn, he wanted to.

So much so that he continued to stand there, watching her, when he knew he should leave. Before he went back on his word and did exactly what he'd sworn he wouldn't do.

She swung her legs over the side of the bed and stood. "What if I want to change the rules?"

His heart started pounding in his chest. Urging him to kiss her. To make her his.

It'd be so easy to give in to his heart. But impossible to justify to his conscience.

Unless he was sure this was what she really wanted.

"They're your rules. You're the only one who can change them."

He was right, of course. They were her rules. She was the one who'd insisted there be no intimacy between them. He was just following the guidelines she'd set out for them. And, frankly, it was annoying the hell out of her.

Was it too much to ask—really?—that he just sweep her into his arms and kiss her senseless? Would that really be so hard on him?

For once in her life, she didn't want to think. Didn't want to be the responsible one. Didn't want to have to make a decision.

She knew he desired her. Felt it in his touch and every look. But she wanted more than just desire. She wanted complete and total surrender. She wanted him to be unable to resist her.

There were a hundred ways they were wrong for each other. She wanted them to be right for each other in this one way.

Slowly she stood before him, close enough that she could see his eyes dilate, even in the dim lighting. Close enough to see the individual hairs scattered across his bare chest. Close enough to smell the warm, masculine scent of him. The same scent that had permeated his pillow the night before.

Was it so wrong to want this?

It didn't feel wrong. In fact, nothing had ever felt more right. What could be more right than making love with the father of her child? What could be more natural?

That thought drummed through her mind as she worked up the courage to raise her hand to his cheek. She could feel the pulse at his temple thundering beneath her fingertips. His heart seemed to beat in the

same crazy rhythm as her own. One thump for anticipation, one for fear. One for pure desire.

As her hand slipped down to cup his jaw, she reveled
in the coarse prickle of hair against her palm. Hoping
to tempt him into submission, she stood on tiptoe and
raised her lips to his.

But he stubbornly pulled away. "Don't do this, Kate."

"Don't do what?" Unable to reach his lips, she
pressed her mouth to his jaw. "Don't do this?"

His skin was hot. The stubble of his beard rough
against her lips. She couldn't resist trailing her lips
down the enticing column of his throat. "Or don't do
this?"

There was something heady about the faint saltiness of
his skin. About the feel of his pulse thundering beneath
her lips. Feeling off balance and a little dizzy, she plastered her palms to his naked chest, thrilling at the sensation of his muscles clenching beneath her touch. "Or this?"

He stared down at her with such intensity. Such restrained power.

Honestly, she couldn't have said what appealed to her
more. His sheer strength or the control he maintained
over it.

She only knew, in that instant, that his personality
was far stronger than she'd previously realized. His
laid-back, casual attitude had fooled herself into under-
estimating his strength of will.

That strength spoke to her in a way she never would
have predicted. She was drawn to his strength and power.
Wanting—somewhat desperately—to be *his* weakness.

"Why shouldn't we give in to what we both want?"
she asked.

He clamped his hands over hers, stopping their
progress. "Because it's the middle of the night. People

do stupid things at 3:00 a.m. They don't think right. They're not logical. They make mistakes."

His arguments were certainly reasonable. But she heard the faint tremor in his voice. The underlying roughness that told her she affected him more than he wanted to admit.

"You're right," she admitted, but pressed on before he could assume she was admitting defeat. "Sometimes people do stupid things in the middle of the night. But sometimes they do brave things. Bold things. Things they'd never have the courage to do in broad daylight."

Much to her chagrin, he chuckled. "Katie, you're the last woman I can imagine needing to bolster her courage."

"Just shows you how good I am at faking it." The admission seemed to lift a weight off her shoulders, so she continued, "I've spent too many months worried about making mistakes. But the one mistake I won't let myself make is being too stubborn to admit I was wrong.

"I know I said I wanted no intimacy between us. I know I insisted on that, but I was wrong. I didn't know how hard it would be to live with you. I never imagined how much I'd want you."

That admission seemed to do the trick. In an instant he went from hard and unyielding to completely at her mercy. She saw the acquiescence in his eyes. Felt it in his touch.

This time, when she stood on her toes to kiss him, he lowered his mouth to hers.

She marveled at the mastery of his kiss. How the simple act of pressing his mouth to hers made her blood pulse and desire quicken in her belly.

As soon as he released her hands, she wrapped her arms around his neck, eagerly pressing her body to his. Just a thin layer of fabric separated them, but it felt like too much. As if he read her mind, his hands moved to the hem of her nightshirt. For a second his fingers merely toyed with the edge, tempting her. Teasing her. But then his hand slipped beneath the hem to her hip. His fingers were rough against her already sensitized skin, eliciting a moan from deep within her.

She grew impatient with his gentle coaxing. She wanted his hands on her—all over her—now.

She grasped the hem of her shirt and pulled her mouth from his long enough to yank the offensive garment over her head.

He stepped back, and for an instant she feared he would leave. But his expression told her he had no intention of going anywhere. He merely studied her.

She felt a curious blossoming of pride. His gaze was heated with desire. His expression taut with barely restrained control. He wanted her and made no attempt to hide it.

"Oh, man, you're beautiful." His words were low and rough. And soft, almost as if he hadn't really meant to say them aloud.

He reached out a finger to trace the curve of her breast. She could have sworn there was a slight tremble in his hand as his finger moved down the slope of her breast to circle the nipple.

Her breasts were so tender that when he finally cupped her in his hands, she groaned aloud with a pleasure so intense it was almost painful.

Instantly his hands stilled. "Too much?"

She shook her head. His touch was far too gentle to cause pain. Far too cautious. "Perfect," she gasped. "Just perfect."

There were so many things she wanted to tell him. How she'd dreamed of this moment. Ached for it. How she'd lain awake in her bed, not just because she couldn't sleep, but because she wanted him there with her. Touching her just like this.

He sat on the edge of the bed and pulled her toward him to stand between his legs. At first he merely nuzzled her breasts, licking lightly at her nipples. Testing her endurance. Unable to take any more of his teasing, she ran her fingers through his hair and urged his mouth to her.

As if he read her mind, he clamped his lips down on her nipple, sucking it fully into his mouth. Pleasure spiked through her so intense her knees nearly gave out. Clutching his shoulders, she leaned into him to keep her balance. Soon, even this intense pleasure wasn't enough for her. She wanted—no needed—to feel him inside of her. Needed him to ease the ache that pulsed between her legs.

But she wouldn't beg.

So instead, she took control.

Pushing against his shoulders, she urged him back onto the bed. After slipping out of her panties, she climbed on his lap.

For a moment she had to close her eyes against the pleasure of it. His erection straining against his pajama bottoms pressed into the folds of skin between her legs. The sensation brought momentary relief to her aching flesh. But it lasted only a heartbeat before her desperation redoubled.

She brought her mouth down to his. Into that kiss she poured all the need she wouldn't allow herself to voice. She didn't just want him. She wanted to drive him crazy. She wanted him as out of control as she felt. No, more out of control.

She moved her hands across his chest, reveling in the tensing of hard muscles and the pounding of his heart. But she didn't linger there. Instead she sought the waistband of his pants. Sensing her intention, he raised his hips off the bed long enough to slip the pants down to his thighs.

She didn't give him a chance to do more than that, but immediately sank down to press against his bare skin.

His erection was hot, like the insistent pulsing between her legs. She didn't even try to resist the urge to rub herself against his length, arching her back and neck as she lost herself in the moment of pleasure.

Jake grabbed her hips, stilling her movement. "Wait," he gasped. His voice was deep, his expression taut with desire.

"Too much?" she asked.

"Perfect. Just perfect," he said, echoing her words. "But too perfect. I want to be inside you." He started to roll out from under her. "I think I have a box of condoms somewhere in my—"

Planting her hands firmly on his shoulders, she held him in place. "No need. I'm already pregnant and we were both tested for everything before—" An uneasy stab of something like jealousy hit her square in the chest. "Unless, since then you've—"

"No. I haven't been with anyone else since then."

She knew he hadn't been with anyone since they married, but four months had passed from when he had donated to when they had married. Anything could have happened in those four months.

She leaned over him, mere inches from his face, looking directly into his eyes. His gaze held not even a flicker of deception.

She wanted to believe him. Her gut and intuition—not to mention her years of experience looking into people's eyes to ascertain if they were lying—told her she could trust him.

But a lifetime of being cautious kept her from taking that leap.

She rolled off him to dig through the drawer of her nightstand and pull out a condom. As she tore it open, she met his gaze. Only the slightest hint of an emotion flickered through his eyes, but it was gone before she could even begin to guess how he felt. Holding up the condom, she asked, "Have I ruined the mood?"

Holding her breath, she waited for his answer. And for a second she thought he might not respond. But then he sat up.

Wrapping one arm around her waist, he pulled her to him and brought his mouth to hers.

The kiss was long and deep, like an intimate invasion of her very soul. When he drew back to meet her gaze, she saw no condemnation in his eyes.

"You're a smart woman, Katie. You're independent and strong and very passionate about what you believe in. That's what I admire most about you. So, no. You haven't ruined the mood. I wouldn't expect anything less."

Seconds later, after easing the condom down his length, she lowered herself onto him. The sensation was so intense her head dropped back as she gasped out his name. She felt so completely filled by him.

When he brought his mouth to her breast, all thought fled her mind, including her plan to drive *him* wild. Instead she met him thrust for thrust, each one driving home what he'd said: that he admired her strength. Her passion. Her.

Then every molecule of her body tightened, only to expand a moment later in wave upon wave of pleasure. And in that moment, she'd known only the intense release of her orgasm. And that he'd been right there with her.

Eleven

"You don't think I look too pregnant?"

As Jake pulled up to the stoplight on the way to the barbecue, he slanted a glance in Kate's direction. She was dressed in denim Capri pants—which he could only assume she'd bought as a concession to their discussion about jeans. Her pregnancy was hidden beneath an oversize white linen shirt, which she wore open over a bright red T-shirt, the sleeves rolled up to her elbows. Her hair fell in loose waves about her shoulders. Other than her pinched, nervous expression, she looked gorgeous.

It was all he could do not to turn the car around, take her home and spend all day making love to her. Man, oh, man, how he wanted to do that.

How could he want her again so soon? How could he want her at all, when she was so much the opposite of everything he normally wanted in a woman?

But he did want her. Desperately. This wasn't mere

sexual desire. This was something more. Something he'd never felt before.

He'd known it the instant he stared into her eyes and promised her he hadn't been with anyone else. In that moment he'd wanted her to believe him. To trust him.

And though he didn't blame her for not doing so, something inside him had broken when she'd reached for the condom.

The light changed and he accelerated again. "You look fine. You have nothing to be nervous about."

"Right," she muttered, her hands clenched around the bowl of salad she held in her lap. "Big work-related picnic. All your friends will be there. Nothing to worry about."

Well, he kept wishing she'd show more vulnerability. He just never would have imagined it'd be over this. "Everyone's going to love you."

She let loose a very un-Kate-like snort of disbelief. "I doubt that."

"You met a couple of these people at the wedding and a lot of the guys when they came to help me move. They liked you fine then."

"It's just that I—" she exhaled a puff of nervous breath "—I don't always make a good first impression."

When he glanced in her direction, she was looking at him with a sort of desperate need for affirmation. He tried to inject his voice with the right amount of disbelief. "Really?"

She rushed on nervously, "Beth says she thinks I come off as cold and unemotional. She thinks it makes people nervous and that—" Her expression turned suspicious. "Were you being sarcastic?"

"No."

Damn, he hoped she believed him. He hadn't meant

to sound sarcastic, but he remembered the first time they'd met, at Beth's and Stew's rehearsal dinner. She'd looked beautiful, but at the same time so coolly professional, so completely unemotional, he'd faked shivering for comic effect after they were introduced.

He never would have dreamed that beneath that icy competence lay such a sweet and endearing woman. Or such a passionate one.

"Don't worry. I'll be right there with you. You'll do fine. Just relax, be yourself, and have fun."

Her frown eased slightly. "Are you sure we have to go?"

He couldn't help chuckling at the gleam of hope in her eyes. "It's just a barbecue. Nothing to be afraid of. The Andersons host this every year and I haven't missed one yet."

"But you could go by yourself," she suggested for about the hundredth time.

"Sure, I could," he admitted, trying not to sound irked that she wasn't jazzed about spending the day with him. "But we agreed that would look strange, remember?"

"And I don't look too pregnant?" She waved aside his laughter with an impatient fluttering of her hands. "I know we have to start telling people soon. But I figure the fewer people who know I'm pregnant, the less confusing it'll be when we get divorced and Beth and Stew take the baby." A pained expression crossed her face. "I guess this is going to be confusing no matter how I look. For now, I just don't want your friends to think I trapped you into marrying me by getting pregnant."

"Well, I'm sure they won't. Mostly because it's not 1952. But also because you're gorgeous, smart and successful. If anything, they'll be wondering how I got *you* to marry *me*."

She dismissed his flattery with a roll of her eyes. "Why is it people are always telling pregnant women how beautiful they are? It's as if everyone's afraid our egos are so frail they might shatter under the weight of the pregnancy."

He looked at her as he turned onto the Andersons' street.

He had no idea why other people thought pregnant women looked beautiful. For that matter, he had no idea if other pregnant women were beautiful. All he knew was that Kate seemed to be positively glowing.

Maybe it was that she'd finally caught up on her sleep. Or maybe it was that she was carrying *his* baby.

But he suspected it had everything to do with the mind-blowing release he'd found in her arms last night. And waking up this morning to find her warm and aroused, ready to make love again.

Whatever the reason, she looked more beautiful to him today than any woman ever had.

She might be worried about impressing his friends. But the only thing worrying him was impressing her.

Just relax? Yeah, that was working.

Kate clenched a soda can in her hand and smiled past gritted teeth at the circle of women surrounding her. At least a dozen women—all wives of the men Jake worked with—had cornered her on the back deck. They'd gotten the expected barrage of questions about her and Jake out of the way early, and she only hoped she'd fielded the interrogation sufficiently. Now they were chatting about everyday things—their kids, school taxes, favorite TV shows.

She wasn't quite sure what to make of these women. They all seemed so…happy. Which, frankly, was outside her normal realm of experience. She kept looking for signs of buried resentments and repressed anger but saw none. These women seemed to love their husbands, adore their children and generally be content with their lives.

Kate was a good enough judge of character to know they weren't faking it. Which left her wondering how her view of the world had gotten so skewed. Had her years in the justice system made her so cynical about relationships? Goodness knows her childhood certainly hadn't helped matters, but surely she'd gotten over that by now. Hadn't she?

Her gaze automatically sought out Jake where he stood by the barbecue pit, drinking a beer and manning the hot dog rotation. She couldn't help remembering his words from the previous night. That he admired her strength and independence. Was it really possible that for the first time in her life, she found someone who didn't resent all the qualities she worked so hard to maintain?

Part of her wished he was here with her now, but maybe it was best he wasn't. The only thing worse than having him leave her at the mercies of all these women would be having him standing beside her, always touching her, distracting her to the point she hardly remembered her name, let alone all the details of their fake marriage.

What really drove her batty was not knowing if he kept touching her because he couldn't keep his hands off her or because he was just making sure all of his buddies bought into their marriage. Was his affectionate behavior today just another ruse to make the lie more convincing?

But every time he touched her, she practically trembled, remembering that morning and how wonderful it had felt to wake up in his arms.

Just when she thought she'd crunch her soda can in frustration, one of the women steered her away from the group, saying loudly, "You look like you could use another hot dog."

As they walked down the steps into the backyard, the woman leaned in closer and added, "Actually, you just looked like you could use a break."

Not sure how to respond, Kate mumbled an "I don't know what you mean" and hoped that would suffice.

"Oh, come on. The girls can be great, but this has got to be a little overwhelming for you," she babbled on good-naturedly without waiting for a response. "You've met probably fifty people or so. And everyone's so curious about you…Well, frankly, I'm surprised you haven't flipped out from the pressure. Just remembering the names alone would make me crazy. I bet you don't even remember my name."

"Ah…I…" But what could Kate say? She didn't remember the other woman's name.

"Lisa. Lisa Anderson."

"Ouch." Kate winced. "Forgetting the name of the hostess? That is bad, isn't it?"

Lisa laughed as they reached the buffet table set up under the sprawling live oak. "Don't worry about it. Easy mistake to make when you're trying to remember dozens of names. I only had to remember one name. Which was simple enough to do, since you're the guest of honor."

Kate stopped where she stood, but Lisa didn't notice and rambled on. "Let's see…there are plenty of hot dogs left. But if you want something else, I'd recommend the potato salad. Steer clear of that thing with noodles. I tried it earlier and it was nasty. Don't know who brought—" Just then Lisa turned and must have read Kate's alarm in her expression. "Oh dear, I've put my foot in it, haven't I? That's your dish with the noodles, isn't it?"

"No. I brought the salad." Though, in retrospect,

opening the bag of mixed greens seemed a meager contribution in light of the myriad of homemade goodies on the table. But that was the least of her worries. "I just…I didn't realize I was the guest of honor." To cover her discomfort, Kate grabbed a plate and spooned onto it a dollop of potato salad.

"Of course you are. We do this every time someone at the station gets married."

"Oh." No wonder Jake had been so insistent she come. "He said you did this barbecue thing every year."

"He probably just didn't want you to be nervous. Come to think of it, though, with all the guys that have gotten married, I guess it does average out to be about once a year. You know, it's kind of funny that Jake still comes to these at all."

"Why?"

Lisa forked some broccoli onto her own paper plate. "Well, he moved up to arson…what was that, two years ago now?" She didn't wait for Kate to answer, which was just as well, since Kate had no idea when Jake started working arson. "At the time, I told Bill he'd drift away from the station. New job, new friends. I figured he'd hang out with them on weekends."

Kate could only murmur noncommittally. It hadn't occurred to her that "the guys" Jake was always referring to weren't the guys he worked with anymore.

"Now that you mention it—" she squirted a line of mustard onto the hot dog Lisa had handed her "—I think I've only met one of the guys from the arson department. Someone named Todd who came to the wedding."

"And Todd—" Lisa held up a finger to emphasize her point "—used to work in the station. In fact, he's the one who recommended Jake move into arson once he'd made lieutenant. But that's Jake for you. He has tons of ambition—look at how quickly he moved up through the ranks—but he'd never let that get in the way of his friendships."

Kate could only nod in agreement. It had never occurred to her that Jake was relatively young for his position. Or that he'd made it to lieutenant before moving on to arson.

But she knew better than anyone how loyal and dependable he was. He'd do anything for a friend. Look what he'd done for her.

"Jake really is a good guy," Lisa was saying. "Which is why Bill and I are glad Jake *finally* found someone."

Boy, how could she respond to that without feeling like a fraud? Of course she'd felt like nothing but a fraud since she walked in the door. There was nothing she could say that would alleviate that.

"I…"

"Oh, I've embarrassed you," Lisa said, placing a concerned hand on Kate's arm. "I hope I didn't offend you. I told you I can really put my foot in it."

"No. Not at all," Kate hastened to reassure her. "It's understandable since Jake's not exactly the marrying kind." As soon as the words left her mouth, she realized her blunder and quickly added, "Before he met me, I mean."

Lisa laughed. "Is that what he told you? Boy, men have selective memories, don't they? He was always talking about how he wanted to get married."

Kate stilled, her hand poised over a tray of raw vegetables. "He was?"

"Well, sure. You know what Jake is like."

Kate forced a bright smile and nodded. If she wasn't more careful, Lisa would realize that in fact she did not know what Jake was like. And wouldn't that make for interesting station house gossip.

"Before you, he's always been drawn to women who were…" Lisa paused, obviously searching for a tactful end to her sentence.

Kate just held her breath, waiting. What kind of woman was Jake drawn to? "Women who are…" she prodded.

"Well—" Lisa made a funny face "—weak, I guess."

"Weak?"

"Women who dated him just because he was a firefighter. There are women like that out there, ya know?"

Kate still wasn't sure she did. "You mean groupies?"

Lisa shrugged. "Sure, there are women like that. But worse than that are the ones who date firefighters because they feel like they need to be rescued."

"Oh."

"Jake's such a good guy, he's always been vulnerable to that kind of woman. I guess maybe all firefighters are to some extent. They love being heroes. Thankfully most of them grow out of it pretty quickly."

"But not Jake?" Kate couldn't help asking, even though she was afraid she wouldn't like the answer.

Lisa smiled broadly. "Not until you." She continued to ramble while she filled her plate with foods, blissfully unaware of the chaos her words had caused inside of Kate.

Not until you.

By marrying her, Jake was rescuing her. As surely as if he'd rescued her from a burning building.

In his eyes she needed saving. Just like all the other women he was attracted to. Once this was all over with and her job was secure, he'd realize she didn't need to be rescued. And then where would their relationship be?

Kate tried to keep up her end of the conversation, but

inside, her heart was…well, not breaking—nothing that dramatic—but her heart was definitely crimping. And she couldn't figure out why.

Their marriage was a business arrangement. Nothing more.

That was the rule *she'd* set out.

She certainly didn't harbor any secret hope about this marriage lasting beyond the six months they'd initially agreed on.

Did she?

Did it matter that Jake's ideal woman just happened to be the opposite of her?

No. Absolutely not.

Not one tiny little bit.

But he darn well could have mentioned it before now.

Twelve

"So, you had a good time?" Jake prodded gently.

"Absolutely."

He and Kate had left the party over an hour ago, and Kate had yet to give more than a one-word response to any of his questions. In the car he'd assumed she was just tired. But now that they were home, he realized something more than that was going on.

She was in full, closemouthed lockdown. And for the life of him, he couldn't figure out why.

"You seemed to get along fine with the other women."

"Hmm," she murmured in response.

Even when he hadn't been by her side, he'd kept a careful eye on her, watching for signs she was flailing about in the water, about to go under. He'd seen none.

In fact, the whole afternoon she'd seemed open and friendly, if nervous. The antithesis of how she seemed now as she stirred the milk she was heating on the stove.

"Lisa seemed to like you," he pointed out.

This time she didn't answer, but for an instant she stilled and her hand clenched the wooden spoon she held. Then she began to stir the milk at a more furious pace. When he tried to run his hand down her arm, she deftly stepped out of his way.

Exhaling loudly in frustration, he propped his hip against the countertop beside the stove and crossed his arms over his chest. Ducking his head slightly to study her expression, he said, "Do you want to talk about—"

"No."

Damn, she was not budging an inch. She wouldn't talk to him. She wouldn't let him touch her. Apparently, as far as she was concerned, he couldn't do anything right. And he didn't even know what he'd done wrong.

He pushed himself away from the counter and stalked over to the fridge for a Shiner Bock. He twisted off the top and shot it across the kitchen into the trash can.

Well, he'd tried. No one could say he hadn't.

Logic told him to take his beer to the living room, turn on the TV and veg out until she was over with whatever snit she'd worked herself into. Every scrap of common sense he had told him to just let it go.

But he couldn't do that.

He took a long draught of beer, then said, "You might as well come right out and tell me whatever's got you so pissed off, 'cause right now you're acting like a real pain in the—"

She spun around to face him, a flash of anger in her eyes. "You want to know why I'm angry?"

"Isn't that what I just said?"

"Fine. I'm angry because you should have told me you wanted to get married."

He paused, beer half lifted to his mouth, able only to stare at her in confusion. "Huh?"

Her voice was curt with barely suppressed emotion. "If you wanted to get married, you should have told me. I shouldn't have had to hear it from Lisa today at the party."

He studied her through narrowed eyes. "We are married."

"Ugh!" She turned back around, gave her milk one last stir and then poured it into a waiting mug. "That's not what I meant. Before you and I got married... She said you'd always wanted to get married."

"So?" He had no idea where this was going, but at least she was talking to him now.

She stalked toward the table and yanked out a chair. "I had always just assumed you weren't interested in marriage, that's all."

"I don't see that it makes any difference whether or not I planned on getting married someday."

"Well, it does. If I'd known that, I never would have asked you to marry me."

"Why not?" Jake asked. "It's not like I had a fiancée waiting in the wings who got bumped aside to make way for you."

Kate sighed, wishing she could explain. Or that she could rewind this whole conversation and start over again. This time trying just a little bit harder to sound like a rational human being.

The truth was, it hardly mattered whether or not he wanted to get married. His lie of omission wasn't what had upset her. That was just an excuse. No, her anger was based on something much more complicated than that. Mostly she just felt betrayed. She'd believed him when he said he admired her strength and independence. But what good was his *admiration* if those weren't the qualities he found attractive? And why, for, goodness' sake, had she let herself care what Jake thought about her?

Finding out she wasn't Jake's type fueled all her insecurities. It was like walking into a new foster home for the first time all over again. Once again having her hope and anticipation—emotions she'd fought so hard against—crushed. No way was she about to tell Jake all of that. "Well, you should have mentioned it, anyway," she said huffily.

"It didn't come up. This whole thing happened pretty quickly, if I remember right. And I still don't see why this matters."

She drew in a fortifying breath, flattened her palms on the table and forced herself to meet his gaze. "It matters because it makes our marriage even more of an inconvenience."

"An inconvenience? Is that how you see this marriage?"

"Yes. For you, it has been." She held up a hand to ward off his protests. "Don't bother trying to deny it. You've turned your whole life upside down for me. And now this."

He pulled back the chair opposite hers and sank into it. "And that's why you were so angry? Because you think you've inconvenienced me?"

"Yes. I…I don't know. I suppose," she said, lowering her gaze.

"Kate, I haven't done anything I wasn't willing to do. You didn't force me into anything."

Exactly. He'd stepped in to rescue her. To be a hero. And he didn't have the faintest idea why that bothered her.

He reached across the table and nudged her chin up with his knuckle, forcing her to meet his gaze again. "I could have said no."

"No, you couldn't have." Her disappointment welled up inside of her and came out as a sigh. "It's not in your nature."

"What about you? It's not like this whole thing has been convenient for you. You're the one actually carrying the baby. And it's your job that was at risk."

At the mention of the baby, something inside her chest tightened. She didn't like to think of the baby as an inconvenience any more than she liked to think of their marriage that way. It cheapened both.

Gazing into his eyes, she saw a flicker of confusion cross his face as he dropped his hand and added, "Let's face it, neither of us got what we bargained for when we agreed to help Stew and Beth."

She couldn't help but chuckle. "That's sure the truth." His expression intensified and suddenly laughing was the last thing she felt like doing. "Don't you worry at all about…"

"About what?"

She hardly knew how to finish her thought. Worrying had become nearly a full-time profession for her. Was she sleeping right? Eating right? Getting enough exercise? Too much exercise? And then there was the granddaddy of all worries. Once she had the baby and didn't need Jake to be her hero anymore, how was she ever going to get used to living without him?

For that matter, how was she going to find the strength to give the baby to Beth and Stew when the time came?

She'd tried so desperately to keep her heart compartmentalized, Thinking of the baby, if she allowed herself to think of the baby at all, as Beth's and Stew's.

But the baby was greedy. She kept stealing pieces of Kate's heart for herself. And Jake seemed to be the baby's willing accomplice. And Kate had no idea how to stop the two of them from absconding with her whole heart.

She looked up to realize Jake was studying her, waiting for her to finish her thought.

She opened her mouth, ready to share her fears, but then snapped it closed again. What would be the point? If she told him what she was feeling, he'd only want to help. To try to make things better. To rescue her, dang it.

She stood. "Never mind. I'm just tired. I think I'll go to bed."

She waited to see if he'd respond. When he didn't, she turned and headed for her bedroom. She'd made it halfway down the hall when he spoke.

"You should sleep in my bed. You'll be more comfortable."

His words clutched at her heart. He was just thinking of her comfort. Not her desirability.

Well, she didn't need or want someone to take care of her. She'd been self-reliant for far too long for that. If she needed anything it was for someone to want her…just as she was. But Jake wasn't that person.

No, he wanted her for who she wasn't—someone vulnerable and in need of protection.

"No, thanks, I'll be fine in my own room."

She looked over her shoulder to see him propped against the kitchen doorway, his arm raised over his head, his face lowered, as if he didn't want to look at her. The stance stretched his T-shirt taut across his chest, emphasizing his sheer strength.

And yet, somehow she was left with the impression that her words had hurt him. Made *him* vulnerable.

"No, thanks," she said again, then turned on her heel and escaped into her room.

Thirteen

On Monday morning Kate awakened to find a note from Jake propped on the kitchen table explaining that he'd been called into work during the night and hadn't wanted to wake her. In some ways the news was a relief. After their discussion the previous night, she was no longer sure where she stood with him or how to face him.

Something she never had to do since he didn't arrive home before midnight.

The following day was a repeat. Except he didn't leave a note.

By the third day of the same behavior, the fears and insecurities she'd been holding at bay flooded the common sense that told her he was just doing his job.

Even as doubts about their relationship raced through her head, she was annoyed with herself for giving them credence. This was exactly the kind of weak behavior she despised. She was smarter than this. At least, she'd always thought she was.

How very disappointing to find out after all this time that she wasn't.

If Jake had been avoiding her, it was equally true that she'd been avoiding her sister. But she couldn't any longer.

Kate needed to talk to Beth.

So after work on Thursday, instead of driving to her own little bungalow near downtown, Kate headed out on Williams Drive to the community of multiacre lots and ranch-style houses where Beth and Stewart lived.

She let herself in the side door and found Beth in the kitchen, chopping vegetables to stir-fry. Something inside of her tightened at the familiar scene. Back in the days before the insemination, she'd been a frequent dinner guest at Beth's and Stew's.

When she heard Kate enter, Beth looked up from her task. Almost instantly, her face bloomed into a smile and she practically flew across the room to give Kate a hug. But all too soon, she pulled back from the hug to scowl. "You've been avoiding me."

"I've been bus—"

"You're always busy." Beth clucked disapprovingly. "But you've never gone this long without at least calling. If Stew hadn't been getting regular updates from Jake, I would have been frantic."

"I've been—" She started to voice another defense, but then Beth's words sank in. "Regular updates from Jake? He's been...what? Telling on me?"

Beth chuckled. "He's been keeping us informed. A couple of weeks after the wedding, when I realized you were avoiding me, I had to resort to checking up on you through Stew and Jake."

There wasn't even a hint of accusation in Beth's

voice. Nevertheless, guilt twinged in Kate's belly. "I'm sorry. Things have just been…"

"Complicated?" Beth wiped her hands on a dish-towel before returning to her chopping.

"Yeah, I guess."

For a moment Kate studied her sister. As always Beth had a peaceful aura about her that was only magnified by her pregnancy. She wore a simple, high-waisted dress that emphasized her growing belly. The brown curls framing her face had been clipped back with a barrette, revealing her naturally rosy complexion. No doubt about it. Pregnancy agreed with Beth. Just as mother-hood would.

By comparison, Kate felt bloated, blotchy and gen-erally incompetent. She hated the stab of jealousy she felt. Just as she always did.

With a sigh, she slipped her arms from her suit jacket and draped it over the back of a kitchen chair. Shoving aside the negative emotions, she started to explain, "It's just—"

"You don't have to explain." Beth rinsed a red pep-per in the sink and handed it and a knife to Kate. "It's only natural you haven't wanted to see me. I certainly can't blame you for feeling resentful."

"I don't feel resentful." But she found herself focus-ing on mutilating the innocent red pepper rather than meeting her sister's gaze.

"Of course you do." Beth stopped chopping long enough to rest her hand on Kate's. "After all you've gone through for me and Stew, you'd have to be a saint not to feel at least a little resentful."

Kate looked up at Beth. She toyed with the aban-doned stem of the pepper while studying Beth's expres-sion. There was no judgment there. No annoyance or frustration. Only acceptance. Which somehow only made Kate feel worse.

She shrugged. "I suppose on some level, I have been feeling a little resentful."

To her chagrin, Beth chuckled. "Well, that's a step in the right direction."

Since she'd been feeling so proud of her admission, Kate arched an eyebrow and asked, "Just a step?"

"Oh, come on, Kate. You've given up close to a year of your life for Stew and me. You're having a baby for us. Married a man who was a virtual stranger. And it turns out it was all unnecessary. Of course you're resentful. Maybe even downright angry."

Beth set down her knife and sighed. "And to make matters worse, I handled things very badly." Her voice held an unusual note of self-censure. "When we first found out we were pregnant, I was so happy for us, I let myself ignore what an awkward position I'd put you into." Her hand drifted down to her belly. "I'd forgotten that our dream come true would pretty much be a nightmare for you."

"Well, I don't know that I'd use the term nightmare," Kate said wryly. "It certainly hasn't been all negative."

She'd certainly had her share of positive experiences these past several months. The amazing feeling of having the baby move inside her. The excitement of the baby's sonogram. Living with Jake. Getting to know him and realizing he was so much more complex than she'd thought. Sleeping curled up next to him in bed. Feeling his hands and mouth bring her unthinkable pleasure. All things she never would have experienced if she hadn't become the surrogate mother for Beth and Stew.

In that light, how could she possibly resent Beth for

putting her in this position? And how could she think of her baby as unnecessary?

She loved this baby. She could never regret all she'd been going through to bring this baby into the world.

"There's been a lot of upheaval in my life," she admitted. "But it hasn't all been bad. Not by far."

"I'm glad." Beth smiled. Not her normal, peaceful smile, but one filled with joy. "And what about work? Things haven't been too rough for you there?"

Kate's hand drifted to her own belly. The silk shell she wore untucked over her black maternity pants certainly didn't hide her bulging belly. With the jacket, things were a little more inconspicuous but not much. "A couple of people have noticed, but I haven't made an official announcement or anything."

"And how have people taken it?"

"So far, everyone's been excited and supportive."

"Even Judge Hatcher?"

"Hatcher's been so busy with his campaign he's barely noticed me at all. He's still circling the McCain case like a vulture. The case won't start for another week, so we'll see if he continues to behave."

The funny thing was how unconcerned she was about the case. About work in general. Mere months ago, all of that seemed so important. So completely vital to her life. Now, work was…just work.

She took it seriously. Still did her job to the utmost of her ability. But it was no longer the focus of her life. Other things had taken its place. Her baby. And Jake.

Which brought her to the purpose of her visit. As quickly as she could, she explained to Beth what had happened between them. Beth listened in near silence.

When Kate was finally done, Beth summarized, "And now you think he's avoiding you."

"I don't just think so. He's been working eighteen-hour days. Who does that?"

Beth shot her a wry look. "You, on occasion. I can think of several times you've worked days that long. And he did warn you."

"I know. It's just…" Kate wiped her hands on a dish-towel and propped her hip against the counter. "I just can't help thinking I did something wrong. That I've messed up this entire situation and now he doesn't know how to get out of it."

"I'm sure you have nothing to worry about," Beth said. "Jake is a really—"

"I know. He's a really good guy." Kate sighed. "You're right. He is. That's the problem. That means he's not going to want to do anything to hurt me. That's only going to make him feel more—" The word caught in her throat. "—obligated to stick around."

She didn't want him to feel obligated to her. She wanted him to want her.

Just once in her life, she wanted someone to want her for her.

With a groan she propped her elbows on the counter and sank her head into her hands. "I just hate feeling so damn needy."

Beth had the gall to chuckle.

Kate curled in her fingers to glare at Beth over her knuckles. "This is funny to you?"

Beth shrugged, then nodded. "Maybe just a little." As if she sensed Kate's rising annoyance, she held out her hands in an "I'm innocent" gesture. "Not that I want you to be miserable and needy, it's just—" Beth paused, searching for a word "—reassuring to know you're not always as confident and together as you seem."

"What's that supposed to mean?"

"Kate, you're my sister. I couldn't love you more, so don't take this the wrong way. It's just that you've always seemed so very self-sufficient. Even as a kid, you never needed anyone."

"That's not true."

"Yes, it is. It's one of the things I've always admired about you, but…"

"But what?" she couldn't help asking.

"But it's a little intimidating, too. It's always made me feel a little… I don't know…" Beth gave a self-conscious laugh. "Weak, I guess. By comparison."

Kate felt her heart tighten just a little bit. This time she was the one who reached out and put her hand on Beth's. "You're not weak. You're one of the most loving, generous people I know."

Beth looked up. Her smile held just a hint of self-deprecation. "Thank you. But it's kind of nice having you here asking for advice. I've been waiting all my life to get to be your helpful big sister."

Kate raised an eyebrow. "My helpful big sister?"

"Well, sure. You've always been so independent, I've never had the chance before. I get to take care of everyone else I care about but you. I've missed that."

"I…I don't know what to say. I'm sorry, I guess."

Beth chuckled. "You don't have to *say* anything. Just keep it in mind for the future. Sometimes letting other people take care of you isn't a bad thing. It's not a sign of weakness. It's just a way of keeping the relationship balanced."

By the time she left Beth's and Stew's she felt no better about the situation with Jake. But she felt as if her relationship with her sister had changed forever.

It had never occurred to her that her sister wanted to

take care of her. That her independence deprived people of anything.

She'd certainly never set out to be aloof. It was just sort of a natural defense. At the first couple of foster homes, she'd yearned for love and attention. It hadn't taken her long to realize she wasn't going to get it. Hugs, cuddles and special treats all went to the kids like Beth. The cute little moppets with big eyes and curly hair.

In fact, there had been several foster homes that wouldn't have taken her if the courts hadn't insisted she and Beth stay together.

She'd learned early on that the only person she could rely on was herself. That was what she'd been doing ever since. Her independence—her steadfast refusal to trust anyone else—had protected her, yes. But now she wondered what it had cost her.

Fourteen

Jake didn't like to think of himself as a weak person. Hell, he supposed no one did. But Kate… Kate was his weakness.

She made him question decisions he'd made with confidence. Made him want things he couldn't have. Like her. And their baby.

For the first time in his life, he didn't just want a woman sexually. He wanted her love. Her trust.

Kate didn't trust him.

That much had been obvious the night she reached for a condom even though he promised he hadn't been with anyone else.

And she didn't trust him enough to open up to him.

Jeez, to hear her talk the other night, you'd think the divorce papers were all ready to go, just waiting to be signed. For all he knew, she still planned on filing for divorce the second Hatcher was elected and her career was safe. Hell, it was possible their time together meant nothing to her.

Yeah, it had always been in the back of his mind that this was a temporary situation, but things were different now.

Making love to Kate had changed everything.

But Kate needed some convincing. He needed to prove to her she could trust him. And, damn it, he had every intention of doing just that before making love with her again.

At least, that had been his plan Monday morning when he left the house early and stopped by the doctor's on the way into work. But getting the test results had taken longer than expected. Three days to be exact.

By Thursday afternoon, he had the clean bill of health from his doctor in hand. Just what he needed to prove to Kate that he was trustworthy.

At five-thirty, when she still wasn't home, he wasn't worried. After all, she probably hadn't left work right at five, and she might be stuck in traffic. By seven-thirty he was wearing a path in the rug from the front door to the back. Sure, she'd worked late before, but this was ridiculous. He'd tried her cell several times but either she wasn't answering or she was out of range.

By nine-thirty, he'd planted himself on a kitchen chair, midway between the two doors, and sat with his elbows propped on his knees.

When the front door finally opened at ten to ten, he no longer knew what he felt: fear, anxiety or outright anger.

When she entered the bungalow, her gaze went immediately to his. "You're home," she said, sounding a little surprised.

"You're late," was all he managed to grind out.

She frowned. If he hadn't been so annoyed, he might have found her expression of confusion amusing.

"I had dinner with Beth and Stew."

"You should have called." He didn't bother trying to keep the exasperation from his voice.

But as soon as he said the words, he knew they were a mistake. Her eyebrows snapped together and her shoulders stiffened.

"I didn't call, because I didn't know you'd be here."

Her response set the warning bells in his head ringing, but the surge of emotions roiling within him was too strong to tap down. He just couldn't keep his mouth shut.

"You still should have called."

"*You* didn't call." She crossed her arms over her chest, her gaze narrowing.

"I was at work," he defended. "You knew I'd be late."

Why were they even talking about this when all he wanted to do was pull her into his arms and kiss her? Peel off a couple of layers of clothes and spend the rest of the night exploring her body. Finding all the hidden sensitive hollows.

"Oh, right." Her voice practically dripped with sarcasm. "I was supposed to know you wouldn't be home until after midnight *three* nights in a row because on Monday you left me a note saying you'd be late."

He shoved his hand through his hair. "This isn't what I wanted to talk to you about tonight."

"Then what *did* you want to talk about? I'm sure you can come up with something else to criticize me about. But if you don't mind, I'd rather skip it tonight."

With that, she spun on her heel and headed for her bedroom.

Guilt stabbed through him. How had this gone so badly? Gotten so out of hand?

Hell, he didn't know. All he knew was he couldn't let her storm off to her room again.

He caught up with her in the hallway. "Wait."

Maybe she heard the desperation in his voice or maybe she was just as tired of fighting as he was. Or maybe he was just lucky. Whatever the reason, she stopped.

She didn't turn to face him, but merely cocked her head to the side. Under the circumstances, he was happy to get at least that from her.

"I didn't mean to…"

What? He asked himself. Act like a total ass? Antagonize you? Alienate you?

Finally, in lieu of a babbling admission of guilt, he settled for, "I was just worried."

This time, she did turn to face him. Her expression softened—just a little—but most of the anger had left her voice. "I don't need you to worry about me. I can take care of myself."

"I know." But knowing that didn't ease the powerful urge within him to protect her, to make her his.

He kept that to himself. She was so strong. So independent. She'd never approve of his cavemanlike urges. For that matter, he wasn't sure *he* approved of them. He certainly never would have pegged himself as that kind of guy.

Not wanting to reveal any of that to her, he changed the subject. "I saw my doctor on Monday."

"Your doctor?" Her forehead furrowed in concern. "Why? Is something wrong?"

He pulled the printout of his test results from his back pocket. "I had myself tested again."

He held out the folded paper, but she didn't take it from him. "I don't understand."

"Everything checks out. Got the all clear, so to speak."

Finally, she took the paper from him, but she didn't unfold it or even look at it. "You did this for me?"

"I wanted you to trust me. I wanted you to know I hadn't lied to you."

"Why?"

"Because I want you to know you can trust me. I want—"

"No." She shook her head. "Why does it matter to you?"

It took a second for her question to sink in. "Because I care about you." Since she still hadn't read the test results, he gestured to the paper she clutched in her hand. "Aren't you going to look at them?"

Kate forced herself to unfold the paper and stare at the results. Part of her brain registered the words typed on the page. The all clear, to use his term.

But most of her mind was still focused on his words. He cared about her. He wanted her to trust him.

She thought of what Beth had said just that evening. About how she was too independent.

After so many years of trusting only herself, could she trust anyone else? Could she forgive herself if she didn't at least try?

Carefully she folded the paper and handed it back to him. "Okay."

He narrowed his gaze as if he wasn't quite sure he'd heard her correctly. "Okay?"

She nodded. "Okay. I'll give it a try."

Part of her wished she could give him something more solid than, "I'll try." But he seemed to accept it for the major step it was. The hopeful smile that crept across his face was all the proof she needed that she'd made the right decision.

When he pulled her into his arms, she felt not only the familiar stirrings of desire, but also a tiniest thread of fear. This was all so new. So fraught with emotional sand traps. But she shoved her fear away, burying it deep within.

She'd only said she'd try to trust him. Surely she could do that without getting hurt.

Jake woke to the smell of Kate lingering on his pillow and the sound of her showering in the bathroom.

For a few minutes he lay in bed, just listening and remembering. His erection hardened beneath his cotton boxer briefs as he thought of how responsive she'd been last night. How she'd groaned, deep in her throat, every time he sucked her nipples into his mouth. How her skin had somehow tasted both sweet and spicy. How she'd moaned his name again and again as she rode him to ecstasy.

He'd never forget what it was like making love to Kate. But there was one memory that he'd cherish even more. The tentative smile on her face as she told him she'd trust him.

For the life of him, he couldn't figure out why she got to him in a way no other woman ever had. Maybe it was because she was the mother of his child. But he didn't think that was it. That alone, he could have understood.

But this crazy compulsion he felt not just to make love to her but to protect her and be with her, to dig through the layers of her personality until he really knew her, that was what he couldn't understand.

Until he did, he was more than willing to sublimate all the other stuff for the one urge he *did* understand. The urge to make love to her. To imprint himself on her, body and soul.

He rose from the bed and made his way to the bathroom. Once inside, he realized she was humming so softly, it could barely be heard over the water. The room was thick with steam and the scent of her lavender shower gel.

For a moment he closed his eyes, remembering how he'd once pictured her in a bubble bath, her skin moist and warm from the water, the crests of her breasts just visible above the bubbles.

Someday, once the baby was born, he'd make love to her in the tub, but for now Kate naked in the steamy shower would do.

He stepped out of his boxers. Her eyes popped open at the rattle of the shower curtain against the rod. A faint smile curled her lips as she watched him step into the shower.

Shampoo bubbles mounded on her head. Beads of water clung to her eyelashes and skin, converging into rivulets that sluiced down her chest. Her nipples were hardened, dusky pink against her creamy skin. Her hips swelled gently out from her waist, which still appeared surprisingly narrow given her growing belly.

He wouldn't have thought it possible, but he felt his erection swell even more. Only then did he realize he'd never seen her naked before. Not in the daylight. Not when he could really look at her.

He felt a ridiculous surge of pride as he stared at her ripe body. After a minute, he sensed her stiffening. His gaze returned to her face to find her smile had faded.

"Believe it or not I used to be quite fit."

Part of him wanted to laugh at her obvious insecurity over something he considered so beautiful. But he knew better. *That* would get his butt kicked out of this shower faster than anything.

Instead he closed the distance between them and

cupped her jaw in his hand, urging her to look in his eyes, to see the truth of his words.

"No woman has looked more beautiful to me than you do right now."

"Yeah, right. I'm a real pinup girl. Big hips, bulging belly—"

He pressed his lips to hers to stop her babbling. Despite whatever fears she might be harboring, he felt her mouth melt under his, her body sway against him. The swell of her belly brushed against his erection, sending pleasure arching through his body.

He had to force himself to pull away from her embrace. He did so only because he desperately wanted her to believe him.

"You said you'd trusted me."

A flicker of hesitation flashed through her eyes. Then she nodded. "Yes."

"Then trust that I won't lie to you. Ever."

She seemed to be searching his gaze, looking for insincerity that he knew she wouldn't find.

His hand slipped down to caress her belly. "You can't imagine how the sight of you turns me on. Seeing you like this, knowing that I did this to you, that this is our baby…it's the most erotic thing I've ever seen."

Her mouth once again curved into a smile. A little hesitant. A little bashful. But still so achingly sexy he could hardly stand it.

Once again he pulled her to him, to make her trust his words with his touch. He poured all of his pent-up emotion into his kiss, to let her feel the power she held over him.

With gentle and loving hands he tipped her head back, rinsing the shampoo from her hair. His fingertips followed the trail the bubbles left across her shoulders, down the arch of her back and over the swell of her buttocks.

Her head tipped back exposing the length of her neck to his mouth. Her skin was warm and moist and tasted sweet, like fresh rainwater. He could spend a lifetime kissing this neck. Feeling her pulse leap beneath his lips. Hearing her moan his name. Running his hands across her silky smooth skin and cupping the weight of her breasts in his palms.

He wanted this moment to last forever. He wanted to imprint it on his memory. But an even stronger force drove him on—the urge to make her his, to push himself into the moist folds of her flesh and to bury himself deep inside her.

His hand slipped farther down her body. His fingers burrowed through her curls to the sensitive skin that lay sheltered between her legs.

Her legs parted, granting him access, and he quickly found the hardened nub. Massaging her with his thumb, he sank his finger deep inside her. A low moan tore through her, and he felt her orgasm building with every stroke of his thumb.

He held her in his arms as she trembled with her release, watching every flicker of ecstasy that crossed her face. Knowing he'd brought her to that state gave him a surge of pleasure, as well.

As the last shudders of her orgasm pulsed through her body, he murmured, "I want to be inside you."

"Yes," she gasped. "Now."

He started to reach behind her to turn off the water— they could be in his bed in mere minutes. But before he could, she turned around. Bending over, she planted her hands firmly on the shower wall.

He didn't need more encouragement than that. Nudging her knees slightly apart, he sought and found her entrance. He plunged into her with a single thrust. They both moaned aloud.

The pleasure was so intense, at first he could hardly move. She arched her back, urging him deeper. He slipped his hand around her to once again find her nub before thrusting into her again and again. Her moist folds seemed to cling to him, massaging his shaft, bringing him pleasure unlike anything he'd ever experienced with another woman.

Not that he even remembered another woman. Not when he had Kate. It was only her. Only the water pounding on her back to the rhythm of their movements. Only the thrusting of her hips bringing him closer to ecstasy. Only the feel of her clenching around him. Driving him over the edge.

The intensity of their joining left him shaking. And shaken.

Because with her, it wasn't enough.

It would never be enough.

Fifteen

They'd been sleeping together every night for almost a week now. Ever since he brought home those test results.

He wanted her to trust him, he'd said. And part of her did. She trusted that he would never hurt the baby. She trusted that he wouldn't intend to hurt her. And she trusted that he wanted to be with her.

But she knew better than anyone how temporary desire could be. It was as transient as love or affection. In less than four months, she'd give birth, Beth and Stew would take custody of the baby, and this would all be over.

What would her life be like then?

Probably she'd go back to the way things had always been. Her, all on her own. Completely independent. Protected from life's disappointments and pains because she never let anyone close enough to hurt her. Once she would have sworn that was exactly the way she wanted things. Now it just seemed terribly lonely.

How could she go back to that life now that she'd experienced a baby growing inside of her? Now that she knew what it was like to sleep with Jake curled against her back?

She thought briefly of the McCain divorce that was on her docket for Monday. For years, everyone in Georgetown had seen them as the perfect couple. Well matched in every way. They certainly hadn't started out their relationship intending it to end in a messy divorce. No one ever did.

The thought disconcerted her so much, the comfort of Jake's sleeping embrace started to feel smothering.

As gently as she could, she slipped out from under his arm, but the extra weight of the baby made her clumsy. Before she could exit the bed, Jake was awake.

"What do you need?" He raised up on his elbow, his gaze clear and alert in the darkness.

"I was just going to…" What? Escape to the other room to brood in peace? Fret endlessly over their future? She fumbled for an explanation and finally finished lamely, "…get a glass of milk."

"You're thirsty?"

Thirsty? Panic-stricken? Sure, those were about the same. "Yes."

He rolled off his side of the bed. "I'll get it for you."

She started to follow him, but he stopped her. "No, stay here. I'll bring it back for you."

Before she could protest he started propping pillows behind her and helping her to sit up in bed. "You want milk or something else?"

How about your love?

Oh, crap. Where had that thought come from?

"Milk will do."

She watched him leave the room with a sinking feeling in her gut. Then she flopped back against the pillows and pressed her hands to her face.

"How about your love?" she muttered to herself.

God, she was a mess.

She didn't really want him to love her, did she?

And it certainly wasn't as if she loved him.

Did she?

She didn't give herself time to search her heart. No. She didn't. She wouldn't be that stupid. Not when she'd spent her whole life being so smart when it came to her emotions.

"Here you go."

She pulled her hands from her face and opened her eyes to find him standing over her, a tall glass of milk in hand. "Thanks."

He handed her the glass, then sat beside her on the bed. "Hey, what's wrong?" he said, running a hand up her arm.

A shiver of awareness followed in the wake of his caress. She wanted nothing more than to set the glass of milk aside and lose herself in his touch. To let him banish the worries that kept her up. To make love with him until she was too exhausted to remember all the reasons she was on a collision course with emotional heartache. She didn't let herself do any of those things.

She did, however, avert her gaze. "If it wasn't for me, your life would be a lot easier."

After being in the kitchen, Jake's eyes hadn't fully adjusted to the dark of the bedroom, making it impossible for him to read her expression. But he could hear in her voice that something just wasn't right.

Once again, he marveled at her complexity.

So tough one moment, so vulnerable the next.

There were a hundred things he wanted to say to her. None of them she was ready to hear.

So he settled for, "If it wasn't for you, I wouldn't be about to become a father."

"You're thinking about keeping the baby?"

"Even if I agree to let Beth and Stew raise her, I'll still be a father. After this, I can't imagine not being a part of her life. Can you?"

Instead of answering his question she said, "If you agree? So you are thinking about keeping the baby?"

"You can't tell me you haven't thought about it."

"I…" She frowned, pulling away from his touch. "What do you want me to say? That I'm tempted? Of course, I am. But I know Beth and Stew will be better parents for this baby than I could ever be alone. For that matter, either one of them would be better than I would."

"I disagree."

Obviously frustrated, she swung her legs over the other side of the bed and stood. "It's a moot point. There are two of them and only one of me."

He stood, as well, and caught her in his arms as she rounded the bed. "But there are two of us."

Even in the dark, he saw her gaze widen. "What are you saying?"

What *was* he saying? That he wanted them to be together?

Yes, it was what he wanted, but did *she* want it?

Come on, Morgan, you want to be in the game, it's time to ante up.

"Let's stay married. Let's raise this baby on our own."

He heard her sharp intake of breath. For a second she seemed to be actually considering it. Then she shook her head and pulled away from him. "Oh, Jake, I don't know."

He felt a sharp stab of disappointment. He'd wanted… What? Surely not a declaration of love from her. A little enthusiasm maybe.

But she hadn't said no. Which meant he still had a chance of convincing her.

"What's not to know?" He cradled her face in his hands. "We're good together."

"Sure, in—"

"Not just in bed. In life. I love you. I love the baby."

She pulled away from him, turning her back on his arguments, but just before she did, something in her gaze wavered. Instantly he knew how to win her over.

"Come on, Katie. You care about the baby, too. You can't deny it. She's *our* baby. We can be a family together."

He ran his hands across her shoulders, down her arms, praying his touch would be more convincing than his words.

She stiffened at first, as if to reinforce her defenses against him. Then slowly she relaxed, leaning her back lightly against his chest.

"Okay," she finally whispered. "Let's do it."

He pulled her fully against him, wrapping his arms around her chest. Beneath one palm, he felt the pounding of her heart. Beneath his other lay the baby that had brought them together…and convinced her to marry him.

He'd hated playing that card. Hated manipulating her like this. But not as much as he hated the thought of losing her.

It was day one in the divorce proceedings of the most important case of her career. And all she could think about was Jake.

He didn't really love her. He'd just said that.

How could a man like him—someone who loved being a hero and rescuing people—really love a woman like her? She was the last person in the world who needed saving.

Agreeing to stay married to him had been an extremely stupid thing to do. But how could she resist when he painted such a compelling picture of their future together?

She could see it so clearly in her mind. Lazy Saturday mornings making love with Jake. Lazy Sunday mornings around the kitchen table, she and Jake sipping coffee, a towheaded toddler sitting on his lap, gumming a waffle.

She was on the way from her chambers to the court, smiling at the images in her mind, when the first wave of pain washed over her.

Immediately she put a hand to the wall to brace herself and grasped her belly with her other hand. Her stomach felt unnaturally hard beneath her palm. The muscles taut and cramped.

The pain seemed to last forever before slowly easing. The whole time, she'd breathed out sharply through her mouth. Praying the sensation would pass. Praying this wasn't a sign something was terribly wrong.

As the last of the pain dissipated, she pressed her back against the wall, needing its support to catch her breath. Even after she was breathing normally, she found she couldn't move.

Her heart began pounding, her fear threatening to overwhelm her. Something was wrong. Something was *very* wrong.

She glanced down the hallway toward her chambers. There was a sofa. She could lie down. Drink some water. All of her pregnancy books seemed to recommend drinking water when things were wrong. And call Jake. He would know what to do.

But then her logical mind scoffed.

Yes, he would rush to her side. Be there in an instant

if she needed him, but would having him there really be any more helpful than drinking a glass of water?

She looked to the other end of the hallway. Just beyond a pair of double doors was her courtroom, where the McCains, their lawyers, and a myriad of reporters and sundry people were waiting for her.

All she had to do was walk the twenty meters her courtroom. Then she could spend the next four hours sitting comfortably in her chair. She could drink all the water she wanted.

She'd almost convinced herself it was the right thing to do when Kevin rounded the corner and spotted her leaning against the wall. He practically ran to her side. "What's wrong?"

She forced herself to straighten away from the wall, moving cautiously, terrified the pain would return.

"Nothing," she said, but her voice sounded strained, and Kevin didn't look like he bought it.

"I find you leaning against the wall, gasping for breath, and you say nothing's wrong? Talk to me, Kate. Something's not right."

The concern in his voice tore at something deep inside of her and she felt her fear give way to tears. Furiously she blinked them away. She would not cry. She was not that weak.

"I felt a…" She struggled for the right word. Not wanting to admit, even to herself, how badly she'd felt. Or how badly she wanted Jake there with her. "Tightening. In my belly. I just had to catch my breath."

Kevin's eyes never left her face, but a deep furrow formed between his eyebrows. "A tightening? Isn't that the word women use to describe labor pains?"

Oh, God. Was it?

"I don't know. How do you know?"

"Two sisters. Five nieces and nephews." He placed a hand at her back. "Come on, let's get you back to your chambers. You can lie down on the sofa while I call the doctor."

The thought that something might really be wrong terrified her, so, she automatically protested. "No, it's nothing. It's passed now." She stood up straighter, to prove to herself and him that nothing was wrong. "Besides, it's probably just those fake contractions, right? What are those called? Hicks something."

"Braxton Hicks? Yes, you may be right. But your doctor will know for sure."

"But the trial—"

"Kate, no," Kevin chided, steering her toward her chambers when she would have headed toward the double doors. "The trial will wait."

"But—"

"Stop being so freakin' stubborn. Nothing is more important than this."

He was right, of course. Yet somehow, giving in to him meant admitting something might really be wrong. Despite that, she allowed him to lead her down the hall and into her chambers.

"What's your doctor's number?" he asked, flipping open his cell phone.

She stopped herself just short of giving him Jake's number first. Yes, Jake would rush to her side, but what if this really was just Braxton Hicks contractions? Wouldn't it be better to wait until she knew if she needed him?

As she rattled off the doctor's number, she lowered herself to the worn leather sofa. The moment she sat down a second wave of pain coursed over her stomach. Automatically she curled onto her side, cupping her belly in her hands.

Kevin crouched beside her. "When was the first one?"

At first she couldn't answer. She was panting for breath as fear and pain overwhelmed her. Finally the pain subsided. "I don't know." It seemed as if time was stretching endlessly. As if a lifetime had passed since she left her office. But logic told her it had been mere minutes. "What time is it now?"

He glanced at his watch. "Nine-o-eight."

She'd left for court with a few minutes to spare. "Maybe ten minutes. Maybe a little longer."

Kevin's frown deepened and he snapped the phone shut. When he spoke, his voice was so deliberately calm, she knew how worried he was. "It's still probably nothing, but I'm taking you straight to the hospital."

She wanted to protest but then thought of what Beth had said about letting people take care of her.

But Kevin was right. Nothing was more important than the baby. Certainly not her stubborn pride.

So she let him help her up from the sofa. "My purse and briefcase are in the bottom desk drawer. Can you get them for me? And you'll need to find my bailiff, Celia, and let her know what's happening."

"I'm on it." He dashed behind the desk to grab her bags and met her by the door. "What else can I do?"

"You can call Jake and have him meet us at the hospital."

Sixteen

With his heart pounding and fear choking him, Jake rushed to the hospital.

Nine hours too late.

Guilt tore at him as he ran through the hospital halls to labor and delivery. He'd told Kate he'd be there if she needed him. He'd sworn it. She'd just begun to trust him, and now this?

She'd needed him—their baby needed him—and where was he? At work. Up in the far reaches of the county. Out of cell phone range.

And now he was the last to make it to the hospital. By the time he found her room, Beth and Stew were already inside and Kate was nowhere in sight.

"Where is she?" Jake asked frantically.

Beth sat curled in a chair on the far side of the empty hospital bed, her head tipped back and her eyes closed. Stew, who sat in the only other chair in the room, stood and crossed to his side. Nodding toward the bathroom door, he whispered, "Taking a shower. The doctor gave her permission after dinner. She was having trouble relaxing."

"Is she—" The words caught in his throat. Nearly an hour had passed since he got her voice-mail message, his fear multiplying with every passing minute. He cleared his throat and started again. "She's okay?"

Stew nodded. In his eyes was a mixture of sympathy and censure. "The on-call doctor says she'll be fine. The baby, too." The censure seemed to win out, and he asked, "Man, where were you?"

All the disapproval in the world couldn't make him feel any worse than he already did. "I came as soon as I got the message. But I was out of cell phone range all day. I tried calling Kate's cell as soon as I got the message, but—"

"The nurse made her turn it off," Stew finished for him. "Something about the equipment." He nodded his understanding but didn't really look any more convinced of Jake's innocence than Jake felt. "Anyway, now that you're here, I'm going to take Beth home. It's been a long day."

A few minutes later Stew led a sleepy Beth from the room. Her expression was even less forgiving than Stew's had been. Jake could only imagine how Kate would react to him finally getting here.

But it didn't matter. She was safe. The baby was safe. She could be furious enough to throw things at him. As long as she was safe, he'd happily take it.

After only a few minutes of pacing, he heard the click of the bathroom door opening behind him.

He spun around to see Kate framed in the doorway. She was wrapped in her bathrobe, her hair clipped high on her head a few damp tendrils trailing her neck.

Something inside of him seemed to break at the sight of her. He didn't even try to restrain his urge to hold her, but rushed across the room and pulled her into his arms.

"Oh, God, I was so worried." He pressed a quick kiss to her lips before pressing his cheek to hers. "I've never been so worried in my whole life. But Stew said the doctor said you and the baby would be okay."

Only then did he realize how stiff she felt in his arms. It was like holding a stranger, rather than holding his wife. He pulled back to search her face.

"You *are* going to be okay, aren't you? The doctor—"

"We're fine." She pulled away from him and walked around him. "The doctor wants to keep me here overnight. Just to keep an eye on me. But the baby should be just fine." Clutching the robe tightly across her chest like a shield of armor, she sat on the edge of the bed.

Seeing her, alive and apparently healthy, did little to ease his anxiety. He needed to keep touching her. He crossed to the chair Beth had vacated and laid his hand on Kate's knee. "Oh, Katie, I'm so sorry I wasn't here. I just got your first message—" he glanced at his watch "—about an hour ago."

"It's fine." She moved her knee from under his hand and swung her legs onto the bed.

"There was a fire outside of Jarrell. It looks like someone started it to cover up a homicide. We were up there all day. Out of cell phone range."

"It's fine," she repeated.

But when he reached for her hand, she slid it under the blanket. Further proof that it was, in fact, not at all fine.

"Katie, if I'd known, I would have been here hours ago. I just didn't get the message."

Finally she looked at him. The sparkle that normally lit her eyes had faded. "Don't worry about it. Kevin was with me."

Now that he thought about it, the first of the phone calls had been from Kevin. He didn't know if he should be thankful that Kevin had been there for Kate, or jealous as hell.

Next time, Jake vowed, she wouldn't have to depend on anyone else but him.

"From now on, I want you to carry the dispatch number with you at all times. They can reach me when my phone is out of range."

"That's not necessary. You don't have to be at my beck and call."

The chilly tone in her voice made him almost as nervous as all the don't-touch-me signals. "Yes, I do. That was the point of us getting married. So I could be here if you needed me."

"No, the point of us getting married was to protect my job."

Maybe he had that coming. After all, he didn't mention that mere days ago he'd asked her to stay married to him for the baby, and for love.

"I thought we agreed things are different now."

She continued as if he'd said nothing, "While we're on the subject of my career, we don't really need to worry about me losing my job anymore."

Unsure where she was going with this, he said, "That's good. But why?"

"The McCain case will have to be reassigned to someone else. And even Judge Hatcher wouldn't fire someone on medical leave. He wouldn't get much political mileage out of that. And by the time I'm back at work—"

"Whoa. What do you mean medical leave?"

"The doctor wants me on bed rest. Probably only for a few weeks, but possibly for the rest of the pregnancy.

He's got me on terbutaline, too, to stop the contractions but wants me to stay off my feet."

He sank back against the chair. "You said you and the baby were okay."

"We are okay. And between the bed rest and the terbutaline there's no reason why I can't carry to term."

"But there's a possibility you'll require bed remainder for the rest of the pregnancy?"

"Worst case scenario, yes."

"But that's like four months."

"Which is exactly why I asked to be taken off the McCain case. It wouldn't be fair to have them wait."

"I'm not worried about the case. I'm worried about you." Again he tried to take her hand. Again she pulled away from him. "Your work is important to you. Are you going to be okay with this?"

She gave a faint little laugh, with just a hint of sorrow in it. When she met his gaze, her expression seemed resigned rather than sad.

"Funny, work just doesn't seem as important as it used to."

Even though she obviously didn't want to be touched just now, he couldn't resist brushing her hair from her forehead and pressing a kiss to the spot of skin he'd bared.

"We'll get through this, Katie. I can take time off, if I need to. Or we can hire someone to stay with you during the day. Or—"

"No, Jake. That's what I've been trying to tell you. We don't need to get through anything."

His gut seemed to drop about a foot. "What are you saying?"

This time, her expression was emotionless. "There's no reason for us to be together anymore, Jake."

"Katie—"

"We got married to save my job. But my job isn't an issue anymore."

"What about us?"

"There never really was an 'us.'"

"No. I don't believe that." Unable to just sit there listening to this, he stood and paced to the windows that lined the far wall of the room. "We were going to try to make this work." He turned around, searching her face for any sign that this was tearing her apart as much as it was him. "We were going to be a family."

"I know. I'm sorry," she said, looking away. The breaking of her voice over the word *sorry* was the only sign she felt anything at all.

"No." He paced back to her. Gripping her chin between his thumb and forefinger, he forced her to meet his gaze again. "Sorry isn't good enough. Talk to me. Why are you doing this?"

"I just think that—"

She yanked her chin from his grasp and twisted to stare blankly at the closed door. She seemed to be struggling, either for words or for the strength to say them. Without meeting his gaze, she continued, "I'm not the woman you want."

"That's ridiculous. I—"

"No, it's not." Her eyes slowly filled with tears. "You only married me because you thought it was the right thing to do. You said so yourself. You want some woman you can take care of and protect. Who you can be a hero to. But I'm not that woman."

He couldn't stand to watch her cry. To watch strong, brave, independent Katie cry. "You're wrong, Katie. I don't want some woman I can protect."

"Lisa said—"

"Damn it, forget what Lisa said. Lisa doesn't know what I want in a wife."

"Are you sure *you* know?"

"Look, maybe I did used to date women who are different from you. But what does that have to do with anything? I don't want to be married to some woman who expects me to save her. Why would I want that? That's the kind of relationship my parents had and it didn't work out for them. The only woman I want is you."

Somehow, he thought if he just kept talking, he'd find the right words. He'd say whatever it was she needed to hear to convince her. But she was slowly shaking her head.

"No, you don't. You want someone who will be a good mother. Someone who—"

"Katie, you'll be a great mother." She shook her head, but he didn't give her a chance to protest. "Is that what this is about? That somehow you're afraid you won't be a good mother?"

"I just don't have the instincts to be a good mother. I certainly don't have the genetics for it."

"Being a good mother is more than—"

"Today, when I felt the first labor pains, I almost didn't come to the hospital. I wouldn't have on my own. I was going to try to go to court, but Kevin found me in the hall and made me come in. The doctor said—" Her voice broke and she had to struggle to regain control. "The doctor said I got here just in time. If I'd waited much longer, it might have been too late."

The anguish in her voice tore at his heart. Damn it, he didn't care if she didn't want to be held. He sat on the edge of her bed and pulled her into his arms, cradling her head against his shoulder. To his surprise, she let him. "But you didn't wait. You came at the right time."

"Only because Kevin was there." She sucked in a

deep breath and all but sobbed against his shoulder. "I was just so afraid. I didn't want anything to be wrong. I never want to be that afraid again."

He pulled back to search her face. "So this is about you not wanting to be afraid?"

"Before all of this, I was so in control. I knew exactly what I wanted out of life. I had it all planned and everything was working out just the way I wanted it to, and now…"

"And now what?"

"And now, I just don't know anymore. But I do know I never want to go through anything like that again."

He had no idea what might calm her fears. Or even if there was anything he could say. "All I know is that I love you. I can't promise you'll never be that afraid again. I can't promise that things even worse than this won't happen further down the road. But I believe we can get through anything together. If you really trusted me, Kate, you'd believe me."

Seventeen

It was near dawn and the sounds of the waking hospital were filtering through the thick wooden door. Kate lay in bed, propped up on the raised back, watching Jake sleep, in a nearby chair.

She'd begged him to go home, but he'd refused. She knew how tired he must be.

He'd had a long day at work, followed by the stressful drive to the hospital, the fear for the baby, and then dealing with her hysteria.

Her mind flashed back to the heightened emotions of the day before. Desperately wanting Jake to be there with her. Needing him. Waiting for him. Sure he'd arrive any minute.

But then minutes passed into hours, followed by the heartbreaking disappointment of knowing that—despite his promises—he wasn't there when she needed him.

She understood now why he'd been so late. She

couldn't blame him for it. He had no control over cell phone towers or spotty service areas.

Still, she never wanted to feel that way again. So desperate to be with someone she loved. So afraid he wouldn't be there someday.

No, it was better—much better—to end things now.

Shoving aside her grim thoughts, she searched for something to occupy her mind. She didn't want to wake Jake, so TV was out of the question. She flicked on the small reading light beside her bed. Jake didn't stir. As quietly as she could, she crawled from the bed to retrieve her briefcase from the corner of the room. Surely there was something inside she could read.

The only folder inside contained her notes from the McCain case. She'd read them before. There was really no reason to reread them. Certainly not now that she'd be removed from the case.

And yet, when she returned to bed, she flipped through the pages with a sort of morbid curiosity. Now that she wasn't presiding over the case, she allowed herself to become emotionally involved in the unfolding story in a way she hadn't the previous time she read it.

The McCain divorce wasn't that different from any other she'd presided over in her years on the bench. The couple had married young, had a few children, whom they both seemed devoted to. Success and wealth had taken their toll on their relationship, but there was tragedy, as well. No two people climbed the ladder of success at the same rate, so their competitive natures strained their relationship. The poor health of their youngest child seemed to be the straw that broke their relationship.

In the end they simply hadn't loved each other enough to weather life's disappointments.

For the first time in her career, Kate was looking at

a case not from a professional point of view, when she'd have to decide who was responsible for what and divvy up any assets or children. Instead, she found herself wondering: if the McCains could do it all over again, would they? Was whatever joy their relationship had brought them worth the heartache they were living through now?

She had no way of knowing. And yet... She knew the statistics as well as anyone. Nearly fifty percent of all marriages ended in divorce. She also knew that many of those people married a second or even a third time. Even after living through a tough divorce, most people were willing to risk getting hurt again. Apparently even those people who'd been hurt the worst by love were willing to try again.

So why couldn't she?

She looked over at the chair where Jake was sleeping.

All this time, she'd thought she was being so smart for trying to protect her heart. Now she couldn't help wondering, was she smart or merely a coward?

Hadn't she told Jake she would try to trust him? And yet, at the first opportunity, she'd doubted him and pushed him away.

She'd always thought of herself as so fair, but she hadn't been fair to him at all. She hadn't been honest, either. She'd never even told him she loved him.

Almost as if he sensed her watching him, Jake slowly opened his eyes. It seemed to take him a moment to focus on her face. She quickly looked away, hoping he hadn't seen in her gaze how disconcerted she felt.

He moved to her side. "How do you feel?"

Nervous, confused. "Fine," she said aloud. "Just fine."

"You slept okay?"

She forced a bright smile. "Great."

"Despite the fact that you were up before six doing work?"

She tried not to look too guilty as she shoved the incriminating files back into her briefcase. "Okay. Not great. But good enough."

There was no way he'd get her to admit how much she'd missed having him in the bed with her. How tempted she'd been to wake him in the night and ask him to just lie beside her. No, if she couldn't sleep without his arm draped across her stomach or nestling her breast, then that was her problem.

Since he seemed to be waiting for her to speak, she added, "It's a strange room, and…"

"And you were worried," he finished for her.

"Yes." Though *worried* barely began to describe her mess of emotions. *Worried* was just the tip of the iceberg.

Before she could say more, there was a knock on the door. Without waiting for a response, a nurse swung open the door and rolled in a sonogram machine on a squeaky cart.

"Oh, good, you're up already," chirped the nurse, as if the sound of all that equipment being wheeled in wouldn't have woken them if they hadn't been. "That makes this easier."

Kate had spent most of the previous day being poked, prodded and generally provoked. So she was already used to having no privacy.

Jake, however, crossed his arms over his chest and scowled at the woman. "Is this really necessary at this hour?"

"Absolutely." Nurse Cheerful smiled sweetly. "Just as soon as we get a good sonogram, we'll do some paperwork, and have her ready to go when the doctor stops by to do one last check."

"But—"

Kate gently grabbed Jake's arm. "It's okay. They only wanted to keep me overnight. My doctor will continue to monitor my condition."

Before he could protest more, Nurse Cheerful had whipped aside Kate's gown and was squirting cold blue gel all over her belly.

Since this was her fourth sonogram, Kate was familiar with the process. Blue gel on her belly plus the plastic wedge-shaped wand equaled cool black-and-white shots of the baby.

No matter how aloof she tried to remain, she couldn't help but feel a jolt of excitement every time she caught a glimpse of the baby's face or a delicate hand opening and closing. Today was no different. Except today, Jake was with her.

Nurse Cheerful flipped on the machine and unceremoniously began rubbing the wand over Kate's bared belly. As she worked, the nurse rattled off a series of questions: Have you felt the baby moving today? Have you felt any more contractions?

Kate answered without really paying attention. She kept glancing from the sonogram monitor to Jake. She hardly knew which brought her greater joy—the flickering images of their baby or the expression of absolute awe on Jake's face.

At first he could only stare in openmouthed wonderment. Then finally he murmured, "My God."

She couldn't help smiling a bit at his open amazement. It so completely reflected how she felt. Without even considering the consequences, she slipped her hand into his and gave it a squeeze.

He pulled his gaze away from the monitor for a second to stare at her, but a flicker of movement on the screen snagged his attention.

"Is that a hand?"

The nurse moved the wand to home in on the tiny hand. "Yup. And she's moving her fingers. That's a good sign." She moved the wand and the hand slipped out of focus. The image on the screen shifted to include a roundish black splotch, which was divided in two and twitching rapidly. "Heartbeat's nice and strong. Give me a minute and I'll have her heart rate for you."

"That's her heart," Jake mused, squeezing Kate's hand. "That's her beating heart."

Kate tore her gaze from Jake's face to watch the screen. It didn't look like much, but somehow it was one of the most beautiful things she'd ever seen. Their baby was alive and healthy despite all she'd been through.

"Her heart rate is 142. That's good. Pretty relaxed for the day she had yesterday. Looks like you've got a pretty tough little girl on your hands. She's a strong one."

Jake's gaze jerked to the nurse's face. "It's a girl?"

Instantly the nurse turned red. "You kept referring to her as 'her.' I assumed you knew."

"No." Then Jake pinned Kate with a stare. "Did you know?"

"No. But I kind of had a gut feeling, remember?"

Again, Jake squeezed her hand. "Yeah. I remember."

The nurse seemed to recover quickly from her faux pas. "Well, your baby girl certainly seems healthy. The doctor will review this when he gets in. Otherwise, I think we're about done here."

Before Nurse Cheerful could hustle off, Jake stopped her. "Can we see her face?"

The nurse shot him an odd look.

"I haven't been to any of the other sonograms," Jake explained.

Understanding dawned and the nurse went to work searching for a good view of their little girl's face.

As she watched Jake, Kate felt guilt burgeoning within her. She'd had the first sonogram at seven weeks—long before Beth and Stew dropped their bombshell—to confirm the viability of the pregnancy. At that sonogram, Beth and Stew had been with her and it had never occurred to anyone that Jake might be interested in attending. As soon as she'd arrived at the hospital yesterday, she'd had a sonogram to make sure the baby was okay, but he hadn't been there for that one, either.

At eighteen weeks, she'd had a routine anatomy sonogram. She purposely hadn't mentioned it to him. Having him come to doctor's appointments with her seemed entirely too intimate. Too much like what real married couples expecting a baby did.

Now she realized what her defensiveness had deprived him of. An irreplaceable opportunity to see the child he'd helped to create. A child who'd always been his to keep.

His hand was warm and strong around hers. Each time he tightened his grip on her hand, she felt a complementary tightening around her heart.

She looked from his face to the gray-scale face on the screen. The baby opened her mouth to yawn, then curled her tiny fist up to her mouth and popped her thumb inside.

As she sat there, watching her husband watch their daughter sucking her thumb, Kate realized the horrible answer to her question. She was a coward.

But she didn't want to be one anymore.

Eighteen

Jake watched the nurse wheel the sonogram machine from the room with a mixture of excitement and dread.

On the one hand, he wanted to be alone with Kate. To hold her in his arms and talk about the joy of seeing their baby girl's face for the first time.

On the other hand, he couldn't blame her for no longer wanting to be with him. He'd promised to protect her, sworn she could trust him. And he'd let her down. She might never be able to forgive him.

If she still wanted to get a divorce, he'd honor her wishes. After he did everything in his power to convince her she was wrong. But he knew how stubborn she could be. He'd have to act fast.

"Kate, I—"

"Jake—"

They both broke off at the same time. She laughed nervously, but laughing was the last thing he felt like doing.

"You go." She clasped her hands together on top of the blanket in a posture that was—for Kate—practically demure. But she didn't meet his gaze.

This wasn't good. Not at all.

Maybe it would have been polite to let her go first, but screw polite. He was pretty damn certain he didn't want to hear what she had to say. No way was he going to give her the chance to blow him off before he could say his piece.

"Look, Kate, I know you have this whole list of reasons why we should get a divorce, but I think you're wrong."

"Jake, I—"

"Just hear me out. It's only fair that you hear all the reasons why we should stay married."

"But—"

"Come on, Katie, you're nothing if not fair."

She opened her mouth as if to protest, then just shrugged. "Okay, but—"

He didn't give her a chance to launch any more protests. "Things are going to be tougher now than they were before. Even if you hire someone to be with you during the day, you can't hire someone to be there twenty-four hours a day. That's just not feasible. I can be there in the evenings and on weekends."

He studied her expression, looking for any sign she might be receptive. A little frown had settled onto her forehead.

Okay, so she wasn't convinced yet. He'd just have to press on.

"Plus, there's your job to think of. Hatcher could use our divorce against you. He could even use your need for medical leave against you. You don't know what he's capable of."

Kate's frown deepened. "Those are the only reasons you think we should stay married?"

Ah, crap. This wasn't working.

"Well…no, of course not." Okay, Morgan, think. What would convince her? What did she care most about? "Obviously, there's also the baby to think of."

"The baby," she said flatly.

"Sure. If we take care of you, we take care of the baby. And a healthy baby is what's most important to both of us, right?"

"Yes, of course." But he couldn't help notice her hands clenching and unclenching on the blanket over her belly. "You're absolutely right." Suddenly she flipped the covers back and swung her legs over the side of the bed. "I'll go ahead and change. That way I'll be all ready to go when the doctor comes by."

He watched in confusion as she gingerly walked toward the bathroom. She'd almost made it there when he stopped her.

"Whoa. Hold on a minute. Did I miss something?"

"No, not at all."

"So did you just agree we should stay married?"

"Your arguments were very persuasive."

"But did I persuade you?"

He held his breath waiting for her answer. So much was riding on it. So much more than she knew. This wasn't about her job. It wasn't even about the health of the baby. This was about their whole future.

How funny that mere weeks ago, she'd had to convince him to get married and now he was desperately trying to convince her to stay married. And all he could do was wait for her answer and try again if it was "no."

For a long moment she just stared at the floor and

said nothing. Finally she turned to him, her eyes brimming with tears.

"Everything you've said makes sense. But no matter how much we both love this baby, she's not enough to base a marriage on. Not a real marriage anyway. Not the kind of marriage I want."

"What kind of marriage is that?"

"A marriage based on love."

Jake felt as if his heart skipped a beat and he had to suck in a deep breath. "Are you saying that's what you want in *a* marriage or that's what you want from *our* marriage?"

He couldn't take his eyes from her face as he waited for her to answer. It was all he could do not to stride across the room, pull her into his arms and try to coax from her the answer he so desperately wanted.

But he made himself stand still. The time for persuasion was past. Now he just wanted the truth.

"I want both," she said finally, her hand drifting to her belly. "It's great that you love the baby, but that's not enough for me. I need you to love me, too. Really love me. Not just say you do. Because I love you. Goodness knows, I tried not to. But I—"

She was in his arms, his lips moving over hers, before the next words could make it out of her mouth. As they kissed he was painfully aware of the delicacy of her condition. So he poured into the kiss all of the tenderness he felt. All of the love. Because he wanted her to know—unequivocally—how much he loved her.

He brushed his lips across hers one final time, then ended the kiss. Cradling her face in his hands, he gazed down into her eyes, willing her to believe him. To trust him.

"Yes, I love our baby. But I love her even more *because* she's our baby. She's a part of us. And I love that she's a part of you, because I love you." Kate's eyes widened slightly and her lips started to curl into a smile. "If it hadn't been for our little girl, I may never have had the chance to fall in love with you. But I love you—and will always love you—because of who you are. Not because of the baby."

Whatever else he might have said, she cut off by rising onto her toes and pulling his mouth down to hers. She kissed him with none of the tenderness he'd shown, but plastered her mouth and body against his. If she felt delicate or frail, she didn't show it in her kiss.

And her love? That was definitely in her kiss. The pure emotion there left no room for doubt.

Finally, she pulled back just enough to smile and say, "I do believe you've convinced me."

"I know you might have trouble trusting me. But that will never happen again. I promise. And I—"

"Jake, it's okay. Last night, you said you couldn't protect me from everything. And you're right. No one could make that kind of promise."

"Kate, I—"

"I know you'll protect me when you can, but there will be things you can't protect me from. There will be things I can't protect you from, either. The important thing is that we don't let those things drive us apart. If we keep this baby and stay married, yes, there's potential for all kinds of things to go wrong. But there's also potential for all kinds of wonderful things, too. I think I'm finally willing to accept both."

Jake met her gaze, his eyes filled with love and hope. "So you really want to give this marriage a shot? You want to keep our baby?"

In love there was so much potential for pain, but there was potential for great joy, too. It made her so happy, knowing she could make him happy.

She nodded. "I do. We'll need to talk to Beth and Stew of course, but yes, I do." Offering up a tremulous smile, she added, "Jake, all this time I thought I couldn't be the right woman for you because you wanted someone you could rescue."

"But—"

She stopped his words with a finger to his lips. "The thing is, it turns out I do need you to rescue me. I need you to save me from myself. Without you, I might have spent my whole life hiding from life. But now I'm ready to face anything. As long as I have you."

A knock sounded. Then the doctor strolled into the room without waiting for an answer, without even looking up from the clipboard he held open in his arm. "Well, everything here looks good, Ms. Bennet."

By the time the doctor looked up, Kate had stepped out of Jake's arms, but still held his hand in hers. "Actually, it's Mrs. Morgan."

The doctor glanced down at his chart in confusion. "But it…ah, I see. Jake Morgan is listed here as the father." He looked up at Jake. "That's you?"

Kate answered before he could. "Yes. We're the parents. She's our baby girl."

Then she slanted a look in Jake's direction that said much more than that.

* * * * *

LYING IN
YOUR ARMS

LESLIE KELLY

To my sisters, Lynn, Donna, Karen and Cheri.

You are always in my heart.

New York Times bestselling author **Leslie Kelly** has written dozens of books and novellas for Mills & Boon. Known for her sparkling dialogue, fun characters and steamy sensuality, she has been honoured with numerous awards, including a National Readers' Choice Award, a Colorado Award of Excellence, a Golden Quill and an RT Book Reviews Career Achievement Award in Series Romance. Leslie has also been nominated four times for the highest award in romance fiction, the RWA RITA® Award. Leslie lives in New Mexico with her own romantic hero, Bruce, and their daughters. Visit her online at www.lesliekelly.com or at her blog, plotmonkeys.com.

Prologue

The Hollywood Tattler—
Shane Going NC-17?

WELL, LADIES, GET ready to indulge in a sexy lovefest with
superhot movie star Tommy Shane. Word is circulating
that Shane's fiancée, screenwriter Madison Reid, is on
the verge of selling her naughtily-ever-after screenplay
and her hubby-to-be is going to star in it!

Shane, who regularly lands on everyone's sexiest
men alive lists, has played action heroes, romantic
leads and innocent soldiers. But my sources tell me
this next role—as a mysterious, dangerous man who
lures an innocent young woman into his dark sexual
fantasies—will be the edgiest, hottest performance of
his career.

As if women all over the world didn't already have
enough to fantasize about when it came to this golden-
haired Adonis.

Soon, fantasizing will be all other women can do.
Because we're also hearing rumors that Tommy and

his fiancée have finally started making wedding plans for next year. Although Shane and Reid—his childhood sweetheart—live in a swanky beachside house in Laguna, they're heading to the other coast for the nuptial celebration. They will reportedly be having a small, private ceremony with their families in Florida, where they grew up as next-door neighbors.

Can you imagine Thomas Superstud Shane being the boy next door? Be still my heart.

We don't know a whole lot about the beautiful Miss Reid. But we suspect millions of women around the world would give anything and everything to be in her shoes. Or at least in her bed. I mean, who doesn't want to know just how much of her sultry screenplay is based on her real-life adventures with Tommy!

Congratulations and good luck you gorgeous lovebirds. I'll be watching the mail for my invitation.

1

"WAIT, ARE YOU SAYING you *want* me to break up with you?"

Not sure she'd correctly heard the drop-dead gorgeous man sitting across from her, Madison waited for a response from Tommy Shane. Aka her fiancé, aka the handsomest man alive, aka Superstud, aka Academy Award nominee.

Aka the man who wanted *her* to dump *him* right after they'd intentionally leaked details about their hush-hush wedding.

Aka...WTF?

"Yeah, Mad. I do."

She didn't get angry, the way most fiancées probably would. She wasn't the typical fiancée and theirs wasn't a typical relationship. Not by a long shot. If they knew the truth, most people would say she and Tommy put the "dys" in dysfunctional.

So, no, she wasn't angry. She was just confused, not sure what was going on. "You're the one who wanted this engagement."

"I know."

"You're the one who leaked the wedding date to the press."

"I know that, too."

"You're the one who played up the childhood-sweethearts-going-home-to-Florida-to-get-married angle."

"Yes."

"You convinced me to leave New York and move out here."

He shook his head. "But you're glad about that, aren't you? Look how well you're doing. Any day now, you're going to get a call that one of the big studios is going to produce your screenplay."

She wished she could be as sure. Madison had confidence in the story she'd crafted and pitched to the studios, with Tommy's help. But that didn't make it a done deal, even with his name attached to it as the star. Although, that sure didn't hurt.

She hadn't written it with him in mind. She'd seen her possibly murderous hero being someone much more dark and twisted. But he'd read the script, loved it and asked for the role. Who was she to turn down Hollywood's number one box office draw?

"This isn't simply cold feet, is it?" she asked, glancing down at the feet in question. "Make that cold ginormous feet."

"They're warm and toasty," he said with a flirtatious grin that would melt the underwear off any woman. Well, any woman who didn't know him well. "And you know what they say, big feet…"

"Big, fat ego," she said with a definite eye roll. Tommy Shane had long ago lost the ability to flirt his way around her common sense. She liked him—loved him, in fact—but she was wise to his antics and not susceptible to his looks or his charm.

"So, what do you say? Will you dump me, ASAP, preferably in as public a manner as possible?"

"Dude, seriously? I'd be happy to dump you on your ass so hard your butt cheeks will look like pancakes," she said, feeling far more relieved than a supposedly blushing bride should. "But I have two questions. First, will anybody buy it?"

"Huh?"

"I mean, why would any woman ever break up with you?"

"Well, I'm gay."

There was that.

Tommy's legion of worldwide fans wouldn't believe it, but his sexuality hadn't been a secret to her, not for a long time. He might play the part of sex symbol to every woman on the planet, but in his private life, Tommy Shane was strictly attracted to men—lately one particular man—and was very happy about it.

"Yeah, but nobody knows about that. Wasn't your in-the-closet-ness the reason we got engaged in the first place?"

"Of course."

"And haven't we been playing lovebirds to the press to cement your cover story so you can keep those sexy-leading-man roles coming your way?"

He smirked. "Well, it wasn't for your smoking-hot bod."

Chuckling, she placed a hand against her smoking-hot hip, knowing she held as much sex appeal for him as a beach ball. The one time she'd tried to kiss him romantically—when they were in middle school—she'd known they lacked any chemistry. It hadn't taken her long to figure out why. Hell, she should have figured it out in elementary school when the two of them would always fight over who got to be Buttercup when they played Powerpuff Girls.

Although the story they'd fed to the press had been fairy-tale nonsense, there had been some truth in it. They had known each other from childhood. She, Tommy and her twin sister Candace—who'd always played Bubbles to their Buttercup during *The Power-puff Girls* days—had been inseparable growing up. He'd climbed into their window for secret sleepovers, had spent long summer days with them at the beach. He had taught Candace how to dance, and Madison how to give a blow job…using a banana, of course. He'd always loved to perform, but had also been strong—he even punched a guy once who'd groped Madison at a concert. Heck, he'd been the one who'd bought a pregnancy test kit for her when she'd had a late-period scare in high school. He'd even offered to marry her if the stick turned blue!

He was a wonderful, loyal, devoted friend. Which was why she had stepped in and agreed to get engaged to him in his time of need…after her sister, who was *supposed* to be the false fiancée, had gone and fallen in love with her dream man.

No, the engagement wasn't supposed to culminate in a real marriage, but their planned breakup was a long way off. They'd scheduled everything, figuring in shooting schedules and premieres, knowing how long they needed to keep up the pretense. They'd discussed how to pull off a gradual, *friendly* breakup once both of them were in good enough career positions to come out of it unscathed. And now he wanted to ditch all that in favor of an impromptu dumping, before they'd even had a chance to stage a public disagreement?

"Nobody'll buy it. You're the biggest fish in the ocean. What woman in her right mind would let you slip off her hook?"

"They'll believe it once the world knows what a cheating mackerel I am," he said with a simple shrug.

She gaped. "Tell me you're joking. You did not cheat!"

She didn't add *on me*. How could he cheat on her when they weren't involved? Even if the big rock on her finger said otherwise.

But there was someone else he could have cheated on, which would break Madison's heart. Tommy's new guy was wonderful.

"You didn't betray Simon, did you?"

"No, of course not," he insisted, looking horrified.

That made her feel a little better. Tommy wasn't the most reliable sort when it came to his romantic life. If he was stupid enough to screw up this new relationship, she'd personally whack him upside the head with his own SAG Award.

"So you two are still okay?"

"Fine." Tommy smiled wistfully. "He's great, isn't he?"

"More than great." Simon, a neurosurgeon, made her friend happier than she'd seen him in years. "So who'd you cheat on?"

"You."

"You're saying you have another best-friend-turned-fake-fiancée…besides Candace? I mean, I've always forgiven you for cheating on me with my sister, even when we were in third grade and you always picked her first for kick ball."

"Not Candace," he said. "I meant, you tell the world I cheated on you. Since I'm turning over an open-and-honest leaf, you don't even have to say it was with a woman. That'll just be what people will think. Who wouldn't dump me for cheating?"

Huh. He had a point. Technically, that was true.

"People will buy it. We'll be all Rob-and-Kristen-like."

She caught the reference. Madison wasn't a Hollywood insider, despite her engagement to a crown prince of Tinseltown, but who hadn't heard of the scandal surrounding one of Hollywood's "It" couples during the whole *Twilight* craze?

"Okay, so they probably would believe that. People have been wondering how on earth I caught you in the first place."

"Don't sell yourself short, gorgeous."

She shrugged. Attractive? Yeah, she'd cop to that. But gorgeous? No way. She had never felt more inept and lacking as a woman than when she'd attended some of these L.A. parties packed wall-to-wall with women who were pretzel-stick thin, cover-girl perfect and runway model clothed. Oh, and saber-toothed-tiger clawed. Sheesh, the competition out here was insane.

"But even if it works, *why* should we do it now rather than sticking to our long engagement, slow-breakup plan?"

He thrust a hand through his thick, sun-streaked hair, looking boyishly adorable. If there'd been an audience, all the women would just have sighed, every one of them dying to smooth that soft hair back into place. Madison just grunted.

Melodrama over, he said, "It's because of Simon."

"He asked you to do this?"

"No. We've been talking about how important it is to be honest. Me living a lie with you—no matter how good the reason or the fact that you're fine with it—won't convince him I'm growing and becoming true to myself."

"Simon would never want you to sabotage your career."

"I know. But this is a step toward the kind of life I want, and the kind of man I want to be. One who isn't afraid, who doesn't go to crazy lengths to hide who he is."

She rarely heard Tommy talk this way. His blue eyes didn't sparkle with mischief. He didn't appear to be acting. He was just being the sweet boy next door she'd always known, telling her what he really wanted, all the pretense stripped away, all the trappings of his lifestyle shoved into the background. Just Tommy. Just her friend. Her friend who needed her.

She'd always been there when he needed her, and vice versa.

"Besides, you're not being true to yourself, either," he added. "You aren't like Candace. I knew it wouldn't be a hardship for her to go without sex for a while. You, though… I know you're horny enough to climb out of your own skin."

She couldn't deny that; Tommy knew her well. She'd been the first one of the three of them to lose her virginity—at sixteen—and had probably had more lovers than the other two combined. The six months of their engagement had been the longest she'd gone without sex in *years,* and her biggest, naughtiest toys just weren't filling the gap anymore. So to speak.

"You've been a great fiancée. Now you can be off the hook and go out there and *get* some."

"Sure, I'll just find a hot guy and say, 'Do me, baby.'"

"Yep."

"Not so easy."

"Not so hard, either. So, will you dump me? Free us both?"

Hell, she'd gotten engaged to him out of love, hadn't she? Of course she could dump the man for the same reason.

But, she suddenly realized, dumping him might not be in his best interest. Because here was the thing about movie star breakup scandals. It was always the cheater who got slammed, not the cheatee. Frankly, Madison didn't need public approval. They wouldn't pay one moment's attention to a wannabe screenwriter who'd had a fling.

But Tommy Shane? Every woman's fantasy man, every kid's comic book hero, every man's wanna-be-him guy? Well, hell. Tommy Shane couldn't be a cheater. It would be like…like John Wayne turning out to be a secret communist or something.

"We can do this," she told him, slowly thinking it out. "But I have a condition of my own."

"I'll still pay you half of everything I made this year."

"Forget the money." She'd never take another dime from him. Tommy had supported her while she'd finished her screenplay. He'd helped her pay her student loans. And she'd let him, figuring if she was going to give up her life, her job, her home and any other man for the duration of their engagement, she would earn it. She was not coming out of this relationship grasping the short end of the stick.

But she was almost free now. That was worth more than money. She'd gone into this with her eyes open, and didn't regret it, but she couldn't deny a big part of her was ready to be just Madison Reid, writer, not Tommy Shane's fiancée.

And, though she wouldn't admit it, getting to have sex again was a pretty darned big perk, too.

"So what's your condition?" he asked.

"The condition is…I take the heat."

"Huh?"

"I'm the cheater. I'm the bitch. And you break up with me."

He sputtered. "No, you can't do that."

She put a hand up, cutting off his arguments. "Tommy Shane can't be a cheating dog. I can. Nobody'll give a damn."

"You don't know that," he said. "The press can be nasty."

"Why would they? They'll say I'm an idiot for letting you get away and that'll be the end of it."

"What if it's not?"

"Well, then, I'll…take a vacation. You send me somewhere tropical and I'll hide out until they forget all about me."

"You should do that anyway. Find a nice, hunky beach bum to shack up with for a little while," he said with an eyebrow wag.

"I'll think about it. So we're agreed?"

He frowned, clearly not liking the idea, but she wasn't going to change her mind. Tommy would never get through a scandal unscathed, but she would. Who cared about Madison Reid? She could take whatever heat anybody wanted to dish out because it wouldn't last for long.

And if it did? Well…there was always the somewhere-tropical-with-a-hunky-beach-bum idea.

2

"IT'S GOING TO BE one hell of a honeymoon."

Although the driver of the cab looked confused, considering Leo Santori was sitting alone in the backseat, he didn't reply. And it wasn't just because this was Costa Rica and Leo didn't speak Spanish. The driver spoke English, or something very much like it. No, he just seemed to be abiding by the code that said Americans on vacation in tropical paradises could be as strange as they wanted to be. It was all good. No problem.

"All good. No problem," Leo muttered.

All good that he was honeymooning alone.

No problem that he'd been betrayed.

It's really all good that my fiancée cheated on me six months ago so we canceled the wedding, which was supposed to have taken place yesterday. No problem that she kept the ring, the apartment, her yuppy bichon frise—which really was *no problem—and the new KitchenAid mixer, and I kept the nonrefundable honeymoon.*

She'd also kept the best man. The one she'd cheated with.

No problem.

Still, it certainly was not a conversation he wanted to have with anyone. Especially not now that he was here in Central America, ready to embark on some to-hell-with-it adventures. Those would definitely include surfing and zip lining. Good drinks, beautiful beaches, exotic foods.

They also might include getting laid. *If* he happened to meet a woman who was interested in a rebound-sex-fest with a Chicago firefighter who had a slight chip on his shoulder and a honeymoon package created for two but starring only one.

"Here we are, *señor,*" said the driver.

The ride from the international airport in Liberia to this west coast paradise had been comfortable. The driver had pointed out various sights that Leo felt sure he'd explore over the next several days. No doubt about it, Costa Rica was every bit as beautiful—sunny, robin's-egg-blue skies, vivid hills and jungles, perfect eighty-degree climate—as the brochures had said. An outstanding choice for a honeymoon. Even a solo one.

"Thanks, man," he said.

The driver pulled out his suitcase and handed it off to a broadly smiling doorman who quickly swept it through the entrance of the hotel, which, as advertised, looked small, tasteful and upscale. Inside, Leo glanced around, noting that every wall seemed open to the outdoors. But it was still comfortable, a soft tropical breeze blowing through, whispering along the cool tile floors and setting the potted palms in gentle motion.

A bellhop engaged him in conversation in heavily

accented English as they walked to the check-in desk. Leo only understood half of what he said, responding with smiles and nods.

The woman at the desk greeted him. "Welcome, Mr. Santori, we're so very glad to have you with us."

She smiled, obviously noting his surprise at being called by name. Then he thought about it and realized he might very well be the only person checking in today. He remembered from the research he'd done on this place that there were only twenty-four rooms on the whole property. Twenty-four bungalows each with a small, private pool and walled garden, just the thing for a romantic interlude between a new bride and groom.

Christ, what was he doing here?

The middle-aged woman, whose English was only slightly tinged with an accent, glanced past him and looked around the open lobby. "And where is Mrs. Santori?"

He grimaced. Obviously, despite his calls and his emails, word had not filtered down to the front desk that he would be traveling alone.

"Uh…"

"Oh, dear," the woman said, reading something on the screen and biting her lip in consternation. She swallowed, visibly embarrassed. "I'm so sorry, Mr. Santori, I didn't see the notation on your reservation."

Okay, so *somebody* had paid attention when he'd changed the reservation to make it clear he was no longer traveling with a companion. It had just taken her a moment to see the note. He wondered what it said.

Maybe: *attention—pathetic sap was cheated on and didn't get married.*

He doubted it happened often, but he couldn't be the first single-on-a-honeymoon vacationer they'd ever seen.

He didn't ask her to turn the screen so he could read it. His imagination was good enough. "No problem."

She smiled her appreciation. "How was your trip from the airport, sir?"

"Fine, thanks."

"Wonderful." Her fingers continued to click on her keyboard as she finished working on his check-in. "We have you in our Emerald Bungalow. It's one of our nicest on the west side of the property. Sunsets over the Pacific will make you gasp."

Yeah. He was sure he'd be doing a lot of gasping during this trip, just not for the reasons he'd expected. It sure wouldn't be out of breathlessness from the ninety-seven ways he and Ashley would have been having sex.

He pushed her name out of his head. He'd done a great job of that for the past six months, since the day he'd mistaken her phone for his and discovered the kinds of intimate sexting pictures he'd *never* want to see from a guy. Definitely not from Tim, his own old friend…and best man. Especially not when those messages were written to—and welcomed by—Leo's fiancée.

Six months had been enough to calm the anger, soften the insult, heal the heart. For the most part. It maybe hadn't been enough to kill the embarrassment, which was what he most felt these days when he thought about it. Which wasn't often.

It was only because he'd come here, to take advantage of the nonrefundable vacation he'd paid for months before the scheduled wedding date, that he was thinking of his ex. Back home in Chicago, around his big extended family, or the guys at the station or the women wanting to help him jump back into the dating game, he was able to forget there'd ever been an Ashley. Or that he'd ever been stupid enough to think he'd *really* been in love with her. If he'd *really* been in love with her, Tim wouldn't have ended up with a broken nose—he'd have ended up in traction. Or, if his great uncle Marco—supposedly mob connected—had had his way, with a pair of cement shoes.

But no. That wasn't Leo's way. No broken legs or kneecaps, definitely nothing even worse. Ashley just hadn't been worth it. When it came right down to it, he'd known his pride had been a whole lot more bruised than his heart. So he'd walked out on her without a big scene, not moved by her crocodile tears. And he'd let Tim off with a punch in the face…and a warning to watch his wallet since Ashley was a bit of a spender.

Frankly, that was why he figured she'd gone for the guy to begin with. The one place Tim had ever outdone Leo in *anything* was the wallet. Hopefully the lawyer would continue raking in the bucks to keep Ash supplied in the stupid snowmen figurines to which she was addicted. Actually, screw it. He didn't care if she never got another one, or if the freaky-faced little monsters melted. At least he didn't have to look at them anymore.

"Sir?" the desk clerk prompted.

Realizing he'd let his mind drift, he shoved away thoughts of Ashley. He was in paradise and had no room in his head for anything dark. "Sounds great, thanks."

"Here you go," she said, handing him a plastic key-card. She also gave him a map of the property. "I hope you have a wonderful time. There are so many things to do, so many people to meet."

He needed to get away from her slightly pitying expression before she mentioned that she had a single niece or something.

The bellhop approached with his suitcase and led him out of the lobby onto a path that wound through the lush grounds. He pointed out a few conveniences including, Leo thought, directions to the pool area and the beach. Or maybe he'd been pointing out a bird or an outhouse, frankly, Leo had no idea.

Finally, they came to a stop in front of a thatch-roofed cottage. "You," the man said with a big smile.

Nodding, Leo slid his key into the reader. The light didn't turn green, and he didn't hear a click as the lock disengaged.

"Is no good?" the belhop asked.

"Doesn't appear to be."

The worker took the key card, tried himself, several times. It didn't work for him, either.

"Forget it. I'll have them reprogram it," Leo said, not happy about having to trudge back to the lobby. Right now, he just wanted to strip out of his clothes and take a cool shower.

"Here," the bellhop said, pulling out his own master keycard. That would save him the lobby trip for a while, anyway.

Following the man inside, Leo glanced around the room. It was large, airy, bright and immaculate. The vaulted ceiling was lined in pale wooden planks and two fans spun lazily overhead. Sandstone tile floors, peach walls, vibrant paintings of island life…just as advertised. A small café table designed for cozy, intimate breakfasts stood in one corner near a love seat. And the enormous king-size bed looked big enough for four honeymooners. He hid a sigh and shifted his gaze.

The bellhop lifted the suitcase onto the dresser, then headed over to unlock the patio door. He pulled it open and a warm, salt-and-flower-tinged breeze wafted in, bathing Leo's skin. He wouldn't need any AC; the ocean breezes were amazing.

"Pool, is very private," the man said.

"I can see that." Naked midnight swims had sounded appealing when they'd chosen this place. "Thank you," he said, pulling some cash out of his pocket and handing it over.

The man smiled and departed. Alone, Leo walked to the sliding door, glancing outside at the small pool, which was surrounded on all sides by a tall hedge covered with bright pink flowers. The owners had really meant it when they'd promised privacy for the pool. The resort boasted a large one, with a swim-up bar and lounge chairs, but right now, wanting that coolness on every inch of his skin, he figured this smaller one would do the trick. Midnight naked swims? Hell…

with that hedge and the stone wall behind it, daytime ones would be fine, too.

Smiling, he checked out the rest of the suite, pausing in the bathroom to strip out of his clothes and grab a towel, which he slung over one shoulder. He returned to the patio door, put one hand on the jamb and another on the slider and stood naked in the opening, letting that breeze bathe his body in coolness.

Heaven.

He was just about to step outside and let the warm late-day sun soak into his skin when he heard something very out of place. A voice. A woman's voice. Coming from right behind him…inside his room.

"Oh. My. God!"

Shocked, he swung around, instinctively yanking the towel off his shoulder and letting it dangle down the middle of his body. To cover the bits that were dangling.

A woman stood in his room, staring at him, wide-eyed and openmouthed. They stared at each other, silent, surprised, and Leo immediately noticed several things about her.

She was young—his age, maybe. Definitely not thirty.

She was uncomfortable, tired, or not feeling well. Her blouse clung to her curvy body, as if it was damp with sweat. Dark smudges cupped her red-rimmed eyes, and she'd already kicked off her shoes, which rested on the floor right by the door, as if her first desire was to get barefoot, pronto.

Oh. And she was hot. Jesus, was she ever.

Gorgeous, in fact, with honey-brown hair that fell in a long, wavy curtain over her shoulders. Although reddened, her big green eyes were sparkling, jewel-toned, heavily lashed, with gently swooping brows above. Her face was perfect—high cheekbones, pretty chin, lush mouth. That body… Well, he suddenly blessed perspiration because the way that silky blouse clung to the full curves of her breasts was enough to make his heart skip every other beat. And the tight skirt that hugged curvaceous hips and several inches of long, slim thigh— leaving the rest of her legs bare for admiring—was making it skip every one in between.

She was also something else, he suddenly realized. Shocked. Stunned. Maybe a little afraid.

"Hi," he said with a small smile. He remained where he was, not wanting to startle her.

"I… You… You're naked!"

"I am, yes."

Her green eyes moved as she shifted her attention over his body, from bare shoulders, down his chest, then toward the white towel that he clutched in his fist right at his belly. She continued staring, scraping her attention over him like a barber used a blade—close, oh so damned close, and so very edgy.

Something like comprehension washed over her face and her tensed, bunched shoulders relaxed a little bit. "Did Tommy send you?" she whispered.

"Huh?"

"Of course it was Tommy. Or Candace? But, wait, this isn't… I'm not… Look, I don't need you."

"Don't need me for what?" *To do your taxes? Cut your hair? Carry your suitcase?*

Put out your fire?

Oh, he suspected he could do that last one, and it wasn't just because of his job.

"To have sex with me. I don't need to get laid this badly."

His jaw fell open. *"What?"*

She licked her lips. "I mean, you're very attractive and all." Her gaze dropped again, and he noticed the redness in her cheeks, and the audible breaths she drew across those lush lips. "Still, I just don't do that. I couldn't."

He had no idea what she was babbling about. But he was starting to get an idea. The gentlemanly part of him wanted to tell her right away that she was in the wrong room. The *male* part demanded he wait and see what on earth this beauty would say next.

"You couldn't do what?" he asked, letting the towel drop a little bit. Oh, it still covered what he needed to cover, but he wasn't gripping it the way a spinster virgin would grip her petticoats. And when she licked her lips, eyeing the thin trail of hair that disappeared beneath the terry fabric, he couldn't resist letting it slip a little bit more.

He was no flasher. But damn, the woman made it interesting to be ogled.

Her eyes almost popped out of her head. "I couldn't, you know, uh, hire you."

He didn't ask what for. It sure wasn't to trim her hedges. At least, not any green ones. He'd begun to suspect she'd taken him for an escort…or even a gigolo. Why on earth this beautiful woman would need either one, he couldn't say. But he was having fun trying to figure it out.

"I'm not desperate. I would never, uh, have sex with a, uh, professional." Her voice falling into a mumble, she added, "Not even one with the finest male ass I have ever seen in my entire life."

Leo was torn between indignation, laughter and lust. Right now, judging by how he felt about the way her assessing eyes belied every word she said about not wanting him, lust was winning the battle.

"You wouldn't, huh?" He stepped closer, moving easily, slowly, almost gliding.

She did the same, edging closer, her bare feet sliding smoothly over the tile floor. "No. Never."

They met near the end of the bed, both stopping when they got within a couple of feet of each other. She licked her lips, shrugged her shoulders, and said, "So, thanks for the effort, it was a, um, nice surprise. But I think you should go."

"You'd like that, would you?"

Her eyes said *no*. Her lips forced out the word, "Yes."

"I can't do that," he said, his voice low, thick.

He edged closer, unable to resist lifting a hand to brush a long, drooping curl back from her face, tucking it behind her ear. She hissed a little, tilting her head, as if to curve her cheek into his palm.

"Why not?" she whispered.

His tone equally as intimate, he replied, "Because you're in my room."

She froze, eyed him, then quickly looked around. Her gaze landed on his suitcase. She turned to peer into the

bathroom, obviously seeing the clothes he'd let fall to
the floor. Then back at him. "Your…"

"My room," he said, a slow smile pulling his lips up.

"You mean, you're a… You're not a…"

"Right. I'm a. And I'm not a."

She groaned softly, her green eyes growing bright
with moisture. Those shoulders slumped again in pure,
visible weariness and her mouth twisted. She didn't look
so much embarrassed as purely humiliated. Dejected.

"I'm so sorry," she muttered.

She backed up a step, obviously not realizing how
close she was to the bed. Her hip banged into the
wooden footboard, and she winced, jerking away and
suddenly losing her balance. She tumbled to her side,
toward the hard tiled floor.

Leo didn't stop to think. He lunged, diving to catch
her as she fell, letting out an oomph as she landed in
his arms. Her tall, slender body was pressed against
his, fitting perfectly, her head tucked under his chin,
her slim waist wrapped in one arm, her shoulders in the
other. She didn't immediately squirm away. Instead, she
stared up at him, her eyes round, her mouth rounder.

Their stares locked and he found himself trying to
identify just what shade of green those beautiful eyes
were. Emerald? Jade? Jungle? Something like all of the
above, plus they had a tiny ring of gold near the pupil,
looking like a starburst.

She said nothing, just stared at his face. The moment
stretched between them, long, heavy and strange. It
was as if they were communicating on a deep, elemental level, no words being necessary, saying everything

two people who'd just met would usually say. Like they wanted to get the preliminaries out of the way. For what, he didn't yet know.

"Thank you," she said, breathing the words across those lush lips.

If this were a movie, his next step would be to kiss her.

If it were a steamy one, the kiss would lead to so much more. He could suddenly see himself touching her, stroking the tip of his finger down the slick column of her throat, into the V of her blouse. Flicking it open, button after button, and pulling the fabric away from her heated skin.

In a moment as long as a single heartbeat, his mind had filled in all the blanks, seeing what it would be like to touch her, make love to her, without ever even learning her name. As if she were a present who'd landed in his arms just because he deserved her.

His body reacted—how could it not react?—but the position wasn't awkward enough to make it incredibly obvious to her. But maybe she was aware, anyway. A pink flush had risen up her face and her lips had fallen apart so she could draw deep, shaky breaths. He could see the frantic racing of her pulse in her throat, and her body trembled.

Yeah. She knew. And judging by the warm, musky scent of woman that began to fill his every inhalation, he wasn't the only one affected by the shocking encounter.

There's one problem. This isn't a movie.

Right. This was real life, she was a stranger and he,

as far as he knew, was a nice guy. The woman was obviously confused, light-headed enough to fall when she moved too quickly. And she didn't look like the type to have anonymous sex with someone she'd known for five minutes.

Time to end this, he knew. Time to put her on her feet, push her out the door and hope he ran into her again this week when she was steady, healthy and fully in control of her thoughts.

God, did he hope he'd been good enough in his life to be rewarded like that.

"This is a little awkward," she finally whispered, as if realizing the cloud of lust had begun to lift from his brain and reality was returning.

"Easy for you to say. At least you have some clothes on."

A tiny gasp escaped her lips. Reflexively, she cast a quick glance down at the floor. He followed the glance, seeing the same pile of white fabric she was seeing.

His towel. He'd dropped it when he'd lunged to catch her.

Yeah. He was naked. Completely naked, aroused at the feel of hot, musky, soft woman in his arms.

A woman who looked on the verge of…

"Son of a bitch," he mumbled.

Because she was no longer on the verge of anything. The beautiful stranger had fainted.

3

MADISON HAD BEEN HAVING the strangest dream. As she
slowly woke up, feeling coolness on her face, she realized she must have drifted off on the plane. The cool air
had to be coming from the vent over her seat.

She shifted, but didn't open her eyes right away, liking the dream a little too much. In it, she'd already
arrived at her destination—a tropical resort where
she intended to hide out for a week. She'd entered her
room, exhausted, sweaty, miserable and nauseous from
the long cab ride—necessitated by her landing at the
wrong Costa Rican airport. Just another example of how
quickly she'd had to get out of the U.S., how desperate
she'd been to get away.

Things hadn't gotten much better on her arrival. The
doorman had been arguing with a deliveryman, the
guy at the check-in desk barely spoke English and kept
suggesting she wait for a woman who was apparently
on break. She'd lost patience, demanding her key and
dragged her own suitcase through the thickly vegeta-
tive grounds.

Arriving in her room, wanting nothing but a cold shower and bed, she'd entered, kicked off her shoes, and had been stunned to behold a naked Adonis standing with his back toward her.

That was how she knew she'd been dreaming. Men that gorgeous, that utterly perfect, didn't exist outside of dreams and fantasies. Even Tommy, admittedly one of the handsomest men alive, wasn't built like *that*.

The man's hair had been dark, almost black, short, thick and wavy. And his bare body had been a thing of art. Broad shoulders had flexed as he'd leaned in the doorway, as if wanting to soak up the outdoors. His strong back was delineated with muscle that rippled with his every movement. Smooth skin encased a slim waist and hips, and he had an unbelievably perfect butt and long, powerful legs.

He'd turned around to reveal a strong, handsome face, masculine and unforgettable. Broad of brow, with deep-set, heavily-lashed brown eyes, slashing cheekbones, jutting chin with a tiny cleft, and a sexy, half smiling mouth.

Unfortunately, her dream state hadn't left him completely uncovered in the front. Her brain had inserted a coy white towel. She wanted to dive back into the dream to see it drop. Oh, she hoped she didn't have to open her eyes before that towel dropped.

But, wait…it *had* dropped. Hadn't it? For some reason, she remembered it on the floor. But she couldn't remember if he'd let it fall as he took her into his arms to passionately kiss her or what. Stupid dream really needed to come back and fill in all the blanks. Or at least most of them. The most interesting ones. She wasn't going to let herself wake up until it did, not even if they landed and started deboarding the plane.

"Open your eyes."

She growled in her throat.

"Come on, open up. You're okay."

That voice was seriously messing with her good dream vibes. But it was, she had to concede, a nice voice. Deep, sexy, masculine. Was it a flight attendant, rousing her for landing? Or was she still dreaming about Mr. Tall, Dark and Built?

"Come on, sweetheart." Coolness brushed her temples, soft, featherlight, then her mouth. "Take a sip."

Moisture kissed her lips. Was her dream guy giving her champagne? She swallowed.

Water. Not champagne.

And that moisture on her temples was sliding down into her hairline.

And…and…this wasn't a dream.

Her eyes flew open.

Definitely not a dream.

"You," she breathed.

It had really happened. She'd arrived at the hotel, walked into her room, seen a gorgeous stranger, and, what? Fallen and hit her head or something? What other reason would there be for her to be…where was she?

It took only a second for her to gather her wits. Holy shit, she was lying flat on her back in a bed. And this handsome, bare-chested stranger was sitting right beside her, tenderly pressing a damp facecloth to her forehead, eyeing her with visible concern.

"You're okay. Take deep breaths. Drink a little more."

She obediently sipped from the water bottle he placed against her lips, trying to kick her brain back into operation.

"What happened?"

"You fainted."

"I never faint." Girlie-girls fainted, and Madison was not a girlie-girl. She'd never been the type who'd wilt like a flower, especially not in front of some man.

Some man who'd apparently picked her up, put her on the bed and taken care of her.

"There's a first time for everything."

She frowned, still having a hard time believing it.

"Why would I faint?"

"When was the last time you ate?"

"I can't remember."

"Well, that could have something to do with it."

Yes, it could.

"You don't look like you've slept much lately, either."

She couldn't remember the last time she'd had a full, uninterrupted night's sleep. "I slept on the plane. Or… maybe that was a dream of a dream. Hell, I don't know."

"You looked pretty uncomfortable when you arrived. Sick maybe."

Sick? Maybe sick at heart. Heaven knew she had reason, considering what her life had been like in recent weeks.

"Do you think you're going to be okay? Should I have the hotel call an ambulance?"

"Good heavens, no!" That was all she needed. More attention. So much for slinking unnoticed into another country and hiding from the world for a while. "I just… I was really carsick. I guess I flew into the wrong airport and it took hours to get here, with no air-conditioning and tons of twisty roads." Ugh, when she thought about all those ups, downs and hairpin turns, she felt her stomach roll over.

"You need to eat something."

It rolled again. But she knew he was right. Something light would probably be good.

She scrunched her brow, trying to recall the last time she'd sat down for a meal, and honestly couldn't remember. Crackers on the plane probably didn't count, though she'd give her right arm for some right now, if only to settle her churning stomach. Whether it was still churning from the drive here or from the fact that this gorgeous stranger was sitting close beside her on a bed, she had no idea.

"Why don't I order something from room service?"

"You don't have to do that."

"You know what they say, save someone's life and they become your responsibility."

She rolled her eyes. "Saved my life, huh?"

He smiled and a tiny dimple appeared in one cheek, taking that dish of handsome and adding a big heaping helping of freaking adorable on top.

"If I hadn't caught you, you would have cracked your head open. That tile's pretty hard."

She suddenly thought about everything that had happened before she'd tripped. The awkward conversation when she'd rejected his *services*. Services he hadn't even been offering.

The way they'd drawn closer together, even while she'd been saying no, as if some unseen magnetic pull between their bodies was working them into close proximity.

Tripping over her own stupid feet. Falling. Him catching her.

The towel on the floor.

Gasping a little, she immediately looked down, not sure whether to sigh in relief or cry in disappointment that he wasn't naked. At some point, he'd grabbed a pair of jeans and yanked them on. They weren't even buttoned, as if he'd been in too much of a hurry to do more than zip. Maybe because he'd been busy lifting her onto the bed, fetching a cold cloth and water to revive her?

She swallowed hard, her mouth dry despite the water she'd been sipping. Because she had a mad impulse to grab the tab of that zipper and pull it down a little more, to see if he'd taken the time to put on anything else before the jeans. She suspected not.

"Well, you definitely seem to be feeling better."

That deep, husky voice suddenly sounded more amused than solicitous. Madison realized what she'd done—jerking her attention off his face and ogling him like a stripper at ladies night—and gulped. She took a deep breath, then worked up the courage to look up. It was a slow lift of the eyes. She just couldn't resist focusing on his body, so close, so big and warm and spicy smelling. She had to note the flat stomach rippled with muscle, the broad chest, wiry hair encircling his flat nipples. Those powerful shoulders, corded and thick, and on up the throat to the strong, lightly grizzled jaw.

And the face. Oh, lord, that face.

That smiling face.

"You done?"

She took a deep, even breath.

"I'm a little confused," she mumbled, lifting a shaking hand to her head.

"Yeah, right."

Well, damn, so much for her thinking he was a gentleman. He could at least have pretended not to notice she'd been struck dumb by his looks.

Then she remembered the way he'd swooped down to catch her, how he'd put her on the bed and tenderly taken care of her. She conceded he was definitely a gentleman. Just one with a sense of humor. Considering she'd accused him of being a male prostitute, that was a good thing.

"Am I *really* in your room?"

"I think so," he said. Then he frowned. "Although, to be honest, I could be in the wrong one. My key didn't work, so the bellhop let me in. He didn't speak English very well…maybe we got our wires crossed and he let me into the wrong one."

"Well, if that's the case, feel free to stay."

One brow shot up.

She flushed. "I mean, they can put me in another room. You've already settled in."

"I really don't mind being the one to move. You look like you need to stay right in this bed until tomorrow."

Yeah, and she couldn't deny she wouldn't mind if he stayed in it with her. Well, she couldn't deny it to herself, anyway. She'd deny it to her last breath if he accused her of feeling that way.

"Long trip?"

"You have no idea. I've been traveling for what seems like days."

"From where?"

"Hmm, kind of all over," she said, thinking about the crazy whirlwind her life had become in the past few weeks, ever since she'd become the woman who'd betrayed the beloved Tommy Shane. Whore, slut, bitch, user, taker, Jezebel—some preacher had lobbed that one from a pulpit—those were some of the names that had been launched at her.

So much for thinking she would escape the breakup unscathed. Could she possibly have been more naive? She'd never in a million years imagined that by becoming the bad girl who'd broken the heart of Hollywood's golden boy, she would be loathed, vilified and reviled all over the freaking country.

She'd had paparazzi follow her wherever she went. People who recognized her from her picture on the cover of every tabloid on the newsstand greeted her with catcalls and jeers. Her life had been ripped to shreds on blogs and Hollywood gossip shows. A woman had even spit on her while she was grocery shopping.

So she'd taken off to northern California. Unfortunately, everyone knew she had a twin sister who lived in Napa, and she hadn't been hard to find. Poor Candace and Oliver, who liked to live quietly, had come into the limelight, too.

Then it was off to Florida to visit her parents. Same

story. She hadn't stayed there long. It had been way too much to ask for them to play along when they saw how horribly she was being treated. They knew better than anyone that she and Tommy hadn't had a real engagement, and her father had been dying to defend her. Or at least to punch a few photographers. Heaven forbid she be the cause of his next heart attack!

So distraught over the whole thing that he'd decided to come out, Tommy had planned a press conference. Madison had told him to forget it. What he needed to do was buy her a ticket to somewhere warm. Before long, she was headed for the airport again.

Costa Rica. It should be far enough away for her to regain her sanity. Lord, did she hope so. If this scandal hadn't blown over by the time she went home, she didn't know what she would do.

"Hello?"

She realized her mind had drifted. She cleared her throat. "What?"

"Where'd you go?"

"Nowhere I want to return to," she insisted vehemently.

"You're on the run, huh?"

"You might say that." Something prompted her to add, "You, too?"

He nodded. "Yeah, I guess I am."

"Not a bank robber, are you?" she asked, her tone light and teasing, even though the possibility that he was an ax murderer had flashed across her mind. Of course, if he'd wanted to chop her into kindling, he could easily have done it while she was unconscious. Besides, nobody with eyes as warm and kind as this man's could ever be the violent sort. He looked and behaved like a real-life hero.

"No. I stick strictly to convenience and liquor stores for my life of crime."

"Penny ante," she said with an airy wave of her hand.

"What about you? Are you a secret double agent seducing your way into state secrets?"

She batted her lashes. "You think I could?"

"Honey, I *know* you could."

The vehemence in his tone made her smile fade a bit. They were no longer teasing and joking. The attraction between them had been thick from the moment he'd turned around and found her in his room, but they'd been successfully hiding from it. Except, she suddenly remembered, for that long, heated moment when he'd held her in his arms after he'd caught her. She wasn't a mind reader, but she'd had no difficulty seeing what was going through his head. Probably because the same wild, erotic thoughts had been going through hers.

Sex with a stranger. Nameless, guiltless, hedonistic. Wild and unforgettable and something never to be regretted.

Oh, yes. She'd definitely been thinking those thoughts.

The fact that he had, too, and that he hadn't taken advantage of the situation, reinforced her *hero* assessment. She couldn't think of him as merely a nice guy… that didn't do justice to this man. She barely knew him, yet she knew he was ever so much more than that.

As if he'd noticed the warm, approving way she was

looking at him, he cleared his throat and slid off the bed, standing beside it. "Think you can sit up?"

She nodded, knowing she could do it on her own but somehow unable to refuse his help when he bent and slid a powerful arm behind her shoulders. He helped her into a sitting position and it was all she could do not to turn her head and nip at the rigid muscle flexing near her cheek, or to breathe deeply to inhale his musky, masculine scent.

Tommy had obviously been right. She needed sex, badly. And for a moment, she found herself wishing her first impression had been correct and the man had been for hire. Because completely unencumbered, drop-your-pants-right-now-and-make-me-come sex sounded pretty damned awesome right now.

"By the way," he said as he stepped away from the bed, "I'm Leo. Leo Santori. What's your name?"

"My name?" Considering how desperately she'd been trying to evade the scandal her name created lately, she had to think for a second about how to respond.

"You have one, don't you? It's the thing they give you at the hospital before you get to go home."

"I thought that was a blanket."

"I don't think they give you the blankets anymore."

"Pacifier?"

"Judging by the number of kids my cousins have had, I'm thinking they pretty much ship you out the door with just a red-faced mutant and a big old bill."

She snickered, liking the good humor in his tone. Then she seized on the rest of his comment. "So you don't have any of your own?"

"Pacifiers?"

She smirked. "Kids."

"Nope." He hesitated the briefest moment before adding, "And there's no one waiting in the wings to supply any."

So, he was single? How interesting that he'd felt the need to point that out. How fascinating that the knowledge made her heart leap in her chest.

"What about you?"

"No pacifiers. No kids. Nobody trying to get me to have them."

"Well, that covers just about everything," he said. "Except one… Are you going to tell me your name?"

"It's Madison," she said.

She didn't add the last name. No need to tempt fate, right? He didn't look like the kind of guy who followed Hollywood gossip. Nor did he seem the type who would sell her out to the tabloids. But then, the host of that syndicated radio show hadn't seemed like the type who would release her private number on the air so she could be bombarded with hateful calls and texts, either.

If this Leo Santori was the curious type, he could get online—she supposed even this reclusive resort had internet access—and check her out on Google. If he had her first and last names, he'd come up with a ton of hits, none of which put her in a very good light. Any of them would probably tip somebody off that they could make a quick buck selling her out to the tabloids. That was one reason she'd chosen this resort—they apparently catered to wealthy clientele looking for privacy.

Which made her wonder just what Leo Santori did for a living, and what he'd come here to escape.

"Okay, Madison, how about you stay here? I'll go talk to the people at the front desk and try to get this straightened out. And I'll bring you something to eat when I come back."

"I couldn't…"

"Sure you could. Feel free to dive into the pool and cool off while I'm gone. You look like you could use it."

She glanced out the door, seeing the beautiful swimming pool, so secluded in a private, idyllic garden, and realized he was right. Gliding through that cool water sounded like heaven right now.

"You're sure you don't mind?" she asked, feeling badly but also really not wanting to make that long trudge back to the front desk again.

"I'm sure," he said, heading into the bathroom. The bed was angled so that she had a clear view of him standing in front of the large mirror, and she watched as he grabbed a shirt and pulled it on over his massive shoulders.

Gracious, the man's muscles had muscles. Her heart was being all spastic, thudding and skipping along, and she couldn't seem to even out her breaths to get the right amount of oxygen. She felt light-headed, no longer queasy but there were definitely butterflies fluttering around in her stomach. Her legs were quivering a little, and she was hot between them.

The stranger was totally turning her on, like she couldn't ever remember being turned on before. He was like a miracle worker, a sex god who got women all hot and bothered for a living…except he apparently didn't follow through.

Right. Not a gigolo. Check.

Which was too bad.

You're being ridiculous a little voice in her head said. One thing Madison had never been accused of was having a limited imagination. Considering she wrote stories for a living—one of which was an extremely erotic film that would surely earn an NC-17 rating if it ever got made, and that looked pretty iffy right now—she couldn't deny she'd been thinking about wild, wicked sex a lot lately. It seemed the longer it had been since she'd had it, the more it filled her thoughts.

So much for coming to a secret hideaway to get some peace and tranquillity. If this guy's room was anywhere near hers, she would probably turn into some female Peeping Tom before the week was out. Because her mind just wasn't going to stop thinking about that white towel until she knew what was under it.

"What do you do, anyway?" she asked when he returned, carrying his shoes. *Stripper? Male model?*

"I'm a firefighter."

Her jaw fell open, then she snapped it closed. Because, that totally made sense. She could easily picture him carrying ladders and big, thick hoses. He probably carried one around with him all the time.

Stop it. You're delirious.

"A real American hero?" she said, amused that her instant assessment of him was so dead-on. He really *was* a hero.

"I wouldn't say that," he insisted with a self-deprecating shrug.

"Have you ever saved anyone's life?"

Another shrug. He looked embarrassed. "I guess."

"That was a pretty vague answer to a yes-or-no question," she said, her voice wry. "'I guess' is the type of answer you'd give if someone asked you if you had a good time at a party or if you liked a movie. Saving someone's life seems to require a bit more specificity."

"Okay."

"Was that a yes?"

He grinned. "I guess."

She couldn't help chuckling. "Where do you live?"

"Chicago. You?"

Hmm. Good question. She'd been raised in Florida. Then she'd moved to New York after grad school, determined to be a world-class journalist. Only, she'd realized she kind of hated journalists. That was when she'd started writing screenplays. And when she'd gotten engaged to Tommy, she'd moved to Southern California. Now, she honestly didn't know where she was going to live.

"I'm sort of between housing right now."

That dimple reappeared. "That was a pretty vague answer."

"I suppose it was. I've been living in L.A. But I'm not sure what I'm going to do when I leave here. I might go back to New York."

"Chicago's got better pizza."

Her jaw dropped. "You must be kidding. That loaf of bread with cheese on it that they serve in Chicago has got nothing on a thin, crispy slice of pepperoni from Ray's."

He drew up, looking offended. "My uncle and cousin run a pizza place with food that would make your taste buds decide to commit suicide rather than eat pizza anywhere else ever again."

"With all due respect to your uncle and cousin, you're mental cheese has obviously slipped off its crust. Because you're crazy."

"I challenge you to a taste test."

"I don't think we're going to find very good examples of New York *or* Chicago style here in Central America."

"When we get back stateside then."

Implying they might see each other again after they left here? Oh, how tempting a thought. But she forced herself to concede, an impossible one.

"Maybe," she murmured, quickly looking away. A sharp stab of disappointment shot through her because she knew she was lying.

She couldn't see him again. Not at home. Not here. Once he got the room situation straightened out, she needed to avoid him altogether.

Maybe if he'd been the gigolo she'd thought him, she'd take a chance. Or if he'd been anything but the delightful, warm, friendly, protective man she'd already seen him to be. As it was, though, she couldn't get involved with anybody like Leo Santori. Her life was too freaking messed up right now to involve anyone else in it.

"Well, guess I'll head up to the lobby," he said, as if

noticing that she'd pulled away, if only mentally. "And I was serious, feel free to use the pool."

She nodded. "I might do that. Thanks. Maybe you should take my room key, just in case I'm outside and don't hear you knock."

He picked it up off the dresser where she'd tossed it and departed. After he'd gone, Madison thought about his offer to use the pool. She had been serious about how appealing it sounded, though she wouldn't swim the way she suspected he'd been about to. Judging by the towel he'd been oh-so-inconveniently holding, he'd been planning to skinny-dip. That sounded perfect, delightful, in fact. Letting her naked body soak up the breezes and the warmth was just about her idea of heaven.

Of course, she wasn't quite desperate enough to strip out of her clothes and pose in front of the door the way he had. Even if she did have a very nice ass, if she did say so herself. Still, she wasn't about to bare it for some stranger…a stranger she'd already decided she couldn't have, no matter how much she might want him.

Now that he was gone, now that the room wasn't full of his warm, masculine presence, she managed to pull the rest of her brain cells together. It wasn't just that she couldn't trust anyone she met to keep her secret; there was more to it than that. Coming here to Costa Rica had been about hiding out, licking her wounds, staying out of the limelight and being completely on her own. She needed to rediscover the Madison she'd been six months ago, before her crazy engagement, before she'd become chum for an ocean of avaricious sharks.

There was more, though. She just couldn't do that to *him*...or to any man. Because, even if she could keep him in the dark about who she really was—and the scandal she'd hopefully left behind in the states—she'd be exposing him to a lot of danger, too. The last thing she needed was to get involved with some guy, then get tracked down by the paparazzi. Any man she spent time with would be subject to the same vicious scrutiny she'd endured, maybe even accused of being the mystery lover she'd cheated on Tommy with. The one who didn't exist.

She just couldn't put anybody else through that, especially not someone as great as Leo seemed to be. So, no. There was no room in her life for a fling with a hot fireman. None whatsoever.

Even if she desperately wished there were.

4

As it turned out, they'd both been wrong…and right. They were both in the correct room. Apparently, the woman who'd been at the front desk when Leo checked in was the only one who knew how to operate the hotel's computerized system. She'd put Leo in the correct room, even though his key card hadn't been coded properly. Then she'd gone on break, leaving a less-than-capable replacement at the desk. That man had put Madison in Leo's room, too.

Leo couldn't deny that it might be interesting—or, hell, fantastic—to share a bed with the beautiful brunette, but it seemed a bit soon to ask her if she wanted to become roomies.

Maybe by the end of the week…

He'd told the clerk that Madison could keep the room and he'd been assigned to another one. The woman got a twinkle in her eye and offered him a slight brow wag when she noted that Madison was traveling alone, too. Maybe she'd also heard from the bellhop that Madison was young and gorgeous.

Yeesh. He wondered if the clerk had been born a matchmaker or if it merely came with the territory when women reached a certain age. Lord knew there were a lot of them in his family. Of course, even his youngest female cousins seemed to have the gene, so he supposed aging had nothing to do with it.

Heading back to fill Madison in, he couldn't stop himself from thinking about her with every step he took across the grounds.

Madison Reid. She hadn't supplied the last name, the front desk clerk had. He liked it. Liked the woman to whom it was attached, even though he had only just met her.

Leo wasn't a huge believer in fate, but he couldn't deny that this afternoon's incident—them both getting assigned the same room, her walking in on him, him being there to catch her when she fell—seemed pretty out of the ordinary. Like it was meant to happen or something.

He'd come here to enjoy himself, as well as to put the final touches on the coat of I'm-totally-over-Ashley paint he'd been wearing for six months. Truth was, ever since Madison Reid had walked in on him, he hadn't given his former fiancée a moment's thought. And now, as her name crossed his mind, there was only the vaguest sense of recollection, like when he ran into someone he'd gone to elementary school with and couldn't for the life of him come up with their name. He could barely remember what Ashley looked like, or why he'd ever thought he could be happy spending his life with her in the first place.

She'd been beautiful, yes. And pretty successful. But there had been a shallowness to her, not to mention a thin vein of hardness that he'd spotted from the start but had fooled himself into thinking was an indication of strength. Maybe he'd had it all wrong. Maybe the coldness had been a symptom of her weakness, her need to constantly make sure she was the most desired, the most loved woman in the room. Perhaps that was why she'd set out to prove it by getting involved in an affair with his friend. Hell, for all Leo knew, it hadn't been her first.

Funny how easy it was to see her—to understand her—now that the blinders had been so completely torn off his eyes.

Arriving back at his—no, *Madison's*—room, he thrust all those thoughts away. He didn't want to think about his ex now. Not when there were so many other good things to think about.

Lifting a hand, he rapped on the door. No answer. Hoping she'd gone ahead and taken a dip, he inserted her key card and pushed the door open a few inches, calling, "Madison?"

Again, nothing. So he went inside. She wasn't on the bed, and as he crossed the room, he heard a faint splash. Stepping over to the patio slider, which stood open, he glanced outdoors and spotted a dash of red in the clear blue waters of the pool.

A red bikini. God help him.

She was floating on her back, her eyes closed, her arms out to her sides. Her face was turned to the sun and a satisfied smile tugged at those lips. He thought he heard her humming a soft melody.

Madison had been incredibly hot in a skirt and blouse. Now that she'd donned a couple of triangles of scarlet fabric, leaving much of her body bare for his perusal, he could honestly say he'd never seen a sexier female.

Her legs were long—heavenly—and she gently kicked them to keep herself afloat. As he'd noted when she wore the skirt, she had some seriously lush hips, covered only by little sling ties that held her bathing suit together. Those feminine hips were made even more noticeable by the slim waist, flat belly and taut midriff. Her bathing suit top managed to cover only the most essential parts of her full breasts, pushing up those amazing curves, leaving a deep V of cleavage that glistened with droplets of pool water.

All of her glistened. Every inch of that smooth skin, from her pink-tipped toenails on up to her cheeks, on which those long lashes rested, gleamed invitingly. Her thick hair had spread out, floating around her face like a halo, and she looked totally lost to everything but physical sensation as she soaked up the sun and the water.

A sharp, almost painful wave of lust washed over him. His heart thudded, his mouth went dry with a need for moisture only she could provide. His hands fisted at his sides as he tried to push away the images of touching her, stroking her, gliding his fingers along every ridge and valley of her body.

"Oh, you're back!"

He flinched, not having even realized she'd opened her eyes. "Yes. Sorry."

She quickly dropped her legs, standing up in the pool, which was only five feet deep at the most, and smiled up at him. "You were right, this was exactly what I needed. I feel tons better."

"You look better," he admitted through a tight throat. God, he hoped the sun was glaring in her eyes and she couldn't see how taut his entire body was as he tried to keep himself from reacting to her. If she were a couple of feet higher, she'd be eye level with his crotch and would undoubtedly notice the ridge in his jeans. He was hard for the woman, wanting her desperately. Hell, he'd been half-hard for her from the minute he'd caught her in his arms.

"How did everything go with the front desk?"

"All settled. You get the house, I get the kids."

She giggled. The sound was light and sweet, and he liked the tiny laugh lines that appeared beside her eyes. "What kind of mother does that make me?"

"I guess I'm just more soft and nurturing."

Her laughter deepened. "Yeah, you look about as soft as a tree trunk."

Oh, if only she knew.

"What really happened?"

He filled her in on the situation. She didn't seem surprised to hear the guy who'd checked her in had messed things up. But she didn't get all ticked off about it, either. She was calm, chill. He doubted much fazed her... except naked guys catching her when she fell.

He needed to forget about holding her while he was

naked. That was not going to do his pants situation any good at all.

"I brought you back some fruit." The lobby had a large bowl of it available for their guests. It should be enough to settle Madison's stomach until she had a chance to sit down for a real meal.

"Thank you."

"I guess I'll grab my stuff and go. I'm in the Scarlet Room," he told her.

"Maybe the guy at the front desk is color-blind and that's how our wires got crossed. This is the Emerald one, isn't it?"

Grinning, he said, "Yeah, I'm sure that's it."

"Scarlet, huh?" She wagged her brows. "Sounds fit for a sinner."

"Huh, and a little while ago you thought I was a hero."

"I still think that," she said, the teasing note fading from her voice. "I really appreciate you, uh… Where do I start?"

"Flashing you?"

Her sultry laugh heated him more than the late-afternoon sun. "I was going to say catching me, putting me on the bed, putting water on my face, going down to the desk…"

"Not the flashing?"

"I think I fainted before I saw anything."

"You think?"

She gave him a mysterious, half-sideways look. "I'll never tell."

"Thanks for being a gentleman."

"An interesting description for a female."

"I don't know, it just seemed appropriate." Not that anybody would ever mistake her for anything but a pure, sexy woman. "I guess I'll see you later."

She hesitated, her mouth opening, then closing, and then slowly nodded. "Sure. Of course. I'll bet you're tired after your trip."

"Not as tired as you were after yours."

"I really am feeling better." She licked her lips, and furrowed her brow, as if considering something, then added, "I do owe you one for all you've done. How about I buy you a drink sometime this week?"

"I got the all-inclusive package," he said, wondering if she saw the twinkle of pleasure in his eyes.

"So you buy me a drink."

"I could," he said with a bark of laughter, "considering I paid for two packages."

She tilted her head in confusion. Mentally kicking himself for bringing up a subject he really didn't want to discuss, he edged back into her room. "Meet me by the main pool or the beach bar tomorrow and I'll buy you that drink."

"And then you'll tell me why you should be drinking for two?"

"Maybe I will."

"Sorry, that was pushy. You really don't have to."

"Well, then, maybe I won't."

"Touché," she said. "See you later, Leo Santori."

"Bye, Madison Reid."

Her smile faded a little. "How did you know my…"

"Your last name? They mentioned it at the desk."

Realizing she was truly upset about that, he couldn't help wondering why. Was she *really* in hiding? Incognito? He had thought from the moment he saw her that she looked familiar, but had been telling himself it was because she looked like the woman he would dream about if he wanted to have the best, most erotic dreams of his life. But maybe it was more than that.

"Are you famous?"

"Maybe infamous," she mumbled under her breath.

He quirked a curious brow. She didn't elaborate. A long silence stretched between them, and he realized she didn't intend to.

Hmm. Interesting.

But he wasn't here to dig into anybody else's secrets. He'd just wanted to get away from his own drama. No responsibilities, no angst, no worrying about a broken engagement or the fact that his family was apprehensive about him and his friends were insisting he get out there and get laid as some kind of get-back-at-his-ex game.

He wasn't into any of that. Coming here to Costa Rica was about leaving everything else behind and just indulging in some sun, some fun and some pleasure.

And now that he'd met Madison, he began to suspect things were going to be even more sunny, fun and pleasurable than he had anticipated.

BY THE TIME she awoke the next morning, having slept a solid, uninterrupted nine hours—largely because of the fresh air blowing in on her through the screen door all night long, not to mention the utter exhaustion—

Madison woke up the next day a little unsure of what to do with herself.

She'd never been on a vacation alone, though she'd been on plenty of family trips as a kid, of course. And she, Candace and Tommy had gone away together several times, usually on college road trips to dive-places on the beach. There'd also been one skiing trip with a boyfriend. But never had she been in a foreign land all by herself, with nowhere to go, no one to see, nothing to do and no schedule to keep.

All she had to do was stay hidden from the press.

She couldn't help wondering what was going on back in California. She hadn't spoken with Tommy or with Candace since she'd left Florida, although she imagined they'd both tried to reach her. She'd bet there were messages on her cell phone and texts and emails. They'd been so worried about her, for once both of them thinking they had to be the protectors, the caretakers. She suspected they were constantly on the phone with each other, trying to figure out what to do.

Though he'd lived with Madison for the past six months, in some ways, Tommy still seemed closer to Candace. Madison was never envious of that, however, knowing their friendship was very different. With creative, artistic, kindhearted Candace, Tommy could be carefree and a little more whimsical. With Madison— much more no-nonsense and blunt than her twin—he had to man up and take responsibility for what he did. And of course, with him, both the Reid twins could be more daring and adventurous.

As far as she was concerned, the three of them brought out the absolute best in each other.

Four. There are four of us now.

Right. Because Candace—her other half—had gotten herself a *new* other half in the form of a hunky lawyer who'd posed as a gardener and planted baskets of love in Candy's heart. Blech.

Madison liked Oliver. She really did. But she still wasn't sure she would ever get over the feeling that she'd lost something vital when she'd become the second most important person in her twin's life.

It's not four, it's five.

Pesky math. But the addition was right. Because Tommy had Simon, and Madison had the feeling he'd be in the picture for a very long time. Meaning she truly was, she realized, the odd man out. Literally the fifth wheel. It was the first time she'd acknowledged it, and a sudden hollowness opened up within her, swallowing some of her happiness and her certainty that nothing could ever really change the relationships she had with those she loved. Things had changed, and continued to change.

She was the only one who hadn't found that mystical connection called love. Honestly, she wasn't sure she ever would. She'd dated men, she'd slept with men, she'd even lived with one before Tommy. But never had she had stars in her eyes the way her sister did, and never had she tap-danced through her day because the right guy smiled at her the way Tommy did.

"Enough, no more feeling sorry for yourself," she muttered as she forced her mind toward other things.

Like what she could do with plenty of money and an exotic, tropical paradise to explore.

There were a lot of things she could do, and someone with whom she'd really like to do them. But having fallen asleep last night thinking of all the reasons that being with Leo Santori would be a really bad idea, she had pretty well decided not to do them. Or, to do them alone.

Zip lining, ecotouring, bodysurfing…they could all be done alone, or with a professional instructor. But the thing she most wanted to do wouldn't be nearly as fun without Leo.

Ah, well. It wouldn't be the first time she'd had sex alone, that was for sure. Lately it was all she'd had.

Of course, she hadn't exactly tucked any sex toys into her luggage. She wondered how often Customs asked travelers to turn on those odd-looking devices, and was glad she hadn't had to find out. But the point was, she was left totally on her own when it came to dealing with the intense, er, *interest* Leo had aroused in her from the moment she'd first seen him.

Oh, yeah, that picture had been burned in her brain.

Madison had always had an active imagination, and had never needed erotic stories or movies to rev her engines. Lately, just thinking about the hero of the screenplay she'd written was enough to get her going. The dark, angry, possibly murderous antihero liked his sex rough and dangerous, with floggers and leather ropes and lots of "Yes, sirs."

While she'd been writing it, that had been her fantasy: being tied up, forced to be submissive, learning how pain could be pleasurable. Well, maybe not her fantasy, but she'd certainly wondered about it, digging into a deep, previously untapped part of herself to create those scenes that disturbed more than titillated.

But now, with Leo's incredibly handsome face and warm, gentle eyes in her mind, she could only think of long, slow, sexy loving that went on for hours and needed no props, just two slick, aroused bodies bathed in sunshine and warm air. No touch off-limits, no sensation forbidden, every eroticism imbued with gentleness and intimacy. And trust. Lots of trust.

She moaned a little, and began to touch all the places on her body that would have far preferred his hands to hers. Running her fingers over her breast, she plumped it, knowing his big hands would overflow if he were to cup them. She reached for her nipple—hard and filled with sensation. Plucking it, teasing it, she acknowledged that she would never really have lived if that man never sucked her nipples.

She whimpered, one hand gliding even farther, over her hip, and then her belly. Farther. She brushed her index finger through the tiny thatch of hair—the landing strip look that was so popular in Southern California. Madison had gone for it once she'd moved out there, but hadn't had a lover since she'd first begun waxing her pubis, and had wondered, more than once, what it would feel like to have a man's mouth on that bare, sensitive skin. Her own fingers felt divine, made slick and smooth by her body's moisture. She moved them slowly, gently, stroking herself just right. Her clit was hard and ever so sensitive, and she made tiny circles around it, drawing out the pleasure, picturing his hands, his tongue.

Another stroke. She gasped, arching her back, curling her toes. Her climax washed over her, quick, hard and hot, and she sprawled out in the bed, trying to even her breaths and calm down.

It didn't happen. For the first time in her life, masturbating hadn't taken the edge off. Yes, she'd had an orgasm, but it hadn't satisfied her. She was still edgy, swollen and in need, as if she'd been cut off in the middle of intensely pleasurable foreplay.

It wasn't hard to figure out why. She wanted a man. One man. Leo. Her own hands just weren't going to cut it. She wanted him to be the one to make her come, wanted his cock inside her when he did it.

She'd told herself all last evening during her room service meal and the long minutes she'd thought about him before drifting off to sleep that she couldn't have him. Couldn't allow herself to take him. But never had she *really* acknowledged what that meant. Or how incredibly difficult it would be to stick by that decision. Because if she couldn't release this tension, she was going to lose her mind. And the only man who could release it for her was one she'd already decided was off-limits. He was too nice, too good, too heroic. Definitely not somebody who deserved to be tarnished with the scandal surrounding her.

"Damn it," she muttered. "Why did you have to go

and be so wonderful?" If he'd been a jerk or a player, it would have been much easier to let go of her concerns and *take* what she wanted.

There was, of course, no answer. Nothing could possibly explain why she'd met a man so sexy, so delicious, so freaking adorable, now, when she was in no position to have him.

Knowing she couldn't stay in bed and continue to be sexually frustrated, she got up and tried to decide between a shower and a morning swim. She intended to go down to the open-air restaurant for breakfast. From the hotel information sheet, she'd noticed that it adjoined the large resort pool. She planned to lie out beside it, so there wasn't much point in showering first, especially since she'd taken one last night before bed.

But she certainly wouldn't be able to swim naked in the public pool, and right now, swimming naked—letting cool water comfort and soothe her overly sensitized private parts—sounded like the perfect cure for what ailed her.

She'd gone skinny-dipping before; what adventurous, Florida-raised kid hadn't? But she'd certainly never done it in broad daylight. Considering the privacy of her pool, though, she figured she could risk it. Leo certainly had been about to yesterday. Good for the goose and all that.

Decision made, she got up and went into the bathroom to brush her teeth. She scooped her hair back into a ponytail, and grabbed the towel she'd used the afternoon before. The one that still carried the faintest scent of the man who'd been holding it when she'd entered her room.

Yeah, using Leo's towel had been pretty pathetic. It had also been pretty delightful, rubbing it against her cool body, smelling him, remembering him.

"Stop it," she ordered herself, determined to put the man out of her mind for the rest of the day. Hell, for the rest of her trip!

Going to the screen door, she pulled it open and stuck her head outside, peeking around. It felt so strange to step out into broad daylight—God, what a gorgeous, clear, sunny morning it was—not wearing a stitch. She caught her bottom lip between her teeth, glancing back and forth from one side of the walled-hedged area to the other. The tangle of green shrub was thick and practically impossible to see through. Plate-size pink flowers helped, too.

"Just do it. Just jump in!" she ordered herself.

So she did. She dropped the towel and wound her way around the lounge chairs that stood under the covered awning right outside the door. Free, excited and naked, she plowed forward, not thinking, just striding the five steps to the pool and taking a leap of faith.

It should have taken a few seconds for her to hit the water.

It didn't. It took forever, considering time had stopped.

She moved in slow motion, horror washing over her.

Because, after her feet had left the concrete deck—after she was committed to the pool and it was too late to change her mind—she saw a dark shape swimming toward her.

A dark, sinuous shape that hit on every one of her most elemental fears and sent hysteria coursing through her body.

There was nothing else to do. She screamed bloody murder.

5

THE ROOM SERVICE breakfast Leo had ordered lived up to the hotel's reputation for outstanding food. He'd enjoyed every bite of his meal, which he'd consumed outside on his patio, having moved his café table and chairs outdoors. It was midmorning, the sun was shining, the breeze was blowing, and he was on vacation. Life didn't get much better than this, especially when he thought about the chilly autumn and frigid winter that awaited him when he returned to Chicago.

He had made some plans for his first full day in Costa Rica, starting with dropping by his next-door neighbor's room.

He hadn't been able to put Madison out of his mind since he'd left her yesterday afternoon. Especially not once he'd realized the Scarlet Bungalow—his suite— was the very next one down the path from hers. Their private courtyards butted up against one another and he'd heard her humming again as she'd floated the previous afternoon. He'd stayed quiet, not wanting to disturb her, somehow knowing they could use a bit of a time before they saw each other again.

She needed some sleep, some food and some energy. He needed to think about what he was going to do about the incredible attraction he felt for the woman.

Today he'd knock on her door and see where things went.

He'd just finished off the last bite of his toast and reached for his coffee cup, sweetened with raw sugar and thick cream, when the morning silence was pierced by a dramatic, shrill scream.

He flinched, nearly dropping his cup, and was on his feet before he'd made up his mind to get out of his chair. His whole body went on instant alert, like it did whenever the alarm sounded at the station house, not knowing if he would be dousing a small oven fire or battling a monster blaze in an abandoned warehouse.

The scream had been cut off sharply—as if the screamer had run out of breath—and that made things even worse. Because he feared he knew where it had come from.

His stomach churned.

"Madison!" he said, knowing the woman's cry of terror had come from the other side of the hedged wall surrounding his pool.

Not giving it another thought, he ran over to the hedge, shoved his hands into the thick greenery and gripped the cool stone wall behind it. He clambered up, his bare feet and legs getting scratched, his arms covered with sticky green moisture, his face slapped with flowers. He lost his footing once, skidded down a few inches, then gripped the top even more tightly in his hand so he wouldn't go tumbling back down.

As he reached the top of the six-foot-tall wall, he heard splashes and another shriek. Was she being attacked? Drowning?

His heart raced. "I'm coming!" he called as he launched over the top of the wall, flinging himself into her private courtyard. He landed on his feet in the mulch, right beside her privacy hedge, and immediately looked for her. Having heard the splashes, his eyes turned right to the pool.

Madison was in it, her face twisted with fear, her mouth open as she exhaled shallow gasps. She didn't even appear to see him. All her attention was focused on the water before her. She was struggling to back up to the rear edge of the pool, reaching behind her, waving her arms, as if afraid to turn and look for it. Afraid to tear her attention off whatever had grabbed it.

"Madison, what is it?"

Her lips trembled. She cast the tiniest glance in his direction. But she didn't have to answer. He suddenly saw for himself.

"Stay still, don't move," he snapped, seeing the creature swimming in the shallow end of the pool.

A snake. Not huge, but big enough—thick, though not terribly long. Boa constrictor, if he had to guess, though he was no expert.

Jesus, no wonder she was screaming like somebody had come at her with an ax. He might have, too. He liked snakes about as much as Indiana Jones did.

But he needed to keep her calm. If she started flailing around, the thing might notice her and come closer to investigate. And while he would never let it get near her, his Tarzan-snake-wrestling skills were a wee bit rusty. Or nonexistent.

"It's okay," he told her, trying to keep her calm with his voice as he edged along the side of the pool. "He's not going to bother you."

"Snake. Oh, God, a snake. I hate snakes, Leo," she said, whimpering.

"I'm not a big fan either, darlin', but I don't think he's paying too much attention to you. He just wanted to take a swim."

"Aren't there j-jungles, rivers, entire oceans?" she said, panic rising in her voice. "Why my pool? Why now when I'm naked and jumped in without looking!"

His mind tried to make him think about that naked part but he was too focused on the way her voice was shaking and the danger the animal posed to her. If it *was* a boa, it wasn't poisonous, which was a good thing. But he doubted anything he said was going to make her feel better.

"Listen to me now," he said as he spied the pool supply closet tucked up against the corner of her bungalow. Hopefully it would contain a skimmer; he doubted the maintenance men would carry them room to room every day. "I'll take care of it, Madison. But I need you to very *calmly* get to the edge of the pool and climb out."

"I c-can't…"

"Of course you can. I'll watch it so you can turn around."

"No."

"Just move slowly."

"Have you forgotten the naked p-part?" she groaned, though he wasn't sure if her voice was shaking due to fear of the snake or embarrassment over her—*gulp*—nakedness.

"I won't look," he promised.

And he wouldn't. He was focused on the snake and the closet and would not allow himself to cast so much as a glimpse at her lithe form gleaming beneath the water. Not while he still had an unwelcome visitor to contend with.

It was just his luck to catch her skinny-dipping when she was in real physical danger.

He edged sideways, noting there was no lock on the closet and finding himself very thankful for that. Reaching it, he yanked the door open, tore his attention off the snake long enough to assess what was inside and gratefully spotted not only a skimmer on a long pole, but also a sizeable bucket that had once held chemicals but was now empty. A lid lay beside it on the concrete floor of the storage closet.

Looking back to assure her, he realized she had moved closer to the wall but still hadn't taken her eyes off the snake. "Okay, it's time to climb out now, Madison," he told her as he retrieved the items from the closet. "Once I try to grab him, he's going to panic and swim away."

She didn't argue anymore. From the corner of his eye, he saw her do as he'd said and put her hands on the pool's edge. Then his attention zoomed right back to her swimming companion.

He moved to the edge of the pool, placing the bucket

close by and trying to gauge just how quick he'd have to be if he wanted to swoop that sucker up and drop him inside it. Part of him thought about just leaving it, getting her inside and calling the hotel to deal with it. But he knew if he did, she would never have another moment's peace. It could easily slither away and if it did, she'd be envisioning it returning every time she closed her eyes. Hell, his bungalow was right next door…so would he!

"Ready?" he asked, not glancing toward her, though he saw her vague shape standing on the far side of the pool. He had a quick impression of hands crossed in the Eve-old woman's modesty pose, but that was all. "Madison?"

She only groaned.

He took a deep breath, then plunged the skimmer into the water, an inch below the animal, and jerked his arms to lift it out of the pool. It immediately squirmed and almost fell over the side, but luck was with him. He was able to flip it right into the waiting bucket.

The snake immediately began to slither up to escape, but he covered the opening with the skimmer, blocking its exit while he grabbed the lid. Then he switched them, catching the angry animal inside, grabbing a large, decorative rock to place on it so the lid wouldn't pop back off. It had taken no more than thirty seconds, but his heart was racing, and his breaths were choppy and forced, as if he'd just run a block wearing his protective gear and carrying a ladder.

"Oh, my God, thank you, thank you, thank you."

He turned just as Madison threw herself against him,

wrapping her arms around his neck, burying her face in the crook. She shuddered, her entire form quaking.

"It's okay, it's over."

"I hate snakes. I'm terrified of them. When I saw that thing in the pool a second *after* I'd leaped in, I thought I'd have a heart attack and die."

"Well, it's done. I'll call the front office and have them send somebody down to take care of it."

She shivered again. "I can't even look at one of them. I know it's irrational, it's stupid, but I just... I'm *offended* by them, somehow. Does that make any sense?" She pulled back a little and rubbed away some moisture that had appeared in her eyes. "My rational mind understands why snakes are needed for the environment, and I know the chances of ever being bitten by one, much less dying, are slim to none. But they just offend some deep, primal part of me."

He believed her. There was no way he couldn't. Her voice was hoarse, shaking, and her eyes were slightly wild. She looked almost on the verge of hysteria.

He slid his arms around her waist, holding her tightly against him, and stroked his fingertips in the hollow of her back. "It's okay. It's over. Shh."

Her head dropped onto his shoulder, and they stood there for few long moments. He could feel her gasping breaths, not to mention her racing heart thudding against his. He continued to whisper consoling words to her, brushing his lips against her damp hair, then against her temple where the pulse fluttered wildly. He would have thought she would have begun to calm down by now, but if anything her heart seemed to be pounding even harder against his chest.

His bare chest.

Which was pressed against her bare chest.

Which went along with her bare *everything*.

Holy shit. In the excitement, he'd momentarily forgotten what she wasn't wearing. She'd been—and was now—completely naked.

He should let her go, spin around, turn his back and toss her a towel. A nice guy would do that. The hero she'd called him would do that.

Leo didn't do that.

He just couldn't. Not yet. Not when she felt so good—so pliant and womanly. Now, when she was curled up against him like she needed his warmth to revive every cell in her body, how could he possibly step away from her?

He continued to stroke the small of her back, then let one hand glide down to brush against the top curve of her buttock. She sighed against his neck, pressing her lips against his raging pulse, telling him not to stop. Considering stopping hadn't even been on the top ten list of possibilities, that wouldn't be a problem.

Her body was all lush curves and softness, and he loved the texture of her skin beneath his fingers. He continued to stroke the curve of her bottom, tracing a line to her hip, which he cupped in his hand. She was so perfectly shaped, with the indentation of her waist designed to be wrapped in a man's arms, those hips intended to be clung to by someone buried to the hilt inside her.

"Leo," she groaned, kissing his neck again.

Her warm, soft tongue slipped out and tasted his earlobe, and he groaned low in his throat.

Her invitation wasn't voiced, but it was clear just the same. He didn't know whether they would have ended up like this if not for her fright. He had no idea whether she'd been tortured by the same kind of long, restless, sleepless night he had, filled with erotic dreams and even more erotic fantasies. He didn't even know if this was going to go anywhere else. All he knew was he had to kiss her.

So he did. Not saying another word, he lifted a hand to her hair, sliding his fingers into the tangled ponytail, and tugged her head back so she was looking up at him. Giving her face a searching glance, he dropped his mouth onto hers.

Soft at first. A tiny shared breath. Then they both fell into the kiss.

It was easy, so easy. And so good.

Her tongue met his with a languorous thrust, and he drank deeply of her, exploring every bit of her mouth. He found himself wanting to memorize the shape of her, the scent of her, the feel of her. They stroked and licked, tangled, gave and took. She tasted sweet and minty, delicious, and having his mouth pressed against hers felt as natural and right as coming home after a long time away.

His hand still cupped her hip, and he stroked her, held her tightly against him. With his other one, he traced a path up her midriff to the side of a full breast, pressed flat against his chest. He was dying to see her, to let his other senses be filled by her, but right now, memorizing her taste was enough. It had to be enough.

She was groaning, sighing, and her own hands explored, too. She tangled one in his hair, fingering it, twisting it, holding him close as if afraid he might end the kiss before they'd both had their fill.

Her other hand dug into his shoulder before sliding down his arm. Their fingers curled together, then she reached between them to stroke his stomach. Her hand drifted close, so damned close, to his rigid cock, which was so hard, it had pushed up beyond the top of his swim trunks.

"Oh, God," she groaned against his mouth, realizing what had happened as she caressed the swollen tip.

His body was helpless to resist the age-old urge to thrust toward her touch. Those soft, delicate fingers flicked lightly over his skin, the tip of her thumb smoothing out the moisture that seeped from him.

Before he could think or breathe or move, she'd tugged the trunks farther away from his groin, making room for her hand. She slipped it down, rubbing her palm all along the back of his cock, her long nails scraping ever so delicately on his tight balls.

He groaned, again rocking toward her, loving that she responded to his blatant need by wrapping her hand around him, at least as much as she could, and squeezing lightly. He heard her whimper. The sound seemed to convey both excitement and perhaps nervousness, as if she had just figured out, since her fingers couldn't close entirely around him, how much he had to offer her.

She didn't have to be nervous. He could make her

wet enough to take every inch of him. And he was *desperate* to do it. More than he wanted to live until sundown did he want to sink into her—her mouth, her sex, somewhere wet and hot and slippery. And tight. Oh, God, yeah, *tight*.

She stroked him, up and down, matching the movements with each warm thrust of her tongue. He edged away, just enough to slide his fingers over one full breast, until he could tweak the hard nipple between them. She hissed into his mouth as he played with her, stroking her into a series of slow shudders.

She made no sound of resistance at all when he moved his other hand from her hip, back around to her bottom, so he could toy with the seam separating those lush curves. A tiny stroke, another, then she relaxed enough to let him play a little more. She was pliant in his arms, arching a bit in invitation, and he dipped his fingers farther…enough to get wet, to sample the juices of her body, hot and slick and welcoming.

He had time to mentally process the fact that her plump, engorged lips were completely bare—*want, want, want*—when she whimpered. "You— We…"

He didn't know what she was about to say—to ask, to demand. Because before she had a chance to continue, they both heard a thumping sound coming from the ground near their feet.

She obviously realized what it was before he did, because she yanked back and leaped away so fast she almost fell into the pool. Leo got the tiniest glimpse at her utterly gorgeous, naked body—God, those breasts were a thing of art—before he focused his attention on what had made the sound.

Mr. Snake was trying to get out of his container. The lid on the bucket was jiggling up and down, and the whole bucket was a bit wobbly. He pulled his trunks up and retrieved another, heavier rock and replaced the one he'd put on there, being sure to leave uncovered a small hole in the old lid. He didn't like the intruder, but he also wanted to make sure the critter would get enough air during the few minutes it took to get somebody down here to get rid of him.

While he resecured the prisoner, Madison grabbed a towel off the ground and wrapped it around herself, sarong style. By the time he straightened and returned his full attention to her, she was covered from breast to upper thigh. He mourned that he had lost his chance to see that incredible, luscious body he'd felt pressing against him, and he knew there would be no diving back into the crazy-hot kiss they'd been sharing. Much less all the other crazy-hot things they'd been doing...and had planned to do.

"Wow," she whispered, lifting a hand to her mouth. That hand was shaking, those lips were trembling, her voice was quivery. Whether she was more freaked out by the snake or by the embrace, he didn't know, but he sure hoped he had a leg up on the slithery reptile.

"I guess I should apologize," he said, not really sure why. If she hadn't enjoyed that, he'd turn in his membership as a dude.

"For saving my life?"

He rolled his eyes. "I don't think it's poisonous."

"I meant, you saved me from a heart attack. I really don't think you understand how much snakes terrify me."

"I think I have a pretty good idea."

She was already shaking her head in disagreement before he'd finished his sentence. "I'm not just being a wimp. Believe me, I'm not scared of much." She thrust a hand in her hair, knocking the ponytail holder out altogether so that those honey curls bounced around her shoulders in a thick, sexy tangle. "I don't usually go around fainting, and I don't remember another time in my adult life that I have ever screamed with terror. Except, maybe, the first time I went skydiving."

Okay. So she was pretty brave.

"But snakes. Oh, God, snakes. They're my Achilles' heel. My sister, Candace, she can't stand spiders. Me? Hell, a guy I dated had a pet tarantula and I used to walk around with him sitting on my shoulder."

"The guy or the tarantula?"

She punched him lightly on the arm. Frankly, he preferred it when she used that hand to squeeze his cock.

But they'd moved past that moment. It was over... at least for now. Sanity and reality had intruded, and she was going to focus on the snake rather than on the near sex.

Letting her get away with it, knowing she probably needed to regroup and think about what had almost happened, he rubbed his upper arm, as if she'd hurt him, and grinned. "Sorry. I got the point, you're okay with bugs."

"Yeah, no big deal. I'd protect Candace from spiders,

she'd protect me from snakes, and Tommy would protect us both from guys who didn't take no for an answer."

"Tommy? Your brother?"

She opened her mouth, then snapped it shut. Some of the high color began to leave her cheeks, and he watched as she clenched her hands together in front of her.

"No, a friend. Boy next door. We grew up together."

"Okay."

He wondered if that was really all, considering how skittish she'd gotten when she'd mentioned the guy. But it wasn't his place to pry.

"Anyway, I know I have ophidiophobia. It's irrational and I've tried to get over it. I've studied, I even got myself hypnotized once."

One of his brows shot up. "Really?"

"Well, it was at one of those girls' naughty-panty party things, with a bunch of women drinking wine and buying fancy underwear. A friend of one of my college roommates was there and she swore she could hypnotize any of us into losing weight or quitting smoking. So I asked her to try to un-ophidiophobia me."

He was having a hard time paying attention, his mind still back on the whole panty party concept. Jeez, did chicks really do that? And how did one sign up to be a salesperson?

"It didn't work."

"No?"

"When she got me under and told me to visualize a snake curled up peacefully at my feet, I apparently threw up all over the saleslady's panty box."

Oh, did he need her to change this conversation. But

because he was a masochist, he replied, "Guess you bought a lot of underwear that night."

"Yeah, right. You hurl on it, you buy it." She wrapped her arms around herself, clinging to the towel, and continued, "So, you see, it's a big deal to me. I was on the verge of a full-on panic attack, and you saved me, and I appreciated it so much, and that's why I threw myself into your arms. It wasn't… I didn't…"

"I get it. You weren't trying to take advantage of me."

She nibbled her lip. "Right."

"Understood."

"And you're not, uh, mad?"

Oh, sure. Because every dude would be really angry about a beautiful, naked woman throwing her arms around him to express her gratitude. Or half jerking him off until he'd become nothing but nine inches of sensation.

"Not mad. I promise."

She looked relieved.

"Now, how about I go in and call the front desk and ask them to send somebody out here to get rid of our friend."

Her eyes rounded into circles. "I'm not staying out here by myself with that thing! He might tip the bucket over. He could…"

"Come with me then," he said, cutting her off and pulling her into her room. He shut the screen door behind them. "We'll make the call together."

She looked visibly relieved. "Okay. And then you can hand me the phone so I can call the airline. Because

there's no way in hell I'm staying here and risking another run-in with the Creature from the Black Lagoon."

His heart skipped a beat and his stomach turned over.
"You're leaving?"

She blinked, as if finally thinking about the words
she'd said. She glanced at the closed door, shivered, then
looked back at him. "That sounds ridiculous, doesn't
it? I mean, there are snakes everywhere."

"Yes."

"I'm overreacting."

"Just a little."

"The thing is, I really don't know if I could ever
be comfortable walking around the grounds again by
myself."

"I'm sure you could."

"I've never vacationed alone."

"Me, either."

She tapped the tip of her finger on her bottom lip.
"I'm wondering if we could, maybe, vacation alone…
together."

His jaw fell open.

"I mean, it would be nice to know somebody had
your back, wouldn't it?"

"Sure," he said with a nod. "I could totally use somebody to save me from any tarantulas that sneak into
my room."

If he woke up with one of those suckers lying on
top of him, the whole town would hear his screeches.

"And you've proved yourself to be a champion snake
wrangler."

A slow smile tugged at his lips. It was answered by

one from her. Maybe her first real one since he'd heard her scream and ran forward to be her dragon, er, snake, slayer. Well, not slayer—he'd never kill an innocent animal that was just doing what animals did—snake *catcher* would be the better term.

"You asking me if I want to be your vacation buddy?" he finally said.

"Something like that. You know, like in kindergarten when you always had to have a partner to hold hands with in the lunch line."

He grimaced. "I'd never have held hands with a *girl*."

"I don't have cooties."

He grinned and walked closer, lifting a hand to push her hair back over her shoulder. "I can tell."

She stared at him, licked her lips, then edged away, as if confused, a little skittish and shy remembering that heated embrace they'd shared.

Again, he let her get away with it, knowing they'd get back there sooner or later. Right now, she was telling herself, and him, that she was just after a buddy to spend time with and cover her back during her vacation. But he knew deep down it was more than that. The encounter was driving her decisions, even if she hadn't yet realized it. Somewhere deep inside, she wanted more. This was a logical, acceptable way to tell him she wanted to spend time with him.

Of course, shoving her hand down his trunks and grabbing his cock had been a pretty good indication, too. In fact, he preferred it.

"I suppose I could check out your pool every day before you get in it."

She shuddered. "Definitely."

"And come running if you call?"

"How did you manage that, anyway?" she asked, as if finally remembering what had happened before he'd caught the snake. "Where'd you come from? I know my door was locked."

"Over the wall. We're next-door neighbors."

A laugh escaped her lips and for the first time that morning, he began to think she was really going to be all right. Her panic had eased its grip on her and she was regaining her equilibrium.

That was a good thing, even if her cute suggestion—that he be her vacation buddy—was driving him crazy. The idea that he could be buddies with a woman who had every one of his senses, and all of his male chromosomes, on high alert, was ludicrous.

But he knew she was only half-joking. The thought of leaving really had crossed her mind, all because of a run-in with a member of the local population. And he didn't want her to go. He *desperately* didn't want her to go.

So, not even giving it any more thought, he agreed to her suggestion.

"Okay, Madison Reid, you've got yourself a deal."

"I do?"

"Uh-huh. Let's be solo vacationers together."

And see just how long it took for them to progress beyond the holding-hands-in-the-lunch-line stage.

6

THE HOTEL STAFF was incredibly apologetic about the snake incident. After Leo had called the front desk and explained the situation, no fewer than four maintenance men had shown up at her door. They'd deftly taken care of her unwanted visitor, and had then, at Leo's suggestion, looked over every inch of her private courtyard, cutting back some of the lower tangles of hedge to make sure there were no holes, nests or sleeping family members. She had remained inside, unwilling to even look out the door for fear they'd stumble across Mrs. Snake and a passel of little snakelings.

They hadn't. They'd found an indentation under one corner of the wall, where they assumed the wild creature had made its entry, and had backfilled it in with packed dirt and stone. The foreman had gone on to assure her that nothing like this had ever happened before and it most certainly wouldn't happen again.

Right. Just her luck to get the pool with the big honking reptile in it.

Of course, it had also been just her luck to have a big, powerful hunk right next door to save her ass.

Lucky me.

Good Lord, was he big and powerful. Even now, a couple of hours later, she couldn't stop thinking about how his body had felt pressed against hers, so strong and masculine. Not to mention how he'd tasted. How he'd smelled.

How that massive ridge of heat had swelled between them during their passionate kiss, making her legs grow weak and her mouth as dry as straw.

She'd thrown her naked self into his arms, not even pausing to think of how he might react. And he'd reacted. Oh, had he ever. She knew for a fact she'd never been with a man who'd *reacted* more. Or had more to react *with*. Wrapping her hand around him the way she had had taken a lot of gall, and she knew it. But she hadn't cared. She still didn't. She'd wanted to touch him and had been desperate for him to touch her.

No, she wouldn't regret this morning. Not ever.

Unless, of course, it was never repeated.

Then she might regret it, because she would be left wondering just how amazing all the *other* things they could have done together would be.

She lifted her hand and fanned it in front of her face, needing it more for her heated imagination than the warm weather. As they lay on a pair of huge, padded lounge chairs beside the stunning tropical pool that dominated the center of the resort grounds, she found herself continuing to cast glances toward his swim trunks, wondering if the lumps in the fabric were caused by the looseness of the material, or by the fact that he was still half-aroused. As she was, even hours later.

She gulped and forced herself to focus on the book she'd brought along, not wanting to distract herself all over again by remembering how wonderful it had felt to be in his arms. And how wonderful it would be to be in his bed.

That was where they were heading. She could no longer deny it to herself. The attraction was too strong, irresistible, and now that they'd kissed, touched each other, she knew there was only one place this kind of want could take them.

He had to have figured that out, too. But for now, he seemed content to be her "buddy." He'd insisted on escorting her down to the pool, making a big production of showing her how carefully he was inspecting the path in front of them. She'd finally begun to laugh and admitted she might have overreacted just a bit, and had found that laughing with Leo was almost as delightful as kissing him.

"What do you suppose is this surprise the hotel is planning for us?" Leo asked, startling her. She'd thought he was sleeping—his eyes were concealed by dark sunglasses, and he'd been lying quietly for several minutes, which had enabled her to, she thought, sneakily glance at him and wonder how on earth his skin could stretch enough to accommodate all those muscles.

"I'm not sure." Madison reached for her drink—a tall, fruity concoction laced with rum that the bartender kept sending over. Apparently, word had gotten out about her close encounter with nature, and the hotel was bending over backward to make it up to them. "I've been wondering about it, too. Whatever it is, it sounds like it's going to be pretty special."

Not only had she been upgraded to a completely all-inclusive vacation, meaning she wouldn't have to pay for any more meals or drinks, she and Leo had also been invited to a private surprise dinner that evening. The hotel was making all the arrangements and kept insisting it was the very least they could do for the inconvenience.

Personally, she preferred they give her a pair of snakeskin boots, but she supposed that was being a little vindictive and bloodthirsty. She wasn't a subscriber to the adage "the only good snake is a dead snake." She simply didn't ever want to have to see, hear or interact with one again as long as she lived.

"I guess they take their snake incursions seriously," she said.

"I suppose it wouldn't do their hotel any good if word got out that their pools came complete with their own boa constrictors."

She shuddered, hating to even think about it. That thing had been a boa, one of the maintenance men had confirmed it. He'd also said it was extremely rare for them to come out of the jungle, but that they did sometimes enjoy taking a freshwater dip. Again, just her luck. Maybe she had a sign on her back that she couldn't see, saying Fuck with me.

"I'm surprised they didn't just offer you a spa day or something," Leo said. "No need to include me."

"Hey, you were the snake catcher. I just stood there naked and screamed."

He smiled broadly. "Yeah. I remember."

She leaned over and flicked his arm sharply. He just laughed.

"Of course, I have a feeling that the woman at the front desk is doing a little matchmaking," he said.

She gaped. "Seriously?"

"Uh-huh. I wouldn't be at all surprised if this turns out to be some romantic setup."

Hmm. That didn't sound so bad.

"Though, they didn't make it sound like we had to dress up or anything," he said, "which is a good thing since I didn't bring much more than jeans and trunks."

"Me, either."

"So you weren't planning on doing any clubbing or hobnobbing while you were here, huh?"

She snorted. "Definitely not. I planned to do exactly what I'm doing right now."

She just hadn't planned to do it with a hunky fire-fighter from Chicago.

"So why did you decide to take a solo vacation?" he asked, sounding a little puzzled, as if he'd been think-ing about it since she'd mentioned this morning that they were both vacationing alone.

She tensed, but didn't overreact. It was a natural question. Everywhere around them were groups and couples. The airport had been full of them, as had the taxi line. And even here, at such a small hotel, one only saw pairs walking about. Right now, on the other side of the lagoon-shaped, flower-bedecked pool, she saw two cooing couples, one middle-aged, another young and honeymoonish. This wasn't the type of place one vacationed alone.

"I was going through some stuff and just needed to get out of town alone for a while." She shrugged. "As it turns out, it might be a great thing."

He smiled lazily.

"Because now I can finish up a project I'm working on," she said a little teasingly, knowing he'd thought she was referring to him. She had been. But that had sounded a little too fawning.

Besides, now that she'd voiced it, she had to admit, the project idea wasn't a bad one. She might be persona non grata around Hollywood right now, but once the press forgot about her, the studios might remember her screenplay. She needed to do some rewriting, tinkering.

Tommy was still insistent that he wanted to play the lead, and maybe an announcement that the two of them were going to be working together might throw some water on the fiery gossip. Since she hadn't ever conceived of him in the role, she wanted to go back over the script and tweak it, make it more suitable for him.

The more she'd thought about it, the more she'd realized he really would be right for the part. She just needed to change her dark, brooding, angry hero into a golden-haired angel whose good looks hid a dangerous, edgy soul. Plus, at least with Tommy, there shouldn't be any diva actor fits over the homoerotic threesome scene!

"What do you do, anyway?" he asked.

"I'm a writer."

He turned his head to look at her from behind the dark glasses. "Novels?"

"Not yet. I was a journalist when I lived in New York. I worked for one of the big papers and hated it. So earlier this year, I moved out to L.A. to market an original screenplay."

"Wow. Any luck?"

"Yes." *And no.* "There's some interest but nothing concrete yet."

"That's pretty amazing. Have you met any stars? Done the whole elite-Hollywood-decadence thing?"

Chuckling, she admitted, "A few. And maybe a little decadence." Then, remembering what he'd said yesterday about having two all-inclusive packages, she asked the question that had been flitting around in her mind.

"So, what about you? Why the solo vacation—and the two-person package?"

He sighed audibly, turning his head to look at the pool again. She lifted her drink, sucking some of the delicious sweetness through the straw, giving him time. She wondered for a moment if he was going to ignore the question, but finally, he cleared his throat.

"This was supposed to be my honeymoon."

She coughed out a mouthful of her drink, spewing it onto her own bare shoulder. Sitting up straighter in the chair, she coughed a few more times.

"Are you okay?" he asked.

He'd sat right up and swung around to face her, patting her back as if helping a kid spit out too big a mouthful of food. Well, she had to concede, that had been a lot to digest. Even in the crazy moment, when her mind had begun to spin over the whole idea that Leo was supposed to be here with another woman—his *wife*—she had time to think how nice his strong fingers had felt on her back.

"I'm fine," she insisted, nodding and scrunching her eyes closed. Some of her drink had flown out of her mouth, some she'd gulped down, and now she had a damned brain freeze. "I was just surprised."

"Sorry."

Finally, when she felt in full control of herself, she turned to face him. Their bare legs brushed against each other, their feet inches apart on the stone pool deck. The coarse black hairs on his legs tickled her smooth ones, just another vivid example of his maleness compared to her femininity. The soft sensation made her stomach flip and her bathing suit feel a tiny bit tighter against her groin.

She forced those sensations away to focus on their conversation. "You were supposed to be here with your *wife?*"

"I'm not married!" he assured her.

"Good thing. I mean, considering you came on your honeymoon alone. What happened?"

"Same old story. Long engagement, nonrefundable trip paid for, wedding got canceled."

"So, what, she kept the dress and you kept the trip?"

"Something like that. We returned what we could but both of us ate some of the costs."

"That must have been painful."

"Not too terrible, considering we broke up six months before the wedding date."

Six months. So he wasn't exactly on the rebound. That was good to know.

"But you still couldn't get a refund on this?" She gestured around the grounds.

"Nope. I'd prepaid for a whole honeymoon package. Nonrefundable."

Wow, that had been pretty optimistic, considering how frequently people broke up these days.

He must have read her expression. "I know, I know. I can't imagine what I was thinking. I wasn't just being a cheapskate, I swear. I think, deep down, doing it that way was an affirmation that I believed we really would get married, even though, somewhere deep inside, I'd already begun to have doubts."

"So it was a friendly, mutual breakup?"

He barked a laugh. "Oh, hell, no."

She didn't reply, not asking the natural questions. She'd already been incredibly nosy. If he wanted to share more, he would.

"She cheated."

Oh, no. Stupid, foolish woman.

"I'm so sorry."

Those broad shoulders lifted in a careless shrug. "I'm over it. What hurt the most was that she did it with my best man…can you possibly get more cliché?"

"Or more trashy?" she snapped. "What a bitch."

"It takes two…he's a bitch, too."

His tone held no heat; he didn't seem to be bearing any grudges or holding on to any residual anger. So maybe he really was over all that. He'd certainly seemed to be so far. She would never have guessed he'd been recently betrayed and hurt by someone he'd cared enough about to propose to.

It truly boggled her mind. She had no use for cheaters, anyway, something she'd never been more thoroughly reminded of than when she'd become the country's most infamous one. But to cheat on someone like Leo? She didn't get it. He was impossibly handsome. He was thoughtful, funny and heroic. He was built like a god, kissed like a dream and had hands that should be patented. She couldn't even begin to imagine how amazing he would be in bed.... He certainly had plenty to offer a woman there.

So why on earth would anyone risk that for a fling with someone else? Even more—how could anyone who proclaimed to care about him do something so hateful, so hurtful, to a man who was so wonderful?

"She's insane."

He waved a hand. "It worked out for the best. Maybe she sensed I wasn't as emotionally attached as I should have been. I think part of her wanted me to find out, wanted to see how I'd react and make sure she really was the center of my world. If I'd played the part of enraged, jealous fiancé, she might have felt more certain that I really loved her."

"Oh, genius plan," she said with a big eye roll. As if he'd have ever taken her back after she'd played such a game? What man would? "You didn't, I presume?"

He shook his head slowly. "I was embarrassed, and I punched the guy. I think I was more mad at him!"

"Bros before hos?"

He grinned, not appearing to mind that she'd just called his ex a ho. Then again, the ex was a ho.

"I didn't yell at her, didn't fight, just…left. I told her what I wanted out of the apartment and that I never wanted to see her again. The end."

"Wow," she murmured, suddenly imagining how that must have felt. Whatever punishment his ex had gotten, including the embarrassment and the ending of her engagement, must surely have paled next to the realization that Leo didn't give a damn that she'd cheated on him. Madison honestly didn't know if she could have survived that.

Not, of course, that she would ever cheat on someone to whom she'd committed herself. Except, of course, according to every damned tabloid in the United States.

"Well, all I can say is, she's an idiot."

He chuckled. "Thanks."

"And you're better off."

"Oh, no doubt about that. But I can't help wishing I'd figured it out sooner. Ah, well, lesson learned. If nothing else, it reaffirmed how incredibly lucky I am to be surrounded by people who really *do* love each other."

"Who?"

"My family." His laughter deepened. "My big, huge, obnoxious, pushy, bossy, demanding family."

"You have a lot of siblings?"

"Two brothers, one older, one younger. But also a ton of cousins, aunts, uncles, second cousins, grandparents. My family might inspire a sequel to *My Big Fat Greek Wedding,* only with Italians."

Good grief, there were more Leos in the world? It boggled the mind.

"And they're all happily married?"

"There's been one divorce in the Santori clan in the past ten years, and that was a great-aunt and uncle who got tired of waiting for each other to die."

She snorted.

"Otherwise, everybody's faithful, everybody's happy. They're pretty damned amazing and incredibly lucky." He shrugged. "It's set a standard for me. I almost took a step that wasn't living up to that standard, and I got slapped down for it. I won't make that mistake again."

No, she didn't imagine he would. He would never sell himself short again, that was for sure. Even she knew he'd never commit to a woman he wasn't completely sure about.

Her heart almost wept over that. To be the woman a man this steady, this sure, this *wonderful* really loved would be such a gift. What a miracle.

And, for her, what an impossibility.

Because all Madison could bring to Leo was embarrassment and scandal, and it sounded like he'd had enough of those to last his whole life. She might as well be walking around with a big scarlet *A* sewn to the front of her bathing suit. His association with her could only drag him through the mud.

He didn't deserve that. And she didn't deserve him.

She knew that. But that didn't change one damn thing.

She still wanted him desperately. They didn't have much time, only six more days, but the more time she spent here, the more confident she was of the privacy and security of this place. Maybe it was risky, maybe she was being selfish, but she couldn't deny that the thought of spending six solid days on the grounds of this resort, having a wild, passionate affair with the man sitting next to her, excited her beyond reason.

Should she, though? She'd made so many bad calls lately, had misjudged one situation after another, the most recent being just how interested the world might be in her love life. Could she really entice Leo Santori into a wild, passionate, short-term affair that they could both walk away from, unscathed, next week?

She honestly didn't know. Nor did she know whether she should.

She just knew she *wanted* to.

HAVING BEEN TOLD by the staff to come to the lobby at around six, dressed comfortably, Leo knocked on her door at five minutes before the hour.

"Right on time," she said as she answered.

"Promptness is my specialty."

"I thought snake wrangling was your specialty."

"That's another one," he said with a laugh as she came outside, pulling the door to her bungalow shut behind her.

She stepped out onto the path, into the sunlight, and he took a sharp breath, looking her over, from head to toe.

Madison was wearing a silky, wispy sundress, all color and light. It was strapless, clinging to her full breasts, tight down to her hips, then flaring out, falling to her knees. The bright, tropical colors made her newly tanned skin glow. Her brilliant green eyes were made even more dramatic with heavier makeup than she usually wore, and she'd swept her hair up onto her head in a loose bun, leaving several long curling strands to fall over her bare shoulders.

She wore simple sandals with a small, delicate ankle bracelet. Something about it, that tiny strip of gold, made his heart race. He wanted to take it off, wanted to kiss her ankle and lick her instep and taste his way all the way up the inside of those beautiful thighs.

"Do you think I look okay?" she asked, noticing his silence.

"No. Not just okay. I think you're beautiful," he said.

She smiled, pleased at the compliment, then looked him over. "I think you are too."

He hadn't been lying about the limits of his wardrobe, but he had remembered to pack a pair of khakis and one dress shirt. It wasn't exactly Chicago dress casual, considering he had brown leather thongs on his feet, but he figured it would do for whatever the hotel staff had cooked up.

They needed to go—it was at least a five-minute walk to the lobby. But something made him stop. This wasn't a date; they were simply getting comped a meal for what had happened this morning. But he couldn't go another minute without doing what he'd wanted to do ever since she'd left his arms earlier today.

Without saying a word, he slid his hands into her hair, knowing he was probably going to knock down more of those sexy curls and not caring. He pulled her to him, saw her eyes flare the tiniest bit in surprise, then he covered her mouth with his.

She didn't hesitate but slid her arms up to encircle his neck, holding him close. Madison tilted her head, parting her lips, gently sliding her tongue out to welcome his. They tasted and explored, slowly, lazily, and he realized he hadn't imagined how good things had been with them this morning. They had chemistry; it was instant, undeniable, almost heady. The more they kissed, the more they wanted to. She pressed her body against his, the pebbled tips of her breasts and the musky, female scent rising off her telling him she was every bit as ready to turn back around and go into her room, skipping dinner in favor of the most delicious physical dessert.

But he wasn't in a rush. No rush at all.

Leo liked taking things slow. There would be no mad, crazy, gotta-get-in-you-right-now coupling. Not with this woman. Oh, maybe that would happen someday, but for their first time, he intended to savor every inch of her. For hours.

Finally, knowing they were probably already late, he ended the kiss and drew away from her. He patted her hair back into place, fixed one dangling curl, and said, "I guess we should go."

"You still want to?"

He saw the question in her eyes, knew she was ready to say to hell with dinner, let's order room service. But like a kid who looked forward to the raw anticipation of Christmas Eve far more than the present-orgy of the next morning, he held firm.

"Yeah, I do. Let's go see what they've got cooked up for us."

She frowned a little. To make sure she understood this wasn't in any way a rejection, he brushed his lips across her mouth one more time. "I can't wait to take that dress off you."

Her eyes flew open and she gasped. "Do you think you can just…"

"Yeah, I can. You want me, Madison. It's dripping off you."

She opened her mouth, then snapped it shut. How could she possibly deny something so utterly obvious to them both?

"And that's good," he added. "Because I want you, too. All I can think about when I see the way your nipples are pressing against those red flowers on the fabric is that they'll taste like ripe berries against my tongue."

He couldn't resist reaching up and flicking his fingers against those taut tips, feeling her sway in reaction as he plucked and teased. He wanted to cup and stroke and suck her but there was no time. Not nearly enough time.

"Leo!"

"Yeah. You're going to taste better than anything they put in front of us for dinner."

She gulped, closed her eyes, obviously trying to steady her breaths. He noticed the way she clenched a lightweight shawl in her hands and wondered if she was picturing his neck in her grip. She appeared ready to strangle him for teasing her now, when there was no way he could follow through.

Hell, the woman obviously didn't appreciate the fine art of anticipation.

"I'll make it up to you," he told her. "I'll make it so worth the wait, Madison."

She opened her eyes, looking up at him, her frown softening, her lips curving into a trusting smile. Then, just to show he wasn't the only one who could play the game, she whispered, "If you think my nipples will taste sweet, just wait until you taste the rest of me."

It was his turn to pause for a deep breath.

"I haven't been with anyone in six months, Leo, and I'm dying to be explored, tasted, *taken*."

"Six months? Funny, same with me. Maybe six months is our lucky number."

It was as if they'd both taken a time-out from everyone else just so they could build toward this night, this joining.

"Mmm-hmm. And if I don't have you in me in the next few hours, I think I'll just die."

"A few hours, huh?" He glanced at his watch. "That doesn't leave much time for foreplay."

She hissed and grabbed at his arm, as if her legs had weakened.

"But I suppose I can make do."

She swallowed visibly. "Please, let's just skip dinner."

"Not a chance, beautiful."

Smiling, Leo took her arm and physically turned her toward the pathway, leading her to the lobby. She didn't say anything, and her steps were the tiniest bit wobbly, as if she was still affected by the sultry promise in his words.

Because he *had* been making a promise.

Hours of foreplay? Not a problem. As long as he could lose himself inside of her at the end of it.

The realization that they'd both turned the corner and admitted that this night would end up with them in bed was enough to slake his appetite for now. It would build, hour by hour, until they were back here. And by then, he looked forward to adoring every inch of her body the way it was meant to have been adored every day for the past six cold, lonely months.

7

AS IT TURNED OUT, the staff's "surprise" dinner wasn't in the upscale restaurant attached to the hotel. Nor was there a limo waiting to whisk them off to some fancy place up in Santa Cruz. Nor was there a bevy of staff carrying trays of room service for a poolside rendezvous.

Instead, they were told when they arrived at the lobby a few minutes after six that they would be going on a beach picnic.

They were instructed to head down to a small, secluded beach tucked into a private cove below the hotel, reserved only for guests. Leo had read about it in the brochures, and he and Madison had talked about heading down there tomorrow. Today they'd just soaked up some sun by the pool, talking, laughing, drinking. She'd filled him in a little on the Hollywood scene—ugh. He'd told her about life in the Windy City. More interesting were all the things they'd both been thinking about but hadn't discussed. Things like how she tasted, how her body molded so perfectly against his, fitting him like she'd been made to be his other half.

As they followed the directions, walking down the steps carved into the hillside below the resort, he realized the term *beach picnic* was far too simple and mundane for the reality. This was more like a picnic a sheikh might indulge in somewhere along the Mediterranean.

"Wow, this is stunning," she said as they reached the bottom of the planked steps.

"No kidding."

The water was a little rough, white-capped waves lapping ashore, not as gentle and soft as a typical Caribbean resort. He liked this better; the Pacific seemed wild and powerful, as timeless as the earth. There was nothing placid about it. It was full of passion and energy.

The shoreline was a broad swath of pale sand, not sugar fine, but still clean and beautiful where it met the blue-green edge of the water.

Not only did they have the cove entirely to themselves—it was near sunset, and, he supposed, the few other guests were eating in the restaurant or were already out on the town. But they also would be dining in splendor. He could only wonder at all the trouble the staff had gone to, and couldn't decide whether it was more a result of the snake or the matchmaking front desk clerk.

A flowing canopy, white and lacy, stood in a sheltered area of the beach, nestled near the curving hillside. Fabric twined around each of the four legs, and it billowed in the evening breeze. Beneath it were a small café table and two chairs.

A chef stood at a tabletop grill, beside which were platters stacked with skewered meat, marinating fish and fresh vegetables. The man smiled as they reached the canopy tent and immediately began to grill the food as the uniformed waiter led them to their seats.

A pristine white cloth covered the table. The center was taken up with a beautiful vase full of colorful, tropical blooms, and a bottle of champagne was laid on ice, two glasses at the ready.

"Good lord, this is like the deluxe wedding night meal in the brochure," Madison whispered as the waiter pulled out her chair and she sat down.

He took his own seat and nodded. This was feeling more and more like a setup, and he decided he needed to leave a large tip for the desk clerk when he checked out.

When he saw the bed-size double lounger, draped with soft, white fabric, he decided to make it an extra-large one.

"Glad we came?" he asked.

She cast a quick look at the lounger. "I think I'm going to be."

"I have no doubt you're going to be."

She shivered a little, though the evening was still warm, and a lovely pink color appeared on her tanned throat, as if her body was growing flushed. He looked forward to exploring that soft swath of pink skin later.

Before she could say anything else, they were startled by the strumming of a guitar. They hadn't even noticed the musician sitting a few yards away. He smiled and nodded as he began to play softly, the notes riding on the air, mingling with the call of seabirds and the never-ending churning of the ocean.

"Champagne?" the waiter asked.

They nodded, and he popped the bottle of an expensive vintage, then poured them each a glass.

"I suppose we should offer a toast to something," Madison said once the waiter had discreetly returned to the chef's table, leaving them in privacy.

"I don't imagine we should drink to the sn…"

She threw a hand up, palm out. "Don't say that word! No more mentioning him tonight."

"All right. How about we drink to…new friendships?"

"As in, vacation buddies?"

He shook his head. "That's not the term I'd use."

Their stares met, and the table suddenly seemed even smaller, more intimate. Because Madison's green eyes were glowing with something that went far beyond friendship. This was so much more than that. Whatever was happening between them, however long it might last and wherever it might go, it was about a lot more than either of them were probably ready to admit. Every minute they'd spent together had suggested that. The kiss they'd shared outside her room had reinforced it. Their conversation had cemented it.

"Let's drink to new beginnings," he finally said.

That felt right, at least for him. For the past six months, he'd been living in limbo. It was almost as if a part of him had been waiting for the original wedding date to pass so the reality that it would never happen would finalize itself in his mind. Now that it had happened, now that the day had come and gone, he felt no sadness, no wistfulness. There was only freedom. Relief. And, now that he'd met Madison, pure anticipation.

"I like that," she said, as if she, too, had something she wanted to move beyond.

Although they'd talked for hours today, while they'd enjoyed the pool—swimming, sunbathing, eating a light lunch—she hadn't opened up much about her past. But he sensed she had come here to escape from her troubles, much as he had. As well as seeking something new and different.

Well, they'd found it. Because they'd found each other.

Maybe just for the next few days. It was too soon to tell. But starting tonight, he and Madison Reid were going to become lovers. Of that he had absolutely no doubt.

It had nothing to do with the conversation they'd had before leaving her room, or with the romantic setup… although the bed definitely didn't hurt. Rather, it had everything to do with the tension and awareness that had been building between them from the moment they'd met. Hell, even if he'd been fully dressed when she'd walked into his room yesterday, and she hadn't fainted in his arms and there had been no naked embrace this morning, this thing between them would still be happening.

It was overwhelming his senses, answering all the questions he'd been asking himself for the past several months. And it was making him more certain than he'd been about anything that he'd finally met the kind of woman he'd been waiting for. One who he couldn't stop thinking about, who filled his thoughts and fueled his every desire, until his hand nearly shook with the need to reach out and touch her. Take her.

"Leo?" she asked, her voice soft.

He shook his head, realizing she was watching him expectantly, her glass in her raised hand. He lifted his, too.

"New beginnings," she said.

He echoed her words. They clinked glasses, and both drank.

The champagne went down smoothly, and the conversation was just as smooth. They had fallen into an easy rhythm with one another sometime after they'd met, and as they waited for their meal to be prepared, answering the chef's questions about their preferences, they talked about a lot of nothing. But good nothing. Fine nothing.

Over fresh fruit, they compared family stories. He marveled that she was an identical twin—that there was another woman as beautiful and perfect as this one somewhere in the world.

She teased him about being the middle of three boys, correctly assessing that he'd been the easygoing one who was always smiling. Unlike his older brother, who was an Army Ranger, or his younger one who was a cop, Leo had always been the comedian of the family, the peacemaker.

When they moved on to a salad filled with exotic greens, they'd talked politics. Only a bit—enough to confirm they were both the same shade of light purple, i.e. a little of this, a little of that. Neither of them were militant on any point, though it seemed important to her that he agree with her on civil rights and gay marriage, which he did.

They didn't talk much when the grilled mahi, marinated beef skewers and crisp vegetables arrived, too focused on the perfection of the meal. And afterward, when the waiter delivered enormous strawberries freshly dipped in chocolate, he couldn't find anything to say. He was too busy watching the way those full lips of hers looked drenched in chocolate, wondering if she cooed like that and closed her eyes with pure, visceral pleasure when she had sex.

He was going to find out tonight.

Their eyes kept meeting. Their hands touched when they both reached for the butter or the water. Their legs brushed. And minute after minute, the pleasurable tension rose. He felt it. She felt it, too. She broadcast it with every flick of her tongue across her lips, every intentional tilt of her head, sweep of her lashes and the tiny sighs she couldn't contain when he leaned close to taste something off her plate or when she reached over to brush a crumb off his shirt.

Tension. Oh, such delightful tension.

"Would you like coffee?" the waiter asked after he'd cleared away the last of the dishes. The chef had already departed, after they'd extended their sincere thanks, and the musician was packing up his guitar.

"That would be nice, thanks," Madison said. She pulled her wrap around her shoulders. The sun had begun to set, the evening air gaining more of a chill.

After serving the coffee, the waiter walked out from under the canopy to light some tiki torches that had been planted in the sand. When he returned, he said, "Please enjoy the sunset. Staff will be down to clean up later tonight. It's been a pleasure serving you, and again, the management extends its sincere apologies for today's inconvenience."

"Thank you," Madison replied, and Leo echoed the sentiment.

Then the man departed, the guitarist following him. Leo and Madison were left alone on the tiny beach.

Without a word, he rose from his seat and extended a hand. When she took it, he helped her stand and led her to the plush lounger. Pulling her with him, he sat down on it, spread out, and helped her tuck herself in beside him. She was on her side, her head on his shoulder, one thigh lifted and curled between his, her hand traipsing lazy circles on his chest.

The sun slipped farther, ever farther, and they remained quiet, washed in the glory of it. There was no need for conversation. They both simply knew, somehow, that the moment deserved utter silence, the only sounds those of their beating hearts and the churning waves.

Red and orange beams chased each other over the surf as the massive golden orb descended toward the horizon. They began to dance across the water, sent forth from some far-off, mystical place, thousands of lines of light riding the waves and landing close to their feet. The entire world seemed to be made of glistening light, every droplet of water in the spray turned into a jeweled rainbow.

Against his chest, he felt Madison stop breathing, and understood the reason. He found himself holding his breath, too, as that globe dropped what seemed like inches into the vast blue. Farther. Farther. Until at last, with a final wink and a flash, it fell off the edge of the world.

She exhaled in a rush. "Beautiful."

It had been. "A once in a lifetime sundown."

Which seemed appropriate for the once in a lifetime night they were about to begin.

AFTER THE SUN had descended beyond the horizon, Madison remained curled up against Leo, content to relive the beauty of the moment in her mind. She'd never seen a more glorious sunset.

Leo remained quiet, too, content to watch, and to stroke lazy circles on her back with his fingers. Her shawl had slipped down and there was nothing separating his fingertips from her sensitive skin, which grew more sensitive with each gentle stroke.

But despite being gentle, there was nothing simple or innocent about it. The same rapt attention she'd paid to the sunset now shifted and turned, zoning in on the feelings he was arousing in her with that deliberate touch. Every time his hand moved a tiny bit lower, pushing closer to the back of her sundress, she shimmied up a little, wanting those fingers to push the material away, to bare her to the cool evening air and the heat of his touch.

Though the sun was gone, darkness certainly hadn't descended. The sky was still awash with purple, orange and gold. Once it did grow dark, the torches would still provide enough illumination for them, though not for anyone standing high on the cliffs above them to actually look down and see them. Especially not beneath the graceful canopy.

The scene was designed for private seduction. For intimacy. And while she couldn't totally agree that the woman at the front desk was doing some matchmaking, she couldn't rule it out, either. Because this setting was simply too perfect for sensual interludes to be accidental.

"You warm enough?" he asked.

"I'm perfect."

He shifted, rolling onto his side to face her, looking intently into her eyes. "Yes, you are."

Placing the tip of his index finger on her chin he tilted her head up, then bent down to brush his lips against hers.

Madison had been in a state of high alert all evening. Hell, all day—ever since that wild, erotic encounter on the patio. She had been thinking of nothing else but being possessed by him—taken wildly, roughly, desperately.

But now, she realized, she wanted it slow. Wanted a lingering, deep kiss that lasted at least a hundred heartbeats, and wanted it to end only because there was so very much more to explore.

He seemed to read her mind. He kept the kiss slow, lazy and sensual, his warm tongue exploring her mouth thoroughly. He tasted every bit of her, breathing into her and taking her breath.

A hundred heartbeats passed. At least. Or perhaps a thousand. Time began to lose its meaning as darkness fell and the night became lit by only those torches and the glow of moonlight they could glimpse through the fabric of the canopy.

He finally moved his lips away, kissing the corner of her mouth. He moved to her cheek, tasting her jawline, and then her neck, until he was breathing into her ear, his tongue flicking out to sample the lobe.

"I've wanted you from the minute you fell into my arms and fainted," he whispered.

"I've wanted you since I walked into the room and saw you standing there."

"Finest male ass you've ever seen," he said with a laugh.

"I can't deny it."

She stretched a little, arching against him, sliding her bare leg up and down against him. Leo moved a hand down her arm, blazing a trail of heat against her cool skin, awakening every nerve ending. He was still focused on her neck, and he kissed his way down it, until he could bury his face in her neck. There he paused to inhale, breathing her in, as if intoxicated by her essence.

She twined her fingers in his hair, needing something to hold on to when he resumed his slow study of her body. Without a word, he reached up to the elastic top of her dress and tugged it down, following the material, kissing every inch of skin as it was revealed. She arched toward his mouth, her breasts heavy, aching and desperate. When the top hem finally scraped across her nipples and popped over them, she moaned. Every stroke was intense, every sensation built upon the last.

He leaned up on an elbow, staring down at her as he pulled the bodice all the way down, revealing her breasts. Even in the semidarkness she could see the hunger in his eyes, the way he had to part his lips to take a shaky breath.

"Taste me," she ordered, knowing he was dying to. He'd been dying to since they'd left her room.

He reached for one breast, cupping it in his hand, plumping it and lightly squeezing her nipple. Heat sluiced through her, as if there were a wire between her breast and her groin, and she jerked reflexively.

Leo didn't notice, he was far too focused on looking at her, studying her, as if he'd never seen anything more beautiful. The tension stretched and built, and she thought she'd die if he didn't suckle her. When she'd almost reached the point of begging, he bent to flick his tongue over her sensitive nipple.

"Oh, God, yes," she cried, waves of heat washing ever downward.

He needed no more urging, moving to cover her entire nipple with his mouth. His hot breath seared her, then he was closing tight, his lips capturing her, his tongue flicking out to taste. He sucked hard, making all her nerve endings roar.

She reached for his shirt, desperate to feel him, and ripped at the front. A few buttons flew, enough for her to reach in and stroke his powerful chest, feel the sheen of sweat on his body that spoke of hunger and desire and need far more than the temperature of the air.

He continued to suckle her, reaching for her other breast, stroking and squeezing it, playing with her nipple until she shook.

"Berries," he murmured. "Sweet and so pretty."

As if remembering she'd invited him to taste far more than her nipples, he finally moved down and kissed a slow path over her midriff. He sampled each rib, licking each indentation, scraping his teeth across her skin as he pulled the dress out of his way.

When it got down to her hips, she lifted up a little so he could pull it all the way off. Beneath it, she wore only a tiny, skimpy pair of panties, lacy and white, the kind made to be torn off by a hungry man. They might as well have been advertised that way on the package.

"Pretty," he said as he studied them. Closely. His mouth was beneath her belly button, his jaw rubbing against the elastic of her panties. She felt his warm breaths through the nylon, and arched up in welcome.

He moved farther, placing his open mouth on her mound and inhaling deeply, breathing her in through the material.

"Oh, God, Leo," she cried, dying—just dying—for him to lick every inch of her.

As if knowing she'd taken about as much as she could, he began to uncover her fully. But he didn't tear the panties off, he merely tugged them, slowly, inch by inch, watching closely as he revealed her secrets.

"Oh, man," he whispered, his voice shaking as he looked at her.

She smiled. He liked what he saw.

He proved it, pushing the panties the rest of the way off, and then reaching for one of her legs. He stroked her thigh gently before pushing it, parting her legs, opening them so he could enjoy her in all her wantonness.

There was no thought of shyness, no modesty, nothing but heat and desire, natural and earthy. He looked at her as if he'd never seen anything more beautiful and moved immediately to taste her.

His mouth moved to her sex, his lips gliding against her in an erotic kiss that defied description. He licked her thoroughly, scraping his warm, wet tongue all over her outer lips, then slipping into the folds for more.

A helpless, desperate cry escaped her mouth. It was carried off by the night breeze, and she wondered just how many more times the man would make her cry out tonight.

"Beautiful," he said, touching her, stroking her, gently plucking at each secret place so he could study her more intimately.

He flicked the tip of his index finger over her clit, which throbbed with sensation, then moved his mouth to it and sucked it gently. As if he knew her body already, he circled his finger around the base while he flicked her with his tongue. Everything—all sensation, all desire, all need—centered there. It built and throbbed until it finally exploded in a climax that left her shaking so hard her teeth chattered.

He noticed. Kissing his way back up her body, until he reached her face, he murmured, "Are you cold?"

"Oh, God, no," she replied, wrapping her arms around him.

He kissed her deeply, his mouth tasting like sex and desire, and she reached again for his shirt, determined not to be stopped by a few buttons this time.

Leo broke away long enough to take over the task, yanking the thing up and over his head and tossing it to the sand. She bit her lip, watching as he quickly undid his khakis, waiting to see that amazing erection she'd held in her hand just this morning.

He rose onto his knees, pushing his pants down. He hadn't been wearing anything underneath, and all her breath left her body in a deep, hungry groan.

"I didn't imagine it," she managed to whisper.

He didn't say anything, but focused on pushing his pants all the way off. Then he returned his full attention to her.

Madison parted her legs even farther in an age-old invitation to claim her. Fill her.

"I'm on the pill," she told him when he paused, opening his mouth as if about to ask her something. "And there's nothing else for you to worry about."

"Or for you," he said.

Then there was no more talking. Nothing else to say. The only communicating they needed to do was with their bodies.

He moved between her parted thighs, bracing himself above her and staring down at her face. Just to melt her heart a tiny bit more, to reinforce the goodness she'd sensed in the man from the beginning, he asked, "You're sure? No second thoughts, no regrets?"

She reached up and encircled his shoulders, drawing him down to her. "I've never been more sure about anything."

"Neither have I," he admitted as he settled between her legs, nudging her sex with that massive erection that both thrilled and intimidated her.

She shouldn't have worried. He was careful, gentle, and he'd aroused her to the point of insanity. She was dripping wet, soft, welcoming and so ready to be filled by him.

He knew. And he began to fill her.

He slid into her warm opening, the passage easy and smooth. All the feminine parts of her reacted and responded the way they were supposed to, with utter surrender to pleasure. She clenched him, tugging him deeper, both with her arms and with her sex. Leo groaned, letting himself be taken in, still careful, but obviously starting to lose himself to sensation.

"Yes. Take me," she pleaded, tightening her arms around his neck, nipping at his throat. "Take me *now*."

That drove him onward. Without another word, he arched his hips and plunged, driving into her more deeply than she'd ever thought it possible to go. She let out another cry of pure, utter satisfaction, and focused on savoring the sensation of heat and power and such wonderful, delightful fullness.

"Are you…"

"I'm fine," she said, moving her mouth to his and licking his lips for entry.

They kissed hungrily, tongues entwining, and he slowly pulled out of her, only to sink again. She arched up to meet the slow thrust, curving her hips upward, wrapping her legs around those lean flanks.

"Madison," he whispered, still cautious.

"More," she demanded, knowing why he was being so careful, knowing he was afraid to hurt her. "Don't take it easy on me, Leo, I *want* it. Give it to me."

She tightened her hands in his hair, gripping him, almost at the point of begging him to pound and thrust.

And then he began to pound and thrust.

He pulled out and drove back in, going deeper and deeper. The walls of her sex wrapped around him, taking everything, greedy for more. Her heart pounded wildly and she found it hard to catch her breath. She couldn't think, couldn't focus, could only *be*.

Leo had obviously thrown off the last of his restraints, because he suddenly rolled over onto his back, pulling her with him. He sat her up, impaling her on his cock, holding tightly to her hips.

"Yeah, baby, please," she groaned, digging her fingers into the crisp hair on his chest.

He encircled her waist with his hands and thrust up, just as he tugged her down. The intensity was wild, and he bored a path even deeper into her. She let out a little scream, but when he paused, she glared down at him. "Don't you stop. Don't you dare stop."

"Not planning on it, sweetheart," he said between harsh breaths.

The muscles in his chest and arms clenched and flexed and his jaw was like granite. His eyes closed and he dropped his head back as he thrust up into her again. And again. And again.

Although she was on top, he controlled their every move, handling her as easily as if she'd been a doll. But she didn't care. Every movement he made was for her pleasure. As if to reinforce that, he moved one hand between them and rubbed her clit, just to make sure she'd climax again when he was ready to.

The heat began to rise again, the sensations spiraled. She was battered by the cool evening air, completely filled with his rock-hard cock, gripped and held and completely lost to pure sexual bliss.

And when he finally gave a hoarse shout, indicating he'd gained his own, she followed him to an explosive orgasm, and then collapsed onto his body, boneless, weak and exhausted.

8

As it turned out, Leo hadn't merely paid for an "all-inclusive" meal plan he didn't need, he'd apparently paid for an unneeded room, too. After he and Madison had become lovers on the beach, they had, by unspoken agreement, gone back to her room and slept together in her bed.

The sex was phenomenal.

Sleeping together afterward just made it better.

He liked drifting off with her head resting against his shoulder, her arm curled over his middle, their legs entwined. He liked it even better every time he woke up to find her warm beside him, ready for more.

They'd spent the deepest, darkest hours of the night exploring each other in a slow, sultry orgy of lust that seemed to go on forever. Or, at least, as long as he could hold out. Madison had once again proved to be impatient, as greedy in bed as she was generous out of it. At one point, he'd been able to do nothing but laugh—and comply—when she'd demanded that he stop with all the oral sex and just fuck her into the headboard.

Hoping to start the day off the same way, he reached for her as soon as he woke up the next morning. Her half of the bed was empty. It was warm, though, as if she'd just left it a few moments ago. Sitting up, he glanced toward the bathroom. The door was open, but she wasn't inside.

A muffled voice was talking nearby, and he finally glanced out the patio door and saw her sitting in the sunshine, talking on her phone.

She was stark naked.

Damn, he liked this place.

Beams of sunlight illuminated every delicious bit of her, catching all the gold highlights in that honey-brown hair. He'd touched and kissed almost every inch of her last night, but he hadn't seen her in all her glory until this moment, and the sight of her nearly stopped his heart. She was all softness and curves and smooth, silky skin.

And he'd left his mark on her.

Even from here he could see the slightly reddened spots on her throat and breasts, left there by his hungry mouth. There was a small bruise on one hip, and he suspected he'd held her a little too tightly when she'd been riding him.

He didn't feel too badly, though, suspecting that if he looked at his back in the mirror he'd see plenty of war wounds, too. He certainly felt them. But he didn't regret one damn thing. The memory that he could get her out of her mind, raking at him, begging him, and utterly helpless to do anything but take what he gave her turned him on almost as much as looking at her sitting naked in the sunshine.

Smiling, he got up and stretched, not surprised to see he had some major morning wood. Hell, just thinking of her was enough to make him want to go outside and push her legs apart. He couldn't think of a better way to scrape up his knees than kneeling in front of her. Draping her legs over the arms of her chair would put all those beautiful, slick secrets right in front of his face; he wanted to see, explore and taste her all over again.

But she seemed pretty involved in her conversation. So he instead headed to the bathroom to wash up. When he came out, she was still outside, still talking, and he went over and pulled the patio door open.

"No, I swear, I'm fine," she was saying into her cell phone. "You don't need to do anything right now, just let it go. It'll die down, these things always do."

Not sure whether her conversation was a private one or not, he was about to close the door again when she glanced up, saw him standing there and offered him a bright good-morning smile.

"Hi," he murmured, bending down to kiss the top of her head.

"Hi back," she replied before returning to her telephone conversation. "What? Uh, yeah. Someone I met here in Costa Rica."

Ah, she was explaining him to someone.

"Oh, be quiet, you know-it-all," she said good-naturedly. "Of course he's hot."

He snickered.

"Leo. Like the lion."

Rowr.

She sighed heavily, obviously getting the third degree. "No, not DiCaprio for God's sake!"

He laughed.

"Yeah, yeah, you're a genius. It was great advice. Blah, blah, blah."

So this someone had been after her to have a wild, sexy fling during her vacation? Interesting, considering that was also what his friends had told him to do, which made him wonder again what it was that haunted Madison. They hadn't discussed it, beyond her admission that she'd come here to get away from her troubles for a while. What were those troubles, though? Had her friends told her to go off and have an affair to get over a broken heart? And if so, who'd broken it?

The idea of someone hurting her made his whole body stiffen in anger. He walked over to the pool's edge, not wanting her to interpret his reaction as jealousy.

Even if, he had to concede, that might be part of it.

Yeah, he hated the idea that anyone might have hurt her.

But it was more than that. The very thought of any other man having his hands on her, making her cry out in pleasure the way she had for him last night, made him want to punch the bungalow wall. How crazy was that? He was jealous over somebody she might have been with even before she'd met him? He'd only known her a couple of days, but the very idea of it made him more ready to do violence than the reality of his former best man sleeping with his ex-fiancée.

"You are losing it, man," he muttered.

"Did you say something?"

He hadn't even realized she'd ended her call and walked up behind him until she spoke. Before he could turn around, she'd slipped her arms around his waist and stepped in close, hugging him from behind. Every bare inch of her body delighted him, but, to be honest, he'd rather be the one coming at her from behind.

Hmm. Nice mental images filled his head.

"I just checked," he told her. "The pool is reptile-free and ready to go."

She shivered against his back, her pert nipples scraping his skin, driving him a little nuts. "Yikes, thanks for reminding me. I'd managed to forget all about that this morning."

He turned around, lining the hug up better. Full frontal under the full sun…it was kind of spectacular.

"Sorry I slept so late. You didn't have to go outside to take your call," he said.

"No problem. It was just a friend from California." She smiled broadly, her eyes twinkling with humor in the sunlight. "Before I came here, he had suggested I find a beach bum to hook up with on my vacation. He was very happy to hear your voice and realize I'd taken his advice."

Thrusting off the quick flash of jealousy that her friend was male, Leo pretended to be offended. "Beach bum?"

"Well, no, I guess I have *slightly* higher standards."

"I'm going to have to punish you for that."

"Promises, promises." Her saucy tone and pursed lips said she was thinking of naughty punishments.

Which sounded just fine to him. God, how he enjoyed this woman's blunt approach to everything, from life to sex. He'd never been with anyone who was so open about what she wanted and what she didn't. And when she did or didn't want them.

"Are you, by any chance, a little wicked?"

"Haven't you figured that out by now?"

He stared into her eyes. "I'm getting the picture."

"Are you liking what you see?"

"Yeah." He raked a slow, thorough stare down her body, from the long hair draping her shoulders and playing peekaboo with those pebbled nipples, to the slim middle, to those eminently grippable hips and drool-inspiring long legs. All naked. All completely his, for now at least. "Oh, *hell,* yeah."

"Good. As for the punishment, despite some curiosity, I'm fairly certain I'm not into pain," she explained. "If you ever spanked me, I would probably cut your hand off."

Chuckling, he replied, "No interest in spanking, sweetheart."

She continued. "Nor am I into rape fantasies. Any man who tries to force me won't lose a hand, he'll lose what he uses that hand to play with."

He didn't play along by grimacing, cringing or feigning horror at the idea of losing every man's most prized possession. Instead, he grew serious, reaching out to touch her hair. It was warm beneath his fingertips, baked in the sun. "Every Santori man was raised by a Santori mother who taught him how to treat women.

Lesson number one—men who hurt women are cowards," he said. "I'd never do anything to hurt you."

She turned her face to kiss his palm. "I know that, Leo. I know you'd never really hurt me." Her impish smile returned. "But if you wanted to, say, get a little creative with some…"

Positions? Toys?

"…handcuffs…I might not object."

He coughed into his fist. Jesus, the woman was killing him here.

"Problem?"

"Nope. No problem. Kind of hard to get handcuffs down here, I imagine." He could hear the heat in his tone as he speculated, "We might have to make do with silk scarves or something."

It was her turn to look affected by the conversation. She was breathing across open lips and her eyelids had dropped to half-mast. She might have been teasing, trying to arouse him with some suggestive ideas, but those ideas were obviously exploding into full-fledged X-rated movies in her mind.

"That could be arranged."

"And maybe then you'd have to shut up and wait and take what I want to give you."

"Maybe," she said, completely unrepentant for being so demanding.

Oh, hell, who was he kidding? He loved that she was so demanding. Loved that he got her so worked up she couldn't do anything but scream and beg and threaten him if he didn't proceed. She'd gone so far as to call him a clit tease last night. He couldn't say he'd ever heard the expression, but had to admit, he'd found it pretty funny. And he'd been determined to live up to it.

"Maybe I'll punish you by making you wait all day for your punishment."

"That'd be punishment for you, too," she said, her voice almost a purr.

He knew she was taunting him, and decided to pay her back. Not warning her, he swung her up into his arms, bracing her under the shoulder, crossing-the-threshold style. As she squealed, he stepped to the very edge of the pool, dangling her over the crystal clear water. "Ready to get wet?"

"Don't you dare!" She twined her arms tightly around his neck. "It's too early, the water's too cold."

"Not for a beach bum."

"Superhot fireman, that's what I meant to say. Strong, professional, determined, hardworking hero." Loosening her grip, she traced the tip of her finger across his lips. "Please don't throw me into that cold water, Leo. Pretty please?"

"What are you going to give me if I don't?"

She thought about it, tapping the tip of her finger on her mouth. Then, smiling as if the proverbial lightbulb had just gone off in her head, she replied, "A blow job?"

He was torn between laughing and groaning with pure want. He'd already been aroused and another ten gallons of blood rushed to his cock just at her suggestion.

"You always say what you're thinking, don't you?"

"Pretty much," she admitted. "That's why my closest

friends always called me Mad. It wasn't just a shorten-
ing of my name."

"Hmm. Mad. You don't seem like the angry type."

"Not angry. It's short for Mad, Bad and Dangerous
to Know."

"That I can see." He glanced at the glistening water,
as if he really had to think about it, and said, "Okay,
Mad. I guess I won't toss you in this time."

"You really are my hero."

She leaned up and brushed her lips against his. He
immediately opened his mouth and deepened the kiss,
invading her, taking the sassiness right off her tongue.
Madison needed to be kissed, well and often, if only as
a reminder that she wasn't always in charge.

When they finally ended the kiss, they were both
panting. But he wouldn't put her down yet. He liked
holding her, liked being in control for now. She might
demand what she wanted, but he was making it pretty
damned clear that, physically, he had her right where
he wanted her.

She twined her fingers in his hair and looked up at
him, her expression purely happy. "That's a very nice
way to start the day."

"I had another one in mind when I woke up."

"Sorry I wasn't there."

"It's okay. Like I said, I slept too late anyway. I never
sleep so late in the morning unless I'm on nights and
have just gone to bed."

"I figured you could use your rest. You got quite a
workout last night."

He scrunched his brow, as if giving it careful consideration. "Really?" Lifting her up and down a couple of times in his arms like a barbell, he added, "Funny, I feel great."

She squealed a little and hung on to his shoulders, saying, "That's good. Because I think you're going to get another one today."

"One?"

"Four."

He barked a laugh, then thought about it. Four. Hmm. Not very impressive. "Come on, challenge me, babe."

"Am I going to need to do any walking for the rest of this vacation?" she asked.

He tilted his head, as if considering it. "Not that I can think of."

"Okay, then. I *guess* you can go for a world record."

"What's the record?"

"Twenty-seven."

He snorted. "Yeah, uh, by that point you wouldn't be able to put your legs together, much less walk. And I wouldn't have a dick, much less one capable of getting hard."

She licked her lips, her expression evil. "Back to that blow job idea, are we?"

He didn't tease her back. She'd mentioned that one too many times for him to pretend he wasn't dying for her to use her beautiful mouth on every inch of him.

"I think we could fit that in today, if you really want to."

"I already know it's not going to fit," she said with a smirk. "But I do really want to and I'm always ready to give it the old college try."

"Rah-rah. So, where does that leave us? Somewhere between four and twenty-seven, with a blow job and a serious licking in between?"

She swallowed visibly. "*Serious* licking?"

"Oh, very serious."

"I noticed you kind of like that."

"No, honey, I kind of love it. You taste better to me than anything I've ever eaten in my life."

"Mmm." She wriggled in his arms, obviously reacting to this verbal foreplay.

So was he. In fact, he couldn't lower her to her feet right now because, if he did, she would hit a major obstacle on her way down.

"Okay, then. We're agreed," she said, as if firming up terms for a business proposition.

"We are? What's the final number again?"

"Six." She quickly added, "Plus the licking and the blowing."

Six. She was challenging him to make love to her six times today. Plus the...extras.

No sweat.

He was twenty-eight. His job kept him in peak physical condition. Until last night, he'd been celibate for six long months.

And he was hotter for her than any man had ever been hot for a woman.

Six would be absolutely no hardship.

"And if it'll *really* kill you not to suck my nipples until I scream, I guess you can do that, too," she said, doing him a very great favor by offering up her beautiful breasts for his devouring.

He lifted her higher, bent his head and flicked his tongue over one pretty tip.

"Thank you, that's so selfless of you," he murmured as she sighed with pleasure.

"That's just how I roll."

They both started to laugh, softly at first, then growing louder. There wasn't another woman he could *ever* remember talking to like this, especially one he'd been holding naked in his arms, whose nipple he'd just licked. She was so damned open and quick, witty and confident. Most women he'd dated hadn't been able to take a joke that *wasn't* about sex, much less any that were.

Before Madison, sex had always been twice as serious but only half as good. Adding warm humor to intimacy—at least before the brain cells evaporated and lust took over completely—enhanced the experience in ways he'd never thought possible. Hell, just having a woman smile up at him tenderly, twining her fingers in his hair, was incredible all on its own. As demanding as she could be in bed, Madison still surprised him with moments like those. Every woman he'd ever been with before had been entirely serious, and, he suspected, focused on gaining advantage in the relationship outside of the bedroom.

He and Madison didn't have a relationship—not yet, anyway, not in the real world. This was a vacation fling, although something inside him rebelled at calling it that. Still, it was a freeing proposition; neither of them were playing games, keeping score or exchanging in any kind of tit for tat.

It was easy with Madison. Hot, incredibly hot, but just so easy.

"Okay, then, I think we have a deal," he finally said.

"This is going to be quite a day, isn't it?" Her eyes were wide, gleaming with excitement, and she was practically panting each breath. He could feel the thudding of her heart in her chest and drew her a little more tightly against his body, knowing now where he intended to put her down.

On the bed.

"I think it would be quite a day even if we had to stop after one," he replied, wondering if she heard the tenderness in his voice and correctly interpreted it.

He wanted to spend the day with her. Yes, that day would include a lot of mind-blowing sex. But even if it didn't, he would still be looking forward to it. Just being with her, getting to know her, hearing that laugh, watching those green-gold eyes sparkle in the sun…sounded like the perfect vacation day to him.

She nodded slowly, silently agreeing with him. "Maybe we could just go on and on for hours and call it one."

"Sounds good to me."

Slowly loosening her arms from around his neck, she said, "Don't you want to put me down?"

"In a minute."

He walked across the patio and went inside through the open door. Carrying her to the huge bed, he didn't so much lower her as toss her onto it. Madison stared up at him, those eyes flashing in challenge, and reached for him.

He shook his head slowly.

"What?"

"Move up," he ordered her, nodding toward the pillows.

She did, edging closer to the headboard. When she was close enough, he said, "Get all the way up on your knees. Turn around facing the wall and hold on to the headboard."

She caught her lip between her teeth. He knew this was driving her crazy, both with lust, and because his tone of voice brooked no disobedience. He was calling the shots for now. It was about time she figured that out.

She didn't move. Neither did he.

He could outwait her, of that he had no doubt. Knowing how to prove he could take care of his needs a little more easily than she could right now, he reached down and grabbed his cock. Encircling it in his hand, he stroked. It wasn't nearly as good as she would be, but it got the job done. She hissed, her gaze dropping so she could stare, and he saw her lick her lips.

She made as if to move toward him. He put a hand up to stop her. "Me first. Then your turn."

That was when she finally figured out what he wanted. A sultry smile broke over her face. She stopped stalling, rose to her knees and crawled toward the head of the bed.

Just because she was a witch and she knew how badly he wanted her, she put some serious wag in that ass, parting her legs a little more than was necessary. A flash of glimmering pink—oh, how that smooth skin felt against his lips, he could have died of sensory overload last night—greeted him. She was practically daring him to resist. She wanted him to climb onto the bed behind her on his knees and ram into her.

"Later," he promised.

"Everything's later," she grumbled.

"So stop stalling so we can get on to the now," he said with a lazy grin.

She grinned back, admitting she liked this push and pull between them, the sparring over who called the shots.

She finally reached the top of the bed, shoving the pillows out of her way and kneeling. He walked closer, took her hands and rested them on the top of the tall wooden headboard, making sure she remained on her knees but completely upright.

Kissing her on the mouth, hot and hard, he dropped onto his back on the bed and slid up toward her. "Show me, Mad. Show me everything."

She looked down at him, over her shoulder, and slowly eased her legs apart, opening for him.

"Beautiful," he growled, unable to tear his eyes off her glistening, sensitive folds. She was swollen and plump, pink and perfect.

When her knees were far enough apart to accommodate him, he slid all the way up so his head was between her thighs.

"Hold on tight," he said.

"Is it going to be a bumpy ride?"

"Uh-huh."

"Oh, good. That's my favorite kind."

He didn't give her any more time to prepare or talk.

He just couldn't wait to taste her fully. Wrapping his arms around her thighs, he tilted her sex toward his mouth and slaked his thirst for her.

She cried out when he flattened his tongue and licked her from stem to stern. Knowing he had her attention, he slid his tongue deeper, between those luscious folds. He lapped into her, sliding his tongue deep enough to make her sing, then moving out again. She tasted as amazing as she looked, as she smelled, as she felt, and he had to tell her so.

"I could do this every day for the rest of my life and die a happy man," he muttered.

"You're killing me, Leo," she groaned, sounding hopeless and desperate.

Almost laughing, he moved his mouth to her pebbled clit and sucked it between his lips. Her hips jerked, but he held her tight, nowhere near ready to let her do what he knew she wanted to do: slide down his body and impale herself on him. Although part of him would love that, considering his need was almost painful, he wasn't going there until she'd completely lost herself to everything but sensation.

Continuing the relentless assault, he brought her higher and higher. She quivered and moaned, but didn't release her death grip on the headboard. He explored her completely, pleasured her until his tongue ached, until, finally, a cry of utter satisfaction signaled her orgasm.

"Yes, oh, lord, yes," she said, her voice weak.

He moved out from under her, his face wet, his every sense filled with her. Madison sagged against the headboard, sucking in deep, needy breaths, completely wrung out. She made as if to turn around, and he knew she still wanted to use her mouth on him, but he was barely holding it together. He had to be inside her, right now.

Rising to his knees, he moved in behind her. Madison smiled at him over her shoulder, suddenly looking a lot more energetic, and scooted back to meet him, her legs parted invitingly.

"Yes," she told him. "I want you to be buried so deep inside me I'll remember you there for a week."

He smirked. "A week? Oh, please."

She licked her lips and curved that gorgeous ass a little higher in welcome. He didn't need any further invite. Taking her hips in his hands, he held her tight and nudged into her. Pleasure washed over him the moment hot, hard cock met warm, slick channel, and he groaned as he sank deeper and deeper, every inch feeling like a step closer to heaven.

She cried out when he finally sank all the way, making a place for himself deep inside her willing body.

"You okay?"

She literally purred. "So okay."

Not wanting to hurt her, and knowing the angle had to be pretty intense for her, he moved slowly at first. He made easy love to her, caressing her hips, her thighs and the small of her back between each deep stroke. But as the intensity built, as her cries increased and she pushed back ever harder, he knew she was long past any need or desire for gentleness.

Which was good. Because he'd reached the point where he needed to pound into her in a mindless frenzy.

But he also wanted to see her beautiful face, wanted to kiss her and share the gasps as they both hit that cliff and flew off it.

Pulling out of her, he flipped her onto her back. Her eyes were sparkling with excitement and wanton pleasure. Her face was flushed, her every breath a gasp, and her whole body sheened with sweat. They were slick and hot and so well matched he wondered how he'd ever done this with anyone else.

"That was…"

"The halfway point," he muttered, making sure she knew they weren't done. "At most."

A sultry smile widened those lips. "One-twelfth of our day, then, huh? You'd better slow down."

He laughed out loud, but grew serious when she reached for him, wrapping her arms tightly around his neck and pulling him down for a deep, hungry kiss. Her thighs parted again and he settled between them, getting back into her with one hot, hard plunge. He reached for one of her slim legs, lifting it over his shoulder, lightly biting the thigh as he drove a little deeper. The angle was incredible. He felt so completely taken in by her, welcomed and pleasured.

She thrust her hips to meet his every downward stroke. Soon she was rolling her head back and forth on the pillow, biting her lip to try to hold back her cries.

"Nobody can hear you, sweetheart," he told her as he felt waves of heat radiating through his body, preparing him for a mind-numbing explosion.

As if she'd just been waiting for permission, she let out a tiny scream of pleasure with the next thrust. An even louder one followed, and he knew by the way her head fell back and her fingers tightened, digging into his shoulders, that she had come again. Seeing her losing herself to glorious pleasure was enough to send him tipping over the edge, too, and with one more deep thrust, he flew apart as well, coming into her in wave after wave of ecstasy.

He didn't roll off her right away, wanting to watch sanity return to her face and feel the raging heartbeat begin to slow to a normal rhythm. He lowered her leg, keeping himself propped on his elbows so he didn't crush her, sharing heaving breaths and then, when she opened her eyes again, satisfied smiles.

"That," he told her, "was…"

"Number one."

9

ALTHOUGH THEY HADN'T hit the world record—whatever that might be, and she doubted it was anywhere near twenty-seven—Madison still found it deliciously difficult to walk the next day. For thirty-six hours, she and Leo hadn't left her room, except to go out into the private pool. They'd ordered room service when hungry, had slept when exhausted, had soaked in the pool when overheated, and had made love so many times, she'd lost count of the positions, sensations and orgasms.

And throughout all of that, she hadn't given more than a passing thought to all the nonsense going on back home. It was like they were living in a completely different world. Things like tabloids and paparazzi and movie stars didn't exist.

Being with Leo had made her troubles disappear.

He was funny and smart, could be bossy, which she liked, and could also be incredibly tender, which she also liked. He was, without a doubt, the most amazing lover she'd ever had. Patient to the extreme, powerful and exciting. But the sex was also playful and fun.

Honestly, she didn't even want to think about what it would be like to give him up at the end of this vacation.

Not that they'd talked about that. Neither of them had mentioned the real world or going back to it. She knew she might be riding a cloud of sexual euphoria, but she was happy to be airborne and didn't want to come back down to earth.

Of course, *this* wasn't exactly what she had in mind.

"I'm sorry, I changed my mind, I don't think I can do it." She heard the nervousness in her own voice and while she hated herself for it, she couldn't prevent it.

"Come on, I know you're not scared of heights. You've been skydiving," Leo said, looking surprised.

"Over North America. Not over the freaking jungle."

It was probably a bad time to get cold feet, considering they had already ridden the party bus several hours to get here. They'd also already paid the exorbitant fee for the double experience—a treetop tour on some swinging wooden walkways, plus zip lining out to a beautiful waterfall in the middle of nowhere. Not to mention they were already standing on a small platform hundreds of feet in the air, getting strapped into harnesses for their zip-line adventure!

She'd been very excited about it, right up until the moment she'd seen a vine dangling from a nearby tree and had a sudden image of a long, slithery animal.

"It's the snake factor," Leo said, understanding immediately.

Yeah. That. Madison had seen that vine, recalled what kinds of creatures made their home in the jungle, and her feet had turned into icicles.

She gulped and nodded. "I want to do this, I really do. It's gorgeous." She spread her arms wide and looked around them at the incredible green canopy blocking out the blue sky above their heads. She truly had never seen such a remarkable palette of different shades of green—her favorite color. Part of her wanted to soar through the sky, to explore the wonders of nature that made this place so different from anywhere back home.

Part of her wanted to carjack the nearest tour bus and hightail it back to the resort.

Because of those pesky snakes.

The guide—young, cute and English speaking—had obviously overheard. "Oh, no, no snakes to worry about, *señorita*."

Madison just lifted a skeptical brow.

The young man shrugged. "Maybe a few."

She reached for the clasp of her harness, ready to strip out of the contraption.

"But you'll do nothing more than wave to them from the air as you fly over," Leo insisted with a chuckle.

"What if the harness breaks and I fall a hundred feet into a nest of fer-de-lances?"

"That won't happen," the guide assured her.

"Plus, I think if you fell a hundred feet, you'd have more to worry about than some snakes," Leo pointed out. "Broken limbs, crushed skull, that sort of thing."

"Ha-ha."

The guide didn't laugh at that part, either. They'd gone over the rules for this adventure many times; the company prided themselves on their safety record.

"Impossible," the man said, looking offended.

"I know, we wouldn't do it if we didn't think it was safe. It's just, she had a snake encounter at the hotel the other day," Leo explained.

"Oh, then all is well!" he exclaimed. "It is like lightning. You've been struck once, you never will be again."

"Huh." She wasn't buying it.

"He's right, you know. What are the odds?" Leo prodded.

Probably not as good as getting engaged to the tabloid-proclaimed sexiest man alive, yet she'd managed to do that, if only for a very unusual reason.

"Come on, are you really going to let a phobia about something that probably won't happen stop you from doing something you really want to do?" Leo asked.

When he put it like that, it did seem crazy.

"I'll go first if you want, clearing the way."

"My hero."

A grin lifted a corner of his mouth and one of those sweetly sexy dimples appeared. Leaning closer, so the guide wouldn't overhear, he whispered in her ear, "The faster we get back down to earth, the sooner we'll be back at the hotel with those pretty new scarves you bought at the bazaar."

Her heart sped up. The bus had made a couple of stops during the trip here, including one at an open-air market. She'd found a stall selling long, beautiful silk scarves and had bought a few of them, knowing when Leo's brow shot up that he knew why.

"All right, all right. I guess I'll do it."

"Are you sure?" Leo asked, searching her face carefully, all kidding aside. "If you really don't want to, I'll understand."

She gazed at the canopy—all that green—at the zip line extending as far as she could see toward that waterfall, which sounded absolutely beautiful, and nodded. "I'm not going to let a phobia deprive me of something I've wanted to do for a long time."

"Good girl."

Pressing a quick kiss on her mouth, he stepped to the edge of the platform. Within a moment, he was gone, flying like a bird, whooping as he went, his laughter floating back to her on the air.

"Ready *señorita?*" the guide asked.

"Ready as I'll ever be."

She stepped to the edge, took a deep breath and did what she'd been doing ever since she met Leo Santori.

She leaped feetfirst into adventure.

LATE IN THE DAY, after their jungle excursion—which Madison had loved in spite of herself—they boarded the tour bus for the trip back up to their resort. The bus was crowded with other tourists. They'd met some very nice people from various parts of the world. Now, though, after a day with them, she really just wanted some alone time with Leo.

She kept thinking about that beautiful waterfall, and how much she would have liked it if they'd had it all to themselves. Making love in the water, she had recently discovered thanks to her private pool, was one of her favorite things. She could only imagine how it would have felt to stand beneath those cascading sheets of cool liquid and lose herself in his strong arms.

She suspected every other couple there had had the same thought. Unfortunately, nobody'd had the nerve to say, "Hey, how about we take turns, you guys go explore the jungle and give us a half hour." It wasn't like college when they would know by the sock hanging on the doorknob that it wasn't safe to come back yet.

Tucked together on the bus, she and Leo kept their voices low, not talking a lot to the people around them, who were well on their way to being drunk. It was a long drive and the rum punch was complimentary. There was also a guy playing a guitar up front, tourists shouting out windows and being a little stupid. But here in the back, cocooned as they were in their own private little nook, she was able to forget any of them were even there.

"That was pretty spectacular today, wasn't it?" Leo said.

"Definitely."

"Glad you went for it?"

"I am. Thank you for doing it first and scaring the wits out of all the snakes so they got out of the way before I arrived."

"Just call me Saint Patrick."

She sipped her drink, which was heavy on the rum and light on everything else. Half of one was knocking her on her butt, and she couldn't imagine how the people closer to the front, who'd downed three or four, were feeling.

Or, actually, considering they'd had to pull over once for some guy to get sick, maybe she could.

"So, tell me about these Santori men raised by Santori women."

"Huh?"

"You said something about it the other day. About how men in your family learn to treat women right."

"Well, they do," he said with a shrug. "I've told you there aren't many breakups in the family."

"Except for Great-Uncle Rocco and Great-Aunt Gertrude," she said with a laugh, "who got tired of waiting for each other to die."

"Actually, their names are Vinnie and Sarah. But like I said, they're the exception, not the rule. My parents have been married thirty-five years, my dad's brothers even longer. Uncle Anthony and Aunt Rosa just celebrated their fiftieth. All six of their kids, who are happily married, celebrated by giving them a trip to the old country."

"Old country?"

"Italy." The dimple flashed. "I'm Italian, if you didn't notice."

She giggled. Big, brawny, dark-haired, dark-eyed, sexy as hell. Oh, yeah, she'd noticed.

"Are they all Italian? I mean, the wives and everyone?" she asked, hoping he wasn't hearing a question that was dancing around in her brain. That question being—*is one-eighth Italian, by virtue of having maybe an Italian great-grandparent somewhere in the family tree, good enough to get the welcome mat put out by the family?*

She wasn't exactly hinting that they might end up married, but she also wouldn't mind if this vacation fling turned into something more when they got back stateside. She was pretty much homeless right now, and not tied down anyplace, who was to say she couldn't check out the Windy City and decide to stay?

"Definitely not," he said. "Tony's and Nick's wives are—they're also sisters. But most of my other cousins didn't go looking for 'traditional' wives."

She thought, *Good.*

She said, "Interesting."

Although he'd mentioned it, they hadn't talked a lot about his broken engagement. He didn't seem to be dwelling on it, that was for sure, and she hoped it wasn't a sensitive subject. She wanted to know more.

"What did they think of the *former*-future Mrs. Leo Santori?"

It took him a second to process the question and figure out what she was asking. Once he had, he grinned. "My brothers hated her."

"That's not a good sign."

"I know, right? Rafe, my older brother…"

"Army Ranger?"

"Right. He only met her once and told me that she reminded him of a crocodile—big, bright teeth, always ready to bite."

She chuckled.

"And Mike…"

"Cop?"

"Right. He said anybody who took six years to get through college for a degree in decorating was an idiot."

She had to agree with that one.

"So what on earth were you doing with her?"

"I don't know, to be honest." Sounding sheepish, he admitted, "This'll seem stupid, but the truth is, I think she just kind of decided she wanted to get married, I was the one she was dating, and I didn't have much say in the matter."

"Oh, poor wittle you."

"Not saying I was blameless, believe me, I wasn't. I floated into it, having seen all my cousins getting married and pushing out the babies. My mother kept hinting that it was my responsibility to get married first since Rafe was in the military."

Oy. Old fashioned, indeed.

"Looking back, her cheating on me—and me finding out—was the best thing that could have happened. Otherwise, I have no doubt I'd be breaking the Santori family record by being the only one of my generation to get a divorce."

That made sense. Heaven knew, Madison had done her fair share of drifting into things because she had nothing better to do at the time. Look at her engagement to Tommy! Sure, she'd been helping her sister, and helping her friend. But hadn't one small part of her decided to do it because she was bored with her life, unhappy with her job, wanting a change?

"On the plus side, I think my near miss has cooled my mom's jets for a while. She's not going to be pushing any of us anytime soon. Right after the breakup, she called my brother Mike and said, 'Michelangelo, you bring home a girl who spends more money a month on makeup than on food and I'll smack you in the head.'"

Laughing, she said, "Your brother's name is really Michelangelo?"

He shrugged. "Yep."

"And Rafe?"

"Raphael," he admitted.

"Leo…short for Leonardo?"

"Uh-huh." He sighed heavily. "You can say it."

Bursting into laughter, she said, "Your parents named you after Teenage Mutant Ninja Turtles?"

"That's certainly what all my friends thought, growing up."

"They must also have thought you had the coolest parents in the world."

"Well, with that, and my uncle Anthony's famous pizzeria, I didn't lack for friends."

His self-deprecation was cute. The fact that he was a hell of a guy, nice, smart and funny, didn't seem to enter into the equation.

"Truth is, my grandparents emigrated and were very traditional, and my parents wanted to please them. So they went with really traditional names."

"Would there have been a Donatello?"

He shook his head. "Don't think so, though Donato was on the short list when they named Mike."

She twined her fingers with his. "So, Leonardo, huh? That makes you the lead turtle—smart, always has a plan and fights with two Japanese katana swords… cool!"

Lifting a brow in surprise, he said, "You do know your turtles."

"What can I say?" She wagged her brows up and down. "I was into dangerous males from a very young age."

"But not reptiles."

She thrust her bottom lip out. "Turtles aren't reptiles…are they?"

"Amphibians, I think."

"Whew!"

"For what it's worth, I bet those dangerous males were into you, too." His brown eyes gleamed with approval as he stared at her, and she saw his lids drop a little. She had no doubt he was thinking wicked, sultry things, and she wished this bus would hurry the hell up.

He lifted her hand and brought it to his mouth, brushing his lips across her knuckles. His tongue flicked out to taste her—just a tiny flash of moisture—and she quivered in her seat.

"Did I mention that Leonardo was always my favorite?"

He squeezed her hand once more as he lowered it. "Glad to know it. I'd hate to have to katana my brothers' asses if you decided you preferred a hotheaded fighter type like Rafe or a wise guy like Mike."

"Not a chance."

She preferred him. Just him. Over any other man she had ever known.

"We'll be there soon," he said, reading her mind.

As if realizing they both needed to focus on anything other than the cloud of sexual awareness building between them, he went back to what he'd been saying. "So, was your sister a Turtles fan, too? I thought girls preferred Powerpuff Girls."

She laughed out loud. "That's so funny, I was just thinking about those characters!"

"I suppose only people our age would have any idea what we were talking about."

"Nickelodeon generation."

"Exactly. Are there any other ways in which you and Candace were different?"

"She was always very sweet."

A slow, sexy smile. "You're sweet."

He didn't say it, but she knew that somewhere in his mind, he'd reworded that sentence and added the word *taste*.

"I meant well behaved. She was the good girl."

"Making you the bad one?"

"Let's just say I was the one who found all the squeaky floorboards in our house and knew how to avoid them when sneaking out. And was almost always the one who instigated a twin-swap whenever there was a test I wanted to get out of that I knew Candace could do better on."

"Lucky!" he said. "I look a lot like my brothers, but not close enough that either of them could ever bail my ass out when it came time for the next English exam."

Before she could reply, they noticed the bus was stopping. Madison glanced out the window, surprised to see they were still on the road. A long line of cars and trucks were lined up ahead of them.

"What's going on, man? What's the holdup?" one of the passengers asked.

One of the tour company reps, who'd been checking his phone for information, replied, "Angelina and Brad are in town at a charity event! Miles of traffic."

She assumed he meant Jolie and Pitt. Funny how superstars needed no last name, even when in a different country.

"So, you want to stop by and say hi to Brad and Angie?" Leo asked. "You run in their circles, right?"

She snickered. "Not exactly." She'd spied the couple from a distance once at a premiere Tommy had taken her to, but hadn't gotten anywhere close to them.

"But you will be someday."

"You don't know that," she said, wishing the whole topic of Hollywood hadn't come up. That brought back issues she'd been trying very hard to run from this week.

"You never have told me what your screenplay's about," he said. He leaned against the window of the bus in their double seat, turning slightly to face her. His hair was windblown, his face tanned and flushed, his eyes sparkling after their exciting day.

"You don't really want to hear about that," she said.

"Yeah, I really do."

Well, she might not want to discuss why she'd fled Hollywood, but she did like talking about her work. She was proud of her project, protective of every word she'd written, and found herself wanting to share some of that with him. "It's a dark thriller about sexual obsession and murder."

His eyes popped.

"Sorry you asked?"

"Uh, no." He grinned broadly. "As long as you're not here doing research on the murder part of the story."

"No. Just the sex part. Thanks, by the way. I'll be sure you get an acknowledgment in the credits."

"My mom'll be so proud."

"Oh, I'm sure all your friends will line up to see it."

"What will my title be? Maybe gripper. Or best boy." His dimple appeared as he loaded the movie tech terms with innuendo. "I've always wondered what that person did on a movie set."

"It's key grip, not gripper, and *you* don't grip, you caress."

His voice low, he said, "And? What else do *I* do?"

She dropped hers too. "You stroke."

"And?"

"And squeeze."

"And?"

"And pound, and thrust, and kiss, and lick, and hold and…"

He lifted his rum punch to his mouth and took a sip. "I shouldn't have started that."

"No, you probably shouldn't have."

He dropped an arm across her shoulders, tugging her closer so she rested against him. Gently squeezing her, he said, "We haven't talked about this, but…"

"Yes?"

"Well, to be honest, I don't know how I'm going to leave here without you on Monday."

Hearing a note in his voice that said he wasn't finished—and that he might have been thinking about something they could do to remedy the this-was-a-vacation-fling-and-we'll-never-see-each-other-again thing, she said, "I know." Then, thinking a little more, she blinked. "Wait, Monday? You mean, tomorrow?" The idea horrified her.

He appeared puzzled. "No, I mean Monday…four days from now. Today's Thursday."

"No, it's not."

"Uh, yeah, babe, it is."

Not totally believing it, she grabbed the backpack in which she'd carried her wallet and some other stuff from her purse. She found the small calendar that went with her checkbook and looked at it, counting back the days since she'd left California.

He was right. It was Thursday. Good lord, she'd been traveling so much in recent weeks—from L.A. to Napa to Florida to Central America—that she'd totally lost track of not only where she was, but *when* she was. How bizarre!

"See?"

She nodded slowly. "That's so weird, I completely messed up the days. I have no idea why I was so sure today was Sunday."

Of course, it could have been more than the travel and the jet-lag. There'd also been the matter of the stress, the tears, the long, sleepless nights, the races with the paparazzi. All of which had been the driving forces in her life until she'd come here and met *him*.

So yeah, it must have been all those confusing things that had led to the screwup in her internal clock.

But something was niggling at the back of her mind. Some small detail or memory that told her there was more to it. She just couldn't grab the thought, and it was irritating her. She swiped a hand through her hair, loosening the ponytail that had begun to give her a bit of a headache, and tried to focus, but nothing came to mind.

"So, now that you know what day it is, can you tell me how long you're staying?"

"I guess until Monday also. I booked for a week."

Or, well, Tommy's travel agent had booked her for a week. She thought.

It was late in the evening, which meant they had only three more full days. That didn't sound like very much time at all.

Part of her wanted to ask him if he could stay a little longer—if they gave up one of their rooms, perhaps they could put it toward extending their stay.

Another part wanted him to make the suggestion.

You can't hide here forever. You've got to go home and straighten your life out before you can take this thing much further.

"You're sure?" he asked her. "You might want to double-check your reservation."

He was teasing, but only just. And she realized he was right. "I know. At least, I *think* it was a week. This trip was planned on the fly and I've been pretty out of it, obviously."

"Remind me to never let you be in charge of the scheduling calendar."

Scheduling calendar.

That thought whizzed by again. Suddenly, she wrestled it into coherence and when it formed in her brain, she gasped.

"What?"

She didn't answer, bending over to grab her backpack again, worry overwhelming her. *No, you couldn't have been that stupid, right?*

"Madison, what is it?"

She kept digging, looking for a small, hard plastic case. Casting quick glances up at him, hating to admit what was going through her mind, she said, "I had a thought about why I might have had my days mixed up. If I'm right, the bus is going to have to pull over for *me* to throw up this time because I feel just sick about it!"

His worried expression told her he was concerned only for her, not for himself, not for any repercussions. He didn't get what she was worried about.

Hell. If her suspicions were correct, there could definitely be some repercussions for them both.

"What can I do?"

"Pray."

He gaped, obviously seeing how frightened she really was.

Finally, she found the object she'd been looking for and pulled it out of her backpack.

Her birth control pills.

"Are those…"

"Yeah."

She gulped, flipped the lid with her thumb and studied the dial of pills. She was very careful, every month, to set the starting day correctly, because she'd had problems with the pill in the beginning. And there had been that one pregnancy scare in her high school years that she had never wanted to repeat.

According to this package, those pills, and the little days of the week imprinted above them, tomorrow she should be taking Monday's pill. That was why she'd thought today was Sunday.

Only, today was Thursday.

For a second, she prayed she'd taken them ahead of time, too many instead of too few. Crazy hopes blossomed within her and she sought frantically for an explanation. *You took extra protection for all the extra sex, right?*

But she knew she hadn't done that, not consciously, anyway.

Leo had obviously been studying the case, too. His brow was furrowed, his expression serious. "What's the verdict? Are there too few or too many?" he asked, jumping to the same conclusion.

She thought about it. Last week she'd been in Florida, the week before in Napa. She'd started this package of pills while she was still in L.A.

The days rolled out in her mind, and by the time she'd finished calculating them, she realized she was in trouble.

"There are too many pills left," she whispered. "Three more should be missing. So I have apparently missed three doses at some point over the past few weeks."

He was silent. She was silent.

Dropping the plastic case into her backpack, she

threw herself back in the seat and closed her eyes, her mind swimming with confusion.

Three pills. Three little pills. That couldn't be a catastrophe, could it? She'd been on the pill for ten years. After all that faithful service, surely one minor mistake like this wouldn't result in…couldn't mean she was…

"So you could be pregnant."

He'd put it right out there, voicing the words she'd been unable to even think. She flinched, slowly lowering her glass of rum punch and putting it into the drink holder in her armrest. She told herself it was instinct— that she felt queasy. But she couldn't deny that something, some tiny spark of oh-my-God-what-if-it's-true, had thought *this isn't good for the baby*.

"No. Of course not," she insisted. "It's crazy."

He wasn't in a panic and he wasn't angry. Not happy, certainly, but not reacting the way she'd expect most twentysomething single men to react to the news that they might have knocked up a woman they'd met a few days ago.

"It's possible, though."

She gulped and slowly nodded. "I'm so sorry, Leo. It's been… I'm *never* so careless. I've just had an awful few weeks, my mind's been spinning. I screwed up. I totally screwed up."

She finally worked up the nerve to open her eyes again, knowing there were tears in them. Blinking rapidly to hold them back, she looked at him, dreading his reaction. Maybe his was a calm before the storm.

But oh, that warmth, that understanding in his expression. If she'd been standing, she would have lost her legs and fallen to the ground, so overwhelmed was she by the tenderness in his handsome face.

"Shh, it's okay," he insisted. "Stop beating yourself up about it. I'm sure it won't happen. The odds are crazy."

"Right."

"Worse odds than encountering two snakes in Costa Rica."

She forced a chuckle that came out a little like a sob. "Yeah. Of course they are."

He lifted her across the seat onto his lap, wrapping his arms around her and pulling her head onto his shoulder. His hand gently stroking her hair, he said, "It's okay, Madison. It'll be fine."

"I can't believe you're not freaking out."

"Over a mistake that anybody could make that *might* lead to a bigger problem? Why would I freak out over that?"

Amazing. She didn't know any other guy who wouldn't have already started losing it, or stated his stance on abortion, or accused her of dumping pills into the toilet to trap him, or at least calling her careless.

This man was unique and so wonderful. Aside from that, he also calmed her, steadied her. She'd always been told she was too volatile, that she had a temper, that she could be thoughtless at times.

Leo was everything she wasn't. He was like a port in a storm, soothing and so damned strong. She wondered if there was any crisis he couldn't weather, and acknowledged that, God forbid this slipup of hers resulted in pregnancy, she couldn't imagine anyone better to go through it with.

"If there's something to worry about, let's deal with it when it happens," he said, brushing a kiss across her temple. "In the meantime, let's just make sure we stop in my room when we get back to the hotel so I can grab some condoms."

She tried for a real smile. "That's a deal." She promptly ruined that with a big, sad-sounding sniffle.

"And maybe a blue necktie. I can tie holes in it and tie it around my face, and maybe get some fake katanas and *really* be your hero."

The smile was a little more genuine this time. "You already are."

They were silent for another moment.

Finally, he said, "It's really okay. It'll be fine, Madison. Let's not worry about it until next month."

Next month. They hadn't even exchanged phone numbers, yet Leo was assuming they would still be… something. She really believed he thought they were going to have some kind of future after this Monday.

Oh, she hoped so. She most certainly hoped so. Because, no matter what day of the week it was, or how many weeks it had been, she was falling for Leo Santori. Falling head over heels, out-of-her-mind, crazy-in-love with him.

She might have come here to escape and to hide.

Now, she suspected she'd been found…and didn't want to be lost ever again.

10

THEIR THREE DAYS left together flew by way too fast for Leo's liking.

Once Madison had stopped beating herself up about what might happen due to her mix-up with her pills, she'd let him coax her back into a good mood. He'd done it with lots of laughter, long walks on the beach, midnight swims in their private pool, surfing lessons, a wind-sailing expedition, dancing at the club of a big touristy resort nearby. And lots and lots of sex.

Damn, he didn't think he would ever have another week like this in his entire life. And he knew he'd never had one before.

They didn't talk about the birth control pill issue, instead using condoms as a matter of course. He wasn't thrilled about it—having been inside her warm, wet body, skin to skin, he really disliked there being any kind of barrier between them. But there was no sense in taking risks.

Although, to be honest, part of him wasn't sure he minded so much.

Yeah, it was crazy to be thinking about having a kid with a woman he'd met a week ago.

But yeah, he was thinking about it.

Whatever he'd thought about his life, his future, his relationships or his prospects before coming here to Costa Rica didn't matter a damn. Because, since he'd met her—since he'd begun to fall in love with her—he was seeing whole new worlds of possibility. Worlds that included him and Madison, committed, together, bringing more little Santoris into the world. No, he wouldn't have chosen to do it so soon, but he wasn't going to deny that, if it happened, he wouldn't be absolutely devastated.

He just wanted to make sure that Madison wanted him as much as he wanted her…and that, whatever happened between them, *didn't* happen only because of a possible pregnancy. That was why he hadn't pushed her for any confirmations on where things would go after they both left this wonderful place. But now it was Sunday night. And in the morning, they were both going to leave this wonderful place.

It was their last night in paradise, but rather than going out somewhere, they'd decided to have a room service dinner. The hotel might be small, but the chef was outstanding, and, once again, they were served an amazing meal.

They shared it outside on her patio at a small table draped with a snowy-white cloth and lit by a few tapered candles. Again, the staff had gone overboard. He had no doubt word had spread that his bed wasn't being slept in—while hers usually looked like a troupe of monkeys had been doing acrobatics on it all night long.

"What are you thinking about?" she asked.

"Monkeys."

She tilted her head, visibly curious, but he only laughed.

"What about you? What are you thinking about?"

"I'm thinking I want one more naked swim in that pool."

He shifted in his seat.

"And wondering how long we'll have to wait until room service comes to take all this stuff away."

He dropped his napkin onto his plate, reached for his water and finished it, as well. Although they had never even discussed it, neither of them admitting any reason for it, he'd noticed that neither he nor Madison had been drinking any alcohol during the past couple of days. It was as if she were already protective of the life that might be growing inside her. And he... Well, he wasn't sure whether it was solidarity or a desire not to jinx anything, but he was laying off, too.

"There's a Do Not Disturb sign on the door. The waiter offered to put it there and said we can just call when we want them to come back," he said with a suggestive wink.

"Do we need to wait a half an hour after eating before we can swim?" she asked.

"I don't think so, considering the water's not even over our heads."

"Perfect," she said, already rising to her feet and pushing at the straps of her sundress. They fell, revealing those soft shoulders, and then the whole dress dropped with a whoosh.

She hadn't been wearing anything underneath.

He swallowed hard, staring at her, awed, as always, by that perfect body, so curvy and feminine. She was lightly tanned all over, no lines to mark the infrequent presence of her skimpy bathing suits.

"Come and get me wet," she said, throwing him a sassy look.

He played along. "The pool's not too cold this time?"

"Not talking about the pool," she promised.

"Good."

He pushed back from the table and stripped off his clothes, grabbing a condom from his pocket before letting his shorts hit the patio. Madison watched him, her eyes zoning in on all the places on his body that she seemed to like a lot.

He was already as hard as a rock.

"Okay, never mind, I don't think I need your help. I'm already there," she exclaimed with a visible quiver of excitement. She clenched her thighs tight, as if to catch the moisture building between them, and his mouth went wet with hunger.

"I think I should check and make sure."

He walked to her, dropping the condom on the pavement right beside the pool, knowing there would be a lot to do before he would want to put it on. He slid his hands around her waist, stroking her hips, pulling her to him. She tilted her face up and their mouths met in a warm, lazy kiss. Their tongues twisted and mated, each stroke languorous and hungry, each breath shared, their heartbeats falling into the same rhythm.

When they finally broke apart, she whispered, "Thought you were going to check it out."

He nodded. Hiding a grin of mischief, he wrapped his arms more tightly around her and jumped into the pool, bringing her with him.

She came up sputtering, splashing his face with water and swimming away. "That was a dirty trick."

"What? Now I'm positive you're nice and wet."

"Maybe not everywhere."

"Everywhere," he said, totally confident.

"Wouldn't you like to know."

He stepped toward her, enjoying the coolness of the water against his naked skin. "Yeah. I would like to know."

She stopped moving away, her teasing words dying on her lips, as if she knew, as he did, that their time together was too short to delay. They wanted—needed—each other, tonight more than ever, and all the playfulness evaporated. There was just intense heat, and, he suspected, a hint of desperation. They both knew they had to leave in mere hours.

Madison watched Leo approach, and saw the same note of, not sadness, but maybe wistfulness on his face that she sensed was on hers. Saying goodbye to this man would be next to impossible, and frankly, she didn't want to think about it. Not when she still had him for a little while longer.

They came together, their bodies meeting beneath the surface. She loved this sensation, had loved it from the first time they'd swum naked together. Water caressed her, cooled her, even as his slick skin warmed and aroused her. There was no weight, no gravity to combat, and they could float and thrust and twist and love to their hearts' content, wrapped in their own wet world.

"I'm going to miss this," she admitted.

"Me, too."

"Not many opportunities for skinny-dipping in Chicago?"

He didn't smile. "Nobody I'd want to do it with if there were."

Madison sighed a little, loving that admission.

"This has been the best week of my life, Leo," she said, reaching up and wrapping her arms around his neck.

He encircled her waist and held her tightly against him. Bending to kiss her, he replied, "Mine, too."

The kiss was sweeter, soft and tender, and in it Madison read a lot of emotions neither of them had expressed. Although she wanted to express them now, to let him know she longed for so much more than this, she knew she couldn't. There was too much to deal with, too much to fix in her life, before she asked him to be a more permanent part of it.

Not that she was about to let him go completely. God, no. She just wanted to be able to come to him with a clean slate. She longed to admit to him exactly what she'd been running from and why. Until that time, telling him she cared about him—hell, that she *loved* him—seemed unfair.

After the kiss, he said, "Are you cold?"

"No."

He lifted her higher as he dropped lower in the water so he was eye level with her breasts. "You look cold."

She laughed softly. "*So* not cold."

"Maybe I should warm you up, just in case."

"You do that."

He did, lapping up some of the water off the curve of one breast, kissing his way toward its tip. He breathed a stream of warm air over the puckered nipple, and then covered it with his mouth and suckled her.

She threw her head back, groaning with pleasure. Lifting her legs, she wrapped them around him and floated there, rubbing herself against his heat, indulging in all the sensations battering her body. His mouth on her breast, his hand on her hip, another twined in her hair, his big, thick cock between her legs, brushing against her core.

There was nothing better than this on earth. Nothing.

He moved to her other breast, pleasuring her just as thoroughly, and then began to draw her back toward the steps at the end of the pool. She saw the condom lying on the pool deck where he'd dropped it but wasn't ready to lose all that hot male skin just yet.

When they got to the steps and he reached for the packet, she said, "Wait."

He eyed her quizzically.

Giving him her sultriest look and licking her lips, she said, "Sit on the top step."

One brow rose. He did as she asked.

Kneeling below him, most of her body still in the

water, she kissed her way up his powerful leg. The wiry black hairs teased her lips as she nibbled and tasted her way ever higher.

He dropped a hand onto her shoulder and tangled the other in her wet hair, obviously knowing where she was headed. When her cheek brushed the side of his erection, he jerked a little. And when she ran the tip of her tongue all the way from its base to its tip, he groaned out loud.

"Madison…"

"I love how you taste," she admitted, licking the moisture that seeped from the tip of his cock.

"Jesus," he groaned.

He liked it, she knew that much. She'd loved doing this to him at various times this week, but they'd never done it in the pool. And the position was so easy and so perfect, the steps lining up exactly the way she needed them to be.

Opening her mouth as wide as she could, she sucked the thick head of his cock.

His guttural groan told her he liked what she was doing, as did the gentle squeeze of his hand on her shoulder. She slid her mouth down, taking more of him, filling her mouth with him, licking the salt and the chlorine and the *male* right off him.

When she could go no farther, she began to pull away, sliding up, knowing her pace was both a torment and a delight. Another flick of her tongue as she lapped up more of his body's delicious juices, and she went down again. Up and down, slow, then faster, soft, then harder, until her jaw hurt and Leo was thrusting a little with every stroke.

"Enough," he said with a gasp. "Get up here."

She wanted to finish, wanted to swallow him down, but she was also dying to have him inside her. So with one last powerful suck, she released him and kissed her way up his stomach, tracing his abs, licking his nipples, biting his neck.

"You definitely should hold the world record for *that,*" he said before sinking both hands in her hair and dragging her mouth to his.

He kissed her deeply, thanking her with every thrust of his tongue, releasing her only so he could grab the condom. Tearing it open, he sheathed himself and then pulled her onto his lap. She straddled him, her knees beside his hips on the step.

Another kiss, deep and hungry, but also incredibly tender, and he began to ease his way into her. She took him, every inch of him, every breath of him, every ounce of him, grabbing and holding and loving and savoring. Wanting all of him. Wanting this memory to imprint itself on her very soul so she would always be able to return to it and relive such glory.

When they were fully joined, as close as they could be, she looked into his eyes—those beautiful brown eyes—and said all the things she couldn't yet say aloud.

She'd swear he said them back.

REALITY RETURNED WITH a vengeance the next morning. As if to punctuate the regret both of them were feeling, Leo awoke to the sound of rain. It was the first time they'd seen anything but a blue sky, and the weather suited his mood.

They were both ass-dragging, having stayed up way too late last night indulging in a long, lethargic lovefest that had left him weak but utterly satisfied. Because of that, they'd overslept a little.

Not wanting to suffer the long drive all the way back to the airport in San José, Madison had been able to get a ticket on a puddle jumper that would take her from Liberia, the same airport from which he was flying, to the capital. That meant they had a little more time together. During that time, he intended to ask her when they were going to see each other again.

He'd prefer tonight in Chicago. But it seemed pushy to ask. So he would have to settle for the weekend.

She'd admitted she wasn't working on anything right now except her screenplay, and he knew she was between permanent homes, though he'd never found out exactly why. She'd said she was heading back to her parents' place in Florida while she regrouped.

Chicago was a very good place for regrouping, if he did say so himself. Plus, flights between there and Florida were pretty cheap. Hell, if she couldn't come to him, he'd go to her.

When they reached the airport and checked in, they hesitated before going through security. Their gates were far apart and they had some time before their flights would start boarding, though his was earlier than hers.

Sitting together in a bar in the main terminal, each of them drinking a Virgin Mary, he said, "So. Madison."

A tiny smile tugged at the corners of her mouth. "So. Leo."

Their eyes met. He knew she knew what he was about to say.

"Facebook?" she asked.

He barked a laugh. "I'm not on it."

"You're joking!"

"Sorry, I prefer regular media to the social kind. I like actually knowing people I call friends."

She nodded in commiseration. "I guess I understand that. And I was just kidding since I don't have a profile anymore, either."

"Really?"

"I got rid of it once I started getting too much attention."

"Because of your screenplay?"

She nibbled her bottom lip and hesitated, staring at him searchingly. It looked as if she wanted to say more, and he wondered if she was finally going to reveal just what she was running from.

The fact that she was running, and that she'd gotten rid of her Facebook profile because of too much attention, suddenly made a sharp fear stab into him. *Had she been stalked? Was she on the run from an abusive ex?*

His hands fisted on the table, but he covered by reaching for his drink.

"Something like that," she finally whispered.

He knew it wasn't the whole story. But he also knew she wasn't ready to tell him the whole story.

"Just tell me one thing. Are you in any kind of danger?"

Her jaw fell open. "Oh, God, no, of course not."

"Okay then."

"It's…it's complicated," she admitted.

"I hear ya. It's all right. I can wait, though not forever."

"You won't have to, I promise."

Good. Her secret would give them plenty to talk about when they saw each other back home. Tonight or next weekend or next month. Hopefully no longer than that.

"So I guess we'll have to do this the old-fashioned way," he said, trying to lighten the mood. "You're hot. Can I have your phone number?"

Her green eyes twinkled and she replied, "Well, I don't usually give my number out to strange guys…"

"Hey, I'm not strange. Just Italian."

A broad smile. Thank God. "Okay, I *guess* it's okay if you call me." She reached into her carry-on and pulled out her cell phone. "Tell me yours so I can punch them into my address book."

He rattled off his numbers—home, cell and the station, and threw in his uncle's restaurant just to be on the safe side. She was laughing and complaining about sore fingers by the time she'd finished entering. After she was done, she raised an inquiring brow.

"I hate to admit it, but we're gonna have to do this the *really* old-fashioned way. I didn't get an international SIM card, and knew my phone wouldn't work here so I never even took it out of my suitcase."

"Which you already checked."

"Right."

"I'll text them to you."

"No way. I don't trust technology when it comes to something this important. Write them down."

"Okay, but I don't want to hear any excuses about you losing my number," she said. "Remember, I have yours and I can stalk you and be all vengeful if you give me the brush-off."

He reached across the table and took her hand. "Not gonna happen, Madison Reid. That is *never* gonna happen."

Their gazes met and held and he knew that, once again, they were saying a *lot* more things that didn't really need to be verbalized. In utter silence, they were thanking each other for the amazing week they'd shared, and promising each other it would be continued. They were admitting there were feelings and promising they would be explored. All without a word being spoken. Just like when they'd made love in the pool the night before.

Without ever even opening his mouth, he'd told her he loved her. He even suspected she'd heard it. And that she felt the same way.

Someday soon they'd say it out loud.

"Here you go," she said, pushing a small sheet of paper across to him. It contained a number marked "cell," and another marked "parents in Florida."

He carefully folded the paper and tucked it into his wallet, right next to his license and certification cards. No way would he lose it. Hell, he'd probably be digging it out to call her within an hour of landing at O'Hare.

They finished their drinks, not saying much, both

stealing glances at the clock. Until, finally, knowing he couldn't delay any longer, Leo got up and held out a hand to her. She rose, too, sliding up against his body. He felt her, even though an inch of air separated them, vibrating with life and passion. He felt her magnetism even when they weren't touching.

"Soon," he demanded, a wave of want washing over him, the way it always did when she was near.

She nodded. "Soon."

Before he could say more, they were startled by raised voices. A large crowd of people had gathered at this end of the terminal. They stood right outside the bar, which was open-air, separated from the main section of the airport by only a half wall. That might explain why it was so damned loud.

He hadn't been paying attention, but now all those people—most carrying cameras—came to life and began shouting questions and snapping pictures. "What the hell?"

"Angelina and Brad are flying out this morning!" someone at the next table whispered, peering around and out into the main terminal.

He rolled his eyes, not interested in the celebrity stuff and only hoping the rolling out of the red carpet didn't delay his flight.

Hell, what was he thinking? This could go ahead and delay it indefinitely, as long as Madison's was delayed, too. Of course, with their luck, they'd each be on their respective planes when the delay happened.

"Think they're following us?" he asked her, laughter on his lips.

It died when he saw her expression. Her eyes were wide and glassy, her mouth rounded in shock. She was staring at the crowd gathering a couple of yards away and he could actually hear her harsh exhalations as she struggled for breath.

"Mad, what is it? What's wrong?"

"Oh, my God," she whispered. She spun around, burying her face in his neck, hugging him tightly and mumbling, "We should go."

"You going to walk backward?" he asked, placing a gentle hand on the small of her back.

She looked up at him and now he didn't just see shock, he saw something that resembled panic. "I mean, you should go. They'll be boarding your flight any minute," she said, suddenly jerking away from him and giving him a push. "I have a little more time."

He couldn't understand her sudden change in mood, but she was right. They would be calling for his flight soon and he still had to get through security.

"If I didn't know any better, I'd say you were trying to get rid of me."

"I shouldn't have come here with you," she said, casting quick glances over her shoulder. "I should have taken a cab to the other airport." She looked at him, her eyes wide and wet. "I never dreamed they'd find… Oh, Leo, please forgive me. I was being selfish, I just wasn't ready to say goodbye. Now I've exposed you to…"

"Madison, whatever it is, it's okay," he told her. Dropping his hands to her hips, he pulled her close, so their bodies touched from thigh to chest, and dropped his mouth onto hers. He kissed her deeply but gently, saying goodbye and reminding her of all the things they'd be missing until they saw each other again.

He usually didn't make out in public, but kissing Madison always made him a little crazy. He deepened things, liking how she clung to him, kissing him back, wildly, hungrily.

They didn't break apart until they heard someone calling her name.

"Madison!"

Then another voice.

"Over here, Miss Reid!"

And another.

"Is he the guy, Madison? Is this where you've been all this time?"

"Any chance you and Shane will reconcile?"

"What's going to happen to the house you two were sharing in California?"

Looking down at her and seeing the utter misery in her face as she grabbed a sun hat and glasses and pulled them on, he could only stare.

"What's your name, buddy? Where are you from?"

"Are you the one she cheated with?"

"Come on, Madison, lay another kiss on him! The world wants to know who you prefer to Tommy Shane!"

Tommy Shane? The movie star?

His heart stopped and his stomach flipped. The room suddenly seemed to spin and it had nothing to do with the heat. He found it hard to think, hard to see, hard to process much of anything except those voices and those snapping cameras.

And the guilt on her face.

"Madison...?"

"I'm sorry. I'm so sorry you got dragged into this, Leo," she whispered, tears falling from her eyes. "I didn't want this to happen to you, I'd never wish it on my own worst enemy, much less..."

Those awful, intrusive voices continued, digging into his brain like sharp, spiky instruments. "Madison, how did you two meet? When did the affair start? How'd Tommy find out?"

Affair. Tommy.

God.

The pieces started to come together in his mind. Tommy Shane—everyone on the planet knew his name. And while he didn't pay attention to Hollywood gossip or junk like that, he now remembered having heard something about a breakup. He'd been visiting his cousin Lottie. She'd just had her second child and he'd glanced through some gossip rags someone else had brought her to look at while nursing.

She'd gone on an indignant rant about poor sweet sexy Tommy Shane, wondering how any woman could cheat on him. A woman who'd been *engaged* to him.

This woman. The woman he suddenly wasn't even sure he knew.

She'd been engaged to one of the most famous men in America. *She cheated.* She'd been hounded by paparazzi. *She cheated.* She'd fled to Costa Rica. *She cheated.* And put another notch on her bedpost?

She cheated.

Every instinct he had rebelled against the idea, but he could think of no other explanation. She wasn't screaming at these people that they were liars. She looked utterly ashamed. Guilty as sin.

His sweet and sexy Madison had betrayed the man she'd promised to marry and had used Leo to lick her wounds while the scandal died down. It was the only thing that made sense.

What he couldn't figure out, though, was what had happened to her lover. Considering she'd lost Shane over the man, he had to be pretty damned important. Which made Leo wonder what the hell she'd been doing slumming around with *him* for the past seven days. She'd cheated on a man who women threw themselves in front of.

So why had she just spent a week here with him, a regular guy?

"Leo, please, let me explain," she insisted, raising her voice to be heard over the paparazzi.

"How about starting with the basics. Were you engaged to Tommy Shane, the movie star?"

She nodded slowly.

He thought he'd been prepared for the answer, but considering he thought he was going to puke, he guessed he hadn't been.

"You lived with him. That's why you're between addresses now."

"Yes."

It got better and better.

"And you came here to get away from all the bad publicity you were getting because of your breakup."

"Yes, but you don't understand," she said.

His whole body rigid, he stepped away from her.

"Speak up, I'm sure everyone would love to hear the story."

She closed her eyes, shaking her head in sorrow and regret.

He wanted to shake her, wanted to yell at her for lying to him.

Only she hadn't, not really, except by omission. She'd never said anything about a broken engagement or an affair. She'd kept her secrets well. He'd just been stupid enough not to see the truth.

Again.

Christ, what was it with him picking women who couldn't be faithful? Was it some character flaw he had?

Part of him screamed at the very idea of putting Madison in the same category as his ex. But in the end, they weren't much different, were they? In fact, Madison's affair had been a whole lot more public.

"I've gotta go," he said, trying to be heard as the photographers and reporters who'd struck out getting the good stuff on Brad and Angelina pressed inside the bar and swarmed them like flies on meat.

"Yes, you should, get out of here before this gets worse."

"It can get worse?"

"You have no idea," she said, her tone bleak.

He was angry. Furious, in fact. He wanted to walk out and leave her here to deal with her own mess.

But he just couldn't do it. He couldn't walk away and leave her in the middle of this feeding frenzy to be chewed up by these animals, even if a part of him thought she probably deserved it.

"Come on," he ordered, grabbing both their carry-ons. He dropped a possessive arm over her shoulders and pulled her along with him, elbowing people out of the way with every step.

The barrage continued.

"Just tell us your name!"

"Do you have anything you want to say to Tommy? Do you feel bad about stealing his woman?"

"Are you two living together somewhere?"

He ignored them. So did she. Together, fighting for every step, they pushed through the crowd. Leo threw a few elbows at those who wouldn't move voluntarily. Finally, they reached the security area, through which nobody without a boarding pass could come. He waved theirs and jerked a thumb toward their pursuers. "I don't think they're passengers, and they're harassing us."

The guards immediately stepped in, ushering them into a secured line, leaving the crowd behind. Still the shouts continued, and Leo could practically feel the cameras taking pictures of the back of his head.

That finally struck him. It wasn't just the shock and betrayal of her not being who he thought she'd been. He'd now been dragged into this. His picture was going to be plastered on their tabloids, his name, his home, his job, his family…everything was going to be thrown out there for public consumption if they found out who he was.

Fuck.

"Thank you," she said as they finally turned a corner and got out of sight of the crowd.

He immediately dropped his arm and stepped away from her.

"If you can, please keep my name out of it, would you?" he bit out from a granite-hard jaw. "I don't imagine it would go over very well with my lieutenant or with my family."

"I'm so sorry," she whispered, watching him, tears falling freely down her face. "I never imagined that would happen, not in my worst nightmares."

He'd heard enough. He just couldn't listen to any more. So when they reached the end of the first line and he saw that there were several checkpoints, each with its own separate queue, he watched her go into the closest one…and headed for one as far away from hers as he could get.

He told himself it was because it was shorter and his flight would board soon.

He knew the truth, though. He needed to think and to breathe. Needed to absorb everything that had happened in the past ten minutes and figure out what it meant and what he was going to do about it.

He needed to get away from her.

"Leo," she said as he turned his back and began to walk away.

He didn't turn around, not trusting himself to look at her face. Instead, he called, "I can't, Madison. Not now. I just can't."

And he didn't. He didn't look back. He didn't wait for her. He didn't try to find her at her gate.

He simply got on his plane and went home.

11

MADISON MADE THE trip home like a zombie, barely cognizant of her surroundings. She'd been able to focus only on the look on Leo's face when he realized he'd been thrown into the deep end of the ocean by a woman he'd thought he could trust.

Her father picked her up at the airport in Florida. As soon as he saw her by the baggage claim, he pulled her into his arms, hugging her tightly. "I'm so sorry, baby girl. So sorry, honey."

She clung to him, feeling tears well up further.

"It didn't help, huh?"

Had her trip helped? Well, the majority of her week hadn't just helped, it had been downright magical. But the ending had been like something out of her worst nightmare.

"I'm okay, just tired," she said, knowing he would see right through it. Her emotions were spinning wildly, and if anybody would recognize that, it was her wise, attentive father.

"Listen, why don't I get your bag? You duck behind

the escalators, I'll grab the suitcase and go get the car. Once I've pulled up to the front, you can dash right out."

Distressed that he had to go to these lengths, especially considering his recent heart attack, she said, "I shouldn't have come here. I should have just gone back to California."

"Forgedaboutit," he said. "Come on now, get on over there. I've always wanted to play James Bond."

"Did you bring weapons?" she asked, heavy on the sarcasm.

"No, but I brought a new secret-agent-mobile that none of those cockroaches will recognize."

She gaped. "You got a new car?"

"I wanted to be less noticeable when you came back. Traded in the old jalopy." His smile said that hadn't been a hardship.

"You got the SUV you've been bugging Mom about."

"Yup." He hugged her again. "Thanks for the crisis, honey."

Knowing he was trying to cheer her up, she forced a laugh.

"Oh, and if it's okay with you, we're going to head over to the condo instead of the house."

Her parents lived inland, but had bought a place on the beach as an investment years ago. She supposed it was possible they'd planned a beach trip, but she doubted it.

"The reporters drove you out of your house?"

"Are you kidding? You know your mother. She's gotta have those ocean breezes. Can't keep her away."

Probably an exaggeration, but she didn't call him on

it. Her parents were doing what parents did, taking care of their kid in her moment of need. Even if the kid had screwed up royally by getting in a situation she hadn't been prepared for and making a decision she'd pay for until the end of her days.

She wasn't just the woman who would go down in infamy as the cheater who'd broken Tommy Shane's heart. She'd also lost the one man who'd ever made her feel as though she was capable of loving someone with every fiber in her being.

"I'm glad you're here," her dad said. "You can pay me back for the ride by making me one of your chocolate cakes…your mother tries to sneak zucchini and wheat germ into hers."

"Ick," she said with a soft laugh, then murmured, "Thanks, Dad."

Their plan worked. He picked her up outside and she didn't hear anyone demanding answers that were nobody's business. They arrived at the condo, which was gated, making it difficult for them to be harassed if anyone tracked her down.

Nobody did. And for the next several days, Madison began to heal.

There was never a sign of a photographer, and while she saw the photos of herself and Leo on the cover of a tabloid at the grocery store, she didn't see his name. She prayed they hadn't discovered who he was, and so far it appeared their luck was holding.

She couldn't imagine how he was explaining it to his colleagues, or anyone in his family, but hoped they were trustworthy enough not to sell him out to the *Tattler*.

Her mother had seen the pictures, too. They'd been standing in line at Publix, and her mother's gasp had cued her in. But being just as supportive and protective as Madison's dad, she didn't say a word. She instead reached up and *accidentally* spilled her cup of iced coffee on the cover of the tabloid.

She hadn't even asked Madison to explain who it was she'd been kissing in Costa Rica, as if realizing the hurt she was feeling might have more to do with that than with what had happened out in L.A. Not for the first time, Madison acknowledged she had the best parents in the world.

She was loved. She knew that. She'd never doubted it. And out of the spotlight, at the small beach town, she began to find peace, to think about her future and figure out what to do.

Calling Leo had been on her mind a lot. A whole lot.

She couldn't begin to count the number of times she had picked up her phone, looked at his numbers in the address book and thought about dialing.

Would he answer? Would he listen? Would he hang up on her?

Did it matter?

Because, even if he would listen, how could she explain? She couldn't tell him the truth without revealing the nature of her engagement to Tommy. Couldn't drag Tommy out of the closet to someone he didn't know when he'd tried so hard to stay in there for the rest of the world. She had seen her sister go through the exact same dilemma when Candace had fallen in love. She'd just never thought it would happen to her, too. Who could ever have imagined a Leo coming into her life?

Besides, he obviously didn't want to talk to her. She kept her phone nearby but he never called. She checked for messages even though it didn't ring. But nothing. He hadn't tried to reach her.

She didn't blame him. He was too decent a guy to be dragged into her garbage. She should never have let herself forget that.

Sitting on the balcony of the condo, watching the waves churn one evening after she and her parents had shared dinner, she began to drift off to sleep, lulled by the ocean and the call of the seabirds. In that lazy place between asleep and awake, she replayed all the lovely moments the two of them had shared.

Their first meeting. The room mix-up. The lovemaking on the beach. The stupid snake in the pool. The zip-lining tour. The long bus ride back when they'd talked about a lot of nothing.

A lot of...*nothing.*

Her eyes flew open. "Oh, my God," she muttered.

"What, honey?" asked her mother, who'd been sitting nearby doing a Sudoku puzzle.

"What's today?" she snapped.

"Thursday, why?"

Thursday. Of course it would be Thursday. Wasn't it always freaking Thursday? "Do you know the date?"

Her mother told her, and Madison started calculating.

She'd been in Florida for seventeen days. She could hardly believe it. Apparently, she'd been so numb, she hadn't noticed the passage of time. Each lazy day had rolled into the next, none bringing a solution to her problems or offering a glimpse of happiness with the man she missed so terribly.

Seventeen days.

That day on the bus with Leo, she had figured out when she'd started her last pack of pills. The date was emblazoned in her mind and it wasn't hard to count backward to see just how long it had been: six weeks ago.

She was late. Two weeks late.

Calm down. It might not be that. Could be stress, anything.

But Madison was never late—she hadn't been in years. Besides, something deep inside her already knew the truth.

She was pregnant.

Pregnant by a man who obviously never wanted to see or hear from her again for the rest of his life.

"What's the matter, Madison?" her mom repeated.

She couldn't tell her folks—not because they were old-fashioned or wouldn't be supportive, but because she just couldn't drag them into even more of her drama. None of this was their fault; how could she add to the worry that was already making her mother so sad? Put more stress on her father's recovering heart?

"Sorry, Mom, I just remembered some stuff I need to take care of." The next words left her lips without her giving them much thought. "In California."

Her mother didn't look surprised, as if she had already come to that conclusion herself and had just been waiting for Madison to figure it out. "All right, honey."

Yes, it was time to go back to California and deal with this once and for all. With a baby to consider—and she truly believed there was one—she could no longer be the story-of-the-week for the cheap news mags. She would be in no position to run around evading the paparazzi.

Besides, she was a fighter, not a quitter. She was good-and-damned tired of having her life ruled by strangers dying to find out sordid details that were not their concern.

She had to see Tommy—and Candace, who she needed now so much her heart ached—and figure out what to do. It was time to reclaim her life. Maybe by doing so, she could go to Leo and tell him the truth.

She hoped he would not only listen…but that he could deal with the fact that he was going to be a father.

"HEY, BRO, HOW'S it going?"

Leo heard his brother Mike's voice, but didn't slide out from under his truck. He continued with his oil change, wishing his brother would go away but knowing he wouldn't.

"You gonna come out or are you hiding?"

"Bite me," he muttered.

"I did when we were four and six. You gave me a fat lip."

"And mom spanked me," Leo said, smiling reluctantly.

"So are you coming out?"

"If you're here to pump me for information, forget about it. I don't want to discuss it."

"Can't a guy just stop by on his lunch hour to say hello to his brother?" Mike squatted down beside the truck, peering at him. "Seriously, I'm not here to bust your balls. I was in the neighborhood and just wanted to see how you're doing."

He sighed heavily. "Give me a minute." At least Mike hadn't come over here to rag on him about the pictures in the tabloids like the guys at the station did.

It had been a crazy couple of weeks.

He'd been *in a mood,* as his mother would describe it, since the minute he'd left Madison at that airport in Costa Rica. The flight stateside had been miserable. He'd vacillated between anger, regret and humiliation the entire way.

Things hadn't improved much once he got home. His family and friends had noticed, but he hadn't told them anything. He was still too raw, too unsure what to believe, to talk about it.

Once the heat of anger had died down and he'd really begun to think, he'd realized there was no way he knew the whole story. First, he didn't think anybody was a good enough actress to pretend the happiness Madison had seemed to feel when they were together. She hadn't behaved at all like a woman pining for another man— her ex-fiancé *or* her mystery lover.

Second, everything inside him rebelled at the idea that she was the type who would cheat. She didn't come across as anything less than an honest person. The moment he'd met Ashley, he'd seen that tiny hint of selfishness that had made it less of a surprise that she couldn't be faithful. He'd never seen that in Madison. Never.

Besides those factors, he also couldn't stop thinking about one of their first conversations, the one when she'd said she hadn't had sex in six months. That hadn't felt like a lie. Besides, why would she make it up? There would be no need for her to invent a detail like that.

But if it were true...what did *that* mean?

That she was innocent and hadn't cheated?

That she hadn't slept with her fiancé—the sexiest man alive, per magazines—since long before they'd broken up?

Confusion didn't begin to describe the state he'd been in. Finally, knowing he had to get the answers or go crazy, he'd pulled out the slip of paper with her phone numbers on it. It had been late, and he'd been leaving the station after a long twenty-four-hour shift. But he hadn't wanted to wait until morning, knowing that in the light of day, when he was less fatigued, he might rethink the decision.

No answer. He hadn't left a message, instead deciding to try the other number for her parents' house in Florida.

It had been disconnected.

Well, if she really had gone back to their home after the nightmare in Costa Rica, he could understand why the phone was no longer connected. Hell, if the paparazzi figured out who he was and where he lived, he'd not only want to change his address and phone number, he'd want to change his damn face!

The very next day, when he'd been about to try to call her again, the story had broken. Those leeches had published the pictures from the airport. He was officially being called "the unidentified man who stole Tommy Shane's fiancée."

And his life totally went to hell. Everybody saw it, everybody commented on it. He was able to laugh off what he called a "resemblance" to people he didn't know. Those he did know, who were aware he had, indeed, gone to Costa Rica, weren't buying it.

"You need a hand?" Mike asked.

"No, I'm done," he said as he finished tightening the filter. Double-checking the seal, he slid out from under the truck and sat up. "Bring any beer?" he asked his brother.

"I'm working."

"I'm not," he said, enjoying the first morning of his long, three-day stretch off. Rising to his feet and wiping his hands with a rag, he added, "Come on in."

Before they turned to walk through the garage into Leo's small house, Mike dropped a hand on his shoulder. "You holding up?"

"I've been better."

Mike followed him inside, and Leo went to the fridge to grab himself a beer and his brother a bottle of water. Going into the living room, they sat down and eyed each other in silence for a minute.

"So, heard from Rafe lately?" he asked, wondering how their older brother was doing. An Army Ranger stationed in Afghanistan, their other sibling didn't communicate much. The whole family was anxious for him to finish up his tour of duty and get the hell out of there.

"No, not a word. Mom's hoping he'll make it home for Christmas."

"Think that'll happen?"

"I doubt it."

They fell silent again, and Leo knew his brother had something else on his mind. This wasn't just a stop-by-to-say-hey visit.

Finally, Mike spoke. "Have you heard from her?"

Leo merely stared, surprised by the question. It was the first time anybody had asked him that. Most of his friends just ragged on him, trying to get information out of him, asking what it had been like to bang a movie star's ex. His family pretended it hadn't happened, changing the subject, not wanting any details.

Nobody had even asked how they'd met, what they'd done, or how he felt about her. *Really* felt.

"No."

"Have you tried calling?"

"I did before the pictures hit the press."

"And she hasn't called you?"

"I didn't leave a message. The last time we spoke at the airport, I made it pretty clear I didn't want to talk."

"Harsh, dude."

His jaw stiff, he admitted, "It wasn't my finest moment."

"I guess you had provocation."

Maybe. Or maybe he'd just been a jerk, acting like the injured party when he really didn't know what was going on. He should have at least given her the chance to say something—anything. He'd been on autopilot, in shock, operating on instinct and emotion. And he regretted it.

"Was it pretty serious?"

He nodded slowly. "I thought so." Swallowing, he admitted, "To be honest, Mike, I was picturing marriage and babies and all that crap, right up until the minute the press showed up."

His brother leaned forward in his seat, dropping his clenched hands between his splayed legs and hunching over.

"What is it?"

"There's something you should know."

His heart skipped a beat. "About Madison?"

Mike nodded. "And maybe about you." He reached into the pocket of his jacket and pulled out a folded piece of newsprint. "Mom saw this article this morning and asked me to come talk to you. She wanted you to hear it from one of us."

Leo reached for the paper, unsure why his mouth had gone so dry and his heart was beating so fast. Unfolding the square, seeing it was a torn-out page of a tabloid, he felt a little sick, but forced himself to look at the "news" article anyway.

At first, the words didn't make sense. As they began to sink in, though, the world seemed to stop spinning, then to suddenly lurch wildly. He spun with it, unable to do anything but stare at the words on the page.

Who's the Daddy, Madison?

He scanned the article, crumpled the paper in his hand, looked up at his brother and said, "Get me to the airport."

"ARE YOU OKAY?"

Madison awakened from a light nap as her sister

stuck her head into the bedroom, offering her a gentle smile. Candace had flown down the day before yesterday, a few days after Madison had returned to California. They were both staying with Tommy in Laguna Beach.

"I guess," Madison mumbled. "I'm just tired all the time now."

"I suppose that's to be expected," her twin said, entering the room and sitting down on the corner of the bed. Although Candace was concerned, there was also a gleam of excitement in her eyes. Ever since she'd found out that Madison was pregnant, she'd been torn between being upset for her and being utterly thrilled that she would be an aunt in about eight months.

That was now official. The three pregnancy tests she'd taken since she'd arrived in California confirmed it.

She was pregnant with Leo Santori's baby.

"You aren't feeling nauseated or anything, are you?"

She sat up, leaning back against the pillows. "No, not really. A tiny bit queasy in the evenings, but mostly I'm just tired." She rubbed at her eyes and asked, "Where's Tommy?"

"He and Simon are downstairs making dinner."

"Are the shades drawn?" she asked, sounding bitter.

They really didn't need to worry too much about that behind the gates of this secluded mansion. Tommy had bought it for privacy, after all. The front lawn was large and gated, the house set well back from the road. The backyard comprised a steep, rocky hillside that led down to the beach and nobody but a goat could climb it. So, yeah, her comment had just been sarcastic. The paparazzi might be cruising the street in front of the house, but they weren't snapping embarrassing pictures, the way they had when she'd first arrived at Tommy's place a week ago and run the gauntlet to get to the gate.

She hadn't had the stomach to read any of the articles or watch the Hollywood "news" shows since her return. She knew full well everybody was speculating that Tommy, being the great guy he was, had taken back his cheating ex-fiancée.

"I need to talk to you. It's about the press."

"Screw them all," Madison muttered, unable to help it.

Candace reached out and took her hand, which Madison had noticed was actually a bit pale, despite her tan. She suspected she'd lost a little weight and knew she wasn't getting enough exercise. She'd been practically hibernating, consoling herself in the company of her sister and her best friend as they all brainstormed on how best to deal with this.

Tommy had offered to marry her. Same old knight in shining armor. Simon, his partner, hadn't seemed too thrilled about it, but hadn't objected. He knew full well how Madison's life had been shredded because of all of this.

Madison had of course declined. It wasn't the 1950s—she didn't need a father's name on the birth certificate. If there was a name to put on there, she wanted it to be the real one. She only hoped that by the time she'd gotten things straightened out here, Leo would listen to her when she showed up in Chicago to break the news.

This wasn't the kind of thing she could say on the phone, so she'd already bought her ticket. She was leaving in two days. Tommy had told her to tell Leo anything she had to in order to make him understand the truth of the situation. He'd offered to go with her. Hell, he'd offered to hold a press conference to stage a big coming-out party.

All she'd really needed was that permission to share his secret. She didn't want him throwing himself on his sword for nothing. Her real hope was that by staying here with him for a few days, maybe the press and the public would see she and Tommy were still friends. Maybe they'd begin to believe she hadn't broken his heart, that their engagement had just been a mistake.

Maybe they'd let her get her life back.

Get Leo back.

"Mad, something's happened. Mom called this afternoon."

Hearing the note of anxiety in her sister's voice, she gripped her hand tighter. "Is Dad all right? His heart…"

"He's fine. It's just… I don't know how to tell you this."

So it had something to do with *her.* "Just say it."

Candace swallowed. "The *Tattler* has a big story about you."

Oh, great. "What else is new?"

"*This* is new. It seems somebody—probably one of their slimy reporters—dug through Tommy's trash the day after you arrived."

Slimy indeed. She hoped he'd gotten a handful of fish guts.

"Mad, he found the test kits." Candace's hand tightened. "Your pregnancy's all over the tabloids."

She froze, unable to process it, hoping her sister was joking. But Candace was dead serious—the tears and sympathy in her eyes proved it.

"You mean they printed…"

"Yeah. Big headline, nasty article, lots of speculation over who the father is." Candace drew her into her arms and held her tightly, as if fearing Madison was about to break apart.

Funny, though, as the immediate reaction died down, she realized she wasn't devastated, wasn't furious. Mostly, she was just terrified. *What if Leo saw it?*

"I've got to go!" She launched out of the bed. "I have to change my flight to Chicago."

Candace nodded. "I'll call while you pack."

But before they could do either, the intercom in the room buzzed on. Tommy loved the stupid thing and played with it all the time. "You awake?"

"I'm busy."

"Mad, you have a visitor."

"No time," she snapped, wondering who on earth would be coming to see her, and, more importantly, why Tommy would let them in.

"He's coming up the driveway right now. Get your ass down here!"

"He who? What are you talking about?" she asked, finally paying attention.

"A gorgeous Italian guy who demanded to be let in,

and then flipped off a dozen photographers in the street as he drove through the gate."

She gasped. *Leo?*

"Do you think it's him?" Candace asked.

She considered, thought about the articles, remembered the conversation they'd had. He would know the baby was his.

"It's him," she whispered, her hand rising to her mouth as she dashed over to the dresser to check her face in the mirror. "Of course, I haven't bathed in two days and I look like a red-eyed raccoon with these bags under my eyes."

Candace leaped to the rescue. She quickly grabbed Madison's makeup bag and touched up the dark circles. There wasn't much she could do about her hair, so she slung it into a ponytail. It took only a minute or two, but even that was too long.

She hurried downstairs, her heart racing, arriving at the bottom of the steps just in time to see Leo Santori throw a punch at her former fiancé. Fortunately, Tommy ducked to the side and evaded the shot.

"Stop, Leo, don't!" she shouted.

He jerked his attention toward her. His dark eyes studied her, his gaze sweeping over her, from messy hair down to bare feet. She saw the tiny furrowing of his brow and knew he didn't like what he saw. She hoped it was because he was worried about her and not because she looked like total shit. Or because he hated her guts.

"This isn't Tommy's fault," she said immediately, trying to diffuse the tension. "And the papers have everything all wrong."

"Are you pregnant?" he snapped, cutting right to the issue at hand.

She nodded slowly.

"Is it mine?"

Another nod.

His bunched shoulders relaxed a little and the dark frown eased. He didn't exactly look overjoyed about the news or ready to pass out cigars, but at least he no longer appeared about to beat the crap out of Tommy.

"So you're not going to deny it, try to claim it's his?" he asked, jerking a thumb toward Tommy.

"Why would I do that?" she asked, genuinely puzzled.

Candace had followed her downstairs, and Simon had come in from the kitchen. He ignored them both.

"I don't know, Madison, I don't have any idea what you might be thinking. But I do know one of those fucking articles is saying lover boy here can't have kids so you went out and had an affair only so you could give him the baby he wants."

Her legs went weak as dismay washed over her. How could people invent such horrible, vicious lies? She lifted a hand to her forehead, suddenly feeling light-headed.

"Mad?" Tommy said.

Leo didn't speak. When he saw that her weakening limbs were about to betray her, he launched himself forward and caught her in his arms. She fell into them gratefully, inhaling his unique scent, feeling the heat of his body and finally allowing herself to believe he was really here.

And then, for the second time in her life, she fainted.

12

Leo didn't know his way around this gaudy California mansion, so when he realized Madison had passed out from shock, weariness or the pregnancy, he simply strode through the nearest doorway, hoping there was a soft surface on which he could place her.

It turned out to be a dining room. The rich wood table was as big as his own kitchen. Jesus, had Madison really been living like this?

"In here," Shane said, gesturing toward another doorway.

Glaring at the man, not wanting his help with anything, Leo nonetheless carried her into the other room. Spying a large plush sofa, he gently lowered her onto it. "Get her some water and a cold cloth."

"Here." Someone thrust a wet facecloth toward him, obviously having gone for it the moment she'd fallen. He glanced up long enough to realize it had been Madison's twin sister, Candace. He nodded his thanks, thinking she might be identical in features, but she certainly didn't make his heart dance around in his chest the way it did when he looked at Madison.

He placed the cloth on Madison's brow, not liking the paleness in her face and the circles under her eyes. She looked like she hadn't slept at all in the weeks since he'd seen her. There were hollows in her cheeks that hadn't been there before, and her hands and arms looked so much smaller and more fragile than he remembered them being.

"Madison, sweetheart, wake up," he whispered.

Her eyelids fluttered. A pause. Then they flew open. "It's really you. You're really here."

"Yeah. Did you think it was a dream?"

She nodded. "It wouldn't be the first time."

So she'd been dreaming about him? Well, that was only fair, wasn't it, considering she'd inhabited his dreams and his fantasies every day since he'd walked away from her at that airport?

"You haven't been taking care of yourself," he scolded.

"You're not looking so great yourself." She lifted a slender hand and brushed her fingers across his lips. "You've lost weight."

"So have you. And you should be gaining it, shouldn't you?"

Her hand immediately dropped to her waist. She again displayed that protective instinct he'd already seen when there was just the possibility of a baby.

How could she be a cheat and a liar? How was something like that even possible?

He no longer believed it was. Which was why he'd

gotten on that plane this morning, right after Mike had shown him the article, and flown out here to get to the truth.

"I was coming to tell you," she said, as if reading his mind. "I have my tickets booked."

"Really?"

"Really," she assured him. "The confirmation is in my purse. I was coming in two days. I never wanted you to find out about the baby like you did."

"Okay," he said, believing, because, as always, he could sense no deceit in the woman.

"I'm so sorry you had to read about it in the damned tabloids. That's so wrong."

"It's all right. They're like piranhas, aren't they?"

"Wish you'd run a few of them over when you flew through the gate," said the world's sexiest man.

Leo stared up at him, his expression hard and un-yielding. Although the rest of the world was boo-hooing about poor Tommy Shane and his broken heart, Leo knew—*knew*—there was more to this whole thing. Madison was the one who'd been hurt. She was the one who'd been nearly crushed by the weight of all this, and he believed she deserved it about as much as he believed in the Easter Bunny.

"Ooh, fierce," Tommy said. He held his hands up, palms out, in a conciliatory gesture. "Take a breath, big guy."

"What the hell is going on?" Leo asked, looking away from Tommy and down at the woman trying to sit up on the couch. He put a hand under her arm and helped her. "Explain this to me because I've read all the stories and the gossip and the innuendo, and I don't believe a word of it. So somebody needs to start talking."

Madison glanced first at Tommy, and then at the other man, who was dark haired, well dressed and standing close to the famous actor. Then at her sister. "Would you excuse us, please?"

They all immediately mumbled apologies and scurried out of the room, leaving them alone.

Leo ached to reach out and pull her into his arms, to hold her again, this time while she was conscious. He held back, though. They had to clear the air and he didn't want to make this any harder than it was already going to be.

"I've missed you so much, Leo," she said. "I've thought about you every minute of every day."

He dropped onto a nearby chair, surprised those had been her opening words, though he certainly echoed the sentiment.

"Wow. I hadn't planned to start off like that," she said, swiping a hand over her brow. "I'm not trying to manipulate things, gain your sympathy or anything."

He didn't reply, still savoring that admission, still wondering what was yet to come.

"Tommy Shane and I were engaged, but we were never planning to get married. He's been one of my dearest friends all my life, and that's all we have ever been to each other, and all we ever will be."

About twenty pounds of weight lifted off his shoulders. But a lot more remained.

"So why the engagement?"

She gestured toward the window. "You think they're

ruthless now? Imagine what they'd say if word got out that the hottest action star in the country…is in love with a man."

The lightbulb clicked. The presence of the dark-haired guy made sense.

Leo closed his eyes and dropped his head back onto the chair, letting out a heavy sigh. It was as if some-body had set a domino in motion and all the other pieces began to fall down, one after another, everything slid-ing into place.

When he thought his voice wouldn't shake, he said, "You were his beard."

"Exactly. It wasn't supposed to last forever. And when he got serious with his partner, we decided the time had come to break up. Only, we needed a reason. A really *good* one."

"Why?"

"Because what woman in her right mind would break up with the sexiest man alive? Unless he did something horrible. Which would really take a chink out of that superhero-of-Hollywood image."

Right. Nice guys didn't cheat. Not when they had relatively new careers *and* a big secret to hide.

"So you pretended you'd had an affair."

She nodded.

"*You* took the fall, carried the burden for weeks while he…while he…"

"While he offered to come out in the open, to throw away his career and his life and his privacy," she said gently. "Tommy's heart is breaking for me. *I'm* the one who won't let him make this more of a spectacle than it is."

Spectacle. Yeah, that pretty much described the life she'd been living lately.

"To be honest, I also didn't want to let those bastards win. Why should they get their way?" She punched the seat cushion. "Why should they be free to hound people to death, prying in their closets, and under their beds and…and in their trash cans!"

He'd read the articles about her pregnancy and knew where that information had come from. How low did somebody have to be to dig stuff out of the garbage? He supposed only someone who wallowed in it for a living.

"I never thought it would be such a big deal…slow news month, I guess."

"It's not news," he snapped. "It's gossip and slander and they're all sick, miserable people with black souls, no lives, and…small penises."

She smiled weakly, nodding in agreement.

"You went to Costa Rica to hide, didn't you?"

"Yes."

"Never planned on meeting anyone, I'll bet."

She peered at him and her voice throbbed with intensity as she replied, "I never expected to meet *you*. Not in Costa Rica. Not anywhere. Not in my whole life."

She was baring herself, laying out her every emotion, exposing herself to more heartache—on top of the mounds of it she'd already been dealing with. All for someone who'd never once told her how he felt about her.

"And I never thought I'd find you, either," he said softly.

Unable to stay away from her any longer, he rose from his chair and sat beside her on the couch. He put his arms around her and gently—oh, so gently—pulled her onto his lap. She wrapped her arms around his neck and tucked her face next to his.

"I missed you, too, Madison."

He couldn't see her smile. But he could feel it.

Maybe they were being cautious, telling the truth, but not telling all of it. What he felt for her was a lot more than absence making the heart grow fonder. He'd missed her, yeah. Because he loved her like crazy.

Unfortunately, they were in someone else's house, with three strangers right outside the door. They hadn't seen each other in weeks. She was exhausted, pregnant, emotionally wrung out.

And she hadn't said she loved him, either.

She does. He knew she did.

But maybe it wasn't quite time to say it yet.

"I'm sorry I didn't come find you sooner."

"And I'm sorry I didn't come tell you the truth sooner. I was going to, I just had to make sure Tommy knew and understood, since it's his secret that's at risk of getting out."

He thought about her friend, considered the life he led. Tommy Shane was an international sensation. He'd risen out of relative obscurity just three or four years ago and had become a superstar. He made millions, lived in a mansion, had women hanging on his every word, turned down movie offers that other actors drooled for…and could never *really* be who he was.

He never would have imagined it, but he truly felt sorry for Shane. It was one hell of a choice to have to make.

"How are we going to get out of this mess, Madison?" he whispered, tenderly kissing her temple. "Because I want it over. I want you in my life and I want our baby."

"I don't know," she admitted. "I honestly don't know."

ALTHOUGH LEO HAD hit it off with Tommy after Madison told him the truth, and also got along great with Candace and Simon, they decided to leave for Chicago that very night. For one thing, he needed to get back to work, having used almost all his vacation time in Costa Rica. And Madison needed to get out of this atmosphere. It was toxic and she knew it was bad for her health, and for the baby's.

More than that, though, she just wanted privacy so she and Leo could spend some time together in the real world. Time to accept all that had happened, to explore the feelings they had for each other and see if they were really as strong as she suspected they were.

They could also use some time to get used to the idea that they were going to have a child together.

They couldn't do that here, certainly. Nor did Leo intend to leave her here, living like a bug under a microscope, while he went home alone.

They'd thought about how to slip away, and it had been Candace who'd come up with an idea—which was why, late in the day, a limousine with blacked-out windows pulled up in front of the house, parking at an angle to help block the view from the road. Each of them wearing a jacket, hat and dark glasses, Madison and Leo said their goodbyes and dashed to the car. The driver let them in, closing the door behind them.

Some of the photographers ran to their cars as if to follow. But before they'd even left the driveway, Candace had come outside, waving enthusiastically at the limo as it departed.

The press stayed. Madison could see the confusion on their faces as they peered at the limo, trying to see who was inside.

Somehow, they'd missed her sister's arrival the other day and had no idea her twin was on the premises. When she'd shown up, they'd probably just assumed it was Madison—that she'd gotten out of the mansion under their noses and was returning.

Whatever the case, the press mistook the sisters for each other again now. Ignoring the mysterious vehicle, they focused instead on the fresh meat standing in the driveway, waving happily, acting as though she didn't have a care in the world.

Madison glanced back, her heart twisting as she saw her brave sister standing there, sticking up for her. Their lives had gone in very different directions, and she doubted they'd ever live in the same state again. But some things never changed—like the instant connection they shared, the way they would drop everything on a dime to be there for each other.

They had each found love with great men. But they would always be twins.

She continued to stare, sending warm, loving thoughts out to her sibling. Suddenly, Tommy walked out of the house. So did Simon. That hadn't been part of the plan. Both of them walked up to Candace, stood on either side of her, and slid an arm around her waist. They laughed together and all three waved, looking like one happy family.

She giggled. "I have no idea what the vultures are going to make of that!"

"Hopefully it'll give them all aneurysms just thinking about it," Leo said, sharing her laughter as he pulled her close on the leather seat, draping an arm across her shoulders.

"I hope my father doesn't have one," she said, shaking her head.

She'd called Florida right before they'd left. Her parents hadn't been thrilled that she'd run away the moment she'd found out she was pregnant. Nor were they happy to have found out about it from friends who read the tabloids. But she'd heard the excitement in their voices and, at the end of the conversation, they'd admitted they were *thrilled* to be having their first grandchild.

"Let me kiss you, woman," he growled. "It's been way too long."

She didn't hesitate. The privacy screen was up. Needing desperately to feel him, touch him and know he was real, she moved over onto his lap, twined her arms around his neck and pulled him close for a long slow kiss. He cupped her face in his hands in the way she so loved—so tender, yet sexy. Sultry but sweet. They kissed and kissed, laughing and whispering between each brush of their mouths.

"I could get used to traveling like this," he said. "Think he'd drive us all the way to Chicago?"

"Sure. We'll send the bill to Tommy."

Chuckling, he kissed her again. "Don't I wish. I do have to go back to work, though."

"Too bad. We could get him to drive us all the way to Florida. My parents are dying to meet you."

"I'm looking forward to meeting them, too," Leo said, sounding sincere.

"They're wonderful. They'll love you." She sighed heavily. "They've known Tommy forever and are in on his secret, so they won't hate you on sight like your folks will me."

She was more than a little terrified about meeting his family, having them think of her as some tramp loathed by the entire world.

"Stop it," he ordered. "They'll love you as much as I do."

She froze. Still, so still. Surprised, happy. Wondering whether he'd meant those words or they were an expression.

Love. He'd said the word *love*. She hadn't misheard it, had she?

As if reading her mind, he lifted her chin so their eyes met.

"I love you, Madison Reid."

Her heart thudded, practically escaping from her chest. That was fine. She didn't own it anymore, anyway. This man did. "You're sure?"

"I've never been more sure of anything."

Slowly nodding, she allowed the truth of it to fill

her up, let it sink in to all those empty places that had been hollowed out by the days and weeks of being without him.

He loved her.

He'd come for her.

He wanted her and he wanted their baby.

She could face anything.

When she was able to speak, she said, "I love you, too, Leo. I am totally and completely yours."

"I know."

She couldn't help poking him in the ribs. "You cocky Italian."

He grinned up at her, that gorgeous dimple appearing, his face glowing with utter happiness. "Come on, what's not to love? I mean, you'll never do better than me, babe. You must've hated life in that huge mansion with the beach and the pool and the art and the movie stars dropping by all the time."

Giggling, she replied, "Oh, definitely. The horrors!"

"I ask ya, what could be better than a little two bedroom house right around the corner from a noisy fire station?"

"Two bedrooms are enough for me."

In fact, it sounded like heaven to her.

She realized they'd both just assumed she would live with him. This didn't feel like a vacation. It was crazy. She'd left most of her things behind in California or in Florida, but it felt like she was on her way home. At last.

As long as she had a computer on which to write and a phone with which to make and receive calls, she could continue pursuing her screenwriting career. If that didn't pan out, well, there was always the *Chicago Tribune,* or another big city paper. Most of them would probably be chomping at the bit to scoop up a journalist with a masters from Columbia.

"Southern California? Who needs it?" Leo asked as they cruised up the coast. "Limos and Porsches and beaches? Screw that. Nothing beats the Windy City. Lake-effect snow, crime, cold that cuts right through your bones."

"Can't wait," she said with a laugh. "I'll be able to take you up on that pizza challenge."

"You'll love my cousin Tony's food. In fact, you'll love the whole family. And they *will* love you. I swear it."

"You really think so?"

"I know so."

"Even if this whole nightmare doesn't die down? We can't just tell everyone the whole story, you know. I'm sorry, that has to be Tommy's decision."

"I understand. But I'm telling you, sweetheart, there's only one thing my mom'll need to hear—that she's going to be a grandmother."

Remembering her own mother's reaction, she believed that one.

"As for the rest, we tell them it's a bunch of sensationalistic lies. That you and Tommy were childhood friends who decided you just worked better as friends, and the tabloids made a bunch of nonsense out of it. Who doesn't know that, anyway? I mean, really, how many martian spacemen have you seen flinging a Frisbee in Central Park?"

Laughing out loud as she pictured some of the more outrageous tabloid headlines she'd seen, she nodded helplessly. "Okay."

Their laughter faded. Growing serious, as if knowing she needed the reassurance, he said, "They're good judges of character, Madison."

"If they're anything like you, I know I'll love them all." She nibbled her lip. "But Leo, sooner or later, the press is going to figure out who you are. Somebody will out us and the maniacs will descend on us, no matter where we are."

He smirked. "Oh, honey, there's no place in Chicago that the Santoris can't block the press in and stop them from getting anywhere near us."

"There are that many of you?"

"I've got more relatives than a new lottery winner—cops, bodyguards, lawyers, construction workers, business owners, strippers, politicians…"

"Strippers?" she said, gawking.

"My cousin's wife. You'll love her. She also bakes—oh, *madone,* you haven't lived until you've tried her cannoli."

"I'll add it to my list."

"The point is, there's a Santori on every corner, and every one of them will serve as a barricade to anybody who tries to mess with one of their own."

Swallowing, she asked, "And I'll be one of their own?"

He brushed his fingers against her cheek, reached for her left hand and laced their fingers together. He lifted it to his mouth, placing a tender kiss on her ring finger.

She knew what he meant. Knew exactly what he meant.

"You already are, Madison. You're mine."

"Forever?"

"Forever. Rings, vows, whatever you want." He bent to brush his lips across hers, sealing the promise with a gentle kiss. "I'm never letting you get away again."

Epilogue

LEO WAS AS GOOD as his word. The family loved her. And she loved them.

Going from a small family with one sibling and only a few other relations into a clan like the Santoris was a bit of a culture shock. Madison was thrown into a whirlwind of aunts, uncles, cousins and in-laws.

It was crazy. It was wonderful. And Leo was by her side through every bit of it.

Although none of them ever made her feel at all unwelcome, or questioned the story she and Leo had told them, she had to admit she felt a lot better after Tommy's press conference.

The one where he'd shocked Hollywood.

No, he hadn't spilled everything, but he'd come pretty damned close. Telling the world that it was wrong for *anyone* to have to feign an engagement with one of his oldest friends, and then see that friend ripped to shreds in public over it, he asked the media to take a good, hard look at themselves.

Of course, the tabloids wouldn't…they thrived on

gossip. But there had been plenty of supposedly "legiti-mate" news outlets that had ripped them apart, too. So maybe his words would do a little good there.

Lots of people speculated that their fake engage-ment, and his demand for privacy, for the right to live the way he wanted to, meant he was gay. But so what? More fans stepped out in support of him than criticized, and a lot of other celebrities had backed him up with similar comments.

His last film had opened at number one and stayed there for weeks. His career was thriving. He was happy—if discreet—with Simon.

And she and Leo were, blessedly, being left in peace.

"How are you feeling?" Leo asked, coming up be-hind her as she typed the last few words of her screen-play. She'd been doing revisions for a studio that had optioned it, wanting to get all the work behind her be-fore their upcoming trip to California.

"I'm fine," she insisted, hearing the worried tone in his voice. He wouldn't stop worrying until their daugh-ter was safely in their arms and Madison had fully re-covered from childbirth.

If there had ever been a more overprotective father-to-be, she had yet to meet him. Absolutely the only time she could persuade him she wasn't about to break, and was perfectly healthy, was when she seduced him into some seriously naughty sex. Seriously. Naughty.

Yum.

It turned out that being pregnant pumped up her li-bido to astronomical levels. She found herself ripping Leo's clothes off every chance she got.

He didn't seem to mind.

"You're sure you're going to be okay to fly? I'm sure Candace would understand…"

"I'm six months pregnant, not on my deathbed," she said, rolling her eyes as they went over this again.

"Six months. Our lucky number, remember?" he said with a suggestive wag of his eyebrows.

"I can't wait to see what happens six months from now next October." Then she got back to the subject at hand. "But as for now, I am *not* missing my sister's wedding. We're going to Napa. End of discussion."

"Bossy chick."

"Hey, what can I say?" She adopted a fake accent and made a hand gesture she'd seen her new father-in-law make many times. "I'm Italian, ya know?"

He broke up over her awful imitation. "Brilliant," he said.

"Hey, I learned from the best. I guess that's why your bossiness has rubbed off on me."

"Baby, you were trying to run the show from the day we met."

Oh, that wonderful day they'd met. How she loved to think about it, and most of the days that had followed, right up to and including their own special, intimate wedding ceremony here in Chicago a few weeks ago.

Well, it had been private, but it certainly hadn't been small. Her family had come, of course, along with Tommy.

And then there had been the Santoris. All the Santoris.

They'd filled the church without inviting a single outside guest. A few *un*invited ones had tried to sneak in—they followed Tommy everywhere he went and were still looking for dish about Madison. But one of Leo's cousins, Nick, was a former bouncer and ran a popular club. He'd *bounced* one photographer out on his ass and the others had scurried for cover.

"So, you're really feeling all right?"

"Indeed I am."

"Then finish that sentence and come to bed."

She glanced out the window at the bright blue sky and raised a brow. She was only teasing him, of course. She and Leo had never felt the need to restrict themselves to the dark of night. Their baby had probably been conceived in broad daylight in a swimming pool for heaven's sake.

"What's that look?" he asked as he took her hand and helped her out of her chair.

"Thinking of our last vacation."

He closed his eyes, obviously picturing it, too. "Guess we won't be able do that again until the kid's twenty."

Hmm. Maybe not.

They should certainly be able to afford it, anyway. Her screenplay had not only made a splash, it had made a tidal wave. Once Tommy had held his press conference, and she'd been the object of sympathy worldwide, the studios had swooped in and fought like dogs over her work.

She supposed she could have felt a little offended, could have thought about it as a pity bidding war.

But screw that. She cashed the check.

"Maybe we can take her with us and go when she's three or four," she said. "I think she should learn how to swim naked."

He nodded, liking the idea. "As long as she's potty trained."

"Good point."

They were laughing together as he bent down to pick her up. He often did that, sweeping her into their bedroom. She thought she might cry on the day she became too heavy for it and told him so.

"Never gonna happen."

"I'll be big as a house in three months."

"I'll eat my Wheaties." He pressed a kiss on her cheek, on her nose, then a long, lazy one on her lips. "Because I learned a long time ago…when I'm holding you in my arms, I can do absolutely anything."

* * * * *

Give a 12 month subscription to a friend today!

Call Customer Services
0844 844 1358*

or visit
millsandboon.co.uk/subscription

The World of
MILLS & BOON®

HISTORICAL

*Awaken the romance
of the past*
6 new stories every month

**MEDICAL
ROMANCE**

*The ultimate in romantic
medical drama*
6 new stories every month

MODERN™

*Power, passion and
irresistible temptation*
8 new stories every month

By Request

*Relive the romance with the
best of the best*
12 stories every month

Have you tried eBooks?

With eBook exclusive series and titles from just **£1.99**,
there's even more reason to try our eBooks today

Visit www.millsandboon.co.uk/eBooks
for more details